Who Was That Masked Woman?

Who Was That Masked Woman?

NORETTA KOERTGE

St. Martin's Press New York

Design by MARY A. BROWN

10 9 8 7

Library of Congress Cataloging in Publication Data
Koertge, Noretta.
Who was that masked woman?
I. Title.
PS3561.0345W5   813'.54   80-28471
ISBN 0-312-87033-7

Who
Was That Masked
Woman?

1 The Identity Problem

> Can the Ethiopian change his skin, or the leopard
> his spots?
> —*Jeremiah*

> There is as much difference between us and
> ourselves as between us and others.
> —*Montaigne*

"TRETONA! TRETONA GETROEK." An unfamiliar voice.
I automatically turned toward the sound—no familiar face.
Puzzled, I continued walking toward my office and then a man
caught me up: "Tretona, it's Jackson—Jackson Parr." More
firmly: "You know, Jackson Parr from Cheaney."

"Jackie?" It seemed unlikely. I scrutinized his face, his
posture, his gestures. No aspect of this chunky, bearded man bore
any resemblance to the little boy who was my best friend when he
was three and I was eleven. Yet he pronounced the name of our
hometown correctly, as if it were spelled "Chainy," and chatted
with authority and familiarity about Jackie's parents, Brother
Don and Sister Naomi.

I wondered if he remembered how he used to masturbate in
the back row at church: standing astride my lap, rubbing his
crotch against my sternum. I felt vaguely embarrassed by it. But
how else was he to be entertained after we had been through
handkerchief dollies, cootie catchers folded from old Sunday
school papers, and bridges constructed out of hymnals? No toys
were allowed in church and the Cheaney farm folks liked long
sermons. Brother Don preached and Sister Naomi played the
piano, so I always took care of Jackie.

I could still picture him clearly—prominent eyes ("bug-eyed"
my mama said and predicted goiter problems), the characteristic

Parr nose (Brother Jode Parr had one, too), jet black, stubborn hair. It was incredible that this rather bland-faced, red-bearded "Jackson" creature was related in any way to my Jackie.

But now I had to stop staring and say something: You've really changed. Wouldn't have recognized you. Must get together sometime, I said. And he said, Sure and then, with feeling: "Boy, I would have known you anywhere."

The remark was obviously true. At forty, I had increased my Levi size by five inches in the waist, but I still wore blue round-toed tennis shoes (always had, even when polka-dotted pointy toes were in fashion), and the short red hair, cowlicks, and freckles were all intact.

So the skin and the spots were the same, but inside I felt completely transformed. If I were to lose my memory, I decided as I crossed over the Jordan River that cut through campus, there would be no overlap between my present self and that fifteen-year-old who ran away from home the night before she went to college, in order to say good-bye again to Jackie and Don 'n' Naomi. Tretona-15 was recluse, shy and socially inept, preoccupied with guilt about religion, sex, and work, and convinced that if there were any answers to her pain and inadequacy, science alone would provide them.

And Tretona-40? Well, I still had problems, I suppose, but both their content and my way of dealing with them seemed radically different. Now I liked and relied on people a lot. I was successful in my field and felt pretty good about my life all in all. And I sure didn't look to science for answers to personal problems.

And yet Tretona-15 was no stranger to me. I could still conjure up with frightening intensity the dumb inarticulate shame and hurt she felt that last night before college when her mother came in the car to take her back from the parsonage. Don and Naomi hadn't realized she was there without permission and they watched in amazement, but didn't intervene, as Mrs. Getroek dragged her off the porch and made her ride the bicycle home in front of the car. When Tretona got tired after a mile and slowed down, her mother nudged the back bicycle tire with the car bumper. Tretona was tempted just to skid in the gravel and let her mom run over her: "Then she'd be sorry." But *would* she? Anyway, Tretona-15 never fought back. She rarely even felt angry, consciously. She just brooded and sulked and blamed herself for being awful, bad, careless, dumb. . . . (Check one or all of the above.)

Tretona-40 emerged from her flashback and shuddered with relief. That was all over now—she was a different person. But *was* she, I wondered. And if she was, how did the transmutation take place?

Can it really be that there were no happy moments in my first fifteen years? A rather careful scan of my most vivid memories reveals none. There is the memory folder called "Bad Times in School," which includes: wetting my pants in the fourth grade, having to be partners in Run Through with fat, ugly Murl Cotterell in eighth grade, unsuccessfully tattling on Donnie Spillman for going into the girls' outdoor toilet (he claimed he only went into the toilet courtyard to retrieve a foul ball), chickening out of a fight when Janie Cotterell kicked me in the groin (she was Murl's little sister), and feeling repulsed by Miss Fillmore's warm, plump thigh (my brother and I rode to school with her and he would never take his turn at sitting in the middle).

There is an even bigger collection of memory recordings featuring emotional disasters at home: whippings that I thought were undeserved, present-less birthdays, dogs that died through my father's carelessness, and long conferences on the north side of the house with the dog that didn't die ("Just you wait, Tippy. When I grow up we'll run away and I'll get you out of here. I promise I will.")

Even the snapshot album where most of the pictures are intended to record moments of triumph shows lots of little (and later, not so little—I was five feet ten inches tall by age eleven) smiling, strained Tretonas with characteristic worry wrinkles in her forehead, hunched slightly forward (at first to protect the heart, later to deaccentuate the breasts), legs a little too far apart to be ladylike. Here is Tretona-9 who has just won the Kiwanis Club essay prize for "What Americanism Means to Me" (partly, she said, it means being able to paint your mailbox purple regardless of what the neighbors think) and Tretona-11 playing a trumpet solo (her band teacher introduced it as "a fantastic musical achievement") and then a pile of clippings showing Tretona-14 winning the county, sectional, and state Elks Club essay contests on the topic, "How American Youth Can Prepare to Take Their Place in This Changing World." (Tretona said they should keep faith with time-honored American traditions, such as being able to paint your mailbox purple, but at the same time be open to modern, scientific innovations.) The Elks liked it $1500 worth and Vernon Crowder, the district representative, read it into the *Congressional Record.*

But Tretona was embarrassed by all these honors: She knew the essays were corny (she wrote them only because her mother insisted) and just because she was fast at picking up the trumpet didn't mean she was really any good at it (she could never hit the high notes and finally switched to trombone). The public recognition didn't increase her self-respect one iota; it only made all the kids (and their parents) think she (and her parents) were stuck-up.

But if this selection of memories was truly representative, surely little Tretona would have died by her own childish hand long ago. Think. Where are the happier moments of the past hiding? There were certainly some times that were at least relatively free of pain: pretending to be Jack Armstrong while bicycling up to get the mail (our non-purple mailbox was a quarter of a mile away), sneaking out of the house while everyone was still asleep and getting my shoes wet walking back to the pond, climbing way up in the maple tree with my telescope and looking at the weathercock on Andy Jack Stallard's barn, cracking hickory nuts in the basement when no one was around and eating all the big pieces first.

And now I have even dredged up a genuinely happy event: Tretona-9 saved up her allowance and ordered water wings one Monday morning from the "Monkey Ward" catalog. Her mother said they would never get there in time for the swimming expedition on Sunday. (This was before we got a holiness preacher and had to give up movies and going anywhere fun on Sunday.) However, Tretona had faith and checked out the mailbox every day just in case. Well, on Friday they came! Not Saturday, mind you, but Friday—a whole day early, as if to prove she was right all along.

But one pair of prompt water wings can't have been enough to have floated Tretona through a fifteen-year-long slough of depression. Happy times are not as pushy and intrusive as their painful counterparts. This circumstance has some survival value since we generally learn more from our mistakes than from our successes. Yet depressing past identities still cast their shadows on our present. Thus, I set out to uncover more of the early Tretona, to seek out the shy happy times as well as admitting the despair, and to analyze where the despair came from and how it was finally dispelled.

2 Chickens, Jimsonweeds, and the Lone Ranger

Happy [s]he who knows the rural gods—Pan, and old Sylvanus and the sisterhood of Nymphs.

—Virgil

No one would choose a friendless existence on condition of having all the other things in the world.

—Aristotle

TRETONA GETROEK SQUIRMED rhythmically in her baby bed. One of her long tan cotton stockings had fallen down from the side railing. Tretona had threaded it between her legs and was now sawing it gently back and forth. As her mother opened the door to the back bedroom, Tretona instinctively froze under the covers. "Are you asleep?" Tretona was silent but couldn't stop a little smile. "Someone's playing 'possum. Try to go to sleep now." When the door closed, Tretona got back to work with the sock but made sure the springs didn't creak.

Tretona slept in the baby bed in her parents' room until her first baby brother was born. She never heard them having sex; it may be that her presence was part of the reason it was four and a half years before Stanton came. But very early one morning, her mother heard Tretona.

Now Tretona is standing on a chair by the dining room stove, whimpering. Her pajama pants are gone and her mother is bathing her crotch over and over again with a cold wash rag. The

6

chair is white, but the green paint underneath shows through in the chipped spots. The chair is freezing cold because it came from the kitchen and in the wintertime the kitchen is closed off at night by a heavy blanket. Tretona starts to shiver.

"It's naughty and it's dirty—that's why I'm washing you," says her mother. "It will make you very nervous if you don't stop it right away." Tretona begins to shake more violently. "You see? It makes you nervous."

Her mother wrings the rag out in the enamel dishpan. The enamel is chipped and a hole in the bottom has been mended with a metal washer and nut. The mother half smiles as she starts sponging Tretona some more: "We'll cool this little thing off." For an instant, the mother's tongue was visible but then she drew her thin lips tightly together.

Tretona would see that same expression again when her mother forbad her to suck on wet washrags or to eat bananas in a certain way or to pull popsicles in and out of her mouth. Later on, she would take it for granted that some things inexplicably spooked her mother. But right now she was genuinely confused as to why her mother should think that anything that felt so good (and that she herself *knew* felt good) was so bad.

Tretona grew up doing all the things that farm kids do— watching her dad milk cows (he sat on a one-legged stool with his head leaned against the cow; occasionally he squirted milk on his hands to lubricate them), helping take care of runty little pigs and looking on stoically when her dad pulled their teeth with pliers (so they wouldn't bite the sow and get rolled on). She was good with the baby chickens (one had to move very quietly in the brooder house so as not to frighten them into the hot stove) and she loved teaching them how to eat. They came from the hatchery in boxes of fifty, scratching and cheeping and poking their little heads out of the ventilation holes. You picked them up one at a time, oh so gently, and dipped their beaks first in water and then in feed. As soon as they got the taste of it, they would eat on their own and could be turned loose. Life was tough for baby chicks. Sometimes a rat would get into the brooder house; and if a chick accidentally got a sore spot, the others would peck at it until it died.

She learned not to walk on sticker weeds or yellow jackets' holes. She stepped on rusty nails and had tetanus shots. She squashed big green worms from the tomato plants and poked at their yellow-green guts with a stick. She threw rocks into fresh cow dabs and listened to them splat. Once she dropped a brick on her toe and the nail turned black and eventually came off. When she found a nest of baby rats in the empty corncrib she was using as a playhouse, her father stunned them by swinging them by the tail and hurling them against the wall. Then the barn cat ate them. She built dams across Muddy Crick until her father complained about the flooding.

She learned that boars and bulls were called "male animals" when her mother talked on the phone or to men other than Daddy. She knew that male animals were always trying to climb up on the other animals so she didn't understand why her mother hit Winky Dinky and Britches, the male kittens, with a broom when they mounted each other. Her mother just said they were naughty and swept them off the front porch.

Like all farm kids, Tretona always had chores to do. When she was young, they were very simple—picking up corncobs to use as kindling in the Franklin heating stove and drying the silverware. Later on, she was permitted to clean the chimneys of the kerosene lamps with newspaper (Tretona's family didn't get electricity until she was eleven). Another job that took special care was gathering eggs (Tretona was always afraid of being pecked by the old setters, so she would put on her dad's gloves and pry the hens off with boards).

Tretona complained a lot about chores—she always seemed to put off hauling in wood until the Jack Armstrong program came on—but she didn't really mind doing them as long as they didn't involve housework or gardening. (Tretona somehow decided early on that women's jobs were no fun.) Later on, when the doctor found she had allergies to housedust, detergent, and many fresh vegetables, she became officially exempt from almost every job she particularly hated. Getting that medical report was almost as satisfying as having the water wings arrive early.

Tretona's big complaint about the farm was the fact that there weren't any kids to play with. When she was three, Melvin Conover, who was four, lived up by the mailbox. They were good buddies. Tretona's dad chuckled over the time they were found naked in the play wigwam he had rigged up under the maple tree in the front yard. Each mother grabbed her own kid and ran to opposite sides of the lawn, he claimed. And then Tretona went through a phase of riding her tricycle up the road to see Melvin until her mom tied her to the gate with a rope. (Mercifully,

Tretona couldn't remember this incident but she always went wild when people would chain dogs up to the clothesline.) But then Melvin moved away and only came to visit when his father came to help cut pigs or make hay.

Tretona liked and admired Melvin a lot. Already at age eight he got to drive the car around the barn lot and on lanes going along the fields to the back forty. There he was, propped up with feedsacks, holding himself up by the steering wheel, his toe barely reaching the clutch. Tretona had to wait until she was ten, though she got to drive the tractor before that, of course.

Her mama thought it was awful letting little kids drive but it became a competitive thing among the men as to whose kid could do things the youngest. Tretona's dad must have set two records—one when Tretona drove the kids to Bible school when she was only eleven, the other when her six-year-old brother Stanton drove a tractor home from the Sand Place in high gear.

Tretona could remember Stant's feat more vividly than her own. She was out in the barn lot with the threshers when someone looked up and said, "It looks like Getroek's kid is driving the tractor alone!" Sure enough, there was Stant, front tooth out, bare-footed, freckled everywhere except where his shorts protected him, his face intent under his straw hat. He was pulling an enormous load of hay, which dwarfed the tractor, which in turn dwarfed him. He was in fourth gear and coming fast. The barn lot gate was plenty narrow and some people had already scraped off a few bundles while making the turn.

Tretona felt the still tension in the men, but then Stanton made it okay and brought the tractor and wagon to a stop. Tretona's dad came in with the next load (he had been riding with Stant, but had jumped off to close a gate). "That kid of yours ain't a bad driver, Getroek," said Melvin's dad. "Well, he's learning, I guess," Tretona's dad said.

Tretona realized that a point had been scored and she beamed with pride for her father and even for that little squirt, Stant, who evidently could do some things right after all. "Come on, Melvin," she said. "Let's go have a contest throwing rocks at cow dabs."

The problem of finding friends to play with didn't get much better when Tretona started going to school. Somehow, she just never could make friends at school. Her mom said it was because everyone was jealous on account of her being so smart and besides, her father was on the school board. It was true that Tretona won the Friday afternoon ciphering matches and always had the longest list of book reports after her name. She played the piano for singing except when someone requested "Down in the Valley," which wasn't in the book. Agatha Waites always took over for that because she could play by ear. Tretona was glad to share the job—she didn't much like sitting up in front all the time. But then she couldn't resist picking out the melody by ear one recess and when the teacher found out, Tretona had to play all the time.

As soon as Tretona got into the Big Room (grades five to eight), she always had to do arithmetic with the eighth grade. Tretona never learned about not showing off. For example, when the teacher confessed she had forgotten how to extract square roots, Tretona immediately went home and got her mother to show her how and then the teacher found out and Tretona had to explain it to the whole eighth grade class, not just that year but *every* year she was in the Big Room.

Tretona couldn't understand why the kids—and even the teacher sometimes—were so dumb about schoolwork. But neither could she understand why they cared about her being good at it. Lots of things in life were a lot more difficult—like throwing a softball straight or learning to run in a darting fashion so you didn't get tagged out in Dare Base. Tretona was no great athlete, but she wasn't nearly as bad as the other kids' jeering would indicate. She was always chosen last unless the teacher was out on the playground. The teacher even let her be pitcher once when Cheaney entered a team in the county tournament on the last day of school.

Most of the time Tretona played with her brothers and sisters. Stanton was four years younger, then Norva and Troy came in quick succession. They called themselves "The Gang" and each had an alias. Stanton was "Watermelon Belly" because he could swell up his skinny little stomach in an unbelievable fashion. He was also the best at farts and belches. Norva was called "Old White Dirty Pants" because her dresses were short and if she sat in anything wet or dusty, it showed. Norva wore glasses and was a bit of a sissy.

Troy's name was "Out-House Mouse" because he liked to go into the toilet and lock the door and stay there even when someone else needed to get in. Tretona liked him best because he was smart and wasn't afraid to talk back to anyone, even their mother. Tretona was "Goose," which was short for "Goose Cake," which was a transformation of "Boose, 'Tona, Cake," which is what one-year-old Tretona had shouted from her high chair when Aunt Beulis brought her a birthday cake.

The Gang spent a lot of time running around in a pack and hiding from Indians and pirates. Sometimes, especially at dusk, they were spies and would play Sneak Up. The main idea was for one person to sneak up on their parents without being seen and report back on what the grown-ups were doing. The Gang built a lot of forts. Some of the best ones were made by cutting down jimsonweeds and piling them up so that the sticker balls were all on the outside.

Tretona always bossed The Gang and never had much trouble keeping things running smoothly, except when her mom would look out the window and intervene. Then peace was destroyed and Tretona generally got into trouble.

I remember one case in point. Tretona-8 and Stanton were playing in the sandpile with tin ice cream spoons. Stanton was trying to collect them all. Rather than have a confrontation, Tretona would secretly throw one over her shoulder from time to time, so she could pick them up later.

"Tretona, what are you throwing out of the sandpile?" a voice yelled out the window. "Rocks," said Tretona, trying to avoid a second confrontation. "I think you're lying," said her mother and came out and gave Tretona a whipping with the flyswatter. It was a homemade swatter and the rough edges of the screening wire scratched up Tretona's legs.

When it came time to go to Bible school that afternoon, Tretona was feeling abused (after all, it was really Stant's fault for trying to pig the spoons and her mother's fault for butting in), so she protested that she couldn't go because people would ask about the scratches. "Nonsense," said her mother. "We'll put talcum powder on them and if anyone should ask, just say, 'They look like blackberry briar scratches, don't they?'"

Tretona still felt abused, but now she also felt triumphant over her mother and she went off to Bible school quite satisfied with herself.

Tretona finally made a friend. Bernice lived in the Asbury Hill school district but came to the Cheaney church. She was a big, good-natured girl and had big, good-natured parents. Tretona loved to go home with Bernice after Sunday school. They would play Lone Ranger and Tonto for hours, galloping around saying "kemo sabe" and humming the theme song. (Years later when an older Tretona heard the *William Tell* Overture played by a Swiss band in Grindelwald, she could hardly keep from visualizing a masked man and his Indian companion riding across the north face of the Eiger.) Sometimes Bernice's cousin, Dottie, was there and she always had to be Dan Reed. (Bernice and Tretona agreed that the Lone Ranger's nephew was too goody-goody and stupid to be taken seriously.)

They were too old to play doctor but sometimes they played school teacher. The victim would lie across the bed, close her eyes and moan while getting paddled gently on the bottom with a Ping Pong paddle.

Sometimes Tretona would stay with Bernice on Saturday night and then she would get to go along with the Gump family to the Cheaney store to loaf. On Saturday night most of the farm families went to the general store to buy groceries and any number of other things, such as chicken feed, rubber boots, garden seeds, and rope. Then they would "set a spell and talk." There was a big stove in the middle with a shiny chrome railing that you could rub your stockinged feet on. It was surrounded by church benches. The men sat on one side and the women on the other. The kids squirmed around or went over by the candy case to do some window shopping. Almost everybody treated himself to a bottle of pop.

The talk was mostly about the weather, who was sick, who was getting married, and whether the preacher was any count. Whenever anyone came in the door, there would be a lull while everyone turned around to see who it was, then there'd be a rather awkward exchange of "howdies" and the talk would gradually start up again.

Tretona's family rarely stayed to loaf (buying pop for six people would have been too expensive and her mom found the talk boring), but Bernice's family always stayed until the end. Sometimes it was eleven o'clock before Tretona got to bed!

Once when Bernice stayed at Tretona's house, Tretona showed her a sock full of nickels and pennies that she had saved up. Bernice was really impressed so Tretona got another sock and gave her some, but when Bernice got ready to go home, Tretona's mom insisted the money be returned. Bernice's mom agreed, but

Tretona felt humiliated. It was supposed to be *her* allowance to spend as *she* liked. As usual, grown-ups were spoiling everything, and just as she was finally getting a friend.

That night Tretona's mom went with her to the outdoor toilet. It was a crisp fall evening and they sat on the adjacent holes looking out at the barn lot and the stars. They talked about the war, about how good it was that her dad was a farmer and didn't have to go in the army, and how lucky cousin Eldon had flunked out of pilot's school and had a safe desk assignment. Tretona was worried about the food rationing, but her mom said they could grow everything they needed on the farm—except for salt maybe. Her mom said the war would probably be over soon anyway. She was more concerned about the Russians and whether they would remain friendly after the war.

Tretona liked it when her mother talked calmly and said important things. When they got back to the house Tretona climbed up the steep stairs to the loft and crawled into bed. Out of habit she lay on her stomach and stretched out her hands and feet in four directions as her mother always told her to do. It was supposed to be a healthy way to sleep. Suddenly, she remembered Bernice and the money sock and began to cry. Instinctively, she curled up into a ball and put her left hand between her pajamaed legs. Slowly the soothing rocking motion began. It was like using your whole body to suck your thumb. After a while the tears stopped and Tretona fell asleep.

3 Blood Will Tell

As is the mother, so is her daughter.
                                          —*Ezekiel*

That which comes of a cat will catch mice.
                                          —*Proverb*

THUS FAR IN my attempt to reconstruct the child Tretona, I
have stuck closely to memories. But these are the memories of
Tretona-40 and even their freshness and vividness cannot guarantee that they haven't been retouched. In addition, the process of
selection and ordering inevitably is that of Tretona-40. Of course,
we should not assume uncritically that Tretona-10, if she were
here to be questioned, would have a better theory of her own
identity than does Tretona-40—or the reader for that matter.
Proximity to an event guarantees neither accuracy of observation
nor astuteness of insight.

All of the above is an apologia for my now proceeding to tell
you what Tretona-child *must* have been thinking and what her
biggest projects were, although I cannot remember specific
instances of her having had exactly these thoughts.

Tretona's central concern was *not* to be like her mother. She
was 100 percent sure she didn't want to be like her, but also afraid
that she might be. She looked a lot like her mother—"just the
spittin' image of Corinne"—everyone said, and unfortunately the
old Thacker photo album, which showed her mother as a child,
bore out the claim. When she talked on the phone, she sounded
like her mother—even her father sometimes mixed them up when
he called home from the store to see if they needed any groceries
for dinner. And her mother was always drawing parallels between
her own childhood and Tretona's: both were good readers; both
skipped two grades and went to high school early; both were

nervous children and had to have enemas a lot; both plagued their mothers by misbehaving ("You'll never know till you have a child of your own; I didn't until I had you"); both had ruined their mothers' health in childbirth, etc., etc.

Tretona was determined that she would not be another link in the chain of nervous, smart, redheaded women that went back at least to her great-grandmother Raelene Wiesner (who, by the way, didn't sound half-bad: she had buried four husbands and there were all sorts of stories about her which involved wolves, covered wagons, burning houses, and quicksand). For one thing, Tretona probably wasn't going to get married—she announced that kissing was unsanitary. And if she did, she was going to insist that her husband be sterilized. (Her mother laughed and said she was clever not to have said "castrated." Tretona didn't actually know the difference, but she stuck to "sterilized" because it sounded cleaner.)

Tretona hated the way her mother got almost hysterically angry and threw things and whipped the kids too hard and in general lost control. In a way, her mother's mad fits were impressive (if one wasn't directly involved), for no one could control them—she even chased Tretona's dad around the house with a hoe. Tretona wanted to be like the stoic, stone-faced Indians she'd read about in *The Deerslayer* and *Last of the Mohicans*. She resolved to show no anger or any other signs of weakness, but also never to forget or forgive the crimes that the "white man" had committed against her rights.

Tretona hated her mother's general inefficiency and her constant complaining about housework. There would be a crisis right at meal time whenever company came to dinner. And the house was always such a mess that no unannounced visitor could be invited in. Tretona's mom would leave the caller standing on the porch and talk out through a half-opened screen door. Periodically, Tretona's mom would get sick and go to bed and read old issues of the *Saturday Evening Post* (it always seemed to happen when a special occasion was coming up). At first, Tretona didn't mind—her mom was very nice when she was sick and read Tretona stories and laughed a lot. Furthermore, either her dad or a hired girl would come in to clean up the house and they were always really jolly and efficient. But then as Tretona got older, she had to take over. She generally could make the kids behave (though they wouldn't help any), but she couldn't get much straightening up done because her mother was always shouting out new jobs from the bedroom and asking for toast or a clean snot rag (around the house the Getroeks used old diapers as handkerchiefs).

Tretona also hated her mother's crude and earthy ways—she was fat and wouldn't get her hair done (she said it cost too much, but Tretona thought she probably just didn't care). When it was hot she ran around in holey underwear and scratched her piles, even when people were looking, and soaked her "granny rags" in a bucket in the basement for days after her menstrual period was over. Tretona just couldn't understand why her dad ever wanted to kiss such a creature. He was lean and good looking. He always slicked up and put on fresh overalls before he went to town (if there *were* any—her mom was generally behind on the washing and ironing).

But no matter how hard Tretona tried to be different from her mother, the fear of imitating her was always there—for Tretona, too, was on the chunky side and she was sloppy at penmanship and always smeared her pilgrims during art class. And then there was the "scientific" theory, which her mother was always citing, to the effect that "blood will out": "Now I don't want you boys being too friendly with Lottie Nork. She may act like a nice girl now, but she's an illegitimate child and her mother was illegitimate, too, and her grandmother, Norene Doss, is a churchgoing woman now, but she was just a whore when she was younger. Mark my words, Lottie Nork will go that way, too—it's in her blood."

Somehow, it never crossed Tretona's mind that she had some of her father's blood, too. She tried to emulate him, but it always seemed she was swimming against the tide—she just didn't feel like her dad. It wasn't so much that she was a girl—Stanton was like her mother, too. Maybe it was because she looked so much like her. It seemed that Troy, the one kid who didn't have red hair, might be the only one who had a chance to become a Getroek instead of a Thacker.

4 Jesus Has a Table Spread

Almost persuaded, now to believe.
Almost persuaded, Christ to receive.
                    —*Revival Songbook*

When nothing else would help
Love lifted me.
                    —*Songs of Praise*

TRETONA GETROEK WAS at her first teenage wiener roast. "The fellows will bring the hot dogs—you girls bring your buns," said the bad boys on the schoolbus. The women who ran the Young People's Sunday school class had organized the games and now as a forfeit Tretona had to go for a walk in the woods with Lee Kiplinger. Lee was shorter than she was (even though she was only eleven Tretona was taller than most of the freshman boys), but he had lost no time in getting his arm around her and his hand under her new sweatshirt, which had a Bushnell Bulldog on it. Tretona had quickly put a stop to that—mainly, she was embarrassed because she didn't wear a bra yet and didn't want anyone to find out. Now they were leaning against a tree and Lee was holding her hands gently behind her back and rubbing her shoulder with his forehead. She liked the smell of his hair oil and sort of felt like touching the back of his neck with her lips, but she didn't, of course. No words were spoken—there was just the sound of crickets and Lee's breathing. Suddenly, Lee expertly pinned her arms against the tree and stuck his right hand down the front of her jeans. Tretona quickly struggled loose but not before his fingers parted her legs and slid along smoothly from

17

bottom to top. They walked in silence back to the campfire. Tretona's cheeks were on fire—and it felt like someone had broken a warm raw egg in her pants. As they went back to their separate places in the circle, Tretona noticed that Lee casually drew the fingers of his right hand under his buddy's nose. It was only then that Tretona felt a bit ashamed—the buddy was Melvin.

Then Fern Baltzell, one of the youth leaders, had everyone stand up, hold hands, and shut their eyes for their prayer song: "Now I Belong to Jesus." Tretona felt cozy all over as the whole circle began to sing: "Jesus my Lord will love me forever. . . ."

The new revival spirit had hit Cheaney when Reverend Tingly came to town preaching about the second blessing. Tretona's dad reckoned he had the right name because he sure made the ladies all tingly. Reverend Tingly said that being saved, baptized, and a member of the church wasn't enough—one had to be sanctified, too. When you got saved, you confessed all your sins and tried hard to be good. But later on, when you got sanctified, God purified you and removed even the desire to sin. One was still tempted, of course, and could make mistakes (he told long, lurid stories about a mother feeding her sick baby arsenic instead of aspirin), but sanctified people never sinned *on purpose.*

To get sanctified one had to go back up to the altar a second time and a lot of the older church members didn't like that idea. Going to the altar was for kids and sinners, not respectable Sunday school teachers. They also thought it sounded too much like what the Church of God people did. Methodists were almost as critical of the Church-of-Godders as they were of unbelievers. Those Pentecostal people were too radical—they washed each other's feet in church and had to tithe 10 percent. They spoke in tongues and went into trances when they got the third blessing.

When some Methodist ladies got up and sang "Lord Build Me Just a Cabin in the Corner of Gloryland" as a special number, Tretona's mother said it was a theological objection to the preacher who was always talking about not remaining at the fringes of Christianity or just sipping from the cup of God's grace. Tretona's dad said that it was just a nice peppy song and that no protest was intended.

In any event, the new revival spirit took over. Tretona's mom was sanctified at home while she was mopping the floor; her dad went quietly to the altar one Sunday morning. As a result there were no more free Saturday night movies on the Cheaney school playground in the summertime and the Getroek kids barely got to see *Quo Vadis* and *The Robe.* (Movies were wicked because movie stars drank and got divorced.) Tretona's mom couldn't hang out wash on Sunday, but her dad continued to haul in hay or plant beans sometimes, if it was a real emergency and rain was forecast. For a while, Tretona was afraid she wouldn't be able to get a high school class ring (the Church of God kids couldn't), but someone finally found a Bible passage which seemed to imply that decorating your body was okay as long as it didn't involve any graven images or made you look like a whore. Lipstick was forbidden—too sexy—but Tretona thought it looked weird with her red hair anyway.

The best thing about the new revival spirit was that the district superintendent appointed Sister Naomi and Brother Don as the new preachers. Brother Don preached sanctification and holiness doctrines (which pleased the evangelistic people in the community), but his style was very soothing, so he didn't antagonize people who liked a more formal church service. Tretona fell in love with the whole family, especially Sister Naomi.

Sister Naomi played the piano by ear with all sorts of extra runs and lots of pedal. Tretona thought she was the best piano player in the world—even better than the woman on the Old Revival Hour radio program. She could transpose songs into any key (even keys with lots of sharps and flats) and that made it a lot easier for the congregation to sing nice and loud. The song leader was always coaxing the congregation to "make a joyful noise unto the Lord." Tretona could sing really loud (maybe it was from yelling at The Gang and playing the trumpet) and sometimes Sister Naomi would hear her clear up at the piano and look back and smile just a little.

Sister Naomi was a bit plump maybe, but she had real nice long, thin legs. She didn't have long hair like most holiness women (the Bible said a woman's crowning glory was her hair). Some people disapprovingly said she probably got permanents, but Tretona believed her hair was naturally curly.

Tretona saw a lot of the new preachers what with morning and evening services on Sunday and Wednesday night prayer meetings. Tretona got Sister Naomi to give her piano lessons—she studied special versions of songs like "The Lost Chord" and

"Jerusalem" and learned how to improvise on regular hymns by playing the melody with the right hand down in the bass and crossing over to chord with the left hand up in the treble. She always took care of Jackie in church, and sometimes she got to babysit in the parsonage. When Jackie was off playing, Tretona would go in the bedroom and look at Don and Naomi's double bed. She ached to lie on it and masturbate, saying, "I love Naomi" rhythmically under her breath the way she did at home, but it somehow seemed sacrilegious so she never did it.

The very best time of all was during the tent meetings in the summer. A big circus tent would be put up on the school yard and for two weeks (or even three, if lots of souls were being saved), Tretona would see the Parrs everyday. Jackie's uncle, Jode Parr, was the evangelist and he was just the opposite of Brother Don. He stood way up on his toes and gestured violently with his arms when he preached. He talked a lot about original sin and claimed it was the devil in them which made little babies cry when you put them down for a nap and tip-toed out the door. He said even little kids would go to hell if they were past the age of accountability and hadn't been saved. (Tretona was a little concerned about Jackie, but Brother Don said not to worry because he had probably been saved once when he was three although they weren't sure he knew exactly what it meant.) Brother Jode said the temperature in hell was even higher than it had been in the middle of the atom bomb and that the burning of flesh and screaming just kept going on and on for all eternity.

Tretona was always relieved when they got on to the altar call. Then Jode's body would relax and he would start talking about how *good* it felt when Jesus came inside of you and filled you with love. Then Naomi would start to play something like "Softly and Tenderly Jesus Is Calling" real quiet and prettylike. Jode would look over at her with the sweat dripping down on his white collar and just smile like an angel. Brother Jode was unmarried and awfully handsome—some people thought he smiled just a little too much at Sister Naomi, but Tretona reckoned it was all right.

All sorts of people would go to the altar—even Bernice's dad went. As a result, he started wearing white shirts to loaf in on Saturday night and people gradually stopped calling him Andy (to go with Gump) and started using his real name, Cliff. Tretona was glad Bernice's dad had got saved, but she did miss looking at the dirty picture books he used to keep hidden behind the seat of his dump truck. They were called "eight-page Bibles." She and Bernice used to pore over the drawings of men and horses with enormous cocks and the big-breasted women who were always smiling as they took it all in.

Once she and Bernice had a big argument over whether Jane Dillard really used Coke bottles. Bernice believed the rumor, but Tretona thought it was implausible—Coke bottles were too cold and hard; besides they might break. Bernice agreed that things like wieners (held under warm water), bananas, candles, Prell shampoo tubes, or the fingers of rubber gloves filled with beans were much better. Tretona believed that Bernice was probably pretty experienced in such matters. Tretona let on like her own activities were quite varied and sophisticated, but in fact what she liked best was just moving against the base of her thumb.

Sometimes when Jode was giving a particularly persuasive altar call, Tretona would put her hands behind her back and hang on to her left thumb. She was always having dreams about getting her thumb cut off and not being able to play the piano. Tretona was very impressed when she learned that one big advantage man had over apes was the opposable thumb.

Tretona liked church because the Parrs were there and people in general at least pretended to be friendly. But high school was a disaster. The long bus ride was the worst. She was among the first to get on the bus when it started its circuit around Cheaney at 6:30 A.M., but it often happened that there would be one person in every row and then no one would let her sit with them. Tretona would try to shove in anyway but they would sit out by the aisle and brace their arms against the seat in front of them and say they were saving the seat for friends. The bus driver, who was Jane Dillard's dad, would slow down the bus and peer anxiously into the rearview mirror as Tretona went up and down the aisle. Finally, he would slam on the brakes and say with exasperation, "All right, *someone* let her sit down." Tretona never quite knew whether he was mad at her for being so unlikable or mad at the kids for saving seats. She generally would end up sitting with Floyd Mushrush, who was fat and tongue-tied. You could hardly understand him when he talked, but Floyd wanted to be a preacher and Brother Jode said that he could be, too—with God's grace. Tretona hated sitting with Floyd Mushrush because all the kids teased them and when they had to sit three-in-a-seat his fat leg felt awful, just like Miss Fillmore's. Then one day, Floyd drew her aside in the corridor at school. His eyes were damp and his speech was thicker than usual. "Tretona," he said, "I want to ask you a favor. I didn't want to say this, but I've prayed about it. Please, don't sit by me anymore. The kids tease me so bad anyway and. . . ." Soon afterward, Tretona got the whooping cough and had to stay out of school for six weeks.

It took a long time, but finally she started to make a few friends. The girl who had a locker next to hers wore a cross around her neck. Tretona had never talked to a Catholic before and they had big discussions about what really went on at Confession and what priests and nuns were like. Tretona started getting along better with the boys, too, because she knew lots of dirty jokes and acted up in class. She wrote an excuse note for Lee when he played hooky, but unfortunately, she misspelled his mother's name (she wrote it "Dorthy") and they both got called down to the principal's office. Once they all had to give a speech in English class on what they wanted to be when they grew up. Tretona wrote a dirty limerick on the back of her note cards, one line per card, and held them up like Burma Shave signs as she was giving the talk. All the kids went into hysterics. Mr. Foxx, who was sitting along the side and couldn't see the backs of the cards, said he didn't see what was so funny about wanting to be a research chemist.

Tretona never had any dates but she often ended up with boys after a football game or band trip or ice skating party. It was always the same—lots of strenuous wrestling during which they would rub her breasts and crotch and Tretona would squeeze the backs of their necks or shoulders. Then they would finally get their hands into her pants. Tretona could stretch things out by putting up a good fight. After they had put their fingers inside for a while, the boys would quit and go behind the car to jack off while Tretona got her clothes straightened out. Then she would get back into the car she'd come in and drive home. The boys never really coaxed her to touch them (Tretona wondered what a cock felt like) and nobody ever tried to kiss her. Tretona knew from talking to Bernice that sometimes boys kissed *her*—Tretona thought maybe it was because Bernice went all the way, although she swore she didn't. Tretona liked the wrestling part and sometimes the boys would be a little friendlier to her on the school bus the next day.

But after a while none of this mattered because Tretona became best friends with Belinda Thacker. It started with a big argument over politics. Belinda liked Harry Truman (whom Tretona and her parents hated), and Tretona soon found out that Belinda's main reason was that Truman was a Democrat (all the Thackers were staunch Democrats). Tretona had a good nose for bad arguments and she immediately attacked the naiveté, even immorality, of blind party loyalty. Belinda was a game opponent and bravely recited all the great things that the Democrats under Roosevelt had done for the country, which Hoover had practically destroyed. Tretona came back with stories of how Roosevelt took away people's freedom and made farmers kill baby pigs (even though people in China were starving) just to drive up prices.

That night Tretona went to sleep thinking about Belinda's snapping green-gray eyes and the fine hair on her cheek in front of her ear. From then on Belinda and Tretona argued every evening on the school bus. They fought over which community was better, Pinkstaff (where Belinda lived) or Cheaney. Tretona said Pinkstaff wasn't nicknamed "Chigger Ridge" for nothing and described in graphic detail all of the illiterate adults and illegitimate children who lived down there in the bottoms. Belinda said Cheaneyites were stuck up just because more people there had electricity. People in Cheaney weren't friendly and didn't have as much religion, as anyone who ever heard them sing in church could tell immediately.

And so then they fought about church music. Tretona said Pinkstaff singing was just "ecclesiastical jazz" (a phrase she had heard at church camp) and not worshipful at all—it almost sounded like Church of God music. Belinda said they were just praising God in a way Cheaneyites couldn't understand because they didn't have such pure hearts. Tretona said, "Judge not that you be not judged" and Belinda said, "Cast the beam out of your own eye. . . ." It was a wonderful argument and practically everyone on the bus was listening.

Then they got into the habit of playing some of the boys' rough games—like Hot Hand. You took turns hitting the back of the other person's hand as hard as you could. If anyone pulled her hand away she got punched in the stomach. Tretona could hit harder but Belinda had the knack of making her wrist limber so that her hand cracked down like a whip. After a while their hands were red and swollen and sweaty.

The best game was Stare. There were two ways to play it. Either you lost by blinking or by looking away. Tretona could generally win at Blink Stare but Look-Away Stare was more exciting. To start with, Belinda's eyes would be hard and combative, but then she would make them go soft and deep. At first, Tretona would get flustered and look away when Belinda did that, but she soon learned to keep on looking. As the game progressed, they would try to distract each other by quick gestures or pinching. Their eyes would lock and then Tretona would brush Belinda's breast with her hand and in retaliation Belinda would dig fingernails into her arm. Tretona's mother was worried about all the bruises and scratches she came home with. Lots of times the other kids thought they were really angry at each other, but Tretona knew better.

When her sophomore year was over and summer came, she really felt depressed because she wouldn't get to see Belinda every day. Always before she had enjoyed the summers—especially since she had been old enough to help her dad with the farm work. There was something soothing about farming—the smell of moist dirt, the mellow buzz of the H tractor (her dad wouldn't have a John Deere on the place because they made a poopy sound), the hypnotic sight of plowshares slicing endlessly through the soil, later the excitement of pacing off rows and counting seedlings to determine whether they'd gotten a good stand.

But this year she was restless. It wasn't so bad disking on the back forty because that field was small and uneven so driving was a challenge, but it got boring working across the road on the old Hollister place where the throughs were a half mile long and straight as a ruler.

Tretona would sit on one buttock for a while and then the other. She practiced steering with her feet until her dad stopped her. (He was particularly nervous because a while back Dell Buck's kid over by Prairie Hall had fallen off a tractor and got an arm cut off.)

So then Tretona decided to work on her tan, taking her shirt off when she was way back in the fields and carefully slipping it on again when she came up toward the road. But her dad put a stop to that, too. "You're too big" was all he said, but she knew better than to argue.

Tretona wished she knew whether her dad liked her or not. True, he never got mad and hit her like her mom did. (Well, once he threw a corncob at her when she was teasing Stant out by the woodpile, but that was the worst.) But he didn't really talk to her much either, at least not about anything important.

And he seemed to get embarrassed if she imitated him. She remembered one time in particular when she was just a little kid. They had walked way back on the Lieb place to look at the new drainage ditch put in by the county, Tretona scurrying along beside him, trying to keep up. When they reached the place where the bulldozers had been working, her dad had slowed down, thrust his hands deep into his overall pockets, and started to whistle. Tretona, who had just learned to whistle herself, joined in though she couldn't trill yet like he could.

Her dad stopped abruptly. "It isn't nice to interrupt someone when they're whistling," he said. "And get your hands out of your pockets—you'll fall down."

Probably her dad would like her better when she grew up and didn't horse around on the tractor so much. Even now, they had pretty good times when they worked away from home and had to take a packed lunch. They would sit under a tree at the side of the field and eat fried chicken and radishes from the garden. They talked about groundhog holes and squirrel's nests and how the crop was going in. Then they would fold up their bread wrappers to be used again (waxed paper was too expensive) and while her dad took a short nap, Tretona would explore a crick bed, looking for arrowheads. Boy, she thought, it would be fun to be a pioneer and lay out the fields just the way you wanted them. There was still ground left up in Alaska—maybe she and a friend, someone like Belinda, could become homesteaders. Of course, you'd have to grow a different kind of crop up there, but you could probably find out what from the Agricultural Extension Agent. She'd better really pay attention now and learn all she could instead of just messing around and driving with her feet like a monkey.

The high point of the farming season was threshing time, and this year Tretona was really looking forward to it. As usual, Melvin's dad came the night before to set up the machine. The thresher was backed up to the barn so that the hay could be blown up into the hayloft. The place where the grain came out had to be cleared of manure and weeds. Her dad lay in a good supply of clean gunnysacks to catch the grain and one of Tretona's jobs was to cut pieces of binder twine just the right length to use as ties for the sacks. She measured the twine carefully and laid the pieces out in rows so that the sacker could grab them.

Early in the morning on threshing day Tretona and the other kids got out the wash tubs and hauled water from the pump. The full tubs were left in the sun to warm up. Just as the dew was pretty well dried off, the threshing gang would start to arrive. It took about twelve hands to run the machine and load up hay fast enough to feed it.

Tretona's job had always been to drive a tractor slowly through the field while the men pitched hay up on the wagon. Sometimes there would be a line of wagons waiting to unload at the threshing machine and then she and Melvin (who was also a driver) would sit up on the big tractor, which powered the threshing machine, and watch the bundles of hay get chomped up by whirling metal hammers. She and Melvin wondered where a person's body would go if it fell into the machine. They decided the teeth and small finger and toe bones would get separated out with the grain while everything else would be blown up into the hayloft.

But this summer her dad said she was not going to help outside—she would stay inside with the women. He had enough drivers, and her mother was short of help. Besides, she was getting too old to be hanging around with all those men—threshers talked pretty rough. Tretona was crushed and hid in the jimsonweed patch behind the chicken house for a long time. Finally, she came out because Sherry Thacker, her cousin's wife, and Fern Baltzell were helping her mom, and she liked them both a lot. It turned out to be fun cooking for so many people—Tretona got everyone to work like they were on an assembly line and it was exciting and efficient.

When it was dinner time the men all came in the yard and washed up in the tubs of warm water. Tretona noticed that Melvin stripped down to his undershirt and washed his neck and shoulders. He was big enough to pitch hay part of the time this year. When the load got high it was pretty easy to get hay down your neck. The older men were loaders. They stood up on top of the wagon and distributed the bundles so that the load was stable.

When the men filed in, they spoke politely to Tretona's mom and looked at their feet. The men and little kids, who couldn't wait, ate first and the women served them. Tretona helped for a while but when it looked like she was going to have to carry Melvin's dessert in to him she couldn't take it and ran off to the chicken house again.

After the men left, the women cleared off everything and prepared to eat at the second table. The men went out and squatted under the sycamore tree. Some of them started to roll cigarettes, but then Brother Don drove up and they stopped. He was in overalls and Tretona was so curious about why he'd come that she went out in the barn lot where the men were. Brother Don had decided to help Brother Getroek out a little, he said. He smiled at Tretona who suddenly felt embarrassed because she was barefooted and wearing a homemade feedsack dress. As she was standing there squirting warm dust between her toes, Melvin came over and said quietly, "I see you aren't working this year— just sitting around in a cool house with the women, huh?" Without a word, Tretona grabbed his straw hat, dipped it in one of the tubs of soapy water, and filled it with sand. Melvin was mad, but he just said, "What'd you want to go and do that for?" Tretona felt like killing somebody, but she couldn't figure out who.

After the hay was in and the corn was too big to cultivate, there was always a lag until soybean time. The kids kept nagging at Tretona to go fishing with them and help out with the new hideout they were building back in Skunk Hollow, but she just didn't seem to have any energy.

Once, though, she rode her bike clear over to the Lieb place. It was a long hard ride, especially since the gravel roads had been graded recently, which meant she had to ride on rocks. Belinda's house was on the way, and Tretona planned to stop and ask for a drink of water. Once she got there, though, she was too shy to stay long. "Nope, I gotta go over and see if the cows've still got water," she said. Belinda was trying to make conversation. "Tretona, are you 'bout ready for school to start?" Tretona just nodded. "*I* sure am," Belinda said brightly. "Mom helped me make some new clothes." Tretona didn't know why she couldn't think of anything to say. Maybe it was because Belinda's little sisters were standing around staring at her.

"That's real nice," she managed—and then with a big effort, "Guess I'll see you before that, though—tent meeting's starting next week."

That summer the tent revival meeting turned out to be real serious. A lady from across the river came to services one night and then drove off the Hardinsville bridge on the way home and drowned. Practically everyone went to the funeral and that night Brother Jode preached about how death could come at any time and how happy we should be that our dear sister had been in church the very night she died and how she was probably now sitting at God's right hand and rejoicing. When he gave the altar call lots of people went up, including Willie Mushrush, who was kind of wild and nothing at all like Floyd. As usual, the church members were invited up to kneel by the penitents. Belinda went because Willie lived in Pinkstaff close to her. Tretona stayed in one of the front pews taking care of Jackie and her little brother. Pretty soon everyone had got saved except Willie, but he just couldn't seem to pray through. Jode went over and told him that *something* was keeping the Holy Spirit out and that he should just ask God to tell him what it was. All of a sudden Willie raised up erect on his knees, took a pack of cigarettes out of his shirt pocket, and threw them in an arc back over his shoulder. "I'll do anything you say, Jesus," he cried and after that he got through right away. As he got up to shake hands with everyone, he told Jode that he felt called to be a preacher.

Tretona didn't file by the altar to shake hands because just then Troy crawled under a bench and got the cigarettes and gave one to Jackie, who promptly put it in his mouth. She had just got him straightened out when Sister Naomi and Belinda approached her. Her face clouded a little as she saw them standing there so close together. Then Belinda said, "Tretona, are you all right?" "You are saved, aren't you?" said Sister Naomi. All of a sudden, Tretona felt confused and said she didn't know for sure. And they both said that if you really were saved, you knew it. God sent the Holy Spirit to take away all doubts.

The next day was Sunday and they just happened to be having the quarterly Communion service. Tretona's mom told her she'd better take the sacraments. During the invocation Tretona got very nervous as the preacher read, "Whosoever taketh of this and is not worthy is in danger of hellfire." Tretona knew she wasn't worthy—she wasn't even sure she believed in hell anymore. She wasn't going to go up but her mother gave her a hard look. Tretona didn't know what to do. If there was a hell, she'd sure go there if she took Communion feeling as she did. But Tretona filed up to the altar. When the bread and wine came by she took them in her mouth and then quietly spit them out into her handkerchief without swallowing them. Later she explained to Sister Naomi that she hadn't really taken the sacraments. Naomi just smiled.

After that, Tretona finally had to admit that she was no longer a Christian. She had been saved once, at the age of ten when Reverend Tingly was still in town. She had gone to the altar at a special service in the Pinkstaff church. She had cried a little and then got up and shook hands with the congregation as they filed by. On the way home her mother said, "You've taken an important step tonight. Hasn't she, Steve?" And her father cleared his throat the way he did when he was a little nervous and said, "Yes, indeed." A few months later she had been baptized in the Ambraw River along with everyone else who had been saved that winter. By then Brother Don was the preacher. He stood out in the river in a suit, and when Tretona's turn came, he put a clean white handkerchief over her nose since she didn't know how to swim yet and tipped her gently back into the water. Tretona sputtered but she didn't choke. One of the church women said afterward that Tretona hadn't gone all the way under because her hair wasn't very wet on top. Her mother got very huffy and said Tretona certainly *had* been totally immersed. On the way home, as Tretona shivered in a blanket in the back seat, her mother was still angry. "Imagine that Gertrude Mundhank trying to insinuate that Tretona's baptism wasn't valid." Her father then told how the Dunkards down by Granddaddy's house baptized people face forward three times (one each for the Father, Son, and Holy Ghost). Tretona thought once was quite enough. Her new white dress never looked the same after being in the dirty river water.

She decided that she had probably been saved then, but she sure wasn't now because she was always thinking bad things about people, like wanting to kill them or stuff their faces in mud. And as Naomi and Belinda had said, being a Christian wasn't the sort of thing you could have any doubts about. If Jesus had come into your heart, you'd know it okay.

After a while, Tretona didn't half mind being classified as a sinner. Naomi often took hold of her hand and said she was praying for her. Don argued with her about predestination, God's omniscience, and free will and loaned her a leather-bound copy of Saint Augustine's *Confessions,* with a silk ribbon book mark. Belinda went out of her way to stand beside her in the Young People's prayer circle before tent meeting and would sometimes whisper, "Oh, Tretona! If only you believed, too!"

By the time school started again, Tretona and Belinda had given up fighting entirely. Now they sat side by side on the bus, their shoulders and thighs touching, and Belinda talked a lot about how sweet Jesus was and how nice it was to know God loved you. If Tretona produced any "atheistical" arguments, Belinda would look infinitely sad and say, "Please don't talk that way—you know it hurts me so," and stroke Tretona's arm.

This might have become boring, but Tretona soon found out that Belinda also liked to hear about sex. First, it was mostly biology, but then Tretona talked about how nice it felt to put your arms around a boy's neck and shoulders and how wonderful it was when they touched you in certain ways. Belinda said she was horrified that Tretona should do such things without being in love, but Tretona could tell that she really liked hearing about it all the same. The more details she gave, the more Belinda would say, "That's really very sinful, Trctona," and the wider her eyes became.

Eventually, Tretona started feeling confused. By now she was convinced that she never could believe in God or salvation or miracles. Yet all the people she really admired (except maybe Mr. Foxx) were fervent believers. And that she remained a sinner obviously hurt Naomi and Don and Belinda. It got so that it was hard for her to sit through church and one night at a special meeting down at Mt. Carmel she just got up and walked out.

It was a chilly fall evening, and Tretona crawled into the back seat of Don and Naomi's car. Suddenly Belinda was there, too, and Tretona could hardly move or think. It was like lead blocks were pushing on her from all sides. Then she must have blacked out for a few seconds—at least there is a gap in her memory—for next she was tongue kissing Belinda and they were lying diagonally across the seat and Tretona was making love to her with her left hand because that was all that was free and Belinda had sweat and maybe a few tears on her face and was holding Tretona's shoulders and murmuring in her neck. Afterwards, as they held each other quietly, Belinda said, "What are we going to do?"

Tretona didn't say anything, but just held her tighter. Right then she felt like she could solve any problem and overcome any barrier. Then church let out and they both went off in separate cars.

By the time she got home, Tretona felt awful. There was blood on her left hand—what a brute she must have been. She was sure Belinda would hate her now. Belinda was clean and pure and without sin—or had been until Tretona had defiled her. Tretona tried and tried to reconstruct how it had happened, but her memory of how they got into each other's arms had gone completely blank. One thing was for sure—Belinda would despise her now. Some sins were too big for even Belinda to forgive.

Tretona was sick the rest of the weekend. Monday morning her mom made her go to school anyway. She sat with a bunch of people way back in the bus and didn't even look up when Belinda got on. They didn't see each other all day because Tretona had chemistry lab and had to eat a late lunch on Mondays. That evening Tretona hung around after band and got on the bus at the last minute. As usual, Belinda was reserving a seat with her books. Tretona couldn't believe it was for her, but then Belinda looked up and gave her a beautiful big smile. Tretona mumbled "Hi" and stumbled back to her seat. And then Belinda laid one hand casually on her thigh and took hold of her arm and started whispering excitedly, "Don't you see! God has chosen *me* as a vessel to bring you His love. Nothing we are doing is wrong since we love each other. This way you won't be sinning with those boys and I'll be better able to help you get saved. Tretona, isn't it wonderful!"

Tretona felt all the tension wires around her head zing away into space. She looked straight into Belinda's eyes and felt her saliva glands twitch and her vagina tighten pleasurably. If anyone could save her, it would be Belinda.

5 If Gold Rusts, What Will Iron Do?

But who would guard the guards themselves?
                                        —Juvenal

Come down and redeem us from virtue,
Our lady. . . .
                    —Algernon Charles Swinburne

TRETONA AND BELINDA had a very jolly junior year. They sat together every night on the school bus (unless Belinda decided to subject Tretona to temporary torture for some minor misdeed). One of them generally managed to get the car for ball games, and they always took each other home last. Tretona talked her dad into getting a "necker's knob" for the steering wheel so she could turn corners with one hand. If Belinda was driving, Tretona caressed her thighs and tickled her underpants so much that she'd give up and let Tretona drive so they wouldn't have an accident.

There were lots of lovers' lanes leading back into the woods or corn fields. One time down in the bottoms they interrupted their lovemaking to watch a raccoon clean its food by the creek bridge. Tretona and Belinda spent a lot of time practicing kissing. They worked on each other's eyelashes and ears and what Tretona later learned in linguistics class were called alveolar ridges. Tretona gave Belinda tiny hickeys on the inside of her elbows. (She never dared bite her neck.) She learned how to mould and tease Belinda's nipples until they were stiff and quivering like tuning forks. Then she would smelt them down into little limp rosebuds with her tongue. She chewed the hair on Belinda's arms and threatened to braid the hair between her legs.

Tretona only let Belinda make love to her on very special occasions. Once when Belinda stayed all night they shared a double bed in the loft. What a luxury after cold nights in the back seat of a Plymouth! They even both took off their pajamas and let their breasts play with each other. Tretona really liked the way Belinda made love to her that night, but it also scared her. When boys rubbed her down there, it was real exciting, but she always felt in control. When Belinda did it, she felt like she was going to burn out something in her brain—maybe go crazy. Besides, it just didn't seem right for Belinda to be doing that sort of thing. She was too good and pure to be involved in initiating sex. Getting swept off your feet wasn't so bad, somehow. The next morning they had to hide the pillowcase because it had bloody handprints on it. It seemed like one of them was always getting her period.

Somehow, miraculously, they were never discovered even though they took more and more chances: bribing Belinda's sisters to go out to play, jumping into their clothes just before her folks came home, passing thinly disguised notes in study hall, and stealing kisses on the bus. One Sunday afternoon in early spring they drove down in the bottoms and started necking. It was so muddy that they couldn't pull off the narrow road. Tretona had her face buried in Belinda's stomach, kissing her navel and Belinda's head was tipped back, her legs spread and her eyes closed. Suddenly, they realized that a man in a pick-up had stopped in front of them and was staring in amazement. Tretona had to back the car up for about a quarter of a mile before there was room for him to pass by. She and Belinda were relieved that he was a stranger, but mortified that they had been so careless.

And yet they wanted to talk to someone about what they were feeling. For hours, they discussed the pros and cons of telling Sister Naomi. Some instinct always stopped them. The events of the following summer proved the wisdom of keeping things secret.

The tent meeting that summer before their senior year was the biggest ever. Brother Jode preached for the second time and Brother Don helped out on the long altar calls—he was more soothing and coaxing than Jode and thus provided a nice counterpoint to Jode's frightening, punitive tone. Sister Naomi was the pianist, of course, but Tretona was the assistant musical director. That meant she got to play for the morning prayer meetings and arrange some special numbers. One evening she and Jackie played "Pass Me Not, Oh Gentle Savior" as a trombone duet. Tretona played the alto part on a real trombone and Jackie carried the melody on a trombone-shaped kazoo. Everyone laughed when they walked out carrying their music racks because Tretona's was so tall and his was so short. But they all shut up when the music began. Jackie got started on the right note and stuck right on the tune even though he was only five and he moved the slide of his toy trombone just like Tretona moved hers. She almost couldn't play for smiling because she was so proud of him.

The biggest attraction of the tent meeting that year was the new song-leading team, James and Lenore Clayton. They were music evangelists from the Nazarene church and, boy, did they get everybody singing and clapping. They would divide the congregation into sections and teach them rounds and question–answer songs. Then they would have contests to see which group could sing loudest. "Praise ye the Lord!" one side would sing. "Hallelujah!" would come the answer. Sister Clayton's group always sang loudest. She was dark skinned and wore navy blue dresses and black stockings. Her thick straight hair was pulled back in French braids and a bun, but wisps would work loose and frame her sweaty face. She had strong cheek bones (Tretona later found out she was part Oklahoma Indian) and rather prominent full lips which were a sort of blue-purple color.

The most remarkable thing about Sister Clayton was the way she moved her body. Her breasts were big and obviously crammed into her crepe dresses. It seemed to Tretona that the dress might split open any minute. She imagined it happening with a slow cracking noise like when you open up a ripe watermelon and loose pieces of juicy heart fall out. After the tightness over the bosom, the dress fell in soft, lazy folds down across her belly and hips. Sister Clayton would sway her lower body back and forth as she directed. Sometimes when she was trying to get everyone to sing louder she would spread her legs slightly and make her thighs tight. You could see them through the dress and also her stomach when she breathed. The louder people sang, the tenser her legs would become. Finally, on the last chorus they would start to quiver just enough so you could notice it. Tretona and Belinda watched pretty carefully and they decided that probably she wasn't wearing a girdle. Tretona's mom didn't like Sister Clayton one bit, but her dad said that Nazarenes just felt the music more than Methodists did.

Tretona also got to observe Sister Clayton in the morning prayer meetings. She was always whispering to people and touching their arms. And she would kneel by folks and comfort them if they had any sins or weaknesses to confess. One morning when Tretona turned around from the piano she saw that her daddy was crying at the altar. It turned out that he had gone into the pool room behind the Cheaney filling station intending to invite some of the crowd there to come to the tent meeting. He was just working the conversation around to the subject when someone started telling dirty jokes. Then he not only lost his nerve, but also laughed at the jokes. Tretona thought it was real nice how Sister Clayton consoled her father, saying that she knew Brother Getroek would be braver next time and that he would surely become a mighty soldier in God's war against evil and filth. Tretona didn't tell her mom about it, though.

One evening during the altar call Belinda and Tretona were side by side in the same pew as usual. They liked to share a hymnal and feel their fingertips touch across the spine of the book. It was also safe to brush their shoulders together and when they stood up sometimes their hips would touch momentarily. Suddenly, their cocoon of blended voices, electric skin, and honeyed underpants was invaded by Sister Clayton. She had come up from the back of the tent and stood behind them in the pew without being noticed. Now she thrust her body between them and whispered harshly, "Okay. Cut it out, you two." She grabbed each of them by the shoulder. Her hips felt firmer than Tretona had imagined. "What do you mean?" said Tretona weakly. "You know very well what I'm talking about," said Sister Clayton. "And to do it in church, too."

During the rest of the service Tretona and Belinda sat far apart. Afterward, they talked about what to do. The next evening during the prayer circle before church Belinda told Sister Clayton that she was only trying to lead Tretona to Christ, but Sister Clayton said, "Sure, kid," and walked away. Then they were really scared about what Sister Clayton might do.

It got more frightening when Tretona found out that the Claytons were coming out for Sunday dinner. The Saturday before she had to babysit Jackie and she tried to calm down and think what to do. She couldn't concentrate though, because Jackie and Troy were in a wild mood. They had decided to play revival meeting and had rolled up all the throw rugs to make an altar and put the davenport cushions on the floor for church seats. Teddy Bear was the preacher and all the Jumbo family were the sinners. "Come to the altar," said Jackie for Teddy. Troy and the stuffed elephants refused. "Bless you," said Teddy, "if you don't get up to the altar right now, I'll come back and kick you up!" A big scuffle ensued. Tretona tried to get them to start over again so she could use Slinky, the loose-jointed green snake, to be Sister Clayton, but Troy and Jackie grew bored and went back to fighting.

When Brother Don came to pick up Jackie, Tretona managed to bring up the topic of Sister Clayton and remarked that she sure seemed to have a powerful imagination. Don looked bewildered, so then Tretona had to mumble something about her big stories about Oklahoma, but Don said that probably things really were quite a bit different down there.

When Sunday came, Tretona decided all she could do was to stick around the house and make sure Sister Clayton didn't get a chance to talk to her mom alone. Dinner went okay. Brother Clayton did most of the talking, punctuating his stories about faith healing and stingy congregations that didn't pay their evangelists well with an occasional, "Isn't that right, Lenore?" Sister Clayton seemed smaller when she wasn't walking around in front of the tent. She sat across from Tretona. Whenever Tretona looked up to pass the noodles or see if her mom needed something brought in from the kitchen, Sister Clayton would be looking at her. Tretona felt flustered, but her experience in playing Stare helped her not to look away. Sister Clayton would give her a funny little smile and then slowly drop her gaze to Tretona's neck and breasts and hands. It happened several times and Tretona was sure she wasn't imagining it.

Tretona managed not to have to talk to Sister Clayton even after the meal when, as usual, Tretona's mom started bragging about her and Tretona had to answer questions about stuff like the essay contests and her classical record collection. (Her mother was so dumb she even wanted her to play some Stravinsky for the assembled group.) But unexpectedly things got out of hand. Troy had gone down to the basement after the noon meal to play. When James Clayton started coughing Tretona immediately

36

figured out what had happened. Troy had her old chemistry set downstairs, and they had supplemented it with muriatic acid from the drugstore, baking soda, lye, cut-up zinc can lids, fertilizer and sulfur disinfecting candles left over from when her mom had had scarlet fever.

Tretona tried to get Troy to be careful, but he liked to make what he called "Mud Pie Mountains"—seething, colored mixtures. The best concoctions were made in the half-gallon glass jar he used as a slop bucket. This Sunday Troy had tried to melt sulfur in a spoon and it had caught on fire. The brimstone fumes got worse and all of a sudden Troy appeared in the gas mask her Dad used when he moughed back hay.

Tretona went down to help Troy air out the basement. When she got back upstairs the men and kids were all out in the yard and her mom and Sister Clayton were in the front bedroom with the door shut. Tretona nearly went wild with worry. It didn't help any when she saw how puzzled her mother looked when the two of them came out. No one said anything but Sister Clayton shot Tretona a triumphant glance. Tretona didn't at all like the looks of the half smile on Sister Clayton's face.

As soon as the company left, Tretona's mom called her dad into the bedroom to talk. Tretona's mind went crazy. What was she going to do? Try to lie? But they wouldn't believe her. Run away from home? But probably Belinda wouldn't go along. Ask Naomi for help? But she wouldn't buy the "leading-Tretona-to-Jesus" argument, either. The only person Tretona could think of who might be willing to take her in was Grandma Getroek, who was really gentle and loving. But then she imagined trying to explain things to Grandma and knew immediately that it would never work.

Suddenly her mind stopped churning over possibilities and got very cold and clear. (1) She and Belinda loved each other. (2) Their love had nothing to do with Jesus. (3) No one would tolerate their love—everyone would try to destroy it. (4) Tretona would never give up that love no matter what, but she wasn't sure about Belinda's being able to stick it out. Tretona pulled her cheeks in tight and made her eyes very hard and dry. She pointed her toes in a little like Indians did, stuck her hands in her back pockets, and looked straight at her folks' bedroom door.

"Oh, there you are, Tretona," said her mother. "We were just discussing what Sister Clayton told us." Tretona was surprised at how calm—even warm—her mother's voice was. "Your father and I have decided we can afford it, if you want to go." And only slowly and with much amazement did Tretona finally understand that Sister Clayton had invited her to go along to a Nazarene music camp for teenagers. And Belinda would go, too. Sister Clayton wanted them to learn some duets and practice leading songs in a team, as she and Brother James did. The camp was clear over by St. Louis, but they could get a ride one-way with Jim and Lenore (her mother seemed to have become quite chummy with the Claytons all of a sudden). "Lenore thinks you have lots of talent and a great future in church music," her mother said proudly.

A question flashed through Tretona's mind about why Sister Clayton was doing this. But she immediately moved on to the problems of making sure Belinda got to go, convincing her folks she had to have new tennis shoes, working up the piano accompaniment to some of the new choruses Jim and Lenore were teaching them, and figuring out what to use as a suitcase. She also noticed that Sister Naomi and Brother Don didn't seem too thrilled about the camp idea, but she reckoned that might be because it was run by the Nazarenes.

A few days later they set off in the Clayton's old Buick. The trip was boring. Jim was a cautious, jerky driver and told lots of long, pointless stories. Lenore was broody and didn't say much. Tretona would have liked to sit close to Belinda, but Sister Clayton had piled some junk in the middle of the back seat, saying firmly, "You'll both want to sit by a window." She and Belinda held hands behind the stuff part of the time but it wasn't very comfortable, and Lenore kept looking back every once in a while and frowning.

They arrived at the camp late on Friday night and the three women were assigned cots in an overflow tent all by themselves. As soon as Jim left, Lenore moved the cots close together and chose the middle one. Everyone turned her back to undress. When they finished Tretona was surprised to see that Sister Clayton was wearing a flowery nightgown. Everyone in her own family wore pajamas. Sister Clayton looked younger when she wasn't wearing navy blue and her face seemed a lot softer and prettier when she undid her hair and started brushing it. Tretona really wanted to kiss Belinda goodnight, but she didn't have a chance.

As soon as the lights went out Tretona felt Sister Clayton's arm under her. Instinctively, she rolled her head up on Sister Clayton's shoulder. Sister Clayton was talking aloud about how much she cared for both of them and how Christ wanted his daughters to love each other. Her voice was soft but Tretona could feel the intensity of her breathing. She laid her arm very casually across Sister Clayton's lower chest. Immediately, Sister Clayton slipped her hand around Tretona's breast.

All of a sudden alarm bells went off in Tretona's mind. What if Sister Clayton was doing the same thing to Belinda? She vaulted over the middle cot and crawled on top of Belinda. "What are you doing?" Sister Clayton hissed. "Just leave us alone," said Tretona. Belinda didn't know what was happening, but she responded to the urgency of Tretona's kisses. Sister Clayton watched for a while, saying things like, "Better come up for air," and then left. Tretona made love to Belinda more fiercely than she ever had before. When they had finished, Tretona covered Belinda for a long time with her entire weight. Then she put their cots side by side and moved Sister Clayton's several feet away.

When Sister Clayton came back she turned the lights on. She was carrying two wet washrags and a towel. "Wash yourselves. It smells like pussy in here." Meekly, like two kids with chocolate on their faces, Tretona and Belinda complied. Nothing more was said and Sister Clayton didn't rearrange the cots. Tretona was surprised at how quickly she fell asleep.

The next morning they all attended the big farewell session for the old campers. Saturday was the day when the old batch left and the new people came in. Tretona and Belinda were very impressed with the way the Nazarenes ran their meetings. There was a band with lots of brass as well as a piano and an organ. The chorus was really peppy and sang lots of fast numbers that had four parts going off in different directions. Tretona's favorite was "Oh, the Glory Did Roll," and she resolved to learn it and to teach it to her brothers and sister. The most unusual part was the Popcorn Testimony Meeting. The idea was that people should pop up and just explode with praise for what God had done for them, preferably several at one time. In no case should one person finish testifying before someone else started. Some people made long speeches about prayers which had been answered. Others just stood up and gave a canned testimony, such as "I'm glad I'm saved, sanctified, and a Nazarene." Tretona felt like getting up and testifying that *she* was glad to be a Methodist, but of course she didn't.

That night the three of them moved into a women's cabin. Not all of the new campers had arrived so they had one corner pretty much to themselves. Sister Clayton and Belinda chose lower beds and Tretona picked the bunk over Belinda's so she could reach down and hold hands with Belinda after the lights went out. Besides, she was good at climbing up on things. Tretona woke up early the next morning just as the night was turning from black to gray. For some reason she glanced down at Sister Clayton. To her surprise, Sister Clayton was awake and staring at her. She was about to turn over and go back to sleep when Sister Clayton slowly pulled her long hair out from behind her head, brought it over her shoulder and arranged it on top of her breast. Then she laid a finger very gently on her lips to signal Tretona to be quiet. Almost as if she were sleepwalking Tretona slipped down off the upper bunk and lay beside Sister Clayton.

Tretona closed her eyes as they began to kiss. Belinda had a cozy moist little mouth and her tongue was always shy and gentle. But Sister Clayton's mouth was large and wet and her tongue was like a wild animal. Tretona felt like she was going to be swallowed alive or turned wrong side out. She got slightly scared when Sister Clayton started pulling her lower lip in between her teeth and biting and chewing on it. In defense, Tretona kissed back real hard and didn't bother to shield her own teeth and she boldly put her hand right up under Sister Clayton's nightgown and into her crotch.

Belinda had a soft little cunt that reminded Tretona of a little moleskin purse with a rabbit fur border. Sister Clayton had wiry hair and her vagina was sort of like the bubbling mud pots in Yellowstone. Tretona thrust in two fingers and then four as Sister Clayton began to buck like a horse. Tretona was afraid some-one—especially Belinda—might wake up from the noise so she tried to hold Sister Clayton down flat. She hooked one foot onto the side of the bunk and tried to pin Sister Clayton's legs. She got her left arm around Sister Clayton's neck in a wrestler's grip. But then somehow Tretona stopped trying to hold her back and really got into the ride. She found that if she moved her thumb around just right, Sister Clayton really went wild and then she started biting Sister Clayton on the neck and holding her breasts really hard and doing all sorts of rough stuff that she never would have dreamed of doing with Belinda.

And then Sister Clayton went stiff and shook like she was having little spastic fits and then her body turned all soft and she kissed Tretona's face all over and kept saying, "You devil, you."

After a while Tretona went off to the john and washed her face and hands and combed her hair. She was surprised at how normal her face looked. Inside, she felt very different. She now realized that Belinda might not be the only woman in the world she could love.

6 Janus Days

You can always tell a junior
By her knowing ways and such.
You can always tell a senior —
But you sure can't tell her much.
                    —*Bushnell High School song*

"I'm afraid I can't put it more clearly," Alice
replied . . . *"for I can't understand it myself to
begin with; and being so many different sizes in a
day is very confusing."*
                    —*Lewis Carroll*

WAS IT GETTING a driver's license on her fifteenth birthday?
Was it sitting on the far left of the study hall with the rest of the
seniors? Was it the confidence she gained from making love to
Sister Clayton (who confided later that Jim didn't satisfy her)? All
I know is that suddenly (although it must have developed
gradually) Tretona stopped feeling like a social incompetent.

Tretona was accepted everywhere now. All of a sudden the
kids on the school bus were friendly. She was in the brass quartet
with three very popular town kids. She wrote a weekly column for
the school paper and managed to smuggle some sexual innuendos
past the faculty advisor. She signed up for a music appreciation
course (even though her mother said it wouldn't help her get into
college) and learned to play some Shostakovich themes on the
piano. She stayed after class to argue with her English teacher
about whether Raskolnikov was mad or wicked or both. She even
stopped being scared shitless of Miss Kirk, the science teacher,
and managed to smile at her once or twice in physics lab.

Best of all, Tretona got a room in town and stayed there from
Monday morning till Friday evening. Her mother would never

have consented, except that Tretona got a big part in the senior play (she was Nora, the Irish maid, who turned out to be the swamp monster and murderer) and the weather was unusually bad that fall. Rather than have Tretona drive on icy, muddy roads, her folks let her stay down in Bushnell.

Tretona thought everything about living in town was wonderful. She stayed with a widow, Mrs. Johnson, whose household included a daughter and a grandson, Jimmy. The Johnsons were different from Cheaney folks. Mrs. Johnson didn't go to church—ever—and her daughter was divorced and worked as a waitress in a place that served beer. They had potato chips and pop in the house all the time and they let Jimmy buy comic books with his allowance—any kind he liked. (The Getroek kids were limited to classic comics—or Donald Duck once in a while.)

When Tretona talked a little about the Johnsons at home (she didn't mention the beer in the fridge or the fact they had a poker deck with real kings and queens instead of just rook cards), her mother got upset about her being in a "low-class environment." But Tretona didn't understand that complaint at all. The only lower-class people she knew were the Grinnegar family who lived in a shack down in the bottoms and drove to Cheaney in a horse and wagon because they didn't have a car. And perhaps the Simmons kids who had boils and got the itch—although maybe they weren't really low class because their mother was always out in the back yard boiling the wash and trying to keep everyone clean. (Mrs. Simmons was a pretty nice women even though she was a little dumb and her eyes were crossed real bad.) Anyway, Tretona thought the Johnsons were very sophisticated—like everyone who lived in town.

Tretona was increasingly impressed with the town kids as she got to know them better. They seemed to be so tolerant. No one teased Roger Farnsworth, the doctor's kid, for being short and playing the piccolo. Richard Darrs even drove around town with a collection of Shakespeare's plays showing in the back window and never got any real flak. Pete Lang wrote poetry and the other kids didn't mind. Mainly, though, he wanted to be a composer.

Not that the town kids were prissy. When Mr. Sharpe sent some of them over to his house to pick up music for the pep band, John Lloyd suggested they search the bedroom for Mr. Sharpe's rubbers. They didn't find any but then John started clowning around with a Tampax from the bathroom cupboard. Tretona had never seen one before, but John claimed that practically everyone used them—unless they were virgins or frigid.

Tretona's favorite town kid was Pete Lang. He sat behind her in study hall and they whispered a lot about his affair with Lynn Ryan. They didn't get to go out too often because she was just a freshman and her folks were against it. (The Ryans owned a big lumberyard and evidently they thought Pete's dad didn't amount to much. Tretona couldn't understand that because Pete dressed nice and was real sophisticated.) As a result, Pete was having a hard time getting Lynn to neck and stuff. He thought maybe he should just write Lynn a note and explain what he wanted. Tretona advised him to be more subtle about it—get the car, park somewhere nice, and sort of gradually seduce her. But Pete said he didn't want to sneak up on Lynn "like she was some old whore."

Tretona was moved by how considerate he was and felt guilty about how she still had to seduce Belinda all the time, but she acted tough and told him that probably Lynn was just waiting for him to be more assertive. Then it turned out that Pete was more worried about something else. "You know why the guys call me Big Phil?" "Sure, your middle name's Philip, isn't it?" "I don't mean the Phil part," he said. And then Tretona finally caught on and covered her embarrassment with a silly argument about how if there was room for a baby to come out there had to be a lot of elasticity down there. But Pete was worried about length, not width, and so finally Tretona just up and asked him, "How long is it, for Christ's sake?"

Well, Pete didn't know exactly but after lunch he came back with a piece of lath board that had two marks on it, one for extended and one for unextended. So Tretona promised to do a little research—not just on herself, but also to ask some of her shorter friends (Lynn wasn't very tall.). Tretona couldn't get over how concerned Pete was about Lynn, and when she had to write a short story for English class, she let the heroine (who was a chemist) end up marrying a composer.

Senior year in high school is a transitional time for planning and self-definition—a sort of nine-month-long period of making New Year's resolutions. Tretona's immediate future was fixed—she had always known she would go to college. But everything else was totally confused. She really loved and admired religious people like Don and Naomi. But Tretona couldn't be like that—

her mind just wouldn't let her believe all that stuff. And she really looked up to town kids like Peter Lang and John Lloyd, so witty, yet gentle and considerate. But she couldn't imagine necking and wrestling with them—they just weren't tough or strong enough. Practically any of the farm boys on the bus were sexier than they were.

But she sure wasn't going to get trapped into being a farmer's wife, the way her mother had. (Tretona's mom had met her father the summer before she was to start graduate school in political science. Her daddy drove a cute little model A Ford and went around the corner on two wheels, and one night in August they both got drunk on Cokes and aspirin and went off to a J.P. and got married).

Neither did she want to be a grumpy old maid like Miss Kirk, who knew a lot about science and never made a mistake, even on the hardest physics problems. She kept all the lab equipment in apple-pie order and could fix anything—from Van de Graaff generators to a bird's broken leg. She went on adventure trips every summer and had been clear to Mexico. But her dresses were way too long and the kids called the shoes she wore Ground Grippers—they were practical but really ugly. She was the harshest disciplinarian in the school and tried to make the kids go downstairs only on the right-hand side, even though that wasn't a rule, and even if no one was coming up the stairs. Tretona didn't know exactly why it happened that way, but all the old maids she knew were really odd and frowned a lot.

She kept hoping that she and Belinda could always be together and love each other. Sometimes the two of them would get passes during study hall and sit in the library drawing floor plans for a dream house. Tretona spent a lot of time on the bedroom and designed twin beds fitted with electromagnets. If both people were in the mood and pushed the right buttons the beds would attract each other and slam solidly together. Afterward, a switch in polarity would cause them to repel and move back apart.

But one day Belinda started to design a nursery and it looked like she hadn't really been planning the dream house for her and Tretona after all. She had always said she was going to marry a preacher (even while swearing she'd never leave Tretona) and now she actually had a candidate—Keith Wartsbaugh. Keith was from Pinkstaff, too, and had curly black hair which reminded

Belinda of Jimmy Dean. Keith was a nice, but tall and clumsy kid who was too shy to talk much—although once he asked Tretona if redheads had red hair down there, too. Tretona told him he'd have to get someone else to tell him. She almost told him to ask Belinda. But he was thinking about being a preacher now (Tretona's mom said he wasn't half smart enough to get through seminary), so of course Belinda got interested in him. Tretona was disgusted when she heard that Belinda sat with him on the bus whenever she stayed in town. Luckily, Tretona got the car a lot and Keith hardly ever did so things didn't get too out of hand.

Spring arrived and with it all the excitement over senior pictures, the class will, and the senior class prophecy. (In the unofficial version, John Lloyd predicted Tretona would be the madame in a whorehouse featuring Peter Lang's erotic music in the background.) Suddenly, the seventy-five graduating seniors all realized how much they liked each other and how high school really hadn't been that bad. They started hanging around the band room and the school newspaper office. They took over the balcony of the old gym at lunch and wouldn't let any non-seniors sit there. Even the town and country kids got together. They managed to get one whole issue of the *Bushnell Bugle* devoted solely to seniors. They felt bad about how depleted the athletic teams and band and chorus were going to be next year. They swore to have their first class reunion picnic in August. And they planned the senior prom.

Tretona hated dances (she had once gone to a mixer at a band contest and danced the two-step with a saxophone player—it was really boring) so she wasn't even thinking of going. But then Bernice told her that the two of them had been invited—by Harry Wiesner and Melvin!

Tretona was too embarrased to tell her mom, so there was no question of getting a long dress. But a lot of the kids weren't going to wear formals anyway; besides, she had a nice new taffeta dress—aqua colored and reaching well down over the knees (something to do with the New Look). She and Bernice talked a lot about whether the boys would get them corsages or not and what they should do about boutonnieres. They figured that Harry would probably get the car—his dad had a new Henry J.—and arranged for Tretona to stay over at Bernice's house in case they stayed out all night and drove down to Evansville for breakfast after the dance. (Bernice's mom knew where they were going.)

Tretona thought a lot about being with Melvin. Somehow, during the four years of wiener roasts and messing around behind the church at cemetery suppers, she and Melvin had never ended up together.

The boys didn't bring flowers. Harry didn't even wear a suit and Melvin took off his tie and jacket right away; the girls soon got hints that they weren't going to the prom after all. Tretona was relieved—she had been worried about dancing with Melvin. After getting cheeseburgers at the drive-in, they drove up to Green Hills State Park. Harry seemed to know exactly where they were going and he parked up at the top by the big cross, which was lit up every Christmas and Easter. He and Bernice immediately got out and walked over toward a picnic table way off in the distance.

Melvin took off his white shirt and folded it. Underneath, he was wearing a sleeveless T-shirt and Tretona could see some of the hair under his arms. Then he took off his suit pants, straightened the creases, and lay the trousers carefully over the front seat. Tretona gasped something about Harry and Bernice, but Melvin said, with a little smile, "They won't be back for a while." Tretona put up a token resistance, but there was never really any question. Melvin never hesitated, never wasted a motion. There was no messing about with breasts or wrestling or giggling or arguing. His legs were smooth, but hard and strong. Every time she moved, her position became more vulnerable— not that he forced anything, it's just that he was completely single-minded and took advantage of every shift. Finally, her right arm was pinned and their left hands were locked above her head. He reached down into his shorts with his other hand and she felt him move it up and down on the outside. Then there was a dull, sharp, cold, hot pain, and then it got a little better and Tretona even raised her hips off the seat. (There was a dirty joke about black girls being able to screw over a bucket of water without getting their asses wet.) Melvin had his forehead on her collar bone and when he stopped breathing so hard, he lay for a minute with the corners of their mouths overlapping. Tretona wondered if that could count as kissing a boy.

It took Melvin quite a while to get dressed—he was whistling a tune under his breath—Tretona thought it was "Stormy Weather." She didn't really have much straightening up to do— her dress was hopelessly wrinkled. Good thing she was staying at

Bernice's house 'cause her mom wouldn't get up when they came home. She got out of the car and peed behind a bush and wiped carefully with her handkerchief, but everything seemed to be okay down there. Pretty soon Harry and Bernice came back, and they did most of the talking on the way home.

The next day Tretona picked out "Stormy Weather" on her trombone and that was when she first thought about getting pregnant. Had Melvin worn a rubber? She hadn't actually seen his penis. Could he have slipped it on with one hand in that brief moment while he was fumbling in his underpants? It seemed unlikely. Maybe he had put it on before they came to pick up the girls. But Tretona had heard that you couldn't put one on before you had an erection and surely he didn't have a hard-on all that time before they went and parked. Had he gone to the toilet at the drive-in? To save her soul, Tretona couldn't remember. Later, she asked Bernice but she just looked baffled and said how the hell should she knew whether Melvin had gone off to take a piss?

The next weeks were agonies of second guessing. Melvin's manner had been so smooth. From the beginning of the evening he had known they were going to go all the way. He and Harry had planned where to park. Surely, they would have laid in a supply of rubbers. But where would they have got them? Both came from big families—probably their dads didn't even use rubbers—and high school kids couldn't buy them in a drugstore. Tretona had heard that you could get them in a machine at a truckstop over in Gosport, but she wasn't sure. Then she tried to remember the feeling when Melvin first went inside her. It had kind of hurt—maybe that was from the rubber. But she had felt awfully sloppy down there afterwards—maybe that was from the sperm. But wouldn't she have smelled it when she went to the bathroom behind a bush?

Tretona started getting headaches everyday on the school bus and Belinda kept asking what she was coming down with. Then one afternoon in gym class Tretona felt sick to her stomach and had to quit early. When Belinda came in from the track, Tretona was already dressed and grinning like crazy. "I got my period," she said. "What's so great about that?" asked Belinda. Tretona felt like she was blushing: "Well, now I won't have it during commencement week."

The more Tretona thought about graduating, the more

confused and frightened she felt. Before, the problem had always been *how* to get what she wanted—whether it was friends, or the front seat of the car on trips, or extra money to spend at the county fair. But now her big problem was to figure out *what* she wanted. Her ideas were like the pieces in a kaleidoscope—one little jiggle and they fell into a totally different pattern.

Take something which looked completely uncontroversial—efficiency. Tretona had always admired the way her dad organized his work, never wasting any motions, while her mother was always doing things the hard way and making everybody cross. Surely, it was good to be efficient. Tretona knew about the end-means distinction and realized that of course it would be bad to be an efficient murderer, but she thought at first that if you had already decided to be a murderer (which was bad), it was good to at least be efficient at it.

But when she read about how organized the Nazis were (the article had pointed out how ironic it was that there was no German word for *efficiency*), she worried because there seemed to be some strange connection between being well-organized and being a cold person. Like Miss Kirk, who had everything scheduled to a T, but then was mean to kids who turned stuff in late, even when they had a medical excuse. Miss Lyttle, on the other hand, was always misplacing their Latin assignments and doing dumb things like wearing her costume jewelry upside down. ("It looked right from up here when I put it on," Miss Lyttle giggled when they told her.) But she'd do anything for you—even for the mean kids who hated Latin. It was the same old paradox that came up with religious people—anyone who had a soft heart also had a soft head. Tretona thought it just wasn't fair.

Tretona also worried about the German problem. She and the other Getroek kids were about five-eighths German, mostly from her father's side. During the war, she had asked about Germans being bad, and her mother had pointed out that there were lots of good Germans, too—like Einstein and her grandmother. But then later Tretona found out that those two were both Swiss and that lots of the great German scientists were actually Jews. She felt funny after the war was over when her grandfather took up reciting poems in German again and bragging about being a good old "Dutchman."

Another spooky thing happened—in English class they read excerpts from *Thus Spake Zarathustra*. Tretona liked it a lot and said so before Mr. Foxx finally told them about the relationship between Nazism and the Superman concept. Tretona had always considered herself to be rather special, though not superhuman, of course, and now she wondered if that was partly due to her German blood. (She even worried a little bit about whether it would be wise to take German in college, but then she remembered she had to have it for a chemistry major.) Tretona became even more confused when she and Mr. Foxx discussed the case of Raskolnikov. (He had recommended that she do a special report on *Crime and Punishment*.) Tretona had always believed you should think for yourself and not pay too much attention to what other people said—in fact, that was the only way that she would have figured out that a lot of religion was bunk. Yet Raskolnikov thought for himself and he'd ended up murdering an innocent old lady with an axe.

Her mother had recently been yelling at her about being too much of a lone wolf and a rebel and told her about how Leopold and Loeb had gotten into trouble because they thought they were smarter than everyone else. Generally when her mother said things like that, she was just trying to get Tretona to fix her hair differently or to dress up more, but Tretona started worrying that maybe she was developing into some kind of monster.

Take the business about honesty. One thing Tretona had always hated was phoniness. It drove her wild when her mother would meet someone important (like the school principal) on the street and all of a sudden put on a fancy accent and start using big words. And she hated it when the gym teacher would break up quarrels over refereeing decisions by calling them all "ladies." Gym teachers also insisted on talking about that "special time of the month" when everyone knew they meant your menstrual period.

But now Tretona would catch herself being dishonest, too. It wasn't lying she worried about—she only lied when forced to for survival—like to avoid really big arguments at home. No, it wasn't the "good, honest lies," as she called them. It was the sneaky, phony business. Like when she wrote a bunch of bullshit on the college admission forms. Or when she argued for something she didn't really believe in in her essays for Mr. Foxx because she knew he'd like it. Or worst of all, the way she would pretty up the graphs in her physics lab reports by not plotting the data exactly right. At this rate, she thought, she would be morally unqualified to be a scientist before she even got to college.

Tretona was also starting to feel bad about disliking her mother so much. She started thinking maybe her mother really couldn't help the way she acted. Maybe she just wasn't cut out to be either a farmer's wife or a mother. Tretona knew her mother had been a good teacher. If her mother wasn't too tired, there wasn't anyone better at making Shakespeare really exciting or explaining advanced algebra. Her mother still knew more Latin that Miss Lyttle did, although she hadn't looked at it for twenty years. So Tretona started trying hard to appreciate her mother's good qualities. In *Little Women,* one of the girls (probably Beth, talking to Jo) had said something about never letting the sun go down on your anger, and so Tretona made it a habit to try to forgive everyone—even her mother—just before she went to sleep every night.

Just before graduation Tretona had a big talk about life and college with Mr. Foxx, and he recommended she read Philip Wylie's *Opus Twenty-One.* When she found out it was in paperback, she bought a copy with her allowance. It was about a writer who ran around voicing opinions on everything—Communism, dumb women, religion, the Kinsey report, you name it. Tretona thought it was fairly interesting but she couldn't exactly figure out why Mr. Foxx suggested it. The author was obviously a show-off, especially when he had clouds in the sky spelling out dirty words. Even when Tretona basically agreed with his criticisms of conventional ways of looking at things, she couldn't understand why he was so obnoxious about it.

But then something happened that made Tretona far more sympathetic to Philip Wylie. Her mother started reading the book and one night Tretona heard her say, "My God, Steve, just read this." Tretona never knew which passage it was, but her father got up out of bed, took the book down, and threw it in the furnace. At that point, Tretona gave up trying to forgive everybody for everything.

7 We Are the Stately Nuns of MMC

Sing a song of colleges
And tell me where to go.
Vassar's for the pretty girls
Wellesley's in the know.
                    —*MacMaster Dining Hall ditty*

Way down in Missouri
Where I heard this melody.
When I was a MacMaster girl
Sittin' on my counsellor's knee.
                    —*MacMaster Serenade song*

"THE BIG PROBLEM about walking down the track," thought Tretona, "is not the tears in your eyes. It's the spacing of the damn railroad ties." You either had to take one at a time and mince along or else double it with giant strides that nearly split your groin in two.

It was an unusually bright and warm Saturday in early March, and technically she was now AWOL from MacMaster College for Women because she had not filled in the sign-out book before going off campus. Cynically, she made up entries to fit her mood: *Destination:* Dereliction; *Accompanied By:* My shadow; *Expected Time of Return:* Never, if I can help it.

Then she ran through her Hit Parade of hated people: this week, Lucy Bentley, the fat little, smug little, rich little Episcopalian preacher's daughter, who was her roommate and had topped the list for at least ten consecutive weeks, had finally been topped by Dean Frysinger, bitch supreme, and defender of the (fanfare) *MacMaster Tradition*. Dean Frysinger had just lectured Tretona about her poor attitude, her lack of cooperation, about the importance of rules in any community, and about the "sanctity and venerability of the customs here at MacMaster." Tretona couldn't decide whether to sneer or vomit, so she just sat, impassive, like Uncas, last of the Mohicans.

Dean Frysinger had surreptitiously hitched up her bra strap (Tretona bet her breasts looked like dried-up cow dabs) and delivered the sentence—an apology to Mrs. Wallace (or "Wall Ass" as the non-*echte* MacMaster types called her) and no off-campus privileges for one week. Tretona was relieved that there had been no talk of cancelling her scholarship, and she didn't mind the apology part too much, for in a way she felt sorry for her housemother who also seemed a little oppressed by the "Mac-Master way." According to protocol, every time she came through the smoker, all the girls were supposed to stand up as a sign of respect, even if they were playing bridge. But there was also a MacMaster tradition that if the housemother held up her index finger as she came in, you didn't have to stand up—you could just hold up your own finger in reply while chorusing "Good morning/afternoon/evening, Mrs. Wallace." (There were even rules about when "afternoon" changed to "evening," so that the chorus would be in unison.)

Well, one afternoon Tretona had everyone down on the floor shooting craps against the wall and when Mrs. Wallace walked in holding her finger out in front like a flagpole, Tretona just couldn't help it and stuck up her giggy finger as she rolled the dice—and of course she got caught.

Tretona could barely stand all the rules, but what really griped her ass were all the MacMaster "traditions." Everytime someone started a sentence with "MacMaster girls. . . ." she got almost sick to her stomach. MacMaster girls practiced sitting down gracefully while holding full teacups. MacMaster girls always took the serving dish in their left hands and passed them on with their right. MacMaster girls never sat on a boy's lap without putting a phone book between their bodies. For a long time Tretona thought that last one was a joke, but then she saw people in the lounge really sitting on phone books. Also, each couple had to keep three out of four legs on the floor.

Tretona stopped to take a cinder out of her tennis shoe. As she felt the callus on her heel, she thought about how much fun it was to go barefoot. At home the crocuses would be coming out and soon there would be baby calves with white faces and the old cows would lick the curly red hair on their little bottoms. Then her father would start getting ready for spring plowing and her mother would be checking the *Farmer's Almanac* to find out when the moon was right to plant cucumbers.

Tretona started whistling "Swanee River" as she reached the lake front. When she got to the part about "far from the old folks at home," it suddenly hit her: These MacMaster types weren't one bit more sophisticated than the folks from Cheaney. When the senior girls came around and serenaded the freshman dorm with "MacMaster, We'll Always Love You" and "Moon Over MacMaster," they were every bit as dopey and sentimental as the people at home who drooled over Jesus. At least religious people were trying to think about serious things. Tretona decided she was like Esau who had sold his birthright. "For a mess of *polish*," said Tretona, pleased with her own cleverness. Then she panicked, because there sitting on the dock was a MacMaster girl— and a senior at that. For all Tretona knew it was one of Dean Frysinger's Gestapo agents, who would report her being off campus; but she decided to just tough it out and so she said hi. Jan Ronsen (Tretona knew her name because she was in the creative writing club, too) looked up in sort of a slow frightened way and made a very gentle gesture for Tretona to join her.

Within two minutes Tretona decided that Roni (as her friends called her) was the most charming woman she had ever met. All they talked about were the ducks and the fine weather, but Roni's voice was so rich and mellow, her posture so elegant (she had unusually broad shoulders and carried them well), her sweater so cozy looking (Tretona found out later it was cashmere) that Tretona fell in love with her on the spot. So she started to show off by making funny, sarcastic remarks about MacMaster. Roni smiled a little as Tretona talked about all the freshman initiation nonsense and would widen her eyes and say half seriously, "But Tretona, dear, it's supposed to make you feel like part of the MacMaster family. And just think—next year you can plan something perfectly vile for the incoming class to do."

Tretona finally caught on that Roni was teasing her for being so concerned about it. So Tretona changed her style a little and eventually got Roni laughing when she confessed that she, Tretona, had been the "Poetess of Porn." For initiation into the

54

Scribbler's Club, everyone had to write poems and go around campus pinning them up on trees like Orlando, or whoever it was, did in *Midsummer Night's Dream*. Tretona thought that was dumb, especially since she didn't even write poetry, so to get even she posted the following stanzas on the beech trees outside the dining hall:

> Suzanne was a lady
> with plenty of class
> Who bowled them all over
> when she wiggled her———
>
> Eyes at the fellows
> as girls sometimes do
> To make it quite plain
> they are aching to———
>
> Go for a sail
> or walk on the dock
> With any young man
> with a sizable———
>
> Roll of bills
> and a pretty good front
> And if he talked fast
> he could feel of her———
>
> Little white dog
> who was subject to fits
> Etc.
> Etc.

Then Roni told her how hysterical Miss Braddle, the faculty sponsor, had been over the poems and how she had wanted to call in detectives "to ferret out and apprehend the perverted individual or individuals who had the audacity to. . . ." but Roni and the other senior scribblers finally talked her out of it by suggesting it was probably high school boys who had done it.

When Roni imitated Miss Braddle, Tretona practically fell off the dock from laughing so hard; when Roni reached out her hand to catch her, Tretona ached to take it, but didn't dare for fear she would turn into jelly blobs or fire crackers or squeeze too hard. As they walked home together, Tretona suggested they go by the road (because it took longer) and when they parted by the hedge behind the chapel (by this time Roni knew that Tretona had to sneak back on campus), Roni said, "Good luck, Little One," and blew her a kiss.

Tretona practically floated back to her room. When ole Lucy Bentley said, "My, you sure look happy for someone who's on probation," Tretona didn't even bother to scowl at her, she was in such a hurry to go sit in a tub of hot water and dream about Roni.

Tretona's pursuit of Roni wasn't very subtle but it sure was persistent. She showed up to watch the fencing club practice and went to the program put on by the modern dance classes. (Roni was a dance major with a phys ed minor.) She hung around the tennis court and talked to Roni as she practiced hitting balls against the wall. She made a Coke date in the refectory with Roni to discuss the possibility of their being able to play boys' basketball at MacMaster. Tretona hated the girls' rules—you could only dribble two times and the guards had to stay down at the opponents' goal. It was bad enough never having tournaments in high school, but now when she finally was at a girls' school where girls got to play, the gym teachers had to go and put in a bunch of dumb rules which took all the fun out of sports. Roni wasn't much help—she talked a lot about not being able to change things overnight and not taking on city hall and about how women *were* built differently from men. Inside, Tretona *knew* that breasts didn't keep you from being able to dribble a basketball and that women weren't so weak that they needed two hits in volleyball, but somehow she couldn't really argue with Roni. Roni wasn't like Belinda, all full of piss 'n' vinegar. She was more suede and silk and when she called Tretona "Little One" again and looked right at her smiling, hell, Tretona didn't care about basketball anymore; and when they started talking about which kind of photography was more artistic, color or black and white, Tretona was careful to give the pros and cons for each instead of just picking one side and arguing to the death for it, the way she usually did.

Then Tretona managed to switch with someone so she could sit at Roni's table in the dining hall. (All the seniors had to be hostesses.) And then she would often spend hours reading the *New Yorker* and the *Saturday Review of Literature*, trying to figure out witty and artistic things to talk about at the table. (She could tell that Roni didn't like people to sit around and gripe about exams and school stuff.) She loved to watch Roni use the serving spoons. Even the way she held her coffee cup was beautiful. And if she ever spilled anything (which was rare, of course), she covered it up gracefully with a little joke.

Then one day Roni invited her to her room and Tretona stopped feeling like an obnoxious puppy dog always hanging around. All the seniors had singles in the best dorm. Tretona was surprised at how bare Roni's room was—she and Lucy Bentley had stuff all over their walls. But here there was just a ukelele and a straw hat (Roni had been in a minstrel show her junior year) and a bud vase with a dried rose in it. In a way it looked sad and lonely, but Tretona sat down, admired the Bates bedspread, and looked at Roni's record collection.

They spent lots of spring afternoons up in Roni's room, listening to the last section of *The Firebird Suite* (Tretona's pick) and songs by Yma Sumac, a woman from Peru with a four-octave range whom Roni adored. And then finally Roni told Tretona about her sad love affair with Barney, a thirty-year-old married man who managed a motel out by the lake. Tretona gathered that Barney was pretty low class and had no intention of divorcing his wife. It sounded as though he and Roni had been sleeping together, but that was about all. They couldn't go to movies or anything, partly because of the wife and partly because Barney wasn't on the List. (MacMaster girls could only date boys on the Approved List and the only way to get someone on the List was for your parents to write a letter to Dean Frysinger. There was one bit of flexibility—once a boy was on the List, anyone could date him.)

Tretona didn't like the way Roni handled the whole business, sitting around moping, waiting for Barney to call, and listening to Johnny Ray sing "The Little White Cloud Who Sat Right Down and Cried" a million times a day just because it was Barney's favorite song. It made Tretona sick to see Roni lose all of her energy and act so dumb. Once she asked her point-blank why she didn't just forget about old Barney, since he obviously was making her miserable, but Roni put on that look of infinite wisdom and sadness which Tretona found so appealing and said, "Oh, Little One—you are too young to understand the agonies of love."

After that Tretona started a big program of cheering Roni up the way she sometimes did her mom. Everyday she told her how nice she looked, and if Roni got in one of her moods, Tretona would change the subject or get her to teach her a new song on the ukelele. On weekends Tretona would spend the night in Roni's room so she wouldn't be depressed. (Lucy Bentley didn't mind and even phoned her up one night when there was an unexpected bed check. Tretona dashed back to her dorm right away, not even stopping to change out of her pajamas. It had rained a lot and fish worms had crawled up all over the sidewalks. She ran barefooted, lifting her knees very high because she didn't want to squish any worms. Luckily, the window with the loose screen was unlocked and Tretona crawled under the covers just before Mrs. Wallace reached their corridor.)

One rainy day in May they decided to turn Roni's room into an Oriental boudoir. They pulled down the blinds, put on "Scheherezade," leaned the bed springs against the wall, and moved the mattresses down on the floor. Roni took off her shoes and started dancing around on the mattresses. After a while Tretona threw a pillow at her and Roni jumped her and they wrestled pretty hard. Roni knew some real holds, but Tretona was stronger so she ended up on top. Suddenly, Roni stopped giggling and Tretona slipped off her and they lay side by side, still panting, and then Roni laid her hand and arm on top of Tretona's. Acting on reflex, Tretona leaned over to—but then Roni said, "But, Little One, I'm not a—" For Tretona, it was like everything in the room had turned to frozen lead. And then Roni restructured the sentence into "I'm in love with Barney, although I love you, too," and put her hand on Tretona's shoulder. But now Tretona knew there were two kinds of women in the world—and Roni was the other kind. And she didn't know where her own kind was.

8 I.D. #238438

Sadness is almost never anything but a form of fatigue.

—*André Gide*

Fatigue is almost never anything but a form of sadness.

—*T. G. at age 40*

TRETONA'S FOLKS DIDN'T like having to pay back the scholarship when she transferred out of MacMaster, but they weren't half as pissed off as she thought they would be. Evidently, Dean Frysinger's remarks about "social ineptness" really got her mother's dander up. Anyway, here she was at the state university and *not* living in a dorm, so she could eat whenever and whatever she wanted to! This was more like it—no set study hours, no dining hours, no room inspections, no dress codes, no rules, and *no traditions*. All you had to do was write your ID number on everything and not cut too many classes.

But by the time her birthday came at the end of October, Tretona finally had to admit that she was miserable. She had gained fifteen pounds and none of her pants fit. She was making C's in both chemistry and calculus and hated school. She was homesick as hell—not just for Belinda and Roni but also for MacMaster—for the Scribbler's Club, The Swing Band, and the basketball tournaments, even if they did play with stupid girls' rules.

"What good is freedom," thought Tretona, "if you don't have any friends?" She looked around the room. It was light and bright enough, but except for her clothes on the floor, anyone could be living there. She hadn't put any stuff up on the walls, partly because the landlady might object, but mainly because there was no point in decorating—no one ever came in her room. There were two other girls staying in the house—they were sisters, maybe even twins. They studied all the time and never talked to anybody. "They aren't friendly like you," said Mrs. Greenley.

It was nice Mrs. Greenly thought she was friendly—no one else did. She'd tried talking to the kids in her classes but they all seemed to be premeds from Chicago. Anyway, they were all boys, and she didn't want them to think she was flirting.

Tretona heard the mail come and decided to go down to get it, even though it meant she might run into the landlady. The old lady had invited her in for crumb cake one day. After talking nonstop about her arthritis for a half hour, she had launched into an attack on the Red Cross as a Communist front and had gone on to say how she would never accept a transfusion from a blood bank—not even if she were dying. "You never knew *whose* blood you might be getting." Tretona had patiently explained about the different blood types and which ones were compatible but that wasn't what was worrying the woman. "But they might give me a nigger's blood."

"So what?" growled Tretona. Mrs. Greenley shot her a quick look and then made a joke: "Well, then I'd turn all chocolate colored, wouldn't I?" and started talking about the brown spots on her hands and Tretona's freckles. After that, Tretona had decided she was a stupid bigot and felt a little ashamed for ever having been nice to her.

But today there was no sight of Mrs. Greenley. There were two cards! Someone knew it was her birthday! Someone besides the university bursar's computer knew that she existed. She opened her mom's first—she recognized the card right away. It came out of the box of twelve assorted greetings that her dad got as a bonus for buying seed corn. "To Our Dearest Daughter" the curly print said. Inside was a message: "Study hard. Love, The Folks." Belinda's inscription was even more depressing: "Sisters in Christ."

Tretona was scheduled to put in extra time at the lab that afternoon but decided to cut it. What the hell, it was Saturday and her birthday. She'd already been to all the good movies downtown, but finally decided to go see a sci-fi film about some kind of strange blob that crept around. It wasn't too bad—for once, the woman assistant to the big research scientist did something more than just look pretty and say, "Dr. Hartley, we're all counting on you." Tretona was starting to get interested in what kind of molecular reactions might be involved in making the blob grow, when someone moved over and sat by her. He was wearing a leather jacket which creaked, and Tretona could smell his hair oil and knew she should move when his knee touched hers, but didn't; and soon her head was on the fur collar of the jacket and he kissed her before moving his hand very gently along her corduroy pants legs. Tretona had never felt so attracted to a boy before—not even to Melvin. When the movie was over, they walked outside and stood blinking in the late autumn afternoon sun, trying not to stare too obviously at each other, but both of them curious as to whom they had picked up.

His name was Joe and he was in the Air Force and his eyes were crossed—not too badly, but one turned out a little bit. Tretona agreed to meet him near the movie house the next evening. After she got home she kept thinking about his eye. It really turned her off and she had about decided not to go, but then felt bad because she was judging people on appearances the way Mrs. Greenley did with Negroes.

When Joe came bounding up the next evening (Tretona had got there ahead of time), he was wearing a heavy sweater and gloves. "Where's your flight jacket?" asked Tretona in her responsible little mother voice. "Pawned it." "Whatever for?" Joe looked shy: "I wanted money to get us a hotel room." Tretona looked at him—shoulders hunched against the wind, just barely controlling his need to shiver. First his one eye and then the other met hers. "That was a dumb thing to do," said Tretona, and went back to Mrs. Greenley's.

Thanksgiving finally came and Tretona got to go home. Everyone talked about how plump and healthy she looked. She lied about her grades, saying she really wouldn't know how she was doing until after finals.

She didn't get to see Belinda until Saturday. Belinda wasn't very happy at college either because Kendrie Theological Seminary taught all sorts of stuff about other religions. (She thought Catholicism seemed more dangerous than the Eastern religions.) They also had to write "dialectical" essays in which they debated the divinity of Christ or the Immaculate Conception. Belinda was afraid she might be tempted into losing her religion. Besides, she hadn't met a single preacher boy she wanted to marry. Tretona sort of half-jokingly brought up the idea of running away together. Belinda didn't take the bait. Instead, she suggested they drive over to Parkersburg to see Don and Naomi and Jackie. Tretona agreed. They disconnected the speedometer on her dad's car so the miles wouldn't show and set off immediately.

The summer before the Parrs had been transferred to another church seventy miles away, but it almost seemed like old times when Tretona and Belinda walked in and saw the same velvety throw on the piano and the big picture of Jesus the Good Shepherd and Jackie's toys all over the couch. Naomi made cocoa and they all sat around and grinned and gossiped about what everybody was doing back in Cheaney. Belinda sat real close to Tretona, closer than she ever had in public. Tretona couldn't get over how much Jackie had grown. Sister Naomi made Tretona promise to go to church at the university and guaranteed she'd meet some nice people that way. Then Belinda started talking about some new interpretation of Revelations according to which the world was going to end during the coming year; Tretona had a fine time putting down prophecy and the credulity of people who believed in it. It was after midnight when Tretona got home, so she got yelled at, but it was worth it.

Back at college Tretona followed Sister Naomi's advice and went off the next Sunday to the campus Methodist church. It was awful, what with the minister talking some garbage about community responsibility and personal growth. All the songs (they called them "hymns") were unfamiliar and the organist played like it was a funeral. That night Tretona went off to the Nazarene church (not knowing whether the Parrs would approve or not, but she was so bored) and that was a lot better. The preacher's wife caught on that she was a newcomer right away and signed her up to play trombone in the church orchestra. But she asked Tretona please not to wear any jewelry on the platform. Tretona didn't know what she meant at first, but then realized the suit she was wearing had an ornament sewn on the lapel. She tried to explain it wasn't really jewelry, but the preacher's wife just said, "That's okay, honey" and gave her a great big hug.

On the way back to her room Tretona felt warm for a moment, but then her mood turned worse than ever—there was no way she could really fit in at the Nazarene church. She had always thought that as soon as people stopped bossing her around she would be happy. But here she was, free to do what she liked, yet completely miserable. "Joe Air Force or the Nazarenes—it looks like those are my only options," she groaned. Maybe having lots of nice things to choose from was just as important as being free to choose. Maybe that had been part of her mom's problem all along.

As final exams approached Tretona felt like she was living in a bowl of molasses. Her limbs were heavy, she slept a lot, she couldn't study much. She stopped even trying to carry on a conversation with the kids in Qualitative Analysis lab—everyone was too busy trying to finish analyzing their unknowns. She got a low grade on her anion sample, having confused bromide with iodide and missed the sulfate altogether. It got so bad she hardly had the energy to clean up her test tubes; she would stand and stare at them and think about how her mother would get immobilized by dirty dishes. Once she went two whole days without saying a single word to anybody, and then she remembered that Raskolnikov used to do that, so she went and sat at the counter at Steak 'n' Shake and forced herself to talk to the waitress instead of just pointing at the Chili Mac Special on the menu.

The Saturday before exam week Tretona decided she had to do something to cheer herself up. First, she went ice skating and then she went to three movies in a row (one was a double feature, so she only had to pay two admissions). She took a late bus home. When she got off and started across the street, there were car lights coming straight at her. Tretona just had time to think, "Maybe Belinda was right. Maybe the world is going to end." Then she came to and tried to crawl out from under the car because the motor was still running and Miss Kirk had warned them about carbon monoxide. She came to again just long enough to tell the intern her university ID number. Then her parents were there and Tretona said, "I really appreciate you. I never really appreciated you before." And when she woke up with tubes up her nose, she pulled them out before the nurse could stop her, and her mom said maybe she doesn't need them now that she's regained consciousness, and the nurse stomped out to get the supervisor as Tretona went back to sleep.

9 Reculer Pour Mieux Sauter

Every [wo]man has [her] own courage, and is betrayed because [s]he seeks in [her]self the courage of other persons.
—*Ralph Waldo Emerson*

The wish for healing has ever been the half of health.
—*Seneca*

SHE NOT ONLY didn't have to take finals, but got a semester's credit anyway, thanks to her mom's having talked to her teachers. And her folks bought a television set when she got out of the hospital (one of the first in the Cheaney community, so Tretona was really excited). The taxi that had hit her was speeding, so there would be a large insurance settlement. Tretona's leg had been smashed into several pieces, but the doctors just threaded all the bits onto a chromium steel rod that went inside the bone from the knee to the ankle. (Tretona borrowed a compass from Miss Kirk, but she couldn't detect it. Either the metal wasn't magnetically permeable or the compass was too weak.) The doctor told her that before the war she would have been kept in traction for six months, but Nazi scientists had developed the Kütschner rod technique by experimenting with American POW's. Tretona wondered whether it had worked right away. How many ex-soldiers were now walking around limping? But then how many more people like herself were up and around in casts instead of being confined to hospital beds? She tried to figure out if it wasn't good after all that the Nazis had done the experiments, although clearly all they had cared about at the time was getting more work out of the prisoners.

Anyway, the accident really wasn't such a bad thing, Tretona decided. She got a big kick out of doing crazy stuff with her casts and crutches, and learned to drive, even shift gears, with one foot and one hand. (Her right elbow was dislocated, too.) When the loafers up at the Cheaney store told her about some one-legged kid who could ride a bicycle, Tretona went home and tried it. She laid her crutches across the handle bars and shoved off. It was fine until she tried to pedal—then she started tipping over toward her bad side. Once again, Tretona felt her mind work very rapidly and logically, as it had when the taxi was coming at her. "I'm only allowed to put ten pounds of weight on my bad foot," she thought. "But as I fall I'm picking up momentum fast. Therefore, I must get my leg out of the way." And so she tucked her leg under her the way they had been taught to do in modern dance class at MacMaster, and she wouldn't have been hurt at all except one of the crutches hit her in the eye.

"Where'd you get that black eye?" asked the orthopedic surgeon the next time she came in. "Just fell off my bike," answered Tretona and wouldn't explain any further.

She felt good about her performance during the accident. She wasn't a coward about pain and doctoring the way her mother was although she still worried whether she would have the courage to stand up to torturers like the Nazis. And it was good to be back home. No chance of getting lonely here, with her kid brothers and sister jabbering all the time. And then lots of neighbors came over to visit. Partly it was to see Tretona. But more than likely it was mostly curiosity about the new TV set. In any case, lots of the neighbors came over to visit. Tretona learned that it was no use trying to carry on a conversation at first, because they would just move their chairs close up to the screen and stare, no matter how boring the program was. Once when the Schoatstalls came Tretona didn't turn the set on and tried to talk, but Flora and Dudge just kept looking over at the dark screen and squirming until she gave in. The second half of the pattern was just as inevitable—after about fifteen minutes, no matter how interesting the program was, people would start to chatter—slowly at first, then at full blast except for occasional eruptions—"Hey, look at that!"

After being in the city for a while Tretona found the neighbors quite interesting characters and didn't look down on them the way she used to. Take Flora and Dudge. Neither one of them was hard of hearing, but somehow they had gotten into the habit of shouting, especially when they spoke to each other. They kept separate pocketbooks and talked about it all the time. Flora had egg money all year round, and in the summer she picked dozens of gallons of blackberries and grew early vegetables to sell to the neighbors. Everyone had a garden but you could always count on Flora Schoatstall to have the first tomatoes and the earliest sweet corn because she lived on a sandy hill and her garden dried out first.

Flora had to pay for all the groceries out of her pocketbook—except for the milk and meat, which Dudge was supposed to provide. Generally they butchered, but one fall the pig they were saving died and they had to buy meat at town. They had a terrible argument right in the middle of the Cheaney general store about who should pay for the lard. Dudge said it wasn't meat, but Flora said it wasn't her fault he didn't have a pig to butcher so they could render their own lard.

Flora was more stubborn and Dudge finally paid, but he was still mad about it. He sat in the Getroek living room and argued his case again, making the old rocking chair creak and creep across the room as he got more and more agitated.

Then they both started talking about how stingy Lois and Sam Mundhank were. They didn't give their cattle enough hay during the winter and kept them outside because they stored machinery in the barn to keep it from rusting. Tretona said something about how cruel it was, but Dudge interrupted with an economic analysis of how much hay cost versus the probability of losing a spring calf on account of the mother's being poorly from their hard wintering.

Flora took Tretona's point about cruelty, though, and told a story about Henry Stoltz and the chicken hawk. Henry Stoltz had a Ph.D. and had gone on to law school, but something had happened (no one knew what), and he came back to Cheaney to live. He had planted an enormous hedge row clear around his house and no one really knew much about him but his cousin, Omer Stoltz (who was also a little strange, although everyone liked the way he and Ivy ran the switchboard all right) went to visit once in a while on business because of their shared inheritance from Grandpa Stoltz. According to Omer, one time Henry was having a lot of trouble with a hawk killing his chickens. After he finally trapped it, he bore a hole through its beak, wired its jaws together, and let it walk around with the chickens until it starved to death.

"Which just goes to show you what lawyers are like," said Dudge. Tretona didn't really believe in race theories anymore, but she made a mental note to ask her mother if the Stoltzes were of German descent.

Tretona's favorite visitor was Uncle Ausby. At first during the visit he would sit rather shyly over in the corner of the davenport and let Aunt Lena sniff and whine about her sinuses. Then the conversation would somehow turn to Delilah, their daughter, who had died of pneumonia when she was only seven. They would talk about how old she would be now—nearly thirty (one year older than Cousin Gene). Aunt Lena would tell what a healthy child Delilah had always been and how much she had loved school and how she had never disobeyed. And then Tretona's mom would remind everybody about the prophetic dreams that Ausby's dad (Tretona's Grandfather Thacker) used to have. In one dream Uncle Ausby was driving a brand new beautiful wagon across the field when suddenly from out of nowhere a big dark wave rolled up behind him and completely engulfed him. "Ausby's gonna have a lot of sorrow in his life," said Grandpa Thacker when he told the dream at the breakfast table.

Uncle Ausby always looked sad when her mom told that story, but then he would change the subject and try to cheer everyone up. Sometimes he would tell stories about "Little Corinne." From him Tretona learned about how once her mom turned around and knocked the glasses off a kid who had yanked her long curls and said, "Sook cow, sook" the way you do whan you're milking. And how the first time she went out with Daddy she was wearing pretty new anklets (just then come into style) instead of silk stockings and how Grandmother Thacker was shocked, and said, "Those naked legs, it'd serve you right if he just felt you up good and proper." According to Uncle Ausby "Little Corinne" had just tossed her head and flounced out. Tretona decided her mom must have been pretty neat when she was younger. She had had a much smaller waist than Tretona and bigger breasts. She only weighed 123 pounds when she got married—now she hit 170 on the scales. No wonder she felt so grumpy, Tretona thought.

Finally Uncle Ausby would get around to telling a story

about shit. (Tretona had just read a big article on Freudian psychology in a *Saturday Evening Post* series called "Modern Philosophies" and she wondered if he had an anal fixation, but he wasn't compulsively neat or anything. Her mom said he just had an earthy sense of humor.) One story was about the time Uncle Alvie ate too many gooseberries. Uncle Alvie was the second child in her mom's family and evidently, he was nervous and uncommunicative, the way Stant, the second Getroek kid, was. Anyway, Alvie got the squits and went down to the outhouse. He got bored sitting there, so he started playing jacks and balls on the toilet bench. The ball rolled outside and Alvie ran after it without pulling up his pants. As he bent over to pick it up, the urge hit him. The shit just shot out and in the confusion Alvie knocked the ball back behind him and as he turned to get it he kept on shitting.

By this time Uncle Ausby was crying from laughing so hard. "That Alvie, he just shit a perfect circle around himself," he gasped. And then her mom, who had been trying hard not to laugh, got tickled and kept saying, "Poor Alvie," while she howled with laughter.

And then her mom told how Uncle Alvie peed through a hole in the wooden fence surrounding the chicken lot and got his penis stuck and started bawling because he was afraid the chickens would peck it. Grandma Thacker had to come out and bathe it with hot and cold cloths before he could get loose. Even Aunt Lena had to smile at that story.

Tretona started to tell about the time her dad fell into the hog wallow when he got mad at an old sow, but her mom quickly interrupted. Tretona guessed that some stories had to sit around and season for a few years before people could see the humor in them.

When the company left, Tretona's mom told her not to mind Uncle Ausby's "rustic" sense of humor and his "bawdy" stories. Whenever her mom used fancy words it was a sign a sermon was coming. And sure enough she talked about how Uncle Ausby never got to go to high school even though he was brilliant at mental arithmetic in the eighth grade and how Tretona should be thankful for the educational advantages she was getting. Tretona was tempted to say something vicious about Henry Stoltz's educational advantages, but decided that was irrelevant and so she swung off on her crutches to work on her German correspondence course. These days Tretona's strategy for avoiding arguments with her mother was to shut up whenever something controversial arose. It made her feel saintly and superior and most of the time it was quite effective. Still she wondered if it wasn't also cowardly and one day that spring they had a confrontation which was scary.

It must have been early in April—the weather was unseasonably warm and sultry. Tretona was sitting on the cistern platform, leaning against the pump, scratching inside her cast with an arrow from Troy's archery set. The light was strange—she wondered how a poet would describe it—liverish, maybe. Of course, a scientist would just give the distribution of wavelengths.

Suddenly her dad came running in from the barn lot. "Get down in the basement," he said. "It looks like tornado weather." Her father never exaggerated, so Tretona headed in the back door right away. She knew that the safest place to be was in the southwest corner of the cellar because tornados always came from that direction, so if the house got blown over it would fall toward the northeast.

Tretona started down the basement stairs, hurrying as much as she could on her crutches. Damn, they were sure no help in an emergency. For a minute she pictured herself trying to crawl out of the rubble with her cast on if the house caved in. Then suddenly she remembered that the new television set might get ruined if there were an electrical storm. She turned to go back upstairs but her mother barred the way.

"Where do you think you're going? Get on downstairs."

"I'm just going to unplug the TV," Tretona said. "In case there's lightning. There's time."

"Don't sass me, young lady," said her mother and hauled back to hit her.

Tretona couldn't flinch and cover her head up as she usually did because she had to hold on to the crutches, so she just looked real hard at her mother and kind of braced herself against the railing.

"You'd just love for me to hit you, wouldn't you?" screamed her mother. "Then you could really hate me. Well, I won't give you the satisfaction." Tretona didn't go up to turn off the TV set. As she went carefully down the rest of the stairs, she remembered the time all the family were out in the barn lot driving cattle and how Old Balky, a crazy, wild brindle cow, had started to run for the gate. Her little sister, Norva, just barely big enough to walk, was supposed to be in the yard but had come wandering out and somehow pushed open the big barnyard gate and now she was standing right in the middle of everything smiling. Old Balky put down her head and charged. Everyone seemed paralyzed, unable to run, scream, or anything. But Norva just looked at Old Balky, unruffled, and suddenly the little kid waved and yelled, "Hey!" The cow stopped, rolled her eyes, and then trotted off.

Tretona decided that's what she had to do with her mom from now on instead of just being quiet and turning the other cheek. She wrote a little memo on her cast, "Remember how Norva stopped Old Balky."

* * *

Belinda would be home soon on spring break and Tretona was desperate to see her again. She had been back for a short visit one weekend just after the accident, and that had been a disaster. Tretona wasn't able to go out yet, so they had just sat around the living room and argued and couldn't even kiss and make up. For one thing, half of Tretona was plastered over. And although Tretona's mom did have the good sense to shut the French doors which separated the living room from the rest of the house, she couldn't resist interrupting every five minutes, either with Seven-Up (they had pop in the house because Tretona was sick) or questions about how Belinda's Great-Aunt Nellie was feeling or with Tretona's bedtime medicine.

Tretona had often worried about whether she and Belinda really had very much more in common than liking to fight and then making out to make up. Now that she was at the state university and Belinda was at Kendrie Theological Seminary, they seemed to be growing farther and farther apart. Still and all, though, now that it was spring and most of her casts were off, Tretona had great hopes for a romantic renewal.

Belinda came home on the Thursday before Easter—just in time for Thelma Mae's funeral, as it turned out. Thelma Mae Thacker Green was Belinda's aunt and Tretona's second cousin. She belonged to the Church of God branch of the Thacker family so Tretona didn't know her well, but she had freckles and long red hair, and looked so much like pictures of her mom when young that she always seemed like a close relation. Thelma Mae was thirty-two when they discovered she had stomach cancer. The doctors wanted to rush her to St. Louis and operate right away and Thelma Mae was all set to go until the Church of God preacher came around and talked her into going to a famous faith healer down in Tennessee instead. The faith healer waved snakes around, pronounced her cured, and told her not to go to doctors again because God would take that as a sign that she lacked faith.

Tretona's mom went crazy when she heard about it. Her own mother had died an awful death from what was probably cancer of the colon. "They didn't know what was going on then," said Tretona's mom, "and they couldn't do anything about it anyway. But now they can—and some ignorant Church of God preacher, who probably never had a science course in his life and couldn't pass one if he tried, has to go butting in."

Tretona urged her mom to talk to Thelma Mae and get her to enter the hospital right away, but her mom said that no, Thelma Mae Green was a grown woman now and she had to hoe her own row. And then miraculously Thelma Mae did stop losing weight and started looking better—for a while. But she turned worse, and the family finally did put her in the hospital, where, in a very few days, she died.

It was a big funeral, so big that they had to hold it in the Methodist Church; the widower, Orville Green, insisted that the Church of God preacher officiate because Thelma Mae would have wanted it that way. He was seated in front with his and Thelma Mae's two little redheaded kids (who looked so much like Norva and Troy that Tretona could hardly stand it). He just sat there stiff as a corpse himself while the preacher talked about how the despair of Good Friday would be followed by the joy of Resurrection Sunday. Then the preacher spoke about how beautiful and strong Thelma Mae's faith was and how we should never resent or try to interfere with God's will. "Who knows what would have happened to Thelma Mae if her well-meaning, but misguided, relatives had not forced her in a moment of weakness to forsake God's way of healing and turn to atheistic doctors?"

There was a sort of animal moan from the front pew and Tretona caught just a glimpse of Orville before he buried his head. It was like a face from the worst nightmare she'd ever had. Then there was rustling around as everyone filed by to view the corpse—casual acquaintances first, then friends, relatives, and finally the immediate family. Everyone looked at Tretona, of course, because she was on crutches; she was a little afraid she might cry. But she got outside of the church all right and was holding up pretty well until Thelma Mae's kids came out, followed by the preacher. Then something snapped and she had to get out of there. Belinda, being a closer relative, had come out of the church after Tretona, but she saw Tretona go around the corner of the church and followed her.

Tretona was smashing at the weather boarding with the top of her crutch. "That fucking, smug, arrogant son-of-a-bitch. I wish someone would destroy that bastard before he gets someone else." Belinda was puzzled and concerned: "Tretona, who on earth are you talking about? What's wrong, for heaven's sake?" Tretona looked up at her, still feeling crazed. "The preacher. The Church of God preacher. He killed her just as surely as if he'd shot her in the head."

And then Tretona felt herself become very calm and clear and strong and alone. It was as if Belinda's reply was coming from another planet. "But Tretona! He's God's delegate on earth. He's here to help us and exhort us to have faith and do God's will. . . ." By then Tretona was getting her crutch back into position and wasn't listening at all anymore.

Belinda came over to visit on Easter Monday, just before she had to go back to Kendrie Theological Seminary. She had Keith Wartsbaugh with her and they didn't stay long. Tretona cried for a while after they left, thinking about how they were probably necking and saying good-bye down in the bottoms in one of the parking places that she, Tretona, had discovered. She took some satisfaction in thinking that Belinda probably wouldn't let Keith touch her anyplace important.

Then Tretona went in and sat down at the piano and played Debussy's "Après-midi d'un Faune" over and over again. She took her new modern art book out on the front steps and looked at the Impressionist paintings. The French seemed to be so much more delicate and civilized in everything they did. And they were brave, too. The *Saturday Evening Post* article on existentialism had talked about the French Resistance movement.

When the cast finally came off, Tretona took an almost gruesome interest in the scar and the flaky skin. Her leg looked like a dead fish's belly, so she rubbed it with mineral oil and spent lots of time sunbathing. She thought about how skin kept dying and getting replaced and how bones could mend, but how when your brain cells died that was it. She wondered if emotional wounds could ever be healed or whether a wounded psyche was

72

irreparable like the brain. Of course, come to think of it, if you didn't believe in souls, the psyche was nothing else *but* your brain. But how could that be right? If the existentialists were correct when they said the distinctive feature of human beings was their ability to make radical choices, then the will couldn't just be part of the brain because the brain worked according to the fixed laws of chemistry and that would mean decisions were predetermined. Tretona wondered if Sartre had ever thought about *that* problem. One thing was for sure—as soon as she finished her German requirement, she was going to study French.

10 Microcosm of the Universe

A University should be a place of light, of liberty, and of learning.
—*Benjamin Disraeli*

I will talk of things heavenly, or things earthly . . . things sacred, or things profane . . . things foreign, or things at home.
—*John Bunyan,* Pilgrim's Progress

"WHOEVER SAID THE university was just a place to escape reality was nuts," thought Tretona. She and hundreds of other students were milling along the boardwalk as classes changed. Sure, there were a lot of real losers here—Greeks, engineers, aggies, and business majors were all completely beyond the pale. Premeds were smart but obnoxious; music majors were nice but awfully vague. But all in all, there were a *lot* of really sharp people here and more interesting stuff to learn than she had ever dreamed of.

Take chemistry—in her very first course in advanced inorganic, she had learned amazing things, like the theory behind the atom bomb (not just the simple stuff about isotopes and free neutrons, which everybody knew, but the fundamentals like nuclear cross-sections, packing fractions, and the principles of transmutation). And even the most ordinary things became exciting when you really understood them—for example, all that stuff about crystal structures and why when you walked in damp sand water collected in your footprints. It was nice to finally figure out why Troy had had that funny explosion down in the basement—he'd probably made an unstable oxide of chlorine.

Now she was studying Thermodynamics, which was really abstract, because the teacher didn't want you to try to visualize enthalpy and entropy, but just work out the equations. Tretona was eager to get back to talking about atoms and molecules again—she had a real feel for that—but still it was a good exercise to do Thermo.

Probably her strangest class was Symbolic Logic. Tretona hadn't thought much about it before but had sort of assumed that everyone just naturally knew the difference between good and bad arguments. But in Logic, you had to justify every step you made. And she liked all the impressive Latin names for fallacies, using them on her mom whenever she went home. ("There you go, Mom, arguing *ad hominem* again." Or, "That's a *petitio principi* if I ever heard one.")

This spell of exaltation and self-congratulation had lasted all the way from Newell Lab to the Union Building. Now it was time to look outside the Commons for Sylvia. Sylvia was one of her housemates at GDI #501 (which stood both for God Damn Independent and Mother Goddard's Den of Iniquity). The house at 501 East Green Street had five bedrooms and housed eleven girls. They were a strange mixture and Tretona liked them all—Michele, the blind girl, who told Tretona she hadn't expected her to be so strong until she felt her arm one day; Judith, the Jewish girl, who kept her pots and pans separate cause she was Kosher; Tiia, the Estonian refugee—she was in the triple with Tretona and Wendy, another Jewish girl from Chicago, who wasn't the least bit Kosher.

But the deepest one was Sylvia. There she was now, sitting on the terrace, her forehead slightly strained, her hand resting lightly on her knee brace ready to lock it when needed. Sylvia had a bad leg. She had told Tretona how it happened last fall. A horse had thrown her, somehow the joint was injured, and her leg stopped growing—it took several operations to save it. She told the story once and then never talked about her leg again. Sylvia was going into biomedical research and Tretona reckoned it was because of her leg.

Sylvia was really a tough-minded, no-nonsense person. Whenever they tried to talk Mrs. Goddard into something at house meeting (like more shelves in the kitchen or extra toilet paper, so they wouldn't run out on weekends), it was Sylvia who would make their arguments stick. The rest of the girls tended either to whine and complain or else get belligerent. But Sylvia would just sit there until the right moment came and then lean forward slightly. "Mrs. Goddard, I know you are a kind and reasonable person. We believe this is a fair and responsible request. All we ask is for you to think about it carefully. I'm sure we will be able to respect your decision." It never failed to work, but Tretona always wondered what Sylvia would do if Mrs. Goddard didn't come to a "reasonable" decision.

Sylvia waved at Tretona—"How you doing, C.T." Ever since Tretona had confessed that some people in high school had called her Carrot Top, Sylvia had taken to calling her C.T., insisting that no one could possibly object to the initials and besides only she and Tretona would know what they meant. Now Tretona liked it so much that she wished she could think up a nickname for Sylvia but so far she hadn't come up with one that was good enough.

"Emma Sue'll be here in a minute. She went off to buy some Cokes and Corn Curls so we can have a picnic." Tretona was just a tad disappointed to hear that Sylvia's roommate was coming too, although she and everyone else knew that Sylvia and Emma Sue were best friends. Tretona sometimes wondered how that had happened. Emma Sue was cute and nice enough, but not half as bright and energetic as Sylvia. She didn't even have plans for what she was going to do after college. Tretona reckoned she'd probably just raise a batch of cute, nice kids in a small town somewhere.

Emma Sue came and the three of them moved over under a big elm tree behind the Union. Tretona took off her shoes, saying that in Cheaney, everyone went barefoot after April 1 whether the ground was thawed or not. Sylvia sat against the tree with her bad leg straight out in front; Emma Sue lay face down on the grass with her chin close to Sylvia's thigh.

Sylvia came straight to the point: "Emma Sue and I decided we wanted to talk to you but we didn't want to do it back at the house where we might be interrupted." Tretona nodded and wondered what new improvement for the house Sylvia had dreamt up now. Or even better, maybe she had a new idea for a practical joke. (Last time they had put Saran Wrap over the toilet bowl under the seat. Judith had been the first to use it. When the pee started running onto the floor she had come shrieking out of the john. Sylvia calmed her while Tretona snuck in and removed the Sarah Wrap. No one ever did figure out what had happened, and Judith was still leery every time she had to go to the toilet.)

But Sylvia looked dead serious. "You know how much Emma Sue and I like each other. Well, we've decided to—actually, she just said yes this morning—anyway, we're going to be together for the rest of our lives." Tretona almost started to ask something dumb about whether that meant Emma Sue was going to medical school, too. But she stopped just in time because Emma Sue was pulling a ring on a chain out from under her sweater. It looked like Sylvia's ring and sure enough Sylvia was wearing Emma Sue's class ring on her little finger.

"We're *so* happy, C.T.," said Emma Sue "and we just had to tell somebody."

"I just had a hunch that maybe you'd understand," added Sylvia. "Something about the way you looked when you talked about that old friend of yours—you know who I mean, Belinda. Well, I just thought maybe you'd understand." Sylvia looked a little rattled.

Tretona felt pretty rattled herself. Finally, she remembered her manners, smiled at Sylvia, and said, "I guess congratulations are in order." Then she turned to Emma Sue: "Since you and Sylvia are going to get . . . going to be. . . ." Tretona couldn't think of the right word, so she just grinned. "Well, anyway, I guess now I better tell you Sylvia's and my secret about what C.T. stands for."

Tretona spent a lot of time in Sylvia and Emma Sue's room after that. They had rearranged things so that their beds were side by side; it was almost as good as a double bed. (Tretona told the other kids it was so that Emma Sue could hand things to Sylvia when she had her brace off.) Sometimes it made Tretona a little sad and envious to see the two of them so happy. But it also gave her hope that maybe she'd find someone someday.

It was strange—all those years she had been dying to tell someone how she felt about Belinda, but now that she had a chance, she just couldn't talk. Sylvia would tease her about it: "Come on, C.T.; spill the beans. When did *you* become a member of the Big H Conspiracy?" Sylvia never said the word—none of them did.

One day Tretona confessed how left out she felt when Emma Sue was rubbing Sylvia's knee and stuff. After that Emma Sue hugged and poked Tretona a lot. Meanwhile, Sylvia put her mind to work on the problem. "The only solution, C.T., is to find someone for you. So how can we do that? In a big city like Chicago, it would be easy, but here. . . ."

Tretona felt embarrassed and started acting sarcastic. "We could always take out a want ad in the paper—'Lonely Redhead, capable of deep and enduring passion, seeks. . . .'" Emma Sue took the ball: "We could get Jeri B.S. Johnson to help. Maybe she could put your picture in the *Daily Stupid.*" Jeri Johnson, one of their housemates, was a gung-ho journalism major. Her real name was Geraldine but she thought Jeri would make a better byline. She ran around all the time with a pencil behind her ear and a camera draped over her breasts like some kind of giant medallion. Sylvia called her B.S. Johnson—short for Brenda Starr, of course.

Sylvia was looking serious. "C.T., I think I've got it." She waited for their attention and then leaned forward as she did in house meetings. "How would you like a beautiful, mysterious, quiet type—someone who is intelligent and cheery, someone who through no fault of her own doesn't have many friends, *and,* someone who already secretly admires you?"

C.T. hesitated, feeling that there was a trick or a tease coming. Sylvia kept going. "Listen, you dumb dodo, the perfect girl for you has been under your nose all along. Literally under your nose—you still sleep in the top bunk, don't you? I mean *Tiia.* She's beautiful under those dumpy clothes she wears and she really likes you. I've seen those sad eyes of hers light up when you're clowning around in the kitchen."

And lo, it came to pass exactly as Sylvia had predicted. No one had paid much attention to Tiia because she was quiet and foreign, but as soon as Tretona showed a little interest in her she opened right up. ("Our C.T. has a green thumb," said Sylvia.) Tiia told Tretona lots of stories about the war—how at first the Estonians liked the Germans because they were better than the Russian army of occupation. How once when she went to the baker's the woman wouldn't give her any bread because she'd forgotten her "Heil Hitler." How after the war in the refugee camp they lived for weeks on catsup and lard sandwiches because the Red Cross got their supplies mixed up. (Tiia claimed she liked the combination now and made a sandwich for Tretona to try—it tasted awful.)

Tiia explained about how Estonian was a Finno-Ugrian language and so it was agglutinative and not like either German or Russian. She sang Tretona little folk songs and was really pleased when Tretona made her write one down in phonetic script so she could learn to sing and play it on the ukelele.

In return, Tretona taught Tiia American slang and talked her into shaving her legs and armpits as Americans did. And once just for fun she got Tiia to try on one of her sweaters—a nice cherry red one—and a pair of Wendy's blue jeans. (Tiia generally wore dark, dowdy skirts and blouses which her mother made for her.) Then she got Tiia to go out on the front porch and took color pictures of her holding Socrates, Tretona's stuffed monkey. They really turned out well, and Tretona had one enlarged and stuck it up on the bookcase above her desk.

It was along about then that Sylvia decided it was time for more action. "Look, C.T., what are you waiting for? You like her a whole lot, right? She likes you, too, and it's obvious she's attracted to you. Look at the way she's always putting her hands on your arms and shoulders and stuff."

But Tretona thought maybe that was just because Tiia was European and more demonstrative. Besides, Tiia was a refugee and it would be terrible if her first American friend pressured her into something she really didn't want to do.

Sylvia wasn't convinced. "You may be right, C.T. But what if you're wrong? It sure would be a shame if this beautiful spring went by, you groaning up in your bunk and Tiia lying awake down in hers wondering why you don't kiss her, wondering if maybe you don't think she's sexy because she wears funny clothes and puts her hair up in braids."

"That's not so at all," said Tretona. "I love her hair and I don't give a shit what she wears." "Tell *her,* not me," said Sylvia.

And so when Wendy went home to Chicago for the weekend, Tretona did tell Tiia—sort of—and they sat on Tiia's bed and looked into each other's eyes. But then Tretona lost her nerve and went to bed in her own bunk. But she felt as though big hot gold rubber bands were pulling at her like an octopus—and she finally said, "Tiia, I can't sleep" and Tiia said, "Maybe you could sleep better down here." Tretona agreed in a flash and found Tiia's body felt even more perfect than it looked—she was solid, yet soft, and not aggressive but not shy, either.

It was like a beautiful dance, with Tiia following Tretona's every move and then intensifying it. At first, Tretona was a little surprised, for with Belinda she had had to work for quite a while to get much response. But Tiia kept right up with her, and what was even more surprising, she touched Tretona every place Tretona touched her. For a little while, Tretona tried to stop her because she was having trouble concentrating on making love to Tiia. But soon they were rolling around like puppies, and Tiia got on top of Tretona and lapped with her tongue all around the back of her neck and ears and Tretona gave Tiia little puppy nips under her breasts and up and down her ribs. Tiia ran her toe up and down the inside of Tretona's leg until Tretona dived down and grabbed it, and then they lay quiet for a minute, heads to toes, letting their pussies nudge and bounce each other in little ups and downs and spirals. And then Tretona had the idea of letting their pussies mouth wrestle the way dogs do and so she slid one leg under Tiia's butt and down her back and up behind her head. Soon their bodies slipped together like two interlocking Ys and their vaginas were kissing face to face, mouth to mouth. It was like Tiia's warmth and moisture was going inside her and around her all at the same time—and she was doing the same to Tiia. Tretona just managed to think, This is a topological impossibility, before a heavy hot surge rolled up along her spine and crashed through her cheeks.

The next morning Tretona was determined not to let anyone know, but as soon as she walked into the kitchen Sylvia cracked: "So it looks like there's been a *rapprochement* between the Old World and the New." "Oh, stop it," said Tretona and loaded up a tray with cereal, milk, sugar and two bowls.

According to her Thermo teacher, the rate of the average chemical reaction doubles with every 10 degrees centigrade increase in temperature; and with catalysts like platinum the rate effects are even more dramatic. Tretona figured that it must be the combination of warm spring weather and Tiia that made her brain run so fast. She just couldn't stop doing goofy things like taking Bonze the goldfish out on the roof to sunbathe and then getting the giggles and knocking over the poor thing's bowl when Tiia showed up.

Tretona's excess energy almost got her into trouble even in class. She started squirting distilled water on Henry Byrd, a serious premed fraternity boy type who worked across the bench from her. He got really fed up with the free showers—especially when he was trying to pour concentrated sulfuric acid dropwise into a separatory funnel. He was too much of a sissy (maybe he would have said gentleman) to complain. He would just get sulky and pack his equipment neatly away in the locker without talking. One day he must have really been shook because he left his sponge out on the lab bench. Tretona waited until he left and then filled the sponge with water and tossed it through the window at him, saying sweetly, "You forgot something, Henry." It made a big wet splotch all over his camel hair sweater when he caught it. To Tretona's surprise he hauled off and threw the sponge right back at her. It sailed in through the window and the lab instructor looked up just as it landed on top of the drying oven. Tretona made a big show of pipetting benzene, and he didn't say a word.

Tretona guessed that part of the reason she kept showing off so much was so she would have good stories to tell Tiia and Sylvia and Emma Sue back at GDI #501. The four of them spent a lot of time in Sylvia's room with the door closed. Sylvia and Emma Sue were getting pretty demonstrative now and sometimes even kissed each other briefly on the mouth. Tretona longed to show some sort of public physical affection to Tiia, too, but something—either in her or in Tiia—held her back. Whenever the longing got too great, she would start tickling Emma Sue or arm wrestling with Sylvia—everything except touching Tiia.

Not that Tiia was untouchable—anything but. When Wendy was in class, Tiia would hide behind the door to their room and spring on Tretona's back like a big, beautiful Siamese cat and they would end up down on the lower bunk bed—or even on Wendy's single—squirming and wrestling and play biting. Then sometimes Tiia would start a little real biting, so Tretona would grab her hands and wrap them up in pajama tops and kiss Tiia until she got loose, and then Tiia's cheeks would get that fierce cherry color. She would hold Tretona very tight and they would make love very quickly so as to be sure and finish before Wendy got back or someone came in.

It was when Wendy got the flu and was bedfast for ten days that Tretona got into real trouble. Wendy was too sick even to have company so Tiia started studying in the library and Tretona took to hanging out across the hall in Jeri Johnson's room. While Jeri rattled on continuously about scoops and deadlines and bylines and headlines, Tretona spent a lot of time staring and then smiling at Jeri Johnson's roommate, Lisa. Lisa was just a freshman whom Tretona had immediately pegged as a dumb southern belle. She was kind of dumpy and had a drawl that sounded real low class to Tretona.

But when Tretona got bored with Jeri Johnson's preoccupation with instant success and yawned and looked to Lisa for confirmation, all of a sudden she realized what an attractive person Lisa was. Maybe it was the way she half-lowered her eyelids and shrugged. "Languid," thought Tretona. Almost as if she were reading Tretona's mind, Lisa got up and put on a record—"One mint julep was the cause of it all." Tretona started to make some flip remark about typecasting and people living up to stereotypes, but then she looked at Lisa who was swaying just the teensiest bit on her straight-backed desk chair. Suddenly it was like that laboratory experiment with tuning forks, where the still fork gets vibrations from the resonator and they both start humming on the same pitch. Suddenly, waves were going back and forth between them and Tretona was recording the color of Lisa's gray-hazel eyes and aching to touch her hair which was slightly kinky. ("Mulatto" crossed Tretona's mind. Maybe that would explain the intense but subtle rhythm in Lisa's body.) The air between them seemed to get as thick as Jello and Tretona could feel every movement Lisa made. She started getting dizzy and couldn't believe that Jeri Johnson was unaware of the oscillations rampaging back and forth between their bodies and eyes and souls.

Then the door slammed and Tiia came running up the stairs. "I'll be damned," said Tiia in her careful birdsong English. "Mrs. Goddard would lock the door in my face." For it was eleven P.M., the hour when all undergraduate women had to be hauled away from the library, the laboratory, the late movie, the lovers' lanes, and locked safely away. And 11:05 was the time when the inhabitants of GDI #501 developed intense longings for unavailable goodies—Hershey bars, crackers, cream cheese with pineapple in it, graph paper for writing up the lab experiment due tomorrow, shoe polish, shampoo, Scotch tape—in short, any of the thousand and one items sold at the little corner grocery which stayed open until midnight. The four young women sat restlessly in Jeri Johnson's room listening to Mrs. Goddard latch the screen door and then double-lock the front door.

"How much I would like a beer," Tiia sighed. She never had been able to understand why Americans were so fearful of

82

alcohol. This town even had an ordinance preventing the sale of any alcoholic beverage within a mile of campus.

Some combination of sexual energy and righteous indignation pushed the words out of Tretona's mouth. "Okay, you want beer? I'll go get you some." Surprised, excited mumbles of "you can't do that—it's after curfew—we aren't supposed to drink up here." Tretona pulled on her sweatshirt and got up. "You guys pop some corn. I'll be back right away."

Then over to the window and out onto the porch roof. The fire escape was right there—it was only fear that kept them prisoner. Tretona crept silently across and started down. A shadow startled her. She looked up to see Lisa—her broad bottom descending toward Tretona's face. "I'm coming, too."

They got safely past Mrs. Goddard's quarters and ran giggling through the alley. Now the main danger was the campus police. Tretona stopped to turn her sweatshirt wrong-side out so the school mascot didn't show. "Let me do the talking at the liquor store," said Lisa. "I'll talk redneck to them." The spring air seemed clearer and headier after eleven. For a moment, Tretona tried to figure out whether the specific gravity of the atmosphere should increase or decrease as the vapor pressure dropped, but then Lisa's shoulder brushed hers and the dizzying waves of desire started up again. She wanted to pull Lisa up against a garage somewhere but some survival instinct warned her that they'd better get back pronto.

The dumb kids at #501 hadn't made popcorn at all. Instead the whole house was in Jeri Johnson's room, looking out the window for them, alternately giggling and hushing each other. "We're in for it," thought Tretona. She and Lisa had just pushed the bag through Jeri Johnson's window when Mrs. Goddard threw open the door.

The next morning Lisa was the first one called in to talk to the Dean of Women. When she came out she had obviously been crying, but her gray eyes were still snappy. Tretona looked up. "Well?" "I'm out," said Lisa. "I was already on academic pro from the first semester." Tretona hadn't been scared until then. She couldn't keep from sucking in her lower lip. "Hang tough," said Lisa. "I'm going to pack."

Dean Eloise Goodbody looked like all the grandmothers in Walt Disney pictures. She had on a blue cardigan and a lacy white blouse. Tretona half expected her to whip out some yarn and a crochet needle. Instead, she went through Tretona's transcript and started grilling her. Why had she taken so many extra phys ed courses? Why did she study both French and German her junior year? Which quantum mechanics course was better, the one in the physics department or the one offered by the chemists? Was she going to graduate school next year? Where?

Tretona answered civilly enough until the subject of grad school came up. "I won't be going anywhere unless I get out of this prison." Suddenly "Grandma" Goodbody looked every inch a dean. "My dear Miss Getroek, since you have a 3.6 average I assume you are intelligent enough to understand that when rules are made for a student body of thousands, they will not always be appropriate for every individual student. There are lots of reasons for having a curfew—one is to encourage people to get enough sleep."

"But the *boys* don't have a closing hour," Tretona snapped. "Even though you're a dean, I assume you're intelligent enough to. . . ." Tretona stopped in panic as she realized what she had just said.

Dean Goodbody looked completely calm. "Of course, it's unfair. We all know that. But many of our parents wouldn't let their daughters come to the university at all if we didn't have a curfew. They think this place is practically as wicked as Sodom and Gomorrah, as it is." Tretona shrugged and wiggled her big toe around under the hole in her tennis shoe. "Well, *do* something if you don't like it. Circulate petitions. I'd be delighted if our student government got interested. Anyway, you'd better go now. You'll be late for your ten o'clock."

"But what's going to happen now? Will my parents be notified?" Tretona's voice was faltering.

"Nothing's going to happen," said Dean Eloise Goodbody. "Case closed. The last thing I'd do is upset your parents with such trivia."

"But Lisa—" said Tretona, gesturing towards the anteroom. "It's not fair that I. . . ."

"Nope, it's not fair," said Dean Goodbody and briskly put Tretona's file in the out box. "Bye now. And good luck in grad school."

On the way over to Newell Lab, Tretona tried to figure out why Dean Goodbody had let her off. She thought a lot about the difference between fairness and justice, and what rules were for and when they were legitimate. She thought about civil disobedience and whether she would have been justified in climbing down the fire escape while carrying a protest sign and ringing a bell. Jeri Johnson had a flash attachment and she could have taken pictures for the D.S. Tretona decided not to tell Lisa or anybody (except maybe Sylvia) how easy she'd gotten off. Then she smiled to herself: "Maybe I'll send that good ole body a post card from grad school next year."

*   *   *

Finals were over and there was just time before commencement to go to Chicago! With Tiia! "To meet the in-laws?" Sylvia had asked. Actually, Tretona was staying at Wendy's house, but they were both invited to an Estonian wedding—Tiia's cousin was getting married—so she would get to see Tiia *in situ* (as Sylvia might put it).

Tretona felt as if she were being rushed from one movie set to another: State and Madison, skyscrapers—even the Chinese restaurant Wendy's folks took them to was *five* stories high. Wendy's mom had lox and bagels for breakfast. (Tretona almost choked because she didn't realize how much chewing the bagel required. It wasn't like any roll she'd ever tasted.) Wendy's house not only had two bathrooms, there was even something called a "half bath" downstairs. In it there were photographs of her mom in the winner's ring at a dog show. It was like a Cary Grant–Katharine Hepburn movie.

Neither Wendy nor Tretona recognized Tiia at first when she came to meet them. She was wearing a kind of headdress as part of her native costume and had on long white stockings. She looked beautiful, though, and Tretona almost collapsed from excitement and longing when Tiia took hold of both of her hands in welcome. Wendy and Tretona were seated at a table with other non-Estonians. Between courses and toasts, Tiia would scamper over and tell them what they were eating and what was happening. She explained how the costumes showed whether you were married, unmarried, widowed, and had children or grandchildren. "What about the man's marital status?" Tretona asked, "How is that indicated?" Tiia laughed. "Well, we don't really need to know that, do we? They always ask us."

By the time the bride and bridegroom got up to lead the first polka, Tretona and Wendy were completely sloshed on wine. Even Tiia's cheeks were flushed as she came over and sat down. The wedding pair were superb dancers, whirling in a cloverleaf pattern, their eyes locked together. When it was over, without thinking, Tretona took hold of Tiia's hand. "That was the most beautiful thing I ever saw," Tretona said. Tiia smiled and touched her cheek to Tretona's shoulder. "You will see," she said. "My wedding dance will be even more beautiful."

Tretona stiffened. "But. . ." she faltered. "What about. . ." and she sort of squeezed Tiia's hand to finish the sentence. Tiia looked at her, with eyes big and clear and completely forthright and innocent. "Yes, my wedding. I could never disappoint my family—my people."

It was like the time the taxi hit her. All bodily defense systems went on alert. Her brain whirred. The lead shield went down behind her eyes and there was no more pain—at least there were no signals getting through. Tretona spent the rest of the evening chatting animatedly about ethnic integrity versus assimilation to Wendy, who was feeling bad about not being Jewish enough. She even kissed Tiia on the cheek when they left.

Tretona thought she would burst into tears when she was finally alone in the guest room back at Wendy's. But nothing happened. She let out a tiny sigh like a polite little balloon going down. "I guess I'm finally growing up," thought Tretona as she fell asleep.

11 Authenticity Among the Test Tubes

Between the amateur and the professional . . .
there is a difference not only in degree but in kind.
                                        —Bernard De Voto

To strive, to seek, to find, and not to yield.
                                        —Alfred Lord Tennyson

TRETONA CLIMBED UP the stairs to Inorganic Preps lab, her briefcase handle straining under the load of the 35th edition of *The Handbook of Chemistry and Physics,* all 3,153 pages of it. "Don't make a handbook out of your head," Professor G. Frederick Smith always told them. Good news for the cranium, but the poor old muscles had to compensate. Tretona wondered if her damn chromium complex would crystallize out this time. Three times she'd made it per directions and three times she'd ended up with a purple-green gunk—nary a crystal to be had. Her lab instructor shrugged: "That's why we're having you check the prep. We want to know if the results from Ohio State are reproducible."

Tretona remembered Sisyphus pushing a rock up the mountain just so it could roll down again. But according to Camus, who was telling the story, Sisyphus finally affirmed his daily existence; "it was *his* rock" was the phrase she remembered. Well, this was *her* purple-green gunk, she thought, as she looked at the tarry watch glass, but she'd be damned if she could "affirm" it. It was *their* journal, *Inorganic Syntheses,* that she was testing the recipe for. But it wasn't even a fair test—if she couldn't get the crystals to form it'd be *her* failure. She was on trial, not the recipe.

Somewhere she'd read a description of scientific experimenting as "putting nature on the rack," thereby extorting her secrets. So far, it seemed to be the graduate students who were put on the rack, not nature. She wondered when, if ever, the emphasis would switch from getting the "right" results to finding out something new—"pushing back the frontiers of knowledge." God, it all sounded so corny and naive.

Still there was a satisfaction in setting up the apparatus efficiently—making a perfect grease seal on the stopcock, titrating with her left hand while swirling the flask with her right, pipetting acetone with the newfangled bulbs with valves in them and hitting the 25-milliliter line with the meniscus on the first try.

The crystals were reported to be rhomboidal and to melt at 115 degrees centigrade. Hell, those people in Ohio couldn't have made the whole thing up. Probably they left out some simple but crucial step in their report.

It was much more fun teaching—being on the other side of the lab bench, as it were. She had a section of C105, the beginning course for chem majors. Even though these kids were mostly bright and had all had chemistry in high school, they sure could goof up in the lab—glass tubing through the palm, letting hot beakers slip out of their tongs, pouring chemicals back into the reagent bottles. They made every mistake in the book.

At first, Tretona about went nuts trying to keep an eye on everything and everybody, but she finally gave up and resigned herself to at least one disaster a week. She even made a joke of it and threatened to award a Chemistry 105 Klutz Prize at the end of the semester.

Tretona smiled. "That's the only prize that Lorrie would fail to win hands down," she thought. Lorrie was her favorite student—and maybe her favorite being in the whole world. Long lanky pony tail, long lanky legs, long slim fingers—everything about Lorrie was extended and light—her slow laugh, shy glances, eye lashes.

Her quiz papers were nearly always perfect and in the lab— Tretona struggled for the right words to express the way Lorrie moved. Like a beautiful thoroughbred colt, past the gawky stage but still not decisively confident. Lorrie seemed already graceful and grown up, but didn't quite realize it yet and so retained a bit of tentativeness that was no longer necessary. "That Lorrie—*she* sure crystallized out beautifully," Tretona thought and then mixed metaphors in her mind: "My chrysalid crystal," which brought to mind "crepitation," which is what these damn chromium crystals were supposed to do when you melted them, which is what Tretona's heart/brain did every time Lorrie asked her a question. It got to be embarrassing—Lorrie's questions were generally hard ones, but even when Tretona knew the answer, more than likely she would end up stammering. Finally, Tretona adopted a formal defense mechanism: "Well, Miss Mills—" (the AI's were all supposed to address students by their last names) "Well, Miss Mills, I'd like to think about that question and get back to you on it a little later."

After a trip to the water fountain, Tretona would be recovered and could then plan the encounter. Generally, she would stand by Lorrie's left shoulder, maybe leaning casually on the lab bench. That way she could calculate or draw graphs on the back pages of Lorrie's notebook and have an excuse to move closer. Sometimes they would need the blackboard and if Tretona was wearing something especially attractive she would go first. Otherwise, she would make a gesture for Lorrie to lead off. Lorrie always seemed a little hesitant about how fast to walk and Tretona ached to just put her arm around her and discharge all the tension.

Tretona sighed. She finished triturating the chromium, set the mixture on a steam bath to digest for ninety minutes, and headed off for a coffee break. On her way to Nick's she resolved to get her feelings under control and stop mooning around. First of all, it wasn't fair to Lorrie, casting all those intense, deep looks sideways at her while ostensibly discussing ionization constants. Poor Lorrie—she'd probably thought that, having a female instructor, for once she wouldn't have to fend off the sweaty glances. Tretona had to admit to being as lascivious as they came, although she hoped she wasn't as pushy and obnoxious about it as boys were.

And it wasn't fair to herself, either. Why should she waste all that time mooning over somebody who a) probably wouldn't even remember her name two weeks after the final exam; b) even if she did like Tretona would never want to be friends; c) even if she did become friends wouldn't dream of kissing; d) even if she did let Tretona kiss her, wouldn't. . . .

Just as Tretona's underpants started to steam up, there was a grotesque snarling noise. It was Emil! Emil, the disgusting leper of Nick's Fountain and Grill. Emil had shaggy hair and pimples and bad teeth and sores around his wrist (he said he was allergic to the ROTC uniform). Emil always hung out at Nick's reading Allen Ginsberg or Ferlinghetti and eating garbage. Literally, garbage. He would creep from table to table cleaning off plates before the waitress could clear them away. Nick didn't seem to mind.

"How is the best mind of my generation?" said Emil.

"Screaming, hysterical, naked," Tretona gave the canonical response and they began to shadow box with arched slashing fingers and great Japanese stomping and prehistoric noises.

Tretona and Emil loved to fight. Once they were wrestling and rolling on the floor at a party with Tretona making gurgles and groans while Emil growled. When some big he-man type tried to rescue Tretona, she and Emil turned on the cheeky intruder and drove him away with banshee cries and then plotted how to put woad in his beer. Emil settled down when they got to Nick's and started looking around for garbage.

"I'm in funds today," Tretona said and casually ordered two batches of French fries.

"Back in a sec," said Emil and reappeared with three half-empty cups of coffee (one had lipstick all over the rim), a cigarette butt, and the catsup-mustard-oil-and-vinegar tray. He bowed to the floor: "A meager and unworthy contribution to Milady's bountiful feast."

Tretona loved Emil, but she wondered if he would go crazy someday—that is, assuming he wasn't crazy already. Emil had a big love-hate thing about science. That was one reason he hung out at Nick's where all the science majors were—that being secondary to the ready availability and superior quality of Nick's garbage, of course. He thought that Einstein had proved that all judgments were *relative* and that according to Heisenberg everything was *uncertain*. He liked to talk a lot about entropy and neg-entropy, time-dilation, mass-energy and the forthcoming heat death of the universe. Tretona concluded that Emil loved science when it seemed to have absurd or counter-intuitive consequences, but hated it when it put limits on possibilities or gave prosaic explanations of things. Emil went wild when Tretona said that no one could build a perpetual motion machine and when she insisted that neither statistical mechanics nor Heisenberg's uncertainty principle provided any loopholes for people who wanted to believe in miracles. "A chance conglomeration of the right kind of atoms," said Emil, "and bingo! We have Christ walking on water. *Deus ex agua*—thanks to Heisenberg who made it all possible."

"But the probability of its happening is vanishingly small," protested Tretona. "Modern physics provides no legitimization whatsoever for all those old fairy tales."

"Tsk, tsk, now don't be sacrilegious," said Emil. "Scientists have wisely conceded that miracles are not only logically coherent but also physically possible. That's real scientific progress."

Now it was Tretona's turn to sputter. She knew Emil was wrong, but he was slippery in his arguments. That's what came from being a philosophy major. She decided to change the subject before Emil started his favorite harangue on transubstantiation and radioactive transmutation.

"Emil, what if you really like someone a lot and you keep looking at them and 'accidentally' brushing against them and stuff, but they don't like you especially—maybe they don't even know you exist. Is that emotional exploitation? Can you—well—sort of rape someone with your eyes?" Tretona expected Emil to come up with something about intentionality or integrity or authenticity or autonomy that would help her sort out the confused feelings she had about Lorrie. But right then, the double order of French fries came and Emil never got around to answering. Anyway, by then it was almost time to go back to the lab.

By the end of the fall semester Tretona had decided grad school was A.O.K. Tretona liked having her own little studio apartment. She liked not having closing hours and being able to work in the lab as late as she pleased. She especially liked getting paid for teaching. Her first purchase was a pair of nice lined winter gloves. (Her mom always thought mittens were more practical.) She was buying a set of the *Encyclopaedia Britannica* on the installment plan. She wondered if that had been rash—the agent had reminded her of the salesmen who came around down home selling simplified translations of the Bible in fancy covers with titles like *The Book of Life*. Anyway, the encyclopaedia (she loved the British spelling) looked spiffy sitting under the double window—and it came in handy for settling arguments.

Lately she had been saving like crazy so she could buy the kids really nice Christmas presents. Troy had just got his driver's license, so he would be easy to shop for. She could get him one of those musical car horns that played "Mary Had a Little Lamb."

But before shopping she had to finish marking the C105 exams. Her kids were doing pretty well. Lorrie's exam got graded first, of course. She made a 98 (two points off for getting an exponent wrong). Tretona had said good-bye to Lorrie after the exam. "Nice having you in class; good luck in C106." She had wanted to add something about keeping in touch, but decided it wouldn't be professional to do so.

In a way she was relieved the semester was almost over. It was going to be rough not seeing Lorrie three times a week, but better than seducing a student. If she ever decided to go into teaching instead of industrial research, she'd have to watch stuff like that. Tretona sighed, got up, took a beer out of the fridge, and then went back to grading the final exams.

Then—a knock on the door, she opened it—there was Lorrie all bundled up in a big coat and stocking cap—confusion, not knowing whether to invite her in or stand like a dolt talking in the doorway.

Then Lorrie was looking straight at her with hazel eyes (funny she never noticed the color before) and saying quietly, but firmly, "I *had* to see you." So Tretona recovered her manners, asked her in, took her coat, started to offer her a beer, then realized Lorrie was a minor, thought what-the-hell and did it anyway. Lorrie refused the drink, so it was all academic. Lorrie sat on the bed so Tretona went back to her desk. There was no place else to sit. "You wrote a beautiful final," said Tretona and apologized for having to take off points for an incorrect exponent. "I know you know how to work with exponents and in a way it's just an arithmetic error, but so many kids never master it, so we have to. . . ."

Lorrie was looking straight at her again, then she gave a coltish shrug and dropped her eyes. "Miss Getroek," she began.

"Hey, the semester's practically over. Call me Tretona," she said and to her great surprise Lorrie did.

"Tretona, why do you look at me that way in lab?"

Tretona's mind whirled like a centrifuge. She started to parry with "What way?" but Lorrie's eyes already were blocking any sort of cop out. So instead she knelt very carefully in front of Lorrie and put her hands first on Lorrie's arms and then around her shoulders and Lorrie's mouth was very gentle and warm.

Lorrie made a little moaning noise. "I knew it. I knew it all the time," she said as Tretona moved her across the bed down toward the pillow end.

After Lorrie left, Tretona made Kraft dinner and carrot sticks. She pulled her desk chair over to the little kitchen table and propped her feet up on the encyclopaedia bookcase. She ate slowly and looked out the window—it was getting dark fast. Why did she feel so numb? After all, Lorrie had come to her. The exams were done. There was no way the happening this afternoon could affect Lorrie's grade one way or the other. "Well, if Lorrie's grade had gone down on the final, I could still have raised it, I suppose." But it hadn't gone down and it was clear that wasn't why Lorrie had come.

Tretona wished she had a cigarette, which made her think, maybe she was having the sort of letdown big game hunters have when they finally kill their prey after stalking it for hours, or days, or even months. She vaguely remembered a Hemingway story about that happening to some guy in Africa.

So was Lorrie her prey? She had been stalking her—no question. And she always used animal images when she thought about Lorrie—colt, antelope, gazelle. "So, deer are in season?" Tretona asked herself. She piled the dishes in the sink, wishing as always that there was a dog to give the leftovers to. As she went down the hall to take a shower, it hit her—she absolutely couldn't afford to get involved with a student in the chemistry department, not a *female* student.

Afterward, she called Emil and asked where the party he had told her about was going to be. Emil was pleased but surprised, "Hey Tretona, this is great. You've really decided to go? Great!" And then, "Are you okay? You sound strange, sort of far away." Tretona felt like saying bitterly, "You schnook, I'm finally taking your fucking advice to meet some interesting men." Maybe that would keep her out of trouble.

Emil walked over to pick her up. Tretona had to stop by the lab and there sitting in the watch glass like some mysterious blue-green omen of good things to come (or maybe it was a recompense for the pain of the afternoon) was a beautiful cluster of chromium crystals. Tretona picked them up oh so gently and put them in a desiccator. These would surely get the lab prep teacher off her back, although the bastard would probably just say, "You finally followed directions, huh?" unless Tretona explained that she'd used a different solvent from the one in the recipe. The crystals were like her feelings—elusive, an unusual shape, hard to replicate.

The party was at Robert Khanna's "flat," as he called it, since he was from the British West Indies. Emil said Robert was half East Indian and half Scots and had come up from Trinidad to study business administration. He raved about Robert, said he was very charming and had great parties, but even so, Tretona was completely unprepared.

First the sound of drums as they walked up on the porch and then a hall full of laughter and tinkling, writhing music. It was a beatniky crowd mixed in with lots of West Indians of all shades and there by the record player leaning against a shelf with candles on it was Robert. He was a perfect toffee color and had black wavy hair and beautiful hands, which he moved very slowly but unpretentiously. Tretona hid behind Emil and refused to be introduced right away, but finally she edged up to hear the conversation. Robert was talking about Voodoo and witching away warts with chicken bones. He claimed it really worked and that the people in the islands who believed in it weren't stupid at all. Robert had been conversing with a beautiful British accent. Now he rolled his eyes and switched to a West Indian intonation: "Oh, mon! When Carnivál come and everyone go Bacchinal, then time for plenty powerful Voodoo. You see."

Then Tretona, who was convinced that no religion could be more primitive than the one she grew up with, forgot her shyness and started telling the story about the time Big Jimmy Haines cursed the Holy Ghost. He had just sold a truck load of cattle and hardly gotten back home before the Church of God preacher showed up to collect his tithe. Big Jimmy said that since they were feeder cattle he should deduct the price he paid for them before taking 10 percent. Evidently, the preacher claimed the tithe should come off the gross, not the net. In any case, Big Jimmy got mad and cussed the Holy Spirit and then the preacher said he had committed the unforgivable sin and would go to hell for sure.

The Methodists said that it wasn't that easy to commit the unforgivable sin—what you had to do was intentionally and deliberately quench that little voice inside. Probably it would take a long time to kill off the Spirit entirely. But Jimmy Haines was a Church of Godder, so he believed the preacher. After that he used to stay home from church on Sunday mornings and listen to sermons on the radio and bawl. Tretona's mom said the very fact he cried so hard showed that he still had a conscience. But no one could console him and that winter he just kept getting more and more poorly. Finally, he developed pneumonia and died.

"So that's the way Voodoo works here in America," said Tretona. She hoped she hadn't stolen the floor for too long but Robert seemed to like the story. He smiled and then guided the conversation onto a discussion of the more jolly side of carnival time—the steel band contests, the dancing in the streets, the flowers. Tretona stopped concentrating on the content and just listened to his voice. She decided it reminded her of Harvey's Bristol Cream Sherry (which she had never tasted, but knew from the *New Yorker* ads).

Then Emil came by and they fell in with some black West Indians who were teasing each other about which was better, Jamaica or Trinidad. They talked about music, dancing, and food, and then started comparing the people. Everyone agreed that it never worked for a Jamaican woman to marry a Trinidadian man, although the reverse was okay. Tretona didn't quite understand why, and so Emil whispered that Jamaica was a matriarchal society while the Trinidadians were patriarchal. Tretona looked over at Robert. He didn't look very patriarchal. His eyes were so warm and he moved so gently; he had hardly any hair at all on his arms or at his neck. During the rest of the party Tretona milled around, hoping to end up in the same circle as Robert but it never happened naturally and she didn't want to push it. Finally, it was getting time to leave so Tretona decided to go up and ask him about the record that was playing. Robert said it was the Duke of Iron singing a calypso about women police in Trinidad. The chorus went, "Woman policeman, hold me tight." You couldn't buy it here, so he offered to lend Tretona his copy. Tretona got flustered and said no, it was too valuable and then Robert said he'd carry it over to her house himself and that way he could help her decipher the words.

Tretona fought to keep from blushing and forced herself not to shuffle around with her right toe on her left instep, which she always did when embarrassed. It seemed hours went by before she could breathe or swallow, let alone say anything. And then her mind and manners came back under control and she said that she'd be gone over Christmas but be back a week early to work in the lab. And Robert said, Super—he'd give her a ring (actually, what he said sounded more like "soup-ah"). She said swell and thanks for the lovely party and Robert said, "Cheerio, old chap," to Emil and "Catch you right after Christmas vac" to her.

About halfway down East Washington Tretona's mood shot down like a polarograph needle approaching the endpoint of a titration. What if Robert was only being polite? What if he never intended to come over at all? She sighed and kicked a piece of muddy ice along the sidewalk. Emil began to giggle. "Sure beats etchings, doesn't it?" "What do you mean?" Tretona demanded. Emil put on a plummy singsong accent. "What say, luv, now wouldn't you like to be comin' up and hearin' my steel band records?" He rolled his eyes at Tretona and started chanting rhythmically: "Gimme a beat on your kimmy kimmy ping pong— gimme a beat." He danced the calypso step looking like Ichabod Crane on snow shoes.

This time Tretona didn't even try to keep from blushing and pretty soon she let out an enormous whoop, "Yeah Carnivál!" and war-danced down the street after Emil. That night as she scrunched down deep under her blankets, Tretona found herself praying. "Dear God," she started to say but then censored it. "Oh my goodness," she said instead, "if only he comes over— even just once—that would be perfect."

And lo, the days passed and the Trinidadian angel did appear and Tretona was sore afraid. "Fear not," said the toffee angel and he brought cut flowers, Swiss chocolate bars, and slightly por-nographic calypso records. And he was polite—not laughing when she put on a commercial album of Harry Belafonte singing West Indian songs, and thoughtful—shaving twice a day after he found out how easily her cheeks got red. And he wasn't at all macho— letting her take charge of the flat tire instead of trying to pretend he knew how to change it. (The chauffeur had always done it at home, he said, or else they called the Royal Auto Club.) He was a very beautiful and romantic lover. Tretona adored him.

And ten months later—it was in October before her birth-day—Tretona lay tossing on the couch in what Robert insisted on calling the "parlor" of their tiny duplex and grimaced as she remembered that little surrogate prayer. "So I said that would be perfect." The bitterness of the memory made her throat swell up. "God if only he, it, everything weren't so perfect maybe I wouldn't be so perfectly miserable."

It wasn't fair—it just wasn't fair. Robert did everything right—he did everything she'd ever dared dream of and more—and still she wasn't happy. He liked her a lot—she was sure of that, though sometimes she wondered why—maybe it was because there weren't any redheads in the Islands?—and she liked him—and yet here she was feeling terrible.

What had gone wrong? Even her mom thought Robert was okay—Tretona had somehow gotten up the nerve to take him home over Easter. Her brothers liked him because he was good at Ping Pong. He would lay back like a sleepy cat, hitting the ball back softly—until he saw an opening and then zap! All without appearing to concentrate. Stanton and Troy huffed and grunted and slammed the ball with big roundhouse strokes—and never did beat him.

Robert was absolutely charming at the dinner table—he seated her mother (who promptly got flustered), asked her father about farming, and obligingly said "ta-mah-toe" and "shed-ule" and "lab-*bore*-a-toree" when Tretona directed the conversation so those words would come up. She groaned now, thinking how happy and proud she had been.

There was only one bad moment during the whole visit. Robert had been out walking down the lane toward the woods with her father. They stopped halfway back—her father was undoubtedly telling about the new drainage ditch that the government had paid for. As the men turned around and faced the house again in the late afternoon sun, her mother shuddered. "For a minute there, he almost looked like a black man," she said. Tretona had never thought about it before, but suddenly she could see what her mother meant. Her father's walk was straight and very solid, his feet crunching down firmly on the occasional clods, sticker weeds, or corn cobs. While Robert, well, it was hard to describe—it's just that he always looked like he was about to turn into a tiger or something beautiful and jungly and wild. On the other hand, if her father ever turned into anything, it would more likely be a Soviet statue—social realism style—or a robot made out of Lego pieces. And though Tretona knew what her mother was talking about, she immediately attacked her on the factual remark and ignored the shudder (which of course was what had really hurt): "Don't be ignorant, Mother. He doesn't look anything like a Negro. He's only half Indian, you know. And

Punjabi at that. The Punjabis are the original Aryans. Not that it would make any difference if he were. . . ."

Now lying on the davenport in the duplex late at night Tretona wondered if it did in fact make a difference. One evening walking up to the lab Tretona had gotten really angry at Robert—she couldn't remember why, something about the way he was carrying her books—and she'd hit him with her slide rule and screamed out, "You're just like a black man. You're no better than a black man." Robert put the books down gently right in the middle of the stairs and walked away. Tretona couldn't move for a minute. She didn't know why she had said it—it was as if her mother had taken over her body and her mother was saying it, not her. Then she chased after him and caught up with him, and she was bawling out stuff about how sorry she was and hugging him around the knees. And Robert was very wise and gentlemanly and said that the words themselves hadn't bothered him, but her intention in saying them did hurt, but that he forgave her and perhaps they should go now and have a nice cup of tea.

He really had been a perfect gentleman. Tretona winced as she remembered it. She still didn't know why she had said it. Had she been trying to taunt him, and break through his perfection—or was she really a racist underneath?

Well, it didn't matter. All she really knew was that she wasn't happy—didn't deserve to be probably. All these years she had felt sorry for herself because she wasn't popular with the boys and no one ever asked her out—literally no one. (Well, Carl Ackerman made a date once in high school but he got drunk and never showed up—and then there was that time she met cross-eyed Joe in the movie theater, but that was more like a pick-up than a real date.) Here she was practically living with an intelligent, cultivated, charming man who probably really did love her—at least he kept talking about how she'd like Trinidad (her mother said he'd probably been sent up to the U.S. to bring home a white girl, but for heaven's sake make him promise to live up here where it was civilized)—and still she wasn't satisfied.

Well, Tretona thought, she might be like her mother in lots of ways but she sure as hell wasn't going to buy into a lifetime of feeling miserable the way her mother had. It was time to get out of this mess right now. Tretona reached for her shoes. Where to go? She could hear Robert breathing regularly and deeply in the bedroom. He had been perfectly reasonable about her wanting to sleep out on the couch. Typical. Back to Jeri Johnson's? (For legal purposes and for her folks' sake, Tretona was technically sharing Jeri's place next door.) Not bloody likely. She'd just head up to campus—something would be open.

But nothing was. By three A.M. Tretona was dog tired and starting to get cold. She was headed over to the chem lab to sleep behind the barrels on the delivery platform in the rear, when she saw a light in the Newman Foundation. Catholic churches were supposed to be open all the time. Maybe she could find sanctuary there.

Into the vestibule, a quick glance at the bulletin board, hesitation, and then Tretona chose the stairs going down. She could always say she was looking for a restroom. Across the dimly lit lounge (maybe the couch in the corner would do?) and she froze. Someone was coming down the corridor. Terrible mutterings approached and then receded. Relief. No, now they were coming back. She started to flee and then bumped into a magazine rack. The mumbling stopped, the double doors flew open and there was a priest. "Good evening," he said. "Or should I say good morning?" Tretona just stared. "I was just saying my office," he explained. "Hope I didn't startle you." Then, "May I possibly be of any assistance?"

"I just wanted to use the restroom," Tretona began. But then it was like when she was a kid and someone stacked her arms full of cabbages out in the garden and they were okay as long as she was walking but when she went to unload them on the kitchen table, as soon as one cabbage became dislodged all the rest tumbled down willy-nilly and it was no use trying to hold them back. And so Tretona found herself babbling all sorts of ridiculous things about authenticity and working in a chem lab and whether it was honorable to love someone if you really weren't right for them and how could you decide what job you were really suited for and how much should you compromise and try to make your parents proud of you and how much should you live your own life, and on and on. Even as she spoke, Tretona couldn't believe what she was doing. These weren't the things she was really worried about—this was all bullshit. It didn't even sound like her voice. It was like some naive, stupid, suck-ass stuffy prude had kidnapped her vocal cords. The real Tretona was sitting back amazed. She didn't have any respect at all for priests. Talk about authenticity—what was she doing talking to a priest?

99

Finally, all the cabbages stopped rolling. The priest waited a while and then spoke in a quiet, matter-of-fact voice: "I have three pieces of advice for you. The first advice concerns tonight: sleep in the restroom here. There's a padded bench inside and a blanket. The second is for tomorrow: go over to the student counseling service and take a vocational aptitude test. The third is for right now and for always: listen more to your conscience. It's wise to seek advice from others and to reflect upon it, but in the end *you* must decide."

Tretona nodded slightly to show that she understood. The priest waited a moment, made a little bow, and disappeared.

The bench in the bathroom wasn't half bad; there weren't even any gruesome sacred heart pictures around. "It's nice that there are sanctuaries," Tretona thought and fell asleep right away.

12 Through the Looking Glass and Beyond

Oh, Dr. Freud! Oh, Dr. Freud!
How we wish you had been otherwise employed!
—Folk Song

The object of homosexual "love" is nothing but a
projection of the client himself as seen through a
dim, disfiguring mirror.
—Psychiatric Monograph

"FATHER O'ROARKE! THAT'S who it had to be. He's the big Christian existentialist over there." Tretona had awakened in time for her birthday breakfast appointment with Emil and had told him a slick version of her adventures in the Newman Foundation. If Emil was concerned about the reasons for her prowling around so late at night, he certainly didn't let on. "A toast! A toast to Tretona on her twenty-second birthday," he cried. Tretona smiled and reached for the orange juice. "No, a real toast," said Emil, solemnly picking up his English muffin.

"What a crummy thing to do," retorted Tretona, and they fell to giggling and bantering.

But Tretona was processing the events of the night before. "Emil," she said, "I've decided to. . . ." she stopped and Emil cocked his head like a big shaggy parrot: "Yes? Go on. All receivers tuned in and open."

"Well, I've decided to . . . to make some new decisions."

"Good," said Emil. "Meta-decisions are. . ." (Perhaps he

was going to say "better than nothing," but what he came out with was) "good decisions to start with."

Tretona pushed on more firmly. "I've decided . . . well, I think I'm going to decide to get out of chemistry—I'm going to take that foreign service exam we saw posted in the Union Building and maybe I'll go see a vocational counselor or something. And I'm going to break off with Robert."

Emil arched his eyebrows and began to drum on the table: "Nothing is the same in Trinidad. Tretona go away, Robert very sad."

Tretona kicked him and Emil stopped and got serious: "All right, you're tired of toffee, fair enough. But what about chemistry? I thought science was your real true love."

Tretona started to explain, but discovered she really didn't know why she wanted to get out of chemistry so she laughed cynically and said the first thing that came to her mind: "Hell, I'm no good at it. Look at Einstein. By the time he was twenty-two he had discovered the theory of relativity plus the photoelectric effect. And even if I did win the Nobel Prize, I couldn't accept it. There's no way I'm going to waltz with the King of Sweden."

Emil seemed relieved that the conversation had lightened. "Maybe I'll win the Nobel Peace Prize at the same time," he said, "for negotiating a truce between the Midwest and the West Indies. And then I will be dancing with the Queen of Sweden and then you and I can snarl and wrestle in the middle of the ballroom floor."

And then the mood was as crazy and wonderful as always. But after breakfast Tretona cut the biochem lecture, something she rarely did. Instead, she went back to the duplex and moved all her stuff back to Jeri Johnson's place. She left a vague cheerful note for Robert. Then she walked over to the student counseling service, took a battery of tests on the spot, and made an appointment to talk over the results with a Dr. Devore.

The aptitude tests were so silly Tretona almost didn't go back. She told Jeri Johnson about them: "Which would you rather do, Jeri, write a complaining letter or call up and bitch at the people over the phone? Which would you rather do, take care of a sick dog or repair a lamp?"

Jeri looked puzzled and tried to figure out the right answers. "Now go slow, Tretona, let me think. It depends, doesn't it—on whether it's my dog or not and whether the lamp is desperately needed right away. As to the mode of complaint, if there's a prospect of litigation, then the letter is preferable. However, if the time factor were important. . . ."

"Oh, shut up Jeri." Tretona was impatient. "You don't understand at all. It was a multiple choice exam. You just get to mark one answer and you're supposed to say what you *like*, not what you ought to do. That's just the trouble with me. I like doing almost anything as long as it's not boring. I would like to be a high school band director like Mr. Sharpe, or a stock car driver (they're having more and more powder puff races these days, you know—it's not impossible), or a cab driver even, or maybe a lawyer (I really like arguing as you very well know), or a preacher (if I really believe in something I can sure stand up and exhort). Maybe I should be an encyclopedia salesman. I *really* believe in books—in reference books, especially."

Jeri Johnson's attention was drifting so Tretona buttonholed her. "Tell me, Jeri. You're really hooked on journalism, have been all the four years I've known you. And now you're keener than ever—you don't even seem to care how fancy a job you get, just as long as you're working on a newspaper. Tell me, how did you make the decision to be a journalist?"

Jeri was baffled. "I didn't decide," she said. "I've always known, ever since I was a little girl and started reading newspapers. I didn't have to decide. Don't worry, Tretona," she continued, "when you finally find the right vocation, you'll know it. I know it sounds corny, but it's true. *Vocation* means calling— what you're supposed to do."

Tretona sighed and went out to finish cooking supper. All these things that people said you'd know when they happened to you: you'll know when you're saved; you'll know when you're sanctified; you'll know when you're in love; when you've had an orgasm, you'll know it; you'll know it when you've found your profession. Things seemed a hell of a lot more complicated than that to her. She pulled the one-egg cake out of the oven and stuck a toothpick in it—then hesitated. Damn it, her mother would know whether it was done or not. Why couldn't she decide? Tretona yelled at Jeri to come take care of the fucking one-egg cake. After all, she shouldn't have to bake her own fucking birthday cake, should she? Then Tretona carried out the garbage and was bundling up old newspapers in the living room when the doorbell rang—flowers from Robert. A tasteful funny note—

something about how he'd felt like cutting off an ear in despair a la Van Gogh, but didn't want to render half of his earring collection redundant. For just a sec, Tretona felt like really cutting off something—a finger maybe—simply for the satisfaction of shaking him up. "What is the proper British response to being presented with a dripping digit?" she wondered. She could practically hear him now: "Oh bother!" (He would stretch out the word with lots of stress on the last syllable.) "What a bloody nuisance." She was glad to be eating her birthday cake here with Jeri and returned to the kitchen in a cheery mood.

* * *

Dr. Devore was neither menacing nor confidence-inspiring. Medium build, tweed jacket, thick glasses, blinked a little (weak eyes or nerves?), and seemed to have just a tiny tendency to stammer (some of his initial consonants were either too slow in coming out or very prolonged). Tretona sat in the chair by his desk and resisted the temptation to move it out at an angle. ("Did that mean she was repressed," she asked herself, "or was it a sign that she had good healthy ego control over her impulses?")

After reading aloud her name, class standing, and major, Dr. Devore leafed through the test results and asked how many hours a week she studied. Tretona stalled while she tried to count up. "Not enough," she said. Dr. Devore nodded sympathetically. "Overachievers always feel anxious about not working enough, when actually they are. . . ."

"Overachievers?" blurted Tretona. "What on earth do you mean?"

He answered patiently. "It's a bit of a misnomer, actually. When a person of average intelligence performs at a higher level. . . ."

"I know what the word means," said Tretona. "What do you mean by insinuating I'm an overachiever? Hell, I'm not half living up to my potential, that's part of my problem."

And again he patiently answered that her score on the quantitative reasoning exam was well within the middle range, but hardly what one typically found among science graduate students.

Tretona was beside herself. "Those problems were something out of *Reader's Digest*. I'd be surprised if I didn't get every single one right."

Dr. Devore's voice firmed. "Now sometimes our hopes and dreams do not match well with our capabilities. In such cases a little reality check, though painful. . . ."

Tretona was thinking aloud: "Check, check. That's it. How do you score those things, anyway? Someone probably made a mistake."

Dr. Devore was plainly exasperated but finally went out and got a template and sure enough the score was wrong, but it was Tretona's fault really, because she had started out on the wrong column (having skipped the sample problems), and so all of her answers were displaced one column to the left of where they should have been.

"So how'd I do?" Tretona asked triumphantly.

Dr. Devore glanced over all the little black pencil marks peeking up through the holes in the stencil. "Quite well, I would say. Yes, very well indeed. Of course, one must wonder about unconscious motivations when a girl as bright as you doesn't follow the instructions properly." Tretona bristled a little; but after all he had been decent enough to recheck the test, so maybe she should bear with him.

He tried a different tack. "I want you to fantasize a little for me. Imagine it's five years from now. If you could be doing anything in the world that you wanted, what would it be?"

Tretona shook her head sadly. "I don't know," she said. "I really draw a blank, I just don't know."

"What do you like most about chemistry?"

"When the lab preps work right, I suppose."

"Are you a good teaching assistant?"

"Oh yes," said Tretona. "My section always does well on the exams. I'm good at explaining things and I think the kids. . . ."

Dr. Devore cut in; "And what's the weakest aspect of your teaching?"

For a moment, Tretona couldn't think of anything and then she knew what it was but she didn't want to say. "Well, it's sort of personal."

Dr. Devore didn't say anything. "It doesn't really have anything to do with my teaching per se. Well, it sort of does, in that it might interfere, but I guess it's not really a deficiency in my teaching—it's sort of—well, it's personal, really." Dr. Devore just sat there.

Tretona took the high road. "It's just that sometimes I feel a

special concern—well, I suppose you could call it affection even—
for a student that surpasses the normal sort of professional
academic concern teachers are supposed to have."

Dr. Devore was blunt. "It's not unusual for a teacher to
develop a crush on a student—or even to fall in love. Tell me
about the student you have special feelings for."

So Tretona told him about Lorrie, not mentioning her name,
of course, and at first avoiding pronouns, but finally Tretona got
her syntax balled up and said something about writing on "her"
homework paper. She stopped then and looked up at Dr. Devore.
He moved his chair back an inch and spoke very carefully. "Have
you ever had crushes on females before?" Tretona nodded.
"Often?" Again a nod. "Now, in early adolescence same-gender
crushes may play a role in the development of a normal sexual
identity. But when they persist into late adolescence or adult-
hood, one must entertain thoughts of l-l-latent l-l-lesbian tendencies."

Maybe it was the stammer that gave Tretona courage. "It
isn't latent," she said. Dr. Devore sat perfectly still for a moment
and then leaned forward.

"Ah," he said, "now we're getting somewhere." He went on
to explain how one could not make satisfactory career decisions
without a strong, well-developed ego. But one's ego could hardly
be intact if one's sexual identity were immature or unhealthy. So
it was hardly any wonder that Tretona couldn't decide whether
she wanted to be a chemist, given her uncertainty about whether
or not she was a real woman. "But don't worry," said Dr.
Devore, "You are a real woman—if I were a psychiatrist and had
an M.D., I could prove it to you." Tretona looked up frightened.
"I mean by examining you here in the office, by taking a mirror
and demonstrating to you each facet of your female genitalia.
Reality check, you know. That's my job—to hold up a mirror so
that you can see yourself as you really are."

Then his voice softened—Tretona relaxed a little just as she
always did when the preacher stopped exhorting and finally
started the altar call. Now Dr. Devore was talking about arrested
sexual developoment not being too serious if you caught it in time
and worked on it. "I gather you do have male friends?" said Dr.
Devore. Tretona nodded. "Boy friends, maybe even lovers?"
Seeing her assent, Dr. Devore brightened noticeably. "Excellent,
excellent. The prognosis is excellent. It'll take some hard work,

mind you, but do not despair, my friend. You had the good sense to seek help in time."

Then mercifully the hour was over. Tretona stumbled out and forced herself to face the receptionist and make another appointment. She automatically headed for the Union but veered off down Wright Street when she realized she might see someone she knew there. Even Wright Street seemed too public, so she turned down a side street. It wasn't latent, that was the trouble. It was quiescent sometimes. Like now it had been eight or nine months since the Lorrie episode. But it was there. Any minute she might meet a woman, take a fancy to her, and then bingo! the flirting, the chase, the intensity, the vulnerability. . . . So far she'd always thought it was worth it, even when she was left finally, it still seemed worth it. But if Dr. Devore was right—if it was messing up her career—then that would be quite a different kettle of fish altogether. Tretona started to shake, so she huddled in a doorway trying to think where to go, what to do. For a minute, she stared unseeingly into the laundromat and then focused on her image reflected in the window. Suddenly it hit her—it wasn't hidden or latent in that sense, either. There she was in standard Getroek garb—the windbreaker (men's small), plaid shirt (her Dad's), jeans (women's large), dark socks (men's medium), tennis shoes (boys' large). Her hair was medium length (she hadn't got it cut since the Robert business started), but it was slicked back behind her ears. The real giveaway was the posture—shoulders hunched, hands in pockets, butt tucked in, feet slightly toed in like an Indian, worried forehead, and pleading eyes. (Jesus, you look like Jimmy Dean.) God, it was so obvious. Everyone must know. Sylvia had known (she said she'd guessed right from the start), and Dr. Devore hadn't been the least bit surprised—he'd probably known all along. That explained everything—why the boys in high school didn't like her, why most of the girls were distant. That's why she never had any friends. Even then they must have all known, or sensed at least, that she was. . . . Tretona hesitated and then her thought shouted out defiantly to the window: "Say it, go on ahead and say it. Queer, queer, you're a queer." Her mind rattled on like a teletype: You always have been. That's what your mom was picking up on when she used to call you a tomboy. That's why you always wore blue jeans. You weren't just trying to be comfortable, or casual, or informal, or Bohemian, or whatever you tried to call it. You were putting on your uniform, you were putting on your true skin, you were revealing your spots—and everyone else knew it all along, but you. God, how they must have laughed at you. How pathetic. And you used to talk about being authentic. "Jesus, what a phony I am," Tretona said aloud and dragged herself back to the duplex. There was no place else to go.

It was a mercy that Jeri Johnson was working late at the *Daily Stupid*. Tretona made some instant rice, put butter and oregano on it, and ate it with two cold hot dogs and a Polish dill. She stole some of Jeri's private gin, carefully topping off the bottle with water (Jeri kept track of things like her gin supply, and how much gum was in her desk drawer), and mixed it with some Welch's grape juice. It tasted almost as bad as lab alcohol. Then she went up to check her closet. She had a bunch of nice wool skirts her mom had bought her last year when she started teaching, but she hadn't worn them much—the dress code for TA's had relaxed practically overnight when Dr. Kaplan, a new hot shot from Cal Tech, came to town and started lecturing in a turtleneck sweater. Tretona held up the skirts—they were the wrong length now, and she didn't have any shoes to go with them. She did have one nice pair of slacks, with a zipper on the side. She put them on and found a sweater to match, even though it was still early in the fall for so much wool. Might as well start now.

It was hard, though. When she sat on the couch to look at the *Time* magazine, she automatically cocked one ankle up on her knee. How else were you supposed to support the fucking magazine? "Don't be stupid," she told herself. "Fifty-one percent of the population manages to read a magazine without propping a shin under it. Surely you can manage." Annoyed at herself, she took one of Jeri Johnson's disgusting menthol cigarettes. "She'll have my ass for swiping all her stuff. I'll have to apologize or make it up to her somehow," thought Tretona—and then realized she had lit the cigarette like a farmer, by shielding the match inside the circle of her hand.

Her face broke and her eyes filled up and then Tretona was pacing back and forth defiantly, deliberately holding her cigarette between thumb and forefinger cowboy fashion and searching frantically for someplace to put her left hand. "Goddamned women's slacks, they never put pockets in them." Dr. Devore said she was a woman and that was true, but she wasn't a lady— never had been and never would be. She wasn't delicate, she wasn't demure, she wasn't incompetent, she wasn't helpless, she wasn't a mechanical moron, she didn't want to get married and have kids. . . . God, maybe she really wasn't a woman, after all. Suddenly an old memory took on a new meaning—Tretona-7 or 8 maybe, out on the north side of the house (that secret, deserted side), all contorted on the lawn trying like hell to kiss her elbow. Her Uncle Floyd had told her that if she kissed her elbow, she'd turn into a boy. Tretona hadn't really believed him, but it would be exciting to try. There she is, first the right elbow, then the left, rotating her left arm with her right hand and then shoving her head down with her right knee, but all in vain. That wasn't the only time she'd tried, either. Hot guilty memories of twisting her arm in bed and then lying on it to stretch the muscles and tendons. It hurt, hot flashes of pain running like lightning up her left shoulder, and then to console herself, the pulsing throbbing thumb—the right one this time, enjoying the unfamiliarity of it, enjoying—yes, enjoying now—the pain jolts as she bounced, enjoying the helplessness she felt in her poor, contorted, bound-up left side and the power and domination in the right half of her body. Even the memory was pretty intense and Tretona could just imagine what Dr. Devore would make of all that. She tried to recall what it had meant to her then, back when she was a naive, innocent child. Well, supposedly that's what children were—naive, at least, if not innocent.

What *did* it mean? Her concentration cleared the masking cobwebs, repressive rubber bands or whatever from her brain and the thought that had been gnawing like a tapeworm finally surfaced. Christine Jorgenson—*transsexual*—that was the word. Maybe she wanted to be a transsexual. No wonder seeing that creature on the Jack Paar show had made her fidgety.

Tretona finished off the watery gin and grape juice and started chewing on the ice: "Now, go slow. Let's have a reality check." (You had to give Dr. Devore credit for that one—a good concept, a good phrase, the basis of science, really.) Whatever it was that she wanted, now or back then when she was trying to kiss her elbow, it wasn't a penis. It really wasn't. Certainly not literally. They weren't very esthetic objects and they just stuck out and got in the way, as far as she could tell. And she didn't like the way penises bossed men around, making them do pushy, inconsiderate things. She didn't like what they symbolized, either—big crude power stuff, big fast dramatic efforts and then total collapse. In a way men were like penises—big, aggressive showoffs, but no patience or staying power when it came down to taking care of squawling babies or picking splinters out of kids' fingers or washing dishes three times every goddamn day. When it came to stuff like that, men were hopeless.

She wouldn't want to have a beard, either—though wait—reality check—there was that time when she was reading *The Rubyiat of Omar Khayam* (she must have been very young—she remembered pulling it out of the bookcase because it had a pebbled leather cover and gold-edged leaves). Anyway, the book had little pastel sketches illustrating the verses. On the overleaf from "A loaf of bread, a jug of wine, and thou. . . ." there was a picture of a sensitive-looking man with a very red beard. She remembered liking it and asking her mother if she could grow a red beard someday. And when her mother laughed, and said, "No," she'd been resentful and said "Why not? It isn't fair!"

Tretona had to admit that she wouldn't half mind a nice long silky beard—but one like the Arabic poet's, not the tough whiskers which real-life men actually had. And then Tretona started to make a composite picture of the Ideal Person. It was a grown-up mental equivalent of the Draw-a-Monster game kids play, where one person draws the head, folds it over so no one can see, and passes it on. Let's see—the hair should be red, of course, not stubborn and straight like hers, but thick and wavy—well, like Robert's. (Tretona had sometimes speculated about what her and Robert's kids would look like. Not that she actually wanted to have any. It was more of a chemist's query: If you mix A with B, what's gonna result? She bet a lot of the reason people had kids was a frustrated combinatorial curiosity. They should take up water colors or kaleidoscopes instead, she thought.)

Anyway, Khanna hair—henna color, strong eye brows, no beard (unless like Omar's), and the shoulders? Well, she liked broad shoulders, so men's shoulders (except Roni's were real nice too), women's breasts for sure, a muscular flat stomach (men had the advantage there), nice round hips (she didn't like men's little pinched skinny butts), strong legs (but not hairy like most men's were—Robert's were smooth, though), good solid feet with well-individuated toes (she hated the way women gave themselves bunions and warped their feet by wearing fashionable shoes).

Just then Jeri burst in the door, made a point of picking up the ashtray with the tell-tale swiped butt in it, started to complain, then switched gears in mid-syllable: "Why the hell are you dressed up? You look *nice*."

Tretona switched gears, too—from self-analysis to ordinary college student dorm banter: "Thought I'd give you a thrill, old thing. I am twenty-two now—can't dress like a teeny bopper all my life."

"God, you look good in slacks. Wish I did. They make me look like a little dumpy sausage. The original pig-in-the-blanket."

Tretona made contradictory noises, although inside she had to admit it was true. The implications of the internal, tacit admission hit her. "But what does it matter what you look like?" she said. "Why are women always so neurotic about looking fashionable?"

"I'm not trying to look elegant or fashionable," Jeri said. "I just want to make the best I can out of what little I got."

"Jesus," said Tretona, "What *little* you've got? Is this my old talented, confident, assertive friend Jeri Johnson, girl reporter, talking?"

"I mean what little I've got as far as looks are concerned— sex appeal, all that. Look honey, I'm no prom queen, so I have to do the best I can."

Tretona was sputtering with frustration, but she couldn't quite pinpoint its source. "But your priorities, everyone's priorities, are so damned fucked up. How is it relevant to your qualifications as a journalist—or as a person for that matter— whether you look like a sausage when you wear blue jeans?"

Jeri peered down over the rims of her glasses with a wiser- than-thou look. "My dear Tretona, come back from outer space or your idealistic ivory tower or wherever you've drifted off to. You know that old formula for success? Well, they left out one crucial ingredient. It's 10 percent inspiration and 90 percent perspiration—*and* 99 percent sex appeal or charisma or magne- tism. Anyway, that's the real recipe—I leave you to readjust the percentages so they add up right." And Jeri went up to bed.

As Tretona sat on the couch inspecting the holes in her tennis shoes, for some reason she thought of the anecdote about Niels Bohr her quantum mechanics teacher had told at the departmen- tal open house. It seems the great physicist had a horseshoe over the door to his office and one day a young post-doc student said, "Pardon me, Professor Bohr, but you don't believe in horseshoes, do you?" To which Bohr had replied, "I understand they're supposed to bring you good luck even if you don't believe in them!" Tretona sighed and straightened the crease in her slacks. Well, it wouldn't hurt to give it a try even if she didn't believe in it.

And try she did. All week she dressed up in sweaters and slacks, worked on her posture, and even put up her hair—not in curlers, but she did put in finger waves while it was wet and tied a bandanna around the bottom so the ends wouldn't stick out like jackstraws. Everyone remarked on how nice she looked—it was embarrassing. Everyone except Emil, that is. He was oblivious to such trivial matters. He did keep an eye out for the well-being of her psyche, however, and questioned Tretona carefully when she announced she was going to a series of evening instruction classes by Father O'Roarke. "Sheer curiosity," said Tretona. "I've been brought up all my life on anti-Papist propaganda. I just want to see what the Church, Big-C Church, that is, is really all about and Father O'Roarke seems like a decent guy. You said yourself that he's an existentialist."

"A Christian existentialist," qualified Emil, "which is almost as absurd as a square circle and other Meinongian impossible objects."

Tretona didn't follow up the hint and ask who Meinong was. Emil had obviously been reading philosophy again and wanted to tell her about it, but she wasn't in the mood. "And the Foreign Service exam is next month," she said. "Who knows, maybe they'll make me Ambassador to the Vatican!" As usual, Emil took the joke to its extreme. "Pax vobiscum, Ambassadress Getroek. You may kiss my ring." He disappeared under the table for a second and then deftly extended a bare foot with a soda straw wrapped around the big toe.

Tretona was embarrassed and delighted. "Emil, don't!" she screamed. A glass of water got knocked over and then they fled before Nick could come over to make them settle down.

Tretona was pretty nervous before her next appointment with Dr. Devore, but it started out okay. He asked how she felt toward her parents and he nodded at almost everything she said. Tretona thought it must all sound frightfully familiar. Then he steered the interview onto the subject of masturbation and somehow elicited the information that she often masturbated while reading about torture. He kept pushing for examples and finally Tretona remembered a story in *The Saturday Evening Post* about putting a bucket over a guy's head and pounding on it with sticks. "And who were you?" Dr. Devore asked suddenly, "the victim under the bucket or the sadistic torturer?"

"Neither one, really," said Tretona.

"I know you weren't *really*," said Dr. Devore impatiently, "But whom did you identify with? Don't block now."

"I wish you wouldn't tell me not to block," said Tretona. "Honestly, I didn't identify with either one—well, not consciously." Dr. Devore waited, and so she continued, "It wasn't only torture stories—it was anything with lots of pain in it—like once I read a story about a missionary in China who walked out of the jungle on a broken leg."

"So there you have an answer," said Dr. Devore triumphantly. "Masochism. It's as clear as can be."

"But I didn't get pleasure from reading about the pain," said Tretona, "It's just that the possibility of intense, unavoidable pain frightens me—and it frightens me even more when I realize that there are people in this world who deliberately torture other human beings—or animals, for that matter. And when I'm frightened I try to distract myself, to console myself—and well, then I masturbate. I'm generally pretty horny anyway—especially if I'm already lying on the bed reading. But isn't that normal? At least for unmarried people my age?"

Dr. Devore ignored the question. "Masochism is an essential ingredient in the neurotic personality pattern of the homosexual," he explained. "So when you said you were homosexual, I immediately deduced you were masochistic. The only questions remaining, and these are big questions, of course, concern the form your masochism takes and how it arose in your childhood."

Tretona was furious. "So all the time you were looking for something to put a masochistic label on? You hardly know me and already you're convinced I'm a masochist. Boy, talk about being objective—talk about reality checks. You sure could use a little. . . ." She stopped, her anger dissipated. She was unsure of whether she'd gone too far and been impolite.

Dr. Devore was conciliatory. "Do you think I've treated you unfairly? Do you think I was unjust right now?"

Tretona was a bit sullen, "Well, a little," she said. "I think you went a little too far in your inferences."

"You tried to provoke me just now, didn't you? Come on, admit it."

"Well, maybe," said Tretona, "But mainly I thought you were jumping to conclusions and since the conclusions weren't very flattering to me—well, I defended myself, that's all. I'm sorry I got angry."

Dr. Devore ignored the apology and continued. "Note the pattern: You provoke someone, they respond negatively, and then you feel abused. It's very typical of the homosexual personality—it's called 'injustice collecting.'"

Tretona wanted to shriek, "You're the one that's doing the provoking," but she controlled herself and said with sarcastic sweetness, "And I detect a pattern, too. It's called *a priori* reasoning. What in the hell makes you think that I make a habit of injustice collecting—anymore than anyone else does?"

Dr. Devore seemed to be enjoying himself and now he pounced: "You're a scientist. Suppose you already knew that the solution in this container was acid. (He tapped the decanter on his desk.) "Would you not then be entitled to infer that this liquid would taste sour and that it would do whatever else acids do?"

"Fizz if you add sodium bicarbonate," said Tretona helpfully.

"Well, fizz—yes, I dare say, whatever else acids do," continued Dr. Devore. "You could infer those properties; you would know they were there even before doing an experiment, wouldn't you?"

"Yes," Tretona said, "but. . . ."

"So that is hardly *a priori* reasoning. That is scientific reasoning *par excellence.*"

"But chemists can do that because they have a good theory about acids and the theory's been checked a million times so it's okay to trust it. But psychology is not a science—I beg your pardon—I mean, it's a young science. . . ." She stopped, flustered.

"You're trying to provoke me again," said Dr. Devore, "but I will not react. One of the things we will do in here is to try to break old patterns by depriving you of the neurotic satisfactions which you have come to expect."

Now it was Tretona who stuck to her guns. "But even if you people had a good theory of homosexuality, not that I think you do . . ."

"Of course we do," snapped Dr. Devore. "Edmund

Bergler's new book lays it all out. The main dynamics are psychic masochism coupled with narcissism. . . ."

"Okay, okay," said Tretona, "even if you have a good theory of homosexuality, the analogy with the acid solution doesn't hold up because you don't know whether I'm a homosexual or not." She pressed on despite his protests. "No. You don't know. How could you, because I don't know. I sleep with men, too. I might be bisexual or pan-sexual or I might even decide to be asexual or . . . who knows? I want you to help me find out, so please don't just keep jumping to conclusions."

"I see that we must go a little more slowly," said Dr. Devore. "Why don't we talk next time about your affairs with men? But in the meantime you may take it on my authority—there is no such thing as bisexuality. You're just fooling yourself if you think there is. But you don't need to take my word for it. I'll prove it to you next time."

And then the hour was over. Tretona staggered out, fuming, flustered, and exhausted. If only there was someone to talk to, someone to help her blow off steam and get her head straight. She wondered what Belinda would think of all this—probably she'd want Tretona to get saved even if it was by Dr. Freud instead of Jesus. Or Tiia? Tiia would probably tell her not to hurt her family. And Sylvia? Sylvia would say to tell Dr. Devore to kiss off, that's for sure. But then what was she supposed to do about choosing a career and making big decisions and finding out who she really was?

And to give old Dr. Devore his due (Tretona slipped and thought "Devil Devore" and then giggled to herself), anyway, he did have some good insights like that time when she was telling him about stealing nickels and dimes off the top of the chest of drawers in her parent's bedroom and he had explained how people often substituted money for love, both in the giving and taking. That was a good point. And what he'd said about having to love or respect yourself before you could love or respect other people. That seemed right.

But he sure wasn't doing much to help her respect herself. What was the phrase he'd used? "Injustice collecting" and . . . psychic masochism—yeah, that was it. Hell, what he was doing was psychic bludgeoning—psychic rape of her being—that's what it really was.

Tretona got so angry thinking about it that she deliberately tried to cool herself off by taking the other side. It scared her to be so angry—and besides, there always are two sides to every question if you look hard enough. Like the business about masturbation and torture. Had she really been candid with Dr. Devore? Wasn't it true that she got some sort of perverse pleasure out of reading about the Nazis and stuff? And that little analysis he gave about how a child could cope with a punishing mother by learning to enjoy the punishment—at least on one level. Wasn't it true that she used to feel smug and superior when her mother whipped her too hard or when she didn't deserve it?

Tretona felt like she was being sucked into a maelstrom. She shook her head around hoping to jar loose some missing piece, some key to the confusion. "Slow down—time for a reality check." The sound of her own voice cleared the air and she looked around. She had walked down to South Campus. Might as well go on down to the Aggie barns now that she'd come this far. "The smell of cow manure will clear my head for sure," Tretona said to herself.

Okay. What was given in the problem? What could be taken for granted?

Point 1: She got sexed up by torture stories, that was a fact. Point 2: She didn't go out of her way to read torture stories—she didn't check them out of the library—but she did go out of her way to get hold of ordinary pornography, like the Henry Miller books. Point 3: She certainly didn't avoid reading torture stories—and she would certainly deliberately go off alone whenever she started reading one because she knew what effect it would have on her. That had to be admitted. Point 4: Now we come to the issue in question. Did the above three facts imply that she was a masochist or neurotic or weird? She didn't think so. She bet that was one reason why torture stories were so popular. But Dr. Devore had said it was neurotic. So who was right? What evidence did she have on her side? None whatsoever and she could hardly imagine asking Jeri Johnson or her fellow students in Non-Aqueous Solvents class (the smell of urea from the pastures reminded her of the lab where they worked with hydrazine and liquid ammonia). She tried out imaginary questions for a sexual Gallup poll: Tell me, my friend, what do you read when you masturbate? Do you think Himmler was sexy? Which is a bigger turn on, cigarette burns on the feet or ice picks under the nails?

Tretona shuddered and realized how disgusting it all sounded. Maybe she *was* perverted, after all. Anyway, Dr. Devore was the authority. He and other psychologists were the ones who talked to people about stuff like this—dozens of people every day, day after day. If he said she was neurotic and a masochist, he surely knew what he was talking about. She was a fool to have argued with him.

Tretona turned in the gate leading to the experimental cow barns. How clean and neat they all were. Suddenly, she started to cry. This model farm, with its concrete floors and shampooed cows and white-washed walls, was so far removed from her daddy's cruddy old farm that it somehow made her feel terribly sad—and inadequate.

She didn't have any evidence at all really that she wasn't a masochist—she'd just been going on her own instincts, as Raskolnikov had done, and look where he ended up. She'd better stop fighting Dr. Devore and get down to cleaning out all those stables she'd grown up with. Still, you had to admit, her daddy's ole cobwebby barn had been a lot homier than these sanitary metal-and-concrete stalls. Tretona sighed and turned around to go back toward campus. She had lots of homework to do.

Tretona went into a decline—everyone noticed it. She stopped wearing slacks and started slouching around in a black imitation leather jacket with rusty zippers, which she had picked up at a second-hand store. She got a bad haircut and her pimples came back.

She started causing trouble in Father O'Roarke's class—saying that if Catholics really didn't worship the Virgin Mary as he claimed, why was it that the statues of the Virgin advertised in the Catholic magazines were taller than those of Jesus? Shouldn't they be about the same height? Then she and Hector (a ne'er-do-well high school drop-out she had started running around with) stole a case of the Communion wine. Tretona held it on her lap on the back of his Lambretta and they went out to the graveyard to drink it, but it was sickeningly sweet.

Both Emil and Jeri Johnson heard about the wine episode and each in their own way made disapproving noises. What they didn't know, but Hector did, was that Tretona had taken up shoplifting. It was almost as if she were applying Dr. Devore's formula whereby you stole material things when no love was to be had.

When Tretona complained to Dr. Devore about her deterioration, he was quite short about it. "Well, you're obviously acting out your true emotional development, which is that of a ten-year-old boy, I would say. Sometimes an open expression of one's present condition is a necessary step toward improvement and eventual cure."

Somehow, Tretona's studies weren't affected. In fact, chemistry, which had started the whole crisis, was the only part of her life which was even halfway stable or satisfactory. Not that there was any joy to be had there, and she dreaded having to choose a thesis topic.

One day Emil formally made an appointment to meet her for coffee. When Tretona arrived at Nick's he was uncharacteristically solemn. At first, Tretona thought he was laying an elaborate foundation for a joke. "Tretona," he said, "I want to discuss the vampire who has come into your life—I mean Dr. Devore, of course."

"Do I look so pale and anemic?" she asked.

"Yes, as a matter of fact you do. Spiritually anemic. I don't know for sure what's causing it—and please believe me, I don't mean to pry, but something or someone is sapping your confidence and—forgive me—I just can't stand by and let your. . . ." She had never seen Emil so moved and inarticulate. "I'm pretty sure Father O'Roarke wouldn't and couldn't do this to you, so I think it's Dr. Devore."

For a split second Tretona left Nick's—she was in a cold gray sea with ice floes, but she was too numb to feel the cold and Emil was standing on the receding shore. "God, I've been seeing too many Bergman movies," she thought.

"Well?" said Emil.

"Uh—no. Dr. Devore is okay. I'll admit sometimes I feel bad when he sticks those funny labels on me." Last week he'd intimated she was frigid because she had admitted that she generally wasn't satisfied when she and Robert made out, no matter how long Robert kept an erection. (He prided himself on being able to hold back.) She had also confessed that sometimes after ejaculation she liked to leave the rubber full of sperm inside of her and sort of wiggle and chew on it with her vagina. (Robert didn't care—he said the Japanese had special gadgets for that very purpose.) Dr. Devore said any sort of vaginal response was to be encouraged—at least at this stage. He had said not to worry—

lesbianism and frigidity went together and although it was difficult theoretically to sort out all the causal interactions, as a matter of clinical experience they also disappeared together.

"Labels?" said Emil. "Oh, you know," said Tretona vaguely, "'neurotic,' 'emotionally immature'—stuff like that." But she couldn't keep her eyes from getting a little wet.

"Tretona," said Emil. "I don't know what kind of filing system that guy's got or where he's trying to fit you in, but promise me one thing." Tretona nodded forlornly. Emil grabbed her arm. "I mean it. Listen to me. You've got a brain. Use it. Get some books and check out all those labels. Don't swallow what that guy says like pablum."

"Okay, I'll watch it," Tretona said. "But right now I've got to get out of here." She wasn't going to break down and cry in Nick's.

She needn't have worried. By the time she got to the street corner she felt taller and firmer than she had in weeks. Hell, she'd fought her way out from under all the religious crap everyone dumped on her when she was a kid, hadn't she? She could tackle this.

Tretona got to Follet's just before they closed and bought a bound notebook with numbered pages like the ones required for lab. She decided to splurge and eat down in campus town. While waiting for the spaghetti dinner to arrive, she carefully wrote her name and address on the inside cover. Then she dated page number 1 and inscribed two mottos in capital letters: BE CRITICAL and BE FAIR. After cleaning up every bit of the sauce with the garlic bread, she headed straight for the library.

It was large and Tretona wondered if she'd be able to find what she wanted. Generally before she had just used the chem library or the reserve room. Tretona remembered the name Dr. Devore had mentioned as Burger, or maybe Burglar, but she couldn't find anything. Maybe the book was too new to be cataloged yet, or maybe it was locked up in some special collection. She was too embarrassed to ask the librarian for help. Then she remembered the subject index and just in case someone was looking she pulled out three drawers from the *H* section. For a while, she stared intently at the entries under "Homologous Series." God, why was her heart beating so fast? It reminded her of looking up "poop deck" in the big dictionary at the back of Miss Fillmore's classroom. It was perfectly safe unless you turned red or giggled—

then Miss Fillmore would be back in a flash and Lord help you if you tried to shut the book too fast.

"Hell, this isn't the third grade," Tretona thought and firmly moved on. There it was—Bergler (no wonder she couldn't find it—German, maybe Jewish? No, not with *Edmond*. Definitely Kraut, though—she should have guessed). The title was to the point. *Homosexuality: Disease or Way of Life?* She giggled at the call number—it started with HQ. For an instant, she almost expected to see Miss Fillmore bearing down on her, but then recovered her nerve and headed for the stacks.

There it was, orange-red cover, gold letters. Her hand trembled a little as she carefully wrote down the complete bibliographic reference on page number 2 of her notebook. Tretona was going to take notes on the preface but it was so emotional she decided it didn't have any scientific merit. Bergler was upset because newspapers and magazines were covering up the big danger to American youth. Homosexuals had always preyed on impressionable young people, but today there was a new danger, *statistical recruitment*. Some intellectuals were using Kinsey's biased data to argue that homosexuality was widespread and hence acceptable. Well, this book was going to prove that it was a disease—that was the truth, no matter how harsh it must seem to some. It could be cured, however—that was the optimistic side of his message.

Having heard Dr. Devore, Tretona found much of the first chapter familiar. There was a specific homosexual personality pattern—unconscious wish to suffer, injustice collecting, in short, psychic masochism. Bergler gave a checklist of the precise elements of the homosexual personality and Tretona copied them down, trying to decide which ones she had: injustice collector, afraid of women (she assumed it would be men in her case) . . . megalomania, inner depression, inner guilt . . . unreliability. And then, in boldface type: **There are no healthy homosexuals.** Tretona sighed and wrote it in her notebook, using underlining to denote the bold letters. She decided to skip the part about the psychogenesis of the disease, at least for the time being, and look at the author's data instead. But there wasn't any! There weren't any questionnaires or protocols. Nothing. The only numbers in the whole book were those he quoted in the preface from Kinsey in order to criticize them. So Tretona went back and carefully noted down Bergler's objection to Kinsey—he'd used a non-representative sample, with too many college graduates and anyway, volunteers couldn't be trusted to talk about their sex lives. Tretona was tempted to write down a comment to the effect that at least Kinsey *had* a sample, but she decided that wouldn't be scholarly.

Bergler did have a few case studies, though. Maybe he reported his findings in that form to make his book more interesting to the general reader. She read about Miss R, the business executive whom Bergler cured (she ended up getting married), and Miss T, who had rich parents, and never got cured. Tretona assumed the point was to isolate those factors that made a cure possible, but the only significant difference Bergler mentioned was the fact that Miss T didn't really want to be cured because she was pretty happy as she was. Bergler hastened to point out that Miss T wasn't really happy because she was neurotic, she just thought she was. Tretona figured there ought to be some other characteristic differences if it was a disease— maybe differences in childhood experiences, something, but she couldn't find any in the case reports.

As she read on, Tretona started getting really upset at how Bergler badgered his patients. At first, she thought it was just part of the therapeutic technique, but it was more than that. He seemed to hate them. Even Miss R, who was going along with his treatment and eventually was cured, was described at one point as (Tretona wrote it down) "a cruel, frequently mean, power-mad, domineering woman. . . ."

Tretona was disappointed. Hadn't Dr. Devore said this was an important new book in the field? Of course, she hadn't read it all, but it was getting late. She decided to skim the chapter on lesbianism. Whereas Bergler thought the numbers on the reports of male homosexuals were exaggerated, he reckoned that lesbianism was more widespread than normally supposed. Probably a good deal of frigidity was due to lesbian tendencies. Then there was another one of his pithy aphorisms: "Lesbianism is not 'woman's love for woman,' but the pseudo love of a masochist woman. The irony is unsurpassed."

Tretona hit the table with her fist—she couldn't help it. "He may be a psychiatrist but since when does that give him the right to judge what love is?" People down at another table were looking, so Tretona pretended she had dropped something, bent down to pick it up, and then went to get a drink. Her brain was still reeling a mile a minute. "What if they"—she took a breath and corrected herself—"we—what if we *are* neurotic—that's not psychotic, and who says neurotics can't love people? There's no love in Bergler, that's for sure. All that talk about *destroying* homosexuality. He talks like it's a cancer. You don't destroy a neurotic personality, you may modify it or heal it—you don't destroy it. His whole choice of words gives him away."

And she wrote in her notebook (but on the left-hand page so as not to confuse it with her notes): "Bergler is an arrogant s.o.b. and he hates homosexuals." After cooling down a bit she decided that the remark was a little too strong for a research notebook, so, smiling to herself, she doctored up her blast by adding at the beginning "Query: Is it the case that [Bergler is . . . etc.]" and tacking on a question mark at the end with some relevant page numbers.

Well, that was enough for one night. As she reshelved the book, Tretona glanced at the surrounding volumes. One, a thick book with a pale gray cover, was well worn. She took it down: Donald Webster Cory, *The Homosexual in America: A Subjective Approach.* She reckoned it couldn't be any more subjective than Bergler's little poison pen monograph—and at least Cory admitted it. Curious, she glanced inside. The dedication was to Howard, *"A filosofia e necessario amore."*

"Ho, ho," thought Tretona, "another country heard from." This one she would check out. After all, Jeri Johnson was used to her coming home with borrowed Henry Millers bound in untitled plain black covers. Since Cory's book was in the library, it could hardly be more shocking than contraband novels.

But Jeri Johnson wasn't home yet, so Tretona sat down on the couch to inspect her find. Yep, Cory was a homosexual— "invert" was the word he applied to himself—and he seemed to be happy, but he was married to a woman! Tretona couldn't figure that one out—she'd have to read the whole thing. But she couldn't help sneaking a peek at the last chapter called "Looking Outward and Forward." It would be nice to end up her evening of existential research on a cheery note.

Cory was anything but optimistic. "Do not feel guilty if you decide to wear a mask," he wrote, "because it's society's fault for not accepting your inversion." She really didn't like that word—it sounded as if homosexuals had everything backwards or upside down. Cory also warned that few straight people could be trusted;

you shouldn't be surprised if even your best friends act weird and drift away if you should tell them. Nonsense, thought Tretona, not if they were real friends. Cory sure was bitter—or sad, that was more accurate. Then she happened to look at the appendix.

There Cory had recorded verbatim the laws against homosexuality in each state. She hadn't even thought about the legal side of this whole business. She quickly scanned the list: "not less than two nor more than twenty. . . .", "hard labor not exceeding twenty-one years. . . ."

Jeez! Did this apply to women too? Maybe it was only for sodomy. But a lot of the laws were against "the infamous crime against nature." What the hell was that? It sounded almost as ineffable as the sin against the Holy Ghost. Wait, here it definitely listed cunnilingus and inciting someone to self-pollution. Oklahoma explicitly included women: "'Mankind' includes male and female." North Dakota prohibited "carnal knowledge of any animal or bird"! (Which reminded Tretona of an old joke about the sex researcher and a farmer. "Sir," said the city slicker, "We've been led to believe that some people around here have intercourse with horses, cows, sheep. . . ." The farmer looked on stone faced. The interviewer continued, " . . . dogs, cats, chickens." "Chickens?" said the farmer excitedly.)

This was really getting absurd. Did this mean that she and Belinda could have been imprisoned for making love? Slowly, she turned to her home state, noting on the way that "any penetration, however slight, is sufficient to complete the crime" and that "emission is not required."

Well, here was the law for her state: "The infamous crime against nature either with man or beast, shall subject the offender to be punished by imprisonment in the penitentiary for a term of not less than one year and not more than ten years." Ten years! If anyone had caught her and Belinda that first night down in the Mt. Carmel churchyard, they could both still be in the penitentiary. No high school graduation. No college. No graduate school. God, that was unbelievable! She read on, carefully tracing out the relevant passages with her finger: "Every person convicted . . . shall be deemed infamous and shall forever thereafter be rendered incapable of holding any office of honor, trust or profit, of voting at any election, or serving as a juror."

Tretona's throat swelled shut. She held out her hand to see if it was shaking but to her surprise it was steady as a rock. No wonder really, because it was like there was a log pressing down on her chest and her stomach felt like someone had put rocks in it and sewn it up. The weight was crushing her. If she could only cry—she tried verbalizing her complaint: "First Bergler claims that I'm incapable of loving anybody and now the law says I'm not fit to vote—ever!" But no sign of tears. Her mouth was dry. It was as if all the water in her body had gone into her bloodstream and was expanding every artery, vein, and capillary.

Maybe anger was a better bet. Who in the hell did those legislators think they were? Hard labor, that was barbaric. But you could even understand that, sort of, if straight people really wanted to stomp out homosexuality. But taking away your voting rights—that was saying you weren't even a citizen. You couldn't even vote to change those barbaric laws. For some reason, Tretona still found no release—maybe she was too stupefied to get really worked up. Her body was quiet as could be, yet inside the tension was tightening, crushing her. She wondered if she might actually implode like one of those evacuated gasoline cans they used in beginning science classes to demonstrate the weight of the atmosphere.

"Well, I better make some hot cocoa or go to bed or take a bath or do something," she said. But the book still lay open—and there was another appendix. "For sure, I'm either compulsive or masochistic," Tretona sighed and turned the page. It was an official document from the United States Civil Service Commission barring homosexuals and "other sex perverts" from employment by the Federal government. There were three reasons: Homosexuals were susceptible to blackmail, showed favoritism to others of their kind, and enticed normal people to engage in perverted practices. The writer summed up: "One homosexual can pollute a government office."

All of a sudden Tretona found a name for the terrible agony she was feeling—it was loss and despair, like when someone dies and is gone forever. Not despair because she was ineligible for the Foreign Service. She could always fake that—wear a mask as Cory recommended. And she wasn't really afraid of getting caught in some Lovers' Lane and being sent to jail, although Lord knows it could happen. No, it was the loss of part of herself that she mourned—the loss of the faith and hope that was expressed in those childhood essays she used to write about Freedom and Americanism and being able to paint your mailbox purple.

She had always believed that the crucial step in the rise of Nazism was the enactment of the racist Nuremberg Laws. If the law of the land became corrupt, there was no hope of justice. How could there be laws like this in America? Why didn't the newspapers say something about them? And she realized that democracy didn't work when there was a minority so totally despised and feared by the majority. That was the flaw in her naive ideas about the democratic political system.

As she walked up to bed she thought about the movie of *Ivan the Terrible,* which was partly in color and partly in black and white. That's what had happened tonight—all the rosy color had gone out of the world. From here on in, it was going to be gray, the color of lead and steel.

13 Beer, Ballads, and a Very Civil Quest for Rights

Democracy is not a static thing. It is an everlasting march.
—*Franklin Delano Roosevelt*

Oh Freedom! Oh freedom!
Oh freedom over me.
And before I'd be a slave
I'd be buried in my grave
And go home to my Lord and be free.
—*Spiritual as sung by Odetta*

FINDING REALLY GOOD people is as rare as finding a four-leaf clover. And like lucky clovers, good people come in clumps—locate one and others are sure to be near by. Tretona's luck started one spring afternoon when she and Hector were riding around on his Lambretta. They stopped out in front of ISCO, the International Students Coop, to watch a volleyball game.

It was a motley crew, but they all seemed to know each other—the noisiest one was a little guy called Bud who had a burr haircut and was aggressive as hell. (Tretona found out later he was an ex-Marine and had a Japanese wife.) The best-natured player was a great big black guy named Leroy who always grinned when he got a good hit. His setter was a tall gentle woman named Ollie.

But Tretona thought the neatest person was Red and when she and Hector finally got rotated in, she chose his side. Tretona was immediately embarrassed because Hector obviously didn't know how to play. He was quick and agile but he kept using basketball-like shots, which were illegal. So the regulars just assumed she couldn't play, either.

Red was playing beside her and he was the pushiest. "That was my ball," Tretona said. And then the next time it happened: "Get back and let me have it and I'll set you up!" But Red kept leaping all over the place at everything that came over the net. So Tretona waited until a particularly blatant transgression occurred and managed to get both a hip and an elbow into him.

"Oof!" said Red, missing the ball.

"That's what happens when you get on other people's segments," Tretona said quietly.

Red looked at her for a minute and then put on a big show. "Hey, everybody. The redhead says we've got to stay on our own segments!" He grabbed a stick and made big lines all over the court. "Here's your segment, here's yours, here's mine. Now everybody stay in your own segment."

He did it in a joking way, but Tretona thought he was a little angry. Anyway, she dug in and played hard and said things like, "Back me up, Red, I have to leave my segment," whenever she chased a ball out of bounds and by game's end they were friends.

Before very long whenever they were on the same team, that team won. Red was good at firing everybody up with his spectacular smashes and sizzling overhand serves, which terrified the opposition. But they made more points when Tretona served—she had a deceptively gentle floater which swerved at the last minute. Her big specialty was running out of bounds to rescue bad passes made by her own team. Once the two of them played alone against a full team ("Red and Redhead versus the Rest of the World") and the game went to deuce before they finally got exhausted and lost.

They started hanging around together off the court too, bicycling, drinking good wine (Red was a connoisseur; he even insisted on using the right glasses), eating out (Red talked her out of being so stingy about food), and mainly talking. They argued about Bertrand Russell's theory of education (too permissive, Tretona thought), Ayn Rand's philosophy of egoism (Tretona said it lacked mercy and compassion), what the purpose of money was (roughly, Red said, it was to spend and Tretona thought it was to save), how to be famous (Tretona said to do something really great, Red said know the right people). But although they argued constantly, they both agreed that they were really as alike as two peas in a pod.

They looked remarkably alike. Some waitresses even thought they were twins, but everyone guessed at least brother and sister. Red was the better athlete and artist (because that's what his dad and mom had encouraged), Tretona was better at analytical thinking and organizing things (because that's what she'd learned from her folks). Both had enormous egos, yet secretly wondered if they would ever amount to anything. Both were still insecure about making friends because of trouble they had had when they were kids. Red had always been considered a "pretty boy" when he was little; Tretona, of course, had been a "tomgirl." When they compared old grade school pictures, they looked less alike than they did now, because Red had curls and wore cute sailor suits while, even then, Tretona had worn plaid shirts and blue jeans whenever she could. Now they both wore cut-offs and T-shirts—and they even wore the same size!

Tretona hoped Dr. Devore woud be pleased to hear that she had a new male friend. Lord knows, it would be nice to find something to lighten up those dreary sessions. She didn't really know why she kept going. After the big night at the library, she had blown up and refused to discuss pseudo-scientific theories of homosexuality any more. To her surprise, Dr. Devore caved in immediately and then asked, "Does this mean that you are now a confirmed homosexual?" Tretona had replied that wasn't the issue—the real questions were about why society stigmatized people and how to change things. But then Dr. Devore had said, "As long as you evade the question of your own sexuality, you can hardly hope to be effective, either professionally or politically." Tretona had to admit he had a point there, so they agreed to explore the question of her sexual orientation in a completely neutral way. Dr. Devore had promised not to try to push her into being heterosexual, but did say that he would ask her to "experiment with alternative conceptualizations of intimate relationships"—whatever that meant.

Evidently her friendship with Red wasn't what he had in mind because Dr. Devore immediately disapproved. "It sounds to me like you're identifying too much with Red. What I want you to try is looking at males as potential mates instead of as models. In a true relationship the partners complement each other."

Tretona thought about that last remark quite a bit. It was true she couldn't imagine being in love with Red—maybe they were too similar. And it was true she hadn't had any female buddies (as opposed to lovers) since Bernice. Well, there was Sylvia—maybe she could have been a buddy, but Jeri Johnson never would be. It seemed like she didn't have much in common with most of the women she met—they were either venus man-traps, sitting around waiting for dates, or emotional prunes like Jeri. But although she always kept an eye out for lovers, she hadn't looked around much for women to be friends with.

Tretona discussed Devore's complementary theory of love with Red and he immediately brought up Plato's fable about how people used to be double in size, with four legs, four arms, two hearts, etc., and how they were cut in two for hubris and went around constantly looking for their other half. "Yeah, I know, I read the *Symposium*," said Tretona, "and according to Plato, the male-male couples were the noblest. So much for that theory."

"Well," said Red, "one could always modify his theory to make it symmetric—maybe it's the homogeneous couples that are the noblest, whether they're male-male or female-female."

"That would fit in with chemistry," said Tretona. "Covalent bonds between like atoms tend to be stronger than ionic bonds." Then remembering Dr. Devore's remark, she made another suggestion: "Wait, now I've got it. Maybe the best lovers of all are physically homogeneous but psychically heterogeneous!"

Red was looking at her intently: "My dear fellow redhead," he said, "that idea is positively subversive."

It was fun being able to kid around with Red. Somehow, without ever explicitly saying it, they had come to an agreement that their relationship would have no sexual component. Once late at a party they had hugged and brushed lips (Tretona had been surprised at the tension in Red's body—he wasn't the least bit cuddly), but that was it. Tretona wondered if Red were a virgin. The only woman he ever talked about was a girl he grew up with, Janet, another officer's kid who had gone off and married a Unitarian minister whose name was Jonathan Moore. Red talked a lot about Janet—and Jonathan, too. Tretona thought she was a childhood sweetheart who got away.

When she teased Red about being celibate, he got very snarky and said he believed in controlling sexual desire, not having it control you. And Red really was in control. Often late at night, after they had been to a romantic movie or maybe listening to a good record, Red would jump up and say, "Well, I'm going over to the gym and work out." Or sometimes he would go to Dean Kroner's house to talk philosophy. Red had got to be friends with Kroner at the men's pool—they were both great swimmers. Tretona was impressed that Red was on such an even social plane with the Dean of Students that he could go over uninvited late at night, but Red shrugged it off. "He's a good conversationalist," he said. "And so am I. We enjoy talking."

"But what do you talk about?" Tretona pushed the point.

"Everything," said Red, "like last time he asked me if I could have my wish, whom would I like to visit as a houseguest for the weekend?"

"So whom did you say?" asked Tretona.

"I thought for a while and finally picked Bertrand Russell and explained why. Kroner thought it was an excellent choice."

"Oh, he did, did he?" Tretona got hostile when Red was so smug.

"Yes, he did. So whom would you have picked?"

Tretona couldn't really think of anyone as neat as Bertrand Russell, so she finally just mumbled "Dmitri Mendeleev" and dropped the subject.

For a while, Tretona made a point of injecting comments relating to homosexuality into conversations whenever she could. The reactions were varied, but rarely positive. When, talking to Jeri Johnson, she brought up the fact that convicted homosexuals were not allowed to vote, Jeri shrugged and said it must be an archaic law which was never enforced because she'd never read anything about any such cases in the newspapers, and then pooh-poohed Tretona's suggestion that newspapers might find it too touchy to print. When she told Red about the law, he snorted and said that only very low types would conduct their private sexual relationships in a public place, anyway. Even without that particular law they could get arrested for public nudity or something. Red seemed annoyed and said it was definitely bad form to get caught in a park or a tearoom. Tretona said you didn't have to be screwing in a coffee shop to get arrested, but he just laughed.

Emil's first reaction was to give an historical lecture on Thomas Aquinas and the Aristotelian concepts of "natural" and "unnatural." Then he went into an esoteric analysis of the law.

130

"Strictly speaking, it doesn't discriminate against homosexuals," he said.

"What the hell do you mean it doesn't?" Tretona flared, ready to argue.

"Now calm down and listen," said Emil. "The way the law is written it doesn't mention homosexuals. It simply forbids certain acts, regardless of the genders of the participants."

"So what?" said Tretona. "Homosexuals are the ones who are affected. If they really want to obey the law, a heterosexual couple can stick to the good old missionary position and stay out of trouble. But no matter what a homosexual couple does, if they have sex at all they're breaking the law. It's bullshit to say that isn't discrimination."

But Emil stuck to his point. "Look," he said, "The law is definitely immoral and almost certainly unconstitutional. I'm on your side. Peace! But you've got to be careful how you attack these things. Take this local barbershop case. The barbers claim they aren't barring Negroes, but all people with kinky hair, race being irrelevant."

That was what happened most often when Tretona brought up the infamous law. Everybody started talking about Negroes. Volleyball Bud was the bluntest: "Hell, Negroes can't even vote. If a goddamn queer keeps his nose clean, he can do anything he damn well pleases. But a black man has no choice. He's marked wherever he goes."

It was ironic. Racial discrimination was so visible and so obviously wrong that it was easier to fight it—in theory at least. Since homosexuals were invisible, the harm they endured was also largely invisible, so nobody got excited about it. And whereas most people these days would at least pay lip service to being against racism (whatever their practice might be), the balance of even enlightened public opinion was probably against homosexuality. Look at the people around here at ISCO—every single one of them militantly against racism, but how would they stand on rights for homosexuals? Vollcyball Bud was a queer-hater if she ever saw one. Like the nasty way he snickered that time he said volleyball was healthier than basketball because it was illegal to break your wrist on a volleyball shot. What about Ollie? She was so gentle and fair-minded that maybe—but wait, she was a biology major and was always evaluating things according to their long-run survival value. So she'd be against it

131

except maybe as a method of controlling population growth. Erwin? He was a psychologist, so he'd probably trot out that old "unfortunate case of arrested development" line. Though it was hard to tell with Erwin. When the city police hired him to draw up a personality assessment instrument for new recruits so they would only induct people with profiles similar to the best officers already in the force, Erwin had sabotaged their plan. The test he designed emphasized conciliation instead of dogmatism, mercy over justice, thinking in shades of gray rather than in black and white polarities. It was a brave and clever thing to do, so she couldn't count Erwin out. He might come through.

And Red? Surely Red, her twin and alter ego, would be an ally. Yet Tretona worried about Red. Sometimes his basic values seemed to have more to do with esthetics and social proprieties than with ethics or politics. Like that time in a restaurant when the guy in the next booth was really bullying his little kid and Tretona had intervened. Red had been furious. At first, Tretona had thought he felt strongly about parental rights or not destroying the child's confidence in his father. But that wasn't the point at all. "You never admit to overhearing a conversation in a restaurant," he'd said. "That is very bad form."

"Your action involves me too, you know," Red had continued. "If the guy gets mad and takes a swing at you, I'm the one who has to respond to the situation."

"No, you don't," said Tretona, "not unless you think I'm right—well, I guess you might because you're my friend."

"My dear Tretona, it is not because I'm your friend that I'd have to help," snapped Red, "but because I'm your escort."

Tretona really didn't understand Red at times like that. Maybe it had to do with being brought up around officers in the Air Force (his dad was a captain) and all that military protocol. But it was more than that. Like now he was bored at the ISCO party because everyone was talking about discrimination in campus barber shops. Furthermore, he assumed that everyone else was really bored too, but was just being polite. Soon he would drift over and get the guitar out of the corner—Tretona had seen him do it before. Then he would sit quietly—so quietly that he would eventually attract the group's attention. And then casually he would start a sea chantey—and Tretona would be the first to join in.

For if there was any team sport which could compete with

volleyball for Tretona's affections, it was folk singing. She loved to rub voices with people. There were the taut abrasive fourths found in mountain music when your voices pulled against each other, or the taffy-toned ascending thirds or sixths of Mexican music—fingerpainting harmonies, everything gooey and parallel—or the feint-parry-riposte of question–answer songs—or the vocal *pas de deux* of melody with obligato.

Tretona loved singing with Red. He had a freckled Irish tenor voice—pure and always right on pitch but with just enough texture to make it interesting. Red always sang lead and Tretona would either buoy him up with a rich chocolaty alto or dance around on top with little soprano riffs or scat noises.

But this night when Red led off with "Drunken Sailor," no one seemed to be enjoying it as much as usual. Suddenly, before he even had a chance to move on to the sequel, "Friggin' in the Riggin'," a clear high voice started a spiritual. It was Ollie's little blonde pig-tailed friend. Evidently she didn't know that Red always led the songs—or didn't care, because now she even reached over and took his guitar. "Tell old Pharoah to let my people go." Leroy's face was beaming and Volleyball Bud was pounding his fist in his palm. Then Pigtails taught them a trilogy of freedom songs. By the end Tretona had found a wonderful little descant part and the two of them spontaneously hummed a little coda just to top everything off.

When there was a break they went up to each other immediately. Tretona couldn't keep from grinning like an idiot.

"Hi," said Pigtails. "My name's Maureen."

"Hi," said Tretona. "I have to sing with you." It was a strange thing to say, but Maureen just smiled.

"I know," she said. "Come over to the dorm and I'll teach you some more songs."

Maureen Cranfield had an Irish mother, an English father, and a New York accent (which got thicker for dramatic purposes). She already had a steady singing partner but since Frances wasn't in summer school, Tretona stepped right in. They spent hours practicing in Maureen's dorm, learning each other's songs, working out harmonies, fussing over guitar strums. Maureen had two guitars so Tretona finally got a chance to play lead on one long enough to learn how. Tretona was enormously attracted to Maureen, but despite her eagerness to invest with deep significance every little brush of Maureen's pigtails or touch of her hand when she suggested a new fingering, Tretona started to admit the possibility that Maureen really wasn't interested in a sexual relationship.

Then one day Maureen actually said so, not directly, but it was clear as could be. Out of the blue Maureen started talking about a new girl who had moved in down the hall from her. "Have you met Lu Rabinowitz yet?"

Tretona said, No, she hadn't, who was Lu Rabinowitz?

"Oh, so you didn't know we have a lesbian living in this corridor?"

Tretona panicked and automatically looked for the door.

"No, no, it's okay. You don't have to close it. Everyone knows. Lu is completely up front about it."

"Wow, that's interesting," said Tretona, "but how do the dormies react?"

"Okay, so far," said Maureen. "You know we're all a bunch of eccentric misfits anyway on this floor. But one thing does freak people out a little. You see, I like Lu a lot. And she likes me and I didn't want there to be any misunderstanding or embarrassment between us. So one day I just came right out and said to her, Lu, I'm straight—irremediably straight—I'm not particularly proud of it, but I am. And I like you a lot and I want to hug you sometimes like a sister. Would that be okay? And Lu really dug it so now we're real affectionate to each other. I think it embarrasses a lot of people, but I'm real glad we got it worked out. I feel sorry for lesbians, you know."

Tretona looked up apprehensively—here comes the crap, she thought.

"No wait," said Maureen, "Let me explain. I feel sorry for lesbians because it's so easy for them to get isolated from straight women. Everyone says it's great how women can touch each other in ways that men can't or men and women can't—at least not without being misunderstood. Don't you see? Lesbians have the same problem with women. If a lesbian even touches a woman, it's almost sure to be interpreted as a sexual overture when it isn't. Sometimes I think even the lesbian herself may get confused and start viewing every physical contact as sexual."

"Yeah, maybe," said Tretona. She was amazed at how much insight Maureen had. She continued, her voice showing genuine awe. "Say, that was really beautiful, what you said about—what's her name—Lu. I bet she really appreciates you being so, well, good about everything." Tretona wished like hell that she could hug Maureen sometimes—like a sister, if that's the way she wanted it. But that was still way too scary. Tretona also wondered if Maureen had an ulterior motive for telling her all this. Had she guessed?

However it was intended, the information was pretty interesting. "Which one is Lu?" asked Tretona, trying to be nonchalant.

"You'll know her when you see her," Maureen said and refused to say more. Again, Tretona felt vaguely uneasy. Was Maureen making an insinuation of the it-takes-one-to-know-one variety?

She wasn't. No special antennae were needed to pick out Lu. If Warner Brothers casting had been asked to come up with a lesbian, they couldn't have done a better job. The first time Tretona saw Lu she was getting out of her white Porsche, which was illegally parked in front of the dorm. She wore a tweed riding jacket with leather trim, breeches, and dress boots. When Maureen called to her, Lu slowly removed her aviator glasses and straightened her ascot before coming over. She shook hands with Tretona (after a studied removal of her right driving glove). Her short hair was very wavy—it threatened to jump out into ringlets any minute. She had a fantastic tan and her lips were so full of color that for a minute Tretona thought she might be wearing lipstick—but she wasn't, of course.

Her eyes were steel blue probes and when she looked at Tretona they seemed to be saying, "Of course, I know you know. What I don't know is what you think about it." And maybe they were also saying (Tretona couldn't be quite so sure), "And you know I know—about you, that is."

But by then Lu had her arm around Maureen and was offering to show both of them the new spotlight she'd just had installed on the car—it operated by remote control and swiveled in all directions. Then the conversation turned to dogs (Lu had a Great Dane at home called Gertrude—she could barely fit in the back compartment of the Porsche) and then to bicycling and then to sailing (Lu offered to teach Tretona). Tretona was nattering away with no problem until Maureen said, "I've got to take care of my laundry. You two wait here—I'll be back in ten minutes." Then Tretona froze and couldn't think of anything to say. Well, not anything she wanted to say. Well, not anything she *dared* to say. What she wanted to say was, "I think it's beautiful the way you dress and move so everyone knows you're homosexual. No, it's not that you advertise, but that you don't disguise. Everything you do suits you so well. But isn't that dangerous? Don't people snicker or throw rocks at your car or try to rape you or lock up their daughters thinking you'll rape them? How can you walk around so cool and elegant?" The questions were pushing so hard at her temples and throat that Tretona was sure Lu must think she was about to have a fit.

Finally, Lu spoke. "Have you known Maureen long?" she asked.

Tretona shook her head, "Nope, we just met at a folksinging session, but we hit it off right away." Lu seemed to be waiting so Tretona added, "Maureen is a very beautiful person." And then thinking that might sound funny, she blurted out, "And her friends are real neat, too; all of them I've met are beautiful." Her eyes dug into Lu's. "Every single one of them."

Then there was silence again. Lu took off her jacket and folded it. Tretona caught the label—Abercrombie and Fitch—and memorized it so she could ask Red what kind of store it was. She wondered if Lu's shirt was real silk, but it wouldn't be polite to ask. She poked at a caterpillar crawling on the dorm steps and searched desperately for something to say. Finally, she blurted out: "The main thing I like about Maureen is her openness—she never hides anything—or if she does, it's out of kindness, not out of fear. Most people are like retarded worms." She nudged the caterpillar along with her ballpoint. "I mean they could be beautiful butterflies, but they get all dry and afraid and never come out of their cocoons." She looked longingly at Lu. "Tell me, what does it take to become a butterfly?"

Lu looked thoughtful for a minute and then stroked her jacket. "I don't really know the secret," she said. Then she grinned, "But it doesn't hurt to have money."

Tretona laughed, but still felt dissatisfied. If there were only some clear issue, some important battle to wage, like Civil Rights. "I'm sick and tired of being a conformist without a cause," she thought.

14 How You Gonna Keep Them Down on the Farm?

If you would be known and not know, vegetate in a village; if you would know and not be known, live in a city.
— Charles Caleb Colton

To say the best, a town life makes one more tolerant and liberal in one's judgments of others.
— Henry Wadsworth Longfellow

COMPREHENSIVE EXAMS—WORDS guaranteed to strike terror in the most accomplished or blasé graduate student. Three written exams—all day for your major area of concentration and a half-day for each minor. And then an oral. There was a rich folklore concerning the different types of mental breakdowns they caused and how to avoid them. Just two years ago a guy over in the isotopes lab had brooded so much over the errors he'd made in the writtens that he drove into the side of a train and never did take the oral. There was an old tale, probably apocryphal, of the student who No-Dozed his way through two nights, then during the exams wrote a whole blue book full of meaningless, endless formulae for nonexistent organic compounds.

Tretona hadn't been raised a Methodist for nothing. She organized her review like a climber preparing to scale Mount Everest. Notebooks, textbooks, reference books all neatly stacked, a spiralling plan of study so she'd be sure to cover everything at least once and then circle back to concentrate on the hard or important topics. The exams were the first week in February and the traditional day to start studying was the Monday after Thanksgiving.

At first, reviewing wasn't too bad. Tretona took a macabre interest in seeing what she had forgotten. She reckoned that if an item really was important, she would remember it and that was generally true, but not always, of course. It was fun, too, seeing all the pieces taught in different courses come together at last. Everyone said that when you finished studying for comps you would know more about chemistry as a whole than you ever would again. From then on it was all specialization—learning more and more about less and less. Tretona dreaded the downhill part to come, but at the moment it was exciting to go for the big picture.

Like a fighter in training, she tried to eat well and not generate any unnecessary stress in her social life. She spent a lot of evenings at Maureen's dorm, strumming through old songs but not learning any new ones and exchanging childhood reminiscences. Tretona loved hearing about life in New York. Maureen could do all sorts of accents—Jewish, black, Puerto Rican, Boston Brahmin. Once she got out her photo album and showed Tretona pictures of her high school gang. Tretona kept picking out one girl and talking about her. "There's something intriguing about her face," said Tretona. "I don't know exactly what it is. Maybe it's the juxtaposition of those enormous sad eyes and that mischievous little smile."

"That's Lara to a T," said Maureen. "She's a sad-eyed brat. And she'll charm you out of your last nickel if you aren't careful."

"I think I'd really like her," Tretona said.

"I bet you would," said Maureen in a funny way that made Tretona look at her. Whatever romantic tension had once existed between them had dissipated. Maureen was dating steadily now— some pleasant nonentity named John. Tretona couldn't believe Maureen really liked him, but they sure went out often enough. If Maureen wasn't home, Tretona always tried Lu's room. Lu and Sonya, her roommate, always seemed to have a party going—or at least the potential for one. Sonya's mother sent her jars of pineapple cheese spread and Lu always had bourbon hidden away someplace where neither the housemother nor Sonya could find it.

And so the weeks went by, Tretona chewing her way steadily

through page after page of chemistry. She even kept going the week after everyone else went home for Christmas holidays. But at 3:10 on the afternoon of December 24, exactly halfway through her study program, she ground to a halt—not gradually, but decisively, definitely, definitively. It was as if a cable had snapped in her brain. There was no way she could go on. And because it was so crystal clear that she literally could not study any more, she didn't feel panicked.

She went over to the Union, not really expecting to see anyone she knew, but there was John, of all people. Since Maureen was the only thing they had in common, they talked about her and about how wonderful New York must be during the holiday season, and by eight P.M. they had each packed a duffel bag and were headed east on the turnpike!

Their excitement lasted into Ohio. Sporadic attempts to make polite conversation persisted a couple of hours longer, and then Tretona settled into a farmer's trance—your unconscious mind attends to the machinery, automatically checking for unusual noises or stumps up ahead, while your conscious mind cuts loose completely. At such times one's thoughts are unusually mobile and alive. She thought of Maureen, how surprised she would be to see them. She hoped Maureen's mother wouldn't mind putting them up. They really should bring her a gift. Maybe nuts or chocolate if they came across a decent place to buy some. She thought about chemistry—not the formulas, but about being a chemist or a chemistry teacher. She couldn't really imagine it— Dr. Getroek—it sounded good, really good, but first she had to make a "significant research contribution." She didn't think about that because it always made her sick when she did.

Dawn found them entering Pennsylvania—John's car was old and he didn't like to drive it too hard. A flat tire ate up another hour. Tretona's body was as saturated with driving as her mind was with chemistry. New Jersey took longer than expected, but finally there were signs to the Lincoln Tunnel and Manhattan was barely visible in the gray evening mist. Somehow they found the Cranfield house in Queens, but then a letdown—Maureen had gone out. John was for waiting there, but when Tretona heard that the party was at Lara Feldman's, she badgered him into crawling back into the car.

Endless navigation and an even longer search for a parking spot. There was the bell—the door buzzed open, up the narrow stairs, sudden shyness, John went first sounding very western as he said, "We're friends of Maureen's," then he spied her and Tretona was left standing looking straight into Lara's face.

"So you're Maureen's redheaded friend," said Lara. "She's told me about you. Welcome to New York." Her hand was cool and soft and their shoulders touched as they went through the door. "This is Trish and Alan and. . . ." Tretona was in a daze of relief at having finally found Maureen and as soon as possible she chose a place on the bed to sit and rested her head against the wall, listening to the music. But burning through the stupor and fatigue was her awareness of Lara—listening to her laugh, watching her move, trying to think of something to talk with her about. Well, the least she could do was wash her face and try to wake up. "Where's the john?" she whispered to Maureen and just as she threaded her way to it, she felt Lara behind her. Not daring to look around, Tretona stumbled into the bathroom and stuck her face under the tap. When she straightened up, chin dripping, Lara was standing beside her holding a towel. Startled, Tretona looked to see if she had left the door open, but it was closed.

"Hi," said Tretona and leaned forward for the towel.

"Hello, yourself," said Lara and kissed her hard on the mouth, then dried her face with little wet puppy licks. Tretona's surprise immediately turned into directed energy and she drew Lara hard against her, hands lifting her buttocks, face down into her breasts. Lara was a gentle, but greedy kitten, lapping up kisses, insisting on more.

An interlude for breathing. "Oh, you really are a wild, wild westerner," teased Lara. Then more seriously, "I'd better go play hostess—they'll miss us."

"Wait," Tretona said. "Don't go."

"Well, then, little Lara will wait nicely for you while you pee. That's what you came in here for, wasn't it?" Tretona nodded dumbly and there was nothing else to do but drop her jeans and sit on the john.

"Go on ahead, tinkle for Lara," she said, stroking Tretona's hair.

"I can't," Tretona said, straining.

"Why not?"

"I just can't, I'm too excited."

"I'll help," said Lara and quick as a wink she hiked up her

140

calico mumu. Tretona saw a flash of knee socks and bare thighs, then Lara was astride her, bouncing a little and holding her face. "Now," said Lara solemnly. "I will make you pee." And before Tretona could bet she couldn't, she felt a gush of warm liquid on her clitoris, drenching, massaging her. Absurdly, an old grade school joke about book titles flashed through her mind (*The Golden Stream* by I. P. Freely), and then everything inside exploded at once.

Lara leaned against her sharing the outburst and relief. Tretona recovered and reached for the toilet paper. "You naughty decadent easterners," she said and dried Lara's pussy very gently but the paper slid so smoothly that she used her fingers instead and then Lara was riding on both thumbs.

"Gently, babe," said Trctona but Lara was already high and wild and away, leaning back so far that Tretona pulled one hand free and held her around the waist and slowly and steadily brought the runaway rider to a peaceful exhausted halt.

Again Lara collapsed against her, the fine hair at her temples and neck wet and matted. Tretona soothed her, combing the damp curly stuff with her fingers as best she could. "Well!" said Tretona, "Well, well, well," but Lara was a dead weight collapsed against her. Then almost imperceptibly, the moist limp body took on form again and when Lara finally did move it was her fingers which Tretona was amazed to find in her crotch! They drummed and stroked and circled all around her vagina, barely brushing her most sensitive spot and then moving on only to return again. Tretona was beside herself.

"Come inside, please. Come inside of me." But the fingers kept up the tattoo, tapping faster and harder. For a moment, Tretona almost got scared. Surely, she would burn out her brain if this teasing continued. But Lara breathed close to her ear, "Don't fight it—just stay with me!" and then Tretona did leave her brain behind and her head crashed into the boxes on the back of the toilet and her feet found the floor and Lara was standing beside her now, the fingers never stopping and then it was like getting rid of all the heavy rocks in her stomach and chest and brain and Lara would take them and then Tretona let it all go up and out and away.

They washed and combed, smiling quietly at each other. "When . . .?" Tretona started to ask.

"Tomorrow," whispered Lara. "Don't worry, I'll fix it."

Judging from the house, Maureen's folks had more money than Tretona had guessed. There was a baby grand in the living room. It turned out that her mom played viola in some string quartet which may have been famous, but Tretona didn't recognize the name. Maureen's dad worked for the city. Tretona didn't want to ask what he did, but since there was an autographed photograph of Mr. Cranfield in a white suit standing by Eleanor Roosevelt at a garden party, it was obvious he didn't collect garbage or clean streets for a living.

Finally (Tretona's eyes were scratchy from fatigue), John was bedded down in the family room and Tretona and Maureen went upstairs. Tretona had already collapsed into the guest bed when Maureen appeared at the door in a nightgown, looking more grown-up than she did in her PJ's at college. "Can I get you anything?"

"Nope, I'm fine," said Tretona, and patted the side of the bed since Maureen looked like she wanted to talk.

"Lara," said Tretona, naming and thereby puncturing the thought barrier between them. "Lara is a—well—a very unusual person." Maureen nodded. "I like her a lot," Tretona continued.

"Oh, I know you do. I knew all along you would, even before you saw her picture." Maureen hesitated. "But Tretona, please be careful."

"What do you mean?" Tretona was cautious.

"Listen, I don't expect you to believe me, but try, won't you? Lara is—well, Lara behaves like an orphan. Everytime someone new comes along she goes all sad-eyed and charming and tries to get them to adopt her .But she doesn't really mean it—she's really much better off where she is. Trish is good for her, I think—a stabilizing influence."

"Who's Trish?"

"You know, she was there tonight. She's Lara's roommate. Actually, it's her apartment."

"Look," Tretona said. "I'm not going to mess up your friend. Believe me, she seems quite able to take care of herself."

"I know, I know," said Maureen. "Look here, you big palooka, it's you I'm worried about." And for the second time that evening Tretona got kissed unexpectedly—this time on both cheeks. And then Maureen was gone.

Sunday morning in Queens. Down to the shopping street for a fat *New York Times* and fresh bagels. For a moment Tretona thought the woman in the deli was just putting on an accent to be funny the way Maureen did until she realized this *was* New York. Mrs. Cranfield made poached eggs (another first for Tretona) and entertained them with stories about Maureen—Maureen at three who had just learned the word "Negro," using it proudly and loudly in public: "A *Negro* just got on the bus." Maureen at nine in a fancy fish restaurant wickedly denying they had a cat when her father asked for a kitty bag. "We did have a cat, as a matter of fact, but Maureen was angry because we hadn't gone to a pizza place."

The conversation was warm and jolly, but Tretona was restless. At last the phone rang. When Maureen hung up, Tretona met her in the corridor. "Miss Feldman requests the pleasure of your company at two o'clock," Maureen said dryly. "Don't worry. John and I will drop you off in plenty of time." Then it was just a question of waiting—and brushing her teeth very carefully and changing clothes twice and wetting down her cow licks.

Trish was just leaving when Tretona arrived. "Bye, bye, dear. See you at six." Lara closed the door and turned to Tretona: "That is when Maureen is picking you up, isn't it?" Tretona nodded and bent to kiss her. They savored each other's tongues and then played hide 'n' seek and tickle all around the gums and soft palate. Lara had a beautiful mouth—not loose and slobbery but moist and elastic, expanding and contracting as the kiss progressed. "Why are we standing here?" she said finally and led Tretona through the apartment. "I've prepared a fantastic nosh for us. But first I want to show you my crazy boudoir."

It was quite a bedroom. The bed itself was enormous and stood in the middle of the room. The surrounding walls were covered with photographs of nude women, singly and in pairs. Tretona, taken aback and not quite knowing where to look, headed for the window.

"The view's inside, my dear," said Lara, closing the blind, and then leading her to the bed.

"It's almost like theater in the round, isn't it?" said Tretona, eyeing the staring photographs, but Lara oozed silence and concentration. She undressed Tretona in a controlled, but intense manner, carefully interspersing kisses and buttons, zippers and caresses.

Tretona stood uncertainly, not knowing what to expect, not used to being around a woman who made the first move. When

Lara's nibbling expedition reached her waist, Tretona tried to regain the initiative. "Don't be so pushy, cowgirl," said Lara. "Put those restless paws inside my old friend, Pussy!" And she produced a beautiful white furry muff. For a moment Tretona felt absurd, standing there naked, both hands shoved into a kid's muff which tickled her stomach. What must the photographs think? But then her concentration rushed in with centripetal force to the place where Lara's hands were parting her hair and Lara's tongue was doing that weird little tap dance. It was as if her whole being were caught in a vortex, circling with Lara around that place too sensitive to touch yet begging to be touched—and kissed and stroked and gently chewed and sucked. Tretona hardly remembered falling to the bed and she had no idea how long that tongue had danced, and the fingers stroked her oval hair line, rosy lips met lilac lips and then she couldn't move, paralyzed, wanting release yet not wanting it to ever stop, and Lara waited and then gently urged Tretona to come off the brink, to fly up and out through mad spaces and finally to land gently on a bed in the middle of a room in downtown New York City.

Tretona looked down at the black wavy hair sandwiching the white pussy muff on top of her stomach. She pulled her hands free and drew Lara's beautiful head up to her. "You're wonderful," Tretona said. The banality of the words broke any remaining aura. My god, I hardly know this woman and yet she has made me feel more . . . Tretona's thought ended in confusion. Suddenly, Tretona felt a need for social intercourse. "The pictures," she said. "I guess then Trish must know."

"Know?" Lara was puzzled.

"Know about you, well, digging women and stuff."

A look of amazement, then amusement: "Tretona," Lara said, "Trish is my lover. She made the photographs. This is our bed." Something on Tretona's face made her stop. "You didn't know? Didn't Maureen tell you? Didn't you guess?"

Tretona felt not only shocked and hurt but stupid. "It doesn't matter," she said, reaching for her shirt and buttoning it all the way up despite Lara's protests. "Hell, we never would have made it anyway, there's just too big a distance between New York City and Corn Country."

But Lara pulled her down and finally Tretona hugged her fiercely and started to make love to her way too rough, but Lara held her face tight and hard and said, "Tretona, stop! Don't be silly. Trish knows I'm with you and she understands. So you should understand, too. Please, you're only here for a few days. Can't we just enjoy each other? I love your body—and I love. . . ." Tretona stopped her from saying any more.

So they solemnly played Follow-the-Leader, touching each other in synchrony, one innovating and the other following so quickly and then so subtly taking over the leadership that it was like a rehearsed ballet. Their bodies formed an X, belly to belly, heads turned left reading the intent in each other's eyes, right hands making music, bodies in unison measuring, pulsing, holding the beat together and steady until the finale where Tretona took off alone on some high tricky obligato riff while Lara went deeper and deeper into rolling swells and crashing two-handed chords.

Then again the return to ordinary space–time, to little nuzzles, and stretching, and the discovery that they both had enormous appetites. The snack Lara had prepared consisted of Arab bread, two dips, and black olives. Tretona approached the dip gingerly. It was a grayish-yellow color and totally unrecognizable. "What is this funny stuff? It's good."

"Baba Gannosh," Lara said and eagerly recited the recipe, but since Tretona had never tasted an eggplant or sesame seed butter, it didn't help much in sorting out the strange flavors.

"Hey, everything about you is pretty exotic, isn't it?" said Tretona. Lara stuck out her tongue.

"Don't give me that big dumb kid act. Maureen told me you practically have a Ph.D."

"Not *practically*, by a long shot," said Tretona. "No, seriously, I don't mean the food so much, though that's great—and very unusual, I think. What I really meant was the way you make love. I mean it. You know—the way you stay on the outside and the fast light rhythm—" Tretona felt like blushing. "Hell, you know what I mean."

"I think I might," said Lara. "Do you mean like so?" and pebbled Tretona's ear with her tongue.

"Cut it out," said Tretona. "I'm trying to conduct a serious conversation and I really am serious about. . . ."

"Well, if you really must know," said Lara, climbing on Tretona's lap, "Trish taught me to make love that way. She doesn't believe in any surrogate penis movements. She thinks lovemaking between women should be free of all phallic content."

"Wow, that's pretty interesting. I don't know about the theory behind it, but the end result—at least when you do it—well, it really *is* superior."

"Speak for yourself," said Lara. "Sometimes I prefer cowgirls." And she began to bounce up and down and nuzzle around until Tretona finally laid down her Arabic bread and made love to her on the spot.

Tretona's mind was still working. "I wonder if Trish is right," she said. "Like just now—do you mind talking like this? Stop me if you do—like just now I made a lot of strong thrusting movements and that's what you wanted. Maybe that was sort of phallic."

Lara seemed close to being angry. "I think that's pure balderdash," she said. "I have never seen a penis. I have no idea how they feel or move. I never dream about one or fantasize about one. What I do take special notice of are women's hands." She traced the contours of Tretona's thumb and fingers. "As I said, I speak from total ignorance of the much admired phallus, but I cannot believe it can come close to the diversity and agility and sensitivity of this organ right here." She kissed Tretona on the knuckles. "As far as I'm concerned, a penis is just a poor imitation of a hand!" The debater in Tretona prompted her to argue, "But of course men have hands too."

Lara's black eyes crackled, "And of course they don't know how to use them—and they have no intention of learning. But that's not the point." Lara started cleaning up the snack stuff. "I was wrong; midwesterners really are dumb after all."

For some reason Tretona got the giggles at that and soon Lara was smiling in spite of herself and then they just had time before six o'clock came for a walk around the block to see Lara's favorite tree.

As far as intimacy was concerned, that afternoon was the last time Lara and Tretona were together. True, Lara cut classes one afternoon (she was studying industrial design at Cooper Union) to help Tretona pick out a guitar (many jokes because she finally selected a Goya) and then the two rode the ferry out to Staten Island with Maureen and John. (It was freezing cold on the deck and stuffy inside.) They held hands when the other couple wasn't looking and necked a bit in the back of John's car. (Maureen only turned around at red lights.) And then it was time for the three of them to head back west. In a way, Tretona was relieved not to be around on New Year's Eve—it would have been too painful at midnight, for Lara would surely have gone to Trish.

On the long drive back to school Tretona had ample opportunity to relive and rethink her hours with Lara. It was funny; she ached to see, feel, Lara again; she had never met anyone so exciting and entertaining. Yet somehow she was also relieved to be going home. Partly it was not wanting to chance spoiling the perfection of the experience. And it had been perfect—no quarrels, no disappointments, no fuckups of any kind. But she was also worried about the Trish business.

When Tretona was driving and John was asleep in the back seat, she brought up the topic. "Maureen, do you know anything about what sort of understanding Trish and Lara have? I mean about having affairs on the side. Lara says Trish doesn't mind."

"Well, Lara is fooling herself, there. From the beginning Lara was very promiscuous—I told you she was like an orphan—and at first Trish raised cain about it, left her twice, laid down ultimatums. But Lara is just that way and finally Trish decided she either had to leave Lara or learn to live with it—there was no third alternative. I guess she's learning to live with it."

"Boy, I bet Trish hates my guts," said Tretona.

"Yeah, maybe," said Maureen, "though she shouldn't really—she knows how Lara is."

"Well, just for the record, I didn't start it, though I sure didn't stop it, either," Tretona said and told Maureen a bit of what happened in the bathroom. Maureen laughed and said how like Lara and then they fell into a comfortable silence.

It suddenly occurred to Tretona how natural and easy their conversation was, even though the whole thing was about—wow, Maureen is really a great friend to have, thought Tretona. And it was such a relief to be able to chat and ramble on about love affairs—like everyone else does all the time, she said to herself with a sigh.

She wondered why Lara was so promiscuous. Maybe Trish didn't pay her enough attention—or satisfy her sexually, given her theory about avoiding male symbolism. Tretona didn't have much sympathy with horny women. Once when she was in high school and her mother wouldn't get up in the morning Tretona had gone into the bedroom and found her mother sitting up in bed looking restless and acting nervous. When Tretona asked what was wrong, she said that Tretona's father was having some sort of middle-aged trouble and couldn't satisfy her anymore. He was taking hormones and he kept trying, but it didn't work and it was driving her mother crazy. Not knowing what her mother expected her to do about it, Tretona just said to get up and get busy and forget it. She reckoned sex was a gift, a bonus, not something you could demand. She hated all that talk about a wife's conjugal duty—and it seemed doubly repulsive to hear a woman talking that way. They at least should know better.

Still it was a shame if Trish had all sorts of rules about what could and could not go on in bed. Things were complicated enough without that. For example, one thing that she had learned from Lara was that people don't always make love the way they would like to be made love to in return. For herself, Lara wanted big, deep movements but what she gave was—Tretona felt a swoon coming on and cradled the steering wheel in her arms. "Bless you, Lara Feldman," she thought, "for breaking the Golden Rule."

Then Tretona sat bolt upright. That was it! She and Lara were refutations to Dr. Devore's mirror theory. Their experience definitely showed that it wasn't a case of displaced narcissism. It couldn't be that they were really making love to themselves while pretending to love the other person, because what each did for the other was significantly different from what she wanted for herself. She could hardly wait to tell Dr. Devore. Maybe he would want to write a paper about it. Maybe she and Lara would become famous like Wolfman! This stuff was really interesting. She should compare notes with Lu and get some more data there.

However, digesting the New York trip had to wait until after comps. It took every ounce of willpower to catch up and complete her review schedule but Tretona did it. And she ate right, got enough sleep, sharpened all her pencils, and sailed through the writtens. Her research director even phoned her at home to say that she had the highest score in her major field exam. But disaster struck in the oral exam. "Not technically, but existentially," said Tretona when she talked to Red about it.

For the first forty minutes everything was hunky dory: "How would you synthesize the *cis* and *trans* isomers of dichlorodinitroplatinate?" And Tretona would tell them if she knew or tell them the principles involved if she didn't know exactly. And then Dr. Molar, who was chairing the inquisition, abruptly leaned back and linked his hands behind his head: "Miss

Getroek, you're an inorganic chemist—or well on your way to being one. Tell me, what *is* inorganic chemistry?"

"And then," Tretona told Red, "it was like a Jack-in-the-Box popped up in my brain, shouting, 'No, I'm not an inorganic chemist. That's not me. That's not what I am at all.' Suddenly it became so clear, so very clear that I am not *really* a chemist. Oh, I know a lot of chemistry and I can do chemistry, but I'm just not a chemist! Do you know what I mean?"

Red nodded and then grinned, "Yeah, I think I know, but I must say, all this stuff about what you *really* are sounds suspiciously like essentialist talk, especially for someone who is supposed to be an existentialist."

"Oh well, translate it for me," said Tretona. "And then I just made a complete fool of myself. I gave them some eighth grade definition of inorganic chemistry and they picked holes in it, of course. Hell, I could have destroyed that answer myself—have, in fact, in my C105 quiz sections. And then I tried to patch it up, but Dr. Molar said with big innocent eyes, 'But what about hemoglobin—it's got iron in it? Yet it's surrounded by an enormous organic chelating agent. Whom does it belong to, those smelly organickers or us nice clean inorganic types?' And then I got mad and said I gave up. Would he please be kind enough to tell me. And so he looked up oh so smug and said, 'In my opinion, Miss Getroek—mind you, this is just my opinion—inorganic chemistry is the object of study of inorganic chemists!' And everyone laughed, of course, and I just felt like one big fool. 'Thank you very much,' I said with all the sarcasm I could muster—and that was the end of the exam."

"And so you passed," said Red.

"I passed with them. But they don't pass with me," said Tretona. "Chemists are the most arrogant, narrow people I have ever met and I'll be damned if I'll be one."

"Oh come on, Tretona. You got snookered in on a trick question, that's all. Remember in Scouts when you always took the new kid on a snipe hunt? Comps are just one more initiation rite. They didn't mean to humiliate you—they were just teasing you a little before making you one of the gang."

Tretona was still fuming. "I should have caught on that it was a trick question. I should have just said that the problem of defining a field is of no intellectual import—it begs for a conventional, though not arbitrary, answer and . . ."

Red interrupted the tirade. "And what do you suppose Dr. Molar would have done then?" asked Red.

"Looked embarrassed, I guess," said Tretona.

"Not on your life," said Red and then he peered over imaginary glasses and spoke in a pompous voice, "'Miss Getroek, I am not interested in *your* evaluation of my question. I would like instead to evaluate your *answer* to it, if you would be so kind as to provide one.' Don't you see, Tretona, there was no way you could win. All you could do was answer straight and then show what a good sport you were later."

"Well, I sure failed the snipe hunt part of the exam," said Tretona. "But I don't know, Red, it kind of worries me how well you understand bureaucrats. I know it's useful, but it makes me a little nervous."

"Hey, just because I understand the Establishment is no sign I'm one of them."

But there was a growing divergence in the way Red and Tretona coped with "them." Tretona became sure of it six weeks later when spring break rolled around. Red was flying off to visit Janet and Jonathan, who had recently been transferred to Texas. When Tretona showed up to drive him to the airport, he was wearing a suit and tie. Red got very touchy at her reaction and said that they would probably be going for drinks at the Officers' Club and he didn't want to embarrass Jonathan. Tretona had to admit he looked great—in a square sort of way—and of course he was still Red whether he was wearing sneakers or wing tips. But nevertheless she felt vaguely betrayed.

By all rights, one should feel a tremendous relief upon finishing the last set of examinations you'd ever have to take in your life, but Tretona fell into a bad post-comp depression. She'd go into the lab late—she just couldn't get out of bed anymore. For a while, she pleaded fatigue and the February weather. Sometimes, she would manage to get an experimental run underway. (Her research involved taking low-temperature spectra of single crystals of transition metal coordination compounds.) But something was always going wrong. The cell window would get fogged with condensation from the liquid nitrogen, or the Carey-500 would run out of chart paper, or the pen would clog, or the crystal would fall off the optical flat or shatter from uneven cooling. Sometimes after a particularly big disappointment, she would try to do something routine and simple, like washing out beakers.

But disaster struck even there—once she cut her hand on a broken stirring rod. There was nothing for it but to go over to the Union for coffee. As time went on, more and more she would go to coffee first in order to calm her nerves—and with any luck, enough people would drop by with interesting things to report that it would be time for lunch. But by two P.M. everybody was gone, and there was nothing to do but drag ass back to the lab. Then the headaches would start and Tretona would fight it with aspirin and a change of scenery down in the chem library, but nothing really worked except a cup of tea at the Union. And people would be dropping by after their classes were done and by evening more than likely the liquid nitrogen would be gone and besides, Tretona needed sleep and had to go to bed early—unless there was a party someplace, of course.

Tretona tried to talk to Dr. Devore about it. Surely, he would have some practical tips about how to get started working again. But Devore seemed to think her grinding to a halt was to be expected. "It's a classic way of manifesting self-hatred," he said. "What better way of punishing yourself than to sabotage your own career?" he said. "Here you are only six or nine months from a Ph.D. You can't permit that to happen, can you? Unconsciously you think you don't deserve it, so you're preventing yourself from succeeding."

"But why *now?*" asked Tretona. "Why is it happening just at this time?"

"It's crystal clear," said Dr. Devore triumphantly. "It's obviously because of your recent affair with that New York woman. There's a perfect correlation—for two years, you've been seeing me, right? And for two years you've abstained from sexual relations with women, right? In part, because I insisted on it. For two years your studies have been going brilliantly, right? Then over the break I had to cancel two appointments because of the holidays and my professional obligations, so what do you do, but rush off to New York—I suppose you were angry at me—and seduce a promiscuous lesbian. Is it any wonder that you're punishing yourself? The only way to become productive again is to improve your self-concept, to find out who you really are. And the only way to do that is to stop flirting with this homosexuality business. And, as I've said before, the only way to cure that is . . ."

As Dr. Devore commenced the familiar litany, Tretona's

mind suddenly shifted into high gear. "I don't have to put up with this anymore," whirred the wheels. "I don't have to listen to this claptrap anymore. I don't have to argue, I don't have to fight back, I don't have to defend myself anymore." And slowly, carefully, as if in a dream, Tretona got to her feet. She turned toward the door—hesitated for a moment—and then looked back. "I already know who I am, Dr. Devore. I am a grown-up lesbian, not a retarded heterosexual. And I'm not a chemist, either." Her voice surprised her with its strength and calmness. Dr. Devore returned her gaze, started to say something, and then shrugged and flipped shut the manila folder lying on his desk.

Closing the chemistry research notebook took a lot longer. At first, Tretona ran on anger; she'd show him and everybody else that she could do the work. Then there were all the prudential arguments—as Red said, getting the degree didn't mean that she actually had to work as a chemist. Whatever she ended up doing, having those three little letters behind her name sure wasn't going to hurt. Dr. Molar, who finally noticed that she wasn't signed up for the Carey-500, suggested a semester's leave of absence. "Go off and work in industry for a while. Have a change of scene. After all, you've been in school twenty years straight now." Maureen declined to make any comment but the way she refused told all, "You know how goddamn achievement-oriented I am, Tretona. Don't drag me into this; you know I won't understand."

Only Emil was helpful. He came over one evening with his beat-up book of Camus' essays. Tretona popped some corn and together they re-read their favorite, *The Myth of Sisyphus*. At the end there was a long silence etched only by the meditative munching of popcorn, until Emil said, "You see, Tretona, we've all got big rocks to shove around. Let's face it, life is difficult—there's no getting away from pushing and straining and trying hard. But where we have freedom is in our choice of rock. See, here it says Sisyphus affirmed the rock because it was his. All I can say is, don't try to come up with an easy way out, but do keep looking until you find a task in life which suits you—one which you can make yours."

"Thanks," said Tretona. "You're right. It's just that sometimes I'm afraid I won't recognize it when it comes along." And then she got up and made cocoa.

The groundwork for big decisions is always laid slowly and laboriously but the actual moment of decision is as effortless and smooth and rapid as the action of a mercury switch. At least that's the way it was with Tretona. One morning she dragged herself into lab, uncertain as to whether to make up a new batch of crystals, talk to Dr. Edwards about the possibility of switching to a more theoretical topic for her dissertation, or ask Dr. Molar where to get a job. She stoppered the sink, filled it with suds, and slowly started washing the volumetric flasks she needed for the prep. For a lark she filled one clear to the top, put a piece of weighing paper over the mouth, and carefully inverted it. She still felt that childish amazement when the water didn't fall out. Her father had taught her that trick once when they were doing dishes. It was fun washing dishes with her dad. Of course, he didn't have to deal with dishes all the time the way her mom did. Even when she or her dad or the other kids did them, it was still her mom's responsibility to make sure they got done.

Suddenly, Tretona had an image of her mother standing at the sink at home scrubbing a Ball jar with a long-handled brush. Whenever they did canning, her mother complained because her hands had become too fat and arthritic to go down into a quart jar. Then Tretona remembered her mother in an oh-so-familiar pose—she had laid down the dirty jar and her right arm was leaning over the hand pump at the side of the sink. With her other hand, she was brushing the hair off her forehead, too tired to care that her hand was still soapy. As a kid Tretona used to hate it when she came across her mother frozen in a posture of defeat before some simple household task. But now she felt a flash of sympathy for her—after all, here she was being stymied by a bunch of boring, meaningless experiments.

"Maybe there was no way you could get out of housework, Mama. Maybe you were trapped by those dishes and diapers and dust mops. But I'm not trapped. I have no commitment to these test tubes. You couldn't escape, but I can." And after that, it was simply a matter of getting a withdrawal form from the dean's office.

The next question was what to do now—her April fellowship check would be the last. Tretona was surprised to discover that although she hadn't consciously thought about it, nevertheless she already knew. (That's another characteristic of big decisions—one rarely gives up one way of life, no matter how painful or unproductive, without an alternative in hand.) The general plan was clear—she would move to the city and get to know a lot of lesbians. She was tired of this once-every-two-years stuff. But which city? New York seemed the obvious choice. Yet although she tossed in her bed masturbating and fantasizing about Lara, some pyschic survival instinct told her that in the long run being around Lara would mess her up. Besides, New York was too big and too far away.

No, Chicago would be much better—and Lu had already offered to show her the scene there. What was the name of the bar she was always talking about—the Volleyball? It sounded like a good place to start.

15 Mucking about Chi Town

*The finished [wo]man of the world must eat of
every apple once.*
                                          —Ralph Waldo Emerson

Metropolis: *(Zoology) A region or area where a
particular kind of organism lives and thrives.*
                                          —American Heritage Dictionary

HAPPINESS, THOUGHT TRETONA, would be sending out
the same Christmas newsletter to everyone. Imagine having a life
and a set of friends so integrated that you didn't have to keep
them all in water-tight compartments. Luckily, her folks had
come up to see how she was getting along when she still had a
room down by Billings Hospital (she was working there as a
research technician). The place she was living now was close to
the corner of Queerborn and Perversion (the street signs said
Dearborn and Division), and it looked like it. The world's
smallest bulldyke lived on the third floor—she stood all of four
feet, ten inches tall in her combat boots and walked around like
Frankenstein. Richard the Falsetto was always chirping about in
the lounge downstairs. The two lesbians across the hall fought
constantly and audibly—mainly it seemed to be about the dog, a
poor ugly mutt that was too fat and spoiled rotten.

The secrecy worked both ways—she always lied about her
work when she was down at the bar. Lu said that if you had a
good job people would try to panhandle you—you could even get
beat up and robbed. As far as the Volleyball crowd was
concerned, she just washed lab equipment all day long. At the

hospital, she said she spent all of her spare time folksinging (that explained why she lived up on the Near North Side). And at the Old Town School of Folk Music (where she was taking banjo lessons)? Well, there she was just a simple farm girl come to the city to make a living, and they didn't really know where she lived. Maybe with some distant southern aunt on the West Side.

She hadn't intended to have anything more to do with chemistry but had made the mistake of going to an employment agency and she'd been pushed into it—the agency got a percentage of her first month's salary and that's the way they could make the most money. So here she was, doing experiments and learning folksongs, just like college. Only the Volleyball part of her life was different.

Already it was hard to remember how scared and green she had been in the beginning. She had driven up with Lu the weekend after her things were shipped Railway Express. They both stayed at Maria's apartment. Evidently, Maria was an old flame of Lu's. They'd barely got there when Lu went off into the bedroom with Maria, leaving Tretona to sip tequila and run the record player. She couldn't help but hear all the moans and little screams. Lu had a red face when she came out. At first Tretona thought it was from embarrassment or maybe exertion, but Lu said it was a whisker burn. Tretona never would have figured that one out if Maria hadn't said something later about needing to wax the hair off her legs—and elsewhere.

Maria was part Mexican and she sure seemed hot-blooded. She'd barely come out of the bedroom with Lu before she started rubbing around on Tretona, messing with the hair on her arms, poking at the hole in her tennies, and counting freckles on her neck. Maria got excited about the prospects of Tretona's debut at the Volleyball—what was she going to wear? Did she have enough money for drinks? Then: "You are butch, aren't you?" Tretona was confused. She found herself speaking unusually slowly and haltingly (being around these Big City people did that to her):

"Well, I'm a tomboy, I guess. And I dress sort of—well, you can see how I dress. But in bed I like it sort of mutual—well, sometimes at least." Tretona was overcome for a minute by an instant recall of Lara's lovemaking. Maria reminded her a little of Lara.

Maria laughed and bubbled and gave Tretona a big hug.

"Don't worry," she said. "You're plenty butch. It's only Big Bad Butches that won't let their femmes touch them in bed. And they're a rotten bunch, anyway—always acting mean and worrying about their machismo. Now my little Tretona Butchona, take some good advice from Mama Maria," and she proceeded to warn Tretona about not being conned into buying drinks ("unless you really like the chica"), about not messing around with the other butches' femmes ("some of the tough ones carry knives"), about not asking people's last names, where they worked or other details which might be used to identify them ("we're all paranoid"), about carrying legal ID for the cops ("we haven't been raided for a long time, but you never know").

Tretona was worried about the police business. "What are they looking for, people drinking under age or what?"

"Well, that and anything they can harass you about. A while back they were booking people on an old transvestite law, which says you have to be wearing at least three articles of clothing of your own sex." Tretona did a quick check—shirt and jeans, no good. Her black crew socks came from the J.C. Penney's work clothes department—that probably counted as men's. (As if women didn't need work clothes.) Bra, okay. These tennis shoes were okay, but her other boating shoes weren't. "Guess I'll have to wear underpants," she said.

"Why," said Maria. "I love creamy blue jeans."

Tretona ignored the remark. "So I'll be wearing three items of feminine attire!" she said.

"Oooh, now I know for sure she's not a big bad butch," said Maria.

It was a gorgeous spring evening when they set off. Tretona felt every one of her senses was especially alert—and vulnerable to stimulation. The three of them rode in the Porsche, Maria sitting on Tretona's lap, her long black hair flagellating Tretona's face. They drove in from the West Side, along the expressway which literally went through the Post Office building, a tight spiral down to Lower Wacker Drive, in and out of concrete columns and traffic, a tunnel under the river and then up onto Rush Street.

They ate at "La Margarita" and there Tretona discovered that Maria wasn't very Mexican—at least, she didn't seem to know much Spanish when the waiter started talking to her. After dinner they went for a walk around the Near North Side. Maria disappeared into a liquor store and came back triumphantly with a small bottle of gin. "I asked for tequila d'oro," she explained, "and when he went to look for it, I snitched this. Sorry I couldn't get bourbon for you, Lu."

"But what if they'd had that kind of tequila?" Tretona asked. "Then you'd have had to buy it."

"Silly. I checked out their supply yesterday," said Maria. "I knew they were out. It's okay. I buy lots of stuff in there—when I have the money."

Tretona was going to ask Maria what she did for a living but decided that was too nosey.

Lu bought some Schweppes lemonade for a mix and they drove out to Lincoln Point. It was beautiful, sitting on the stone chess tables, watching the moon hang over the lake, picking out some of the big landmarks downtown. "Chicago really is a wonderful town," said Lu. "It might not be safe out here a little later on. But the best time is at dawn—you stay at the Volleyball until it closes, go make mad passionate love to some chica (she pulled Maria closer and tweaked her breast), put her to sleep and then drive out here on your way home about five A.M. There's an all-night carry-out place on North Avenue. Sitting out here in the Porsche with a cup of coffee watching the sunrise—man, that's living."

Tretona was curious. "Is it just not done to stay all night? I mean if you pick up somebody?"

Lu shrugged. "Naw, it's okay. Generally they want you to stay. It's just that, well, hell, there's nothing much to talk about in the morning—and unless they shower, I really don't feel like—"

"Ooh, our little Lulu is so fussy," teased Maria. "But come on, it's time for the Volleyball to meet Tretona Butchona!" So it was back into the car and north a little ways on Clark Street—Lu drove past it and parked. It was only when they walked back and were practically there that Tretona saw the small neon sign. Darkened windows, dark inside, not many people in the front, the first person to come into focus was the bartender—a tall muscular mulatto in white shirt and a dark blue pinstriped vest, who nodded at Lu.

"That's Jackie," whispered Maria. Clumps of women around the bar, lots of denim work shirts topped by long cardigans, even though it was hot in there.

"No one's dancing yet, I knew we were too early," said

Maria. They sat down at the side, Lu went for drinks, and Tretona tried to decide whether she could turn around and look without being rude.

"Why is there a man tending bar?" she asked.

Maria was delighted. "Jackie? Look again, honey."

So Tretona snuck a glance around.

"Jackie's all woman, believe me. But she does pass very well. During the day she's an elevator boy! Wait'll you hear her voice. It's beautiful. Real deep and creamy like it's bubbling up through butterscotch."

Lu dropped off the drinks and went over to play the juke box. Pretty soon several people got up to dance—it was the most overtly sexual dancing Tretona had ever seen ("Of course, I've only been to school dances," she kept reminding herself). Hands cupped under butts and noses in ears—one couple in the corner seemed to be soul kissing. Lu and Maria were doing all right too—some kind of little jitterbug step where Maria straddled Lu's knee and then they switched around the other way all in time to the music.

Tretona finished her drink too quickly and fidgeted around with the ice, trying to decide whether she dared walk over to get a refill. Everyone looked normal and friendly enough, except for a couple of women in motorcycle outfits—Tretona thought one of them had a tattoo on her arm. She reckoned she was stronger than any of the rest of them, though—well, maybe not Jackie—but of course they might have weapons. Geez, why was she thinking about stuff like that? No one was near picking a fight.

"Whacha drinkin', honey?" She was being addressed by a boozy-woozy bleached blonde.

"Gin and tonic," answered Tretona—and then not wanting to be in anyone's debt, "I'm just going for another one. Can I get you something?" God, here I am already buying a lush a drink, she thought. Well, at least she'd get to hear Jackie's sexy voice, but Jackie elicited the order by raising one eyebrow and Tretona paid with a five because she was too shy to ask how much.

It was a bore talking to the platinum blonde, who had evidently never heard the rules about not asking where people were from and what they did and how old they were and does your mother know. After a while, Tretona started lying or evading the questions by saying things like, "Well, it's kind of hard to say," or, "I don't know, really," but the blonde got annoyed at that. Finally, Maria came over and dragged her off to the dance floor.

"Thanks for rescuing me," said Tretona, "but I don't dance. Can we go sit at the bar?"

"Nope, I asked you to dance and you said yes. Come on, it's easy. Just follow everything I do—and don't move anything unless I tell you to." Then Maria poured herself onto Tretona's body, every possible square inch of contact was made—cheeks, breasts, bellies, inner thighs. They just stood there molten together for an interminable period of time, Maria breathing "Hush" when Tretona tried to shift her weight. Then Maria started to move her pelvis—back and forth and a little grind. It was very subtle—maybe no one could see. Tretona bent her knee a little—it improved contact—and when their crotches and thighs were really working well together, Maria locked her arms around Tretona's neck and threw her head back and started writhing wildly with her upper torso. Sometimes their breasts touched, sometimes Tretona's face was lost in a hair storm, sometimes she had to fight to keep Maria from doing a back bend clear to the floor. But what never varied was the base—the legs and hips and thighs, solid together as if they were one, but oh, so obviously not solid as they rubbed and nudged and slid against each other.

The record stopped, and through some impossible feat of will Tretona stopped too and she reached for Maria's hand. Where would they go? The park? Maybe Maria would know a place nearby. But to her surprise, Maria just gave her a little squeeze and said, "Nice, thanks," and went over to talk to someone at another table.

Tretona staggered off to the bathroom. Her crotch was so tense she could hardly walk and her blue jeans were a mess. Inside the john there wasn't any T.P. She finally took off her socks and used one to mop the come off her legs. She waited until no one else was in the john and then snuck out, rinsed the sock in cold water and used it to cool herself off ("Just like my mama taught me to," she thought). She sat in the stall reading graffiti (just like any truckstop, except this was about women lovers—one said "L. is a good cunt kisser"). She wondered if "L" was Lu.

Tretona decided that she'd better take it easy. "You aren't used to all this stimulation. If you don't get a hold of yourself, you'll end up either raping someone or moaning and masturbating all over the john floor." Yep, she'd better watch it or she'd burn out her brain for sure.

She needn't have worried—never again did she get turned on like that at the Volleyball. Oh, she scored all right—the first girl she took home was a skinny little thing who turned out to be on drugs. Just when Tretona thought things were warming up she sat up and took a break to sniff something. It took her a long time to come and Tretona wasn't sure in the end whether it was her or the dope the girl was responding to.

She liked flirting with Maria and eventually they made out, but by then Tretona knew that Maria worked as a hooker and she couldn't help thinking about that, wondering if Maria was faking with her like she did with the men who paid for it.

When Lu moved back to Chicago in the summer, the two of them even made out once. That was strange—they were sitting around Maria's place one afternoon waiting for her to get off work (she waited on tables upstairs at Marshall Fields) and started messing around. Tretona was surprised at how round and soft Lu's body was. At first, it was confusing, both of them being butch really. Finally, Tretona ended up on top, partly because she was bigger, but she was still hesitant to actually touch her until Lu breathed, "If you're going to, now's the time."

So she did and Lu became amazingly femme, melting under her and making funny little cries. When she finished, though, Lu popped up on one elbow right away, tough as ever. "You're good, Getroek," she said in her normal deep voice and Tretona was really pleased by that. Pretty soon Maria came home, but neither one of them told her. Tretona wondered a little why they didn't.

Tretona met one girl at the Volleyball whom she thought she might like. Her name was Natasha, but she said she liked to be called Nat. (Tretona wondered why she didn't just introduce herself that way if that's what she really wanted.) Just to tease, Tretona always called her Nat Tasha. She was full of contradictions—she wore elaborate embroidered tops (ethnic stuff) and had beautiful long hair, looking as femme as you please, but then wore real mean black motorcycle boots. What she drove, though, was a Vespa scooter. She wore eye make-up, carefully done, too, but always had black greasy fingernails (presumably from the scooter).

Tretona chased Nat Tasha for quite a while and even talked

her into staying all night once, but to Tretona's great disappointment Nat brought a sleeping bag and slept on the floor, saying she wasn't interested in intimacy with anyone. Tretona offered to be just friends, but that didn't work out, either.

Then there was Bobbie Rosen (she was half Jewish) who was always hanging around at the Volley, hoping Tretona would take her home. She was short and insecure to boot. Tretona seemed to attract the little mousey types easy enough. What she couldn't find was someone who was—well, more or less her own size and shape, especially emotionally and intellectually, though she was starting to think physical parity was important, too. That was one reason she liked Natasha so much.

But Tretona could never say no, especially when she was feeling horny (which was pretty much all the time, though it seemed to be tapering off a bit), so one night when Bobbie Rosen announced in a meaningful tone that she was going to be home alone all weekend, Tretona finally propositioned her, partly because she wanted to see Bobbie's folks' fancy Edgeware Road apartment.

It was swanky—nineteenth floor, lakeside picture windows, nice big plants, and paintings which were not only expensive but pretty good. Bobbie provided champagne and didn't seem quite so much of a nerd, so Tretona managed to whomp up a real romantic, sustained seduction, making good use of the big white sofa and thick carpets.

Tretona wasn't really sexually involved so she amused herself by trying to make the composition of their bodies against the furnishings as photogenic as possible. She had spread Bobbie's long black hair over her left arm, positioned her own head carefully sideways so that her lips and tongue just touched Bobbie's left nipple and as the imaginary camera panned slowly down, capturing the rise and fall of their rosy bodies against the maroon Oriental carpet, Tretona slowly and gracefully parted Bobbie's legs, keeping her elbow down (no sharp body angles in this shot). She paused at the threshhold, gently asking permission with her finger, seconding the motion upstage with her tongue (though that would be off camera, unless they went to a wide angle lens), listening to Bobbie's breathing, which was rapidly getting faster and harsh, so Tretona accelerated and intensified her probing and soon Bobbie's hips were pumping and heaving (back up camera or the viewer will get seasick) and now was the time for powerful body movements and to be a little rough—there, there she liked that—hold her there hard, high, her breath rasping now, panting like a marathoner—now here it is—her body tense, quivering, hold her, hold her, now a little nudge over the top—and then Tretona was kissing her face and loving her, forgetting about the camera, for she really did love her, loved anyone at that moment. Bobbie's chest continued to heave—she was fighting for breath. "Hey, kid, you must not be in very good condition," said Tretona. But Bobbie just shook her head, struggled to her feet, and rushed into the bedroom.

After a moment Tretona followed and found Bobbie sucking oxygen from a respirator. "I've got asthma," Bobbie finally managed to gasp. "I'm not supposed to get excited." After pills and medicinal spray and much soothing, the attack finally subsided and a very exhausted Bobbie fell asleep. Tretona stood at the window looking down at the three A.M. traffic—sporadic now, but still enough to outline the lake with twinkling lights. What is it about heights, and expanses of water, and celestial bodies near the horizon that puts one in a philosophical mood? Tretona had once decided that such moments were sheer romantic sentimentalism, but after reading that even Bertrand Russell had feelings of "transcendance" on such occasions, she took them more seriously.

Here she was literally above the city and it made her realize how much her existence had changed, how citified she had become. What did her life consist of but prospecting at the Volley (where even the sex wasn't that great), where all the conversations were about the Mafia, who was on belladonna, and the opportunities for lesbian prostitutes? No more long intellectual arguments with Emil, no more jolly spreads in the dorm with Maureen and Sonya and Lu, no more volleyball—her serve was probably rusty as hell—no more exercise, for that matter. But now I am free to be myself, she thought. At least I have sexual freedom. Before, that whole side of me had to hibernate.

It was soon after that that Red wrote he was coming to Chicago for a weekend. Jonathan Moore was flying in for some chaplain's convention and Red was taking the train up. Could Tretona meet him at the Palmer House for Friday lunch? Jonathan would not arrive until three o'clock.

Tretona had almost forgotten what it was like to have feelings of excitement and anticipation that weren't tied up with sex. God, how decadent I've become, she thought, pouring over "What's on in Chicago," boning up on plays and exhibitions and all the things you were supposed to be doing in a big city. It was late August—almost time for school to start. She really must get hold of herself and start going to some cultural things. Once she and Natasha had planned to go to the Art Institute, but they'd ended up at a beach instead.

Red looked younger and thinner. He'd stopped putting stuff on his hair, so it was real soft and fluffy—almost looked like a page boy. And he was wearing a slinky shirt which clung to his torso—the color was nice, too, a pastel paisley print. He gave Tretona a hug—it seemed odd to be embracing someone who was taller and more muscular than herself. Five minutes of delighted grinning at each other and inane conversation about weather, trains and the furniture in the hotel lounge—and then it was okay, both asking questions at once and jabbering on with the intensity of music boxes whose springs were wound too tight. Red was fed up with poly sci and was going to enter law school. "But you still want to be a politician, though?" Tretona asked.

"Probably, but first I want a real profession. I want to really know something. I'm tired of bullshit courses. Give me some facts, man. What about you? Do you like your research job at the hospital? Are you doing relevant stuff now? Big cancer cure on the way?"

But Tretona veered away from talk of her job (which was boring as hell) and talked instead about how liberating it was to be in the city. "Gee, Red, you can't imagine what different sorts of people you meet up here." But when he pressed for examples, she found herself censoring and distorting—mainly changing pronouns. When she told about Arlene (one of the doggy lesbians across the hall) who hit Beth's mistress on the head with a skillet, "Beth" became "Brad" along the way.

Red was restless, looking at his watch. Tretona quickly picked up her end of the conversation. "So you're here to meet Jonathan," she said. "Isn't he the big rival? I always thought Janet was your old flame." Red's eyes froze for a second—then he suddenly bent toward her: "No, Tretona, Jonathan's the one I—" then slowly and carefully, like he was reading it from a prompting card. "Jonathan and I are lovers. We met through Janet—and Janet knows. Jonathan talked to her about it before they got married and she agreed—you know, to help cover for him in the

Air Force." He stopped and stared while Tretona's mind, which had flown away from her heart and body, watched with him, incredulous, as she gasped and bit her thumbnail and groaned, "Oh no, Red, not you," and then she tried to take it back. "I didn't mean that, forgive me, I was just surprised, that's all," and began to cry, but her eyes stayed dry—only bitter squeaks came out.

Somehow, the drinks were paid for and chitchat invented until it wasn't too long before Jonathan would be there and they could decently say "good-bye" and "must keep in touch if you're ever in Chicago or back at school."

Tretona ghost-walked up Michigan Avenue—nothing was left—she was hollow—not even her turtle shell remained. By the time she reached the river the shock was wearing off and pain and self-recriminations started welling up. Why did I do that? Oh, poor Red. It should have been happy news. Why did I say that? And then the brain flew back to its dovescote and briskly began scratching through the rubble. You identify with Red, you always have. And you really aren't too happy with your own situation here, are you? Let's face it, being gay in Chicago isn't quite what you were hoping for. And so naturally you're apprehensive when you learn that Red may also be in for some bad disappointments. And maybe you're a little jealous. Maybe you had a tiny dream stowed away someplace that you and Red would someday fly away on a platonic honeymoon (maybe a weekend together with Bertrand Russell) and now that's gone. Of course, there's the surprise factor—plus deception. All those protestations of celibacy on the way to work out at the gym. He was implicitly lying to you all the way along—just like you lied to him, of course. Because you didn't dare tell him, either.

Satisfied momentarily, the brain stopped pecking and a great groaning troll clambered up over the railing. Brown ugly water—hard to believe it was green on St. Patrick's Day. Must take gallons of dye to change it. What will wash away my sin? Nothing but the blood of. Nothing but blood. Blood, nothing but. Nothing. Nothing, no thing.

"And what do strawberry blondes think of our fine summer weather?" said a young man wearing glasses, his own hair a bit sandy colored. Down, Caliban, fly away, dove. Tretona mother-hubbarded her thoughts back into the proper closets.

"Excuse me. What did you say?"

"I'm a roving reporter," explained the young man, "and I'm doing a story on the nice weather. It's been unusually cool for so late in the summer, you know. Not a very thrilling topic really, but that's what they want. So can I ask you? What are you doing here on Michigan Avenue on a fine Friday afternoon?"

"You can say that I just quit my job," said Tretona. "And I'm looking at the Chicago River trying to decide what to do next."

Tretona did quit her job—well, she didn't explicitly quit— she just didn't go back on Monday, or on Tuesday, and snuck in Wednesday noon to get her slide rule and things. People at the boarding house wrote down lots of phone messages from work, but she ignored them.

She got a job singing folk songs at a coffeehouse on Wednesday and Thursday nights. Ten bucks a time plus snacks and sometimes a bag full of stale danishes. Black sweater, stool, spotlight—it was fun except she didn't like it much when people talked while she was performing. Maybe the trouble was that all her songs were too serious—she wondered how Piaf and Grecco managed. Did people buzz away when they were singing? Surely, no one would dare.

She finally talked to Lu about how to meet other kinds of lesbians. "You hankering after a classy lady, eh?" teased Lu.

"No, I don't care so much about class," Tretona said. "It's just that the people at the Volley are all such derelicts." She saw from Lu's face that that was the wrong word. "What I mean is, they're kind of happy-go-lucky." (Actually, that wasn't at all what she meant—more like sad and desperate.) "I mean that they aren't very serious."

"Look, honey," Lu was in her sophisticated-but-tough mood. "The stable couple types are not going to show up at the Volley. Why should they? They've got their own set and go to a lot of private parties."

"Well, aren't there any nice single people around?" Tretona asked.

"Hell, honey, it takes time. You've only been here—how long—six months? What do you expect, the love of your life deposited on your doorstep C.O.D.?" Then Lu dropped her defensive tone. "Seriously, Tretona, I wish I knew where to find what you're looking for. Believe me, if I did know, you wouldn't catch me at the Volley two or three times a week."

After that Lu and Tretona tried another bar. The Port Hole (or "P-Hole" as the regulars called it) was in a pretty rough part of town near Halstead Avenue. The clientele was a mixture of drunken Irishmen—they were locals, mostly—and WAFs. The Air Force had about a hundred women in some sort of special security division stationed near the city. They couldn't stay too late—morning roll call came early—and they had to drive back to some place out in the suburbs, but they sure lived it up while they were in town, cheering and sassing the strippers and swooning over Janine who played saxophone, had her own band and sang torchy songs like "Are you satisfied?"

The local men either didn't cotton on to the fact that the Maidens in Uniform were queer—or they were too drunk to care. Well, not all of them were queer—just 80 percent, or so Jo reckoned. Jo was an ex-cab driver, now an MP, and had the best uniform—black boots and white spats, night stick, whistle. She tried to talk Tretona and Lu into joining the Air Force. "Practically everyone is gay—it's just one big gay community—well, we have a lot of fights, but you know, that always happens." Jo had an old knife wound across her ribs, which she showed to Tretona in the washroom. Tretona admired the scar and touched it very lightly with her finger. Jo had a beautiful tan all over—no strap marks—even her breasts were Polynesian, except they didn't droop like native women's did. It was hard to concentrate on the story behind the scar, Jo there, pants tucked in boots, belt riding on her hips—she was tanned down as far as Tretona could see. Her shirt was still tucked in but hanging down over her rump. Now she struggled back into it, buttoning up the eagles. "They don't make you wear a bra?" Tretona asked as casually as she could manage.

"Hey, the CO may be a dyke, but inspections aren't that thorough," Jo laughed. "The pockets cover me up okay."

A refrain from one of Robert's calypso records circled around in Tretona's mind: "Woman policeman, hold me tight, hold me tight, tight, tight."

One night after a good session at the P-hole Tretona felt out Lu about joining the Army. "They're a pretty good bunch of women, I think. At least they're functioning—you know, getting up in the morning, eating right, doing their job. That's more than you can say for most people at the Volley." As Lu turned from the wheel and looked straight at her, Tretona suddenly realized that she had just described herself. Now that she wasn't working regularly she was sleeping more and more, later and later. Just last week she had run into trouble getting her new songs memorized and had ended up cutting her second set short. But it turned out that wasn't what Lu's glance meant at all.

"Are you nuts?" she asked. "You wouldn't last two weeks with all that military Mickey Mouse. I know you. Everytime someone lays a rule down, you've got to up and break it. You're religious about it. There aren't any wishy-washy dean types in the Army. They'd as soon throw you in the stockade as look at you."

"But at least there'd be a real community of lesbians," said Tretona. "Whole barracks full. Just think, for once we'd be the majority! Wouldn't that be neat?"

"Well, I expect Jo is exaggerating about the numbers," Lu said. "Anyway, the percentages don't matter. The main thing is, we live in a straight society, and the armed forces are the straightest of all. Jo says her CO is a dyke. That may be so, but let Jo hold hands on base or do something publicly lesbian and just watch that officer slap a dishonorable discharge on her. Individuals can't do anything—not as long as the institutions are fucked up."

Lu was right, of course. Sappho's island wasn't camouflaged as an Army base. As they bounced along Halstead Tretona's thoughts turned sleepily to Jo—Jo driving a jeep, naked except for her hat and boots, flying over a sandy beach, Tretona beside her navigating. "Now turn 23 degrees east, go that way 500 yards, now a sharp right, maybe it's behind that sand dune—yes, there they are!" A panorama of sea, clouds, sky, sand, and Army tents on the beach, and in front of the tents Turkish carpets, harem cushions, waist-high piles of grapes, goatskins of wine cradled on carved wooden stands—and women, beautiful women all sizes and shapes. What did the Sunday school song say? "Red and yellow, black and white—all are precious in her sight . . ." Jo skidding to a halt—everyone excited to see her. She waved regally and then turned to her navigator.

Tretona snapped out of the fantasy—what the hell did that mean? Was that her dream, a sexual monarchy with Tretona cast as helpmate and consort? Geez, it was enough to make you believe in Jungian archetypes. The content was way out—lesbians and all that—but the forms were just the same: domination, master-slave, bosses. No, what you had to do was change both at

168

once. But it was hard—thinking on the level of a whole society. If only she could meet some lesbians who had these things figured out—people who could inspire her, not drag her down.

The light changed and Lu turned north on Chicago Avenue. "That second stripper—the little one—she was okay, wasn't she?" Lu frankly and openly enjoyed watching them dance around. She didn't drool like the men did, but she appraised their bodies and speculated about what they'd be like in bed. She wasn't vicious—Tretona thought maybe that for Lu it was like going to a dog show or a gymkhana; there were objective standards for what counted as a good piece of woman flesh and it was fun judging the exhibitors.

Suddenly, Tretona really laid into Lu. "Yeah, well I thought it was obscene—the way she kept putting things up her twat."

"Hell, that's just one of the things they do for comic relief. Didn't you see the look on that old guy's face when she started talking to him about liking to smoke? How he took the pipe out of his mouth quick as a wink and stuck it in his back pocket? I thought sure he was going to burn his bum or. . . ."

"Well, I'll tell you one thing, it made me sick when you loaned her your chewing gum."

"For goodness' sake, Tretona, I didn't actually chew it after she did her little number with it," Lu said. "I just took it back to be funny, to help out the act."

"That's just the point. Where in the hell do you get off helping out? What are we doing? We all sit there cheering, encouraging some poor woman to make a living by degrading herself like some geek in front of a bunch of drunken workmen and soldiers. Yes, soldiers—that's what they are—I don't care if they are women or lesbians or whatever. They—we—I—all of us were just acting like a bunch of rowdy soldiers."

"Hey kid," Lu said quietly and calmly. "Take it easy. You're not Jesus Christ, you know. Don't try to bear the sins of the whole goddamn world."

"Well, at least I try to bear my own sins." Tretona was sniffling. "At least I don't drive around in a Porsche and silk shirts saying, 'I'm all right Jack, the rest of the world can fuck off.'" Tretona began to bawl and bang her head against the dash. What had she done? First Red, now Lu.

But Lu was calm and friendly. She parked in front of Tretona's house and pulled Tretona over on her shoulder. "Hey kid," she said again. "I know I'm lucky. I've got money—or my family has—I've got a job I like and I know it's mainly just luck and I thank my stars that I'm as happy as I am. But do you know what I'm really thankful for? This may sound conceited, but I'm really thankful I'm not a WASP, that no one laid that big guilt thing on me. You've got to start taking care of good ole number one, Tretona, and stop shedding tears over things that you aren't responsible for, that you can't change—things that probably aren't even any of your business."

"Hell, you make me sound like some would-be saint," sobbed Tretona. "Believe me, I'm as selfish as they come. I'd be very glad to take care of number one if I could. I just don't know how. I don't know what I want. I don't even have a good theory about what might make me happy, let alone any idea of how to get it."

Lu shut up after that outburst and just held and patted her. Tretona noticed that Lu had carefully pulled up the collar of her windbreaker so that her fancy shirt didn't get tear-stained. "Sorry about the salt water shower," Tretona said stiffly and went in to bed.

She woke up early the next morning (well, earlier than usual) and decided to treat herself to lunch at the Bon Ton down the street. The place was run by tough middle-aged women who were Polish or Armenian or something ethnic. Tretona hadn't been there since she'd stopped working (no money) and sleeping so late she generally ended up snacking at odd hours anyway. The waitress recognized her reappearance with a sort of half-friendly grunt. Tretona ordered soup and a piroshky and started drawing a flow chart on her napkin. She put boxes labelled "where I am now" and "where I'd like to be" on opposite sides, leaving lots of space in between for methods of bridging the gap. It was easy enough filling in the "now" box on the left side: broke, blue, lonesome (she scratched that out and wrote "loveless" instead), not getting anywhere (that got corrected to "going downhill"). Luckily, the food came before it got really depressing and the waitress had even brought along her customary side order of sour cream. Tretona hadn't ordered it this time to save money, but she was glad to see it. Between bites she worked on the "like to be" box, but the only thing she came up with was "happy." She thought about writing down "rich" or "quite a bit of money," but she decided that wasn't really essential. As she'd said to Lu, she really didn't know what she wanted.

"Dessert?" barked the waitress. It seemed to be a command rather than an inquiry. Tretona did a mental money count—she could just make it. "What do you have?" she asked to gain time to think. "It's easier to say what we don't have," snapped the waitress. "We don't have apple turnovers and we don't have the mince meat tarts." Tretona ordered cheesecake and smiled at the waitress' gruff manner—"What a way to sell something," she thought. But as she turned back to her homework, it struck her that there was something to be said for taking a negative approach. Right now she could sure say she *didn't* like being broke. And although she hadn't really been satisfied at the university, still she definitely *didn't* like being around non-intellectuals all the time. And she *didn't* like labwork, and she *didn't* like being out of work. And she *didn't* like sex without romance. "Maybe I've been going about this the wrong way," she thought. "Instead of worrying so much about exactly what I want to be, what a perfect life would be like, finding a perfect person to fall in love with, maybe I should just concentrate on avoiding situations I know good and well are going to get me down."

Tretona paid the check, went back to the house to get dressed up, saw the landlady on the stairs and borrowed an alarm clock (hers had mysteriously disappeared; either a visitor had swiped it or some dark Freudian force had been at work), phoned the Old Town School to see if she had any banjo lessons still coming (she'd paid for a bunch but stopped going) and took the bus downtown to the employment agency.

Her little burst of positive energy ran aground there—they were really pissed about the way she had quit the job at Billings. The woman toyed with the little buttons of her left cuff ("She could be one of us," Tretona thought) and said, "I'm sorry, Miss Getroek, but with this work record it's impossible for me to recommend you to any of our clients." Tretona's heart sank.

"Couldn't I try for something not quite so—well, you know—like a waitress job or something?" It seemed like it was the crisp blue suit which gave the negative answer, " . . . overqualified . . . guarantee our clients reliable employees. . . ." Tretona gathered herself together and prepared to snake-belly out the door. "I've got to do something—and right away," she mumbled, "but I understand you can't do anything. Sorry I blew it. Well, bye." The woman nodded and then coughed.

"It's not really professionally correct for me to do this, I suppose. But of course there's nothing to prevent you from going to another agency, one that doesn't have your work record."

"You mean just lie about having worked at Billings?" asked Tretona. As soon as she said it, she realized how naive she was. She covered quickly, "I mean, try to get a fresh start?" For some reason the woman in blue was smiling—even with her eyes. "Tretona," she said. (It was odd that she knew her first name. Of course, people in business were trained to do things like that.) "Why don't you look for a job teaching chemistry? The employment office at your university could probably help you there."
"Yeah, sounds just like what my mom would say," Tretona thought. Still and all, it wasn't a bad idea.

16 Marking Time in Middle America

*[The bourgeois] prefers comfort to pleasure, con-
venience to liberty, and a pleasant temperature to
that deathly inner consuming fire.*
—*Hermann Hesse*

*The unsettled questions are hibernating, probably
to bud and burgeon again at some future season.*
—*Mark Hopkins*

IT HAD BEEN almost too easy—but then everything at Lake
View College happened effortlessly. A call to President Steiner, a
leisurely stroll around campus on the Saturday after Thanksgiving, a pleasant interview in his office with Dr. Kripke, head of the
science division, and—hot damn—she was hired! There was a
tense moment when they asked her if she planned to finish her
Ph.D. She took a deep breath and said, "No." That turned out to
be the right answer. "We want dedicated teachers," beamed
President Steiner. Later, Tretona asked him if one had to be a
Christian to work at Lake View because if so that would pose a
problem and it was his turn to hesitate. "No, not if one shares the
basic principles of Christian ethics," he said, casting a quick look
at Dr. Kripke, who obviously had strong views on this subject. "It
would be more important if you were teaching one of the
humanities," said Kripke. The Reverend Steiner relaxed, and
then said smoothly, "I might remark that Miss Getroek took note
of the Niebuhr portrait in the library, so I gather that she has
some knowledge of theology."

"Knowledge, yes," said Tretona, and that was the end of
that.

The former chemistry teacher, Mr. Thoren, had quietly dropped dead ten days before, so she could start anytime it was convenient—no need to rush, though, Dr. Kripke had the classes well in hand. He had retired early from industry because he felt a debt to his alma mater. "I've been telling them about chemical marketing techniques and they're quite fascinated."

A room within walking distance was located, the college station wagon was made available for moving her stuff from the city, perhaps she would like a salary advance (Tretona had made up a hard luck story about no suitable work being available after the unit at Billings had disbanded). There was one other young woman on the faculty—perhaps Mrs. Steiner could arrange to have them both to tea. And so she was quickly and effortlessly immersed in the cozy Lake View College community.

The students were openly happy to see her. Mr. Thoren had taught from his own ancient mimeographed notes, which contained scientific heresies, such as the claim that the nucleus contained only protons and electrons (neutrons being hypothetical constructs). Tretona promised lectures on radioactivity, put in a rush order for new books, and they were puppy-dog pleased. What a change from the premeds at the university who were never grateful for anything.

The faculty gave her a gracious welcome, too. Tretona was a little hesitant about walking into the lounge the first day, but they all seemed perfectly charming, somewhat reminiscent of her Grandad Getroek and his buddies down at Zahn's Corner. Rudolph Halfner, chairman of Philosophy and Religion, spotted her standing near the mailboxes, introduced himself, and took her by the elbow to meet the others: Fritjof Kubler—History; Karl Spangler—English; the coach—Heinz Nozick (jokes about the football team); and Herr Wahlpuhl, the German professor who was busy opening a package of galley proofs. "You see, Herr Wahlpuhl publishes," said her escort proudly.

"Ant in Inklish, Doktor Halfner," said Wahlpuhl with enthusiasm. Halfner moved her along toward the coffee urn and modulated his voice into a between-you-and-me mode: "It's a textbook, you know." (The word *only* hung in the air between them, waiting to be inserted.) "President Steiner is very proud." Some Byzantine instinct warned Tretona to be noncommital.

"How nice to see things you've been working on in print,"

she said. Halfner looked at her questioningly, she smiled, and he relaxed.

"How nice to find a young person who appreciates the art of pedagogy. I say *art,* not science, deliberately. I have no truck whatsoever with these modern educationists who would analyze and systematize and regularize the mysterious bond between teacher and student. The essence of good teaching is sensitivity—and an instinctive reaction to the needs and wants of the students. The textbook of a born teacher like Herr Wahlpuhl is ten times, a hundredfold, more valuable than these so-called scientific learning programs which treat students like rats instead of the ineffable human ensembles of thought and feeling which they are."

Tretona made a move to take the coffee he had presumably meant to offer her.

"Ah, yes, I am carried away and forget. But it is so delightful to meet a young person, a young lady, who has not been infected with modernism. These modernists want to automate teaching so as to leave themselves more time for their blessed research. Now let me be perfectly clear, I am not against research. What intellectual is not attracted by the charms of pushing into the unknown, delving into nature's little secrets! No, no. I would *love* to do research—and I am constantly thinking, planning for my *magnum opus*—but now I am a teacher and my duties are to those students who pass four short years at Lake View College. You will meet people here who do not share my views or my dedication. They are mostly the younger faculty, I am sorry to say—youth is always vulnerable to modernism—but I think you will observe" [again, his voice became conspiratorial] "that the more they carry on about research and how it is possible to do both, the more they carry on, the less effective they are as teachers. It is an inverse—what do you scientists say?—like a seesaw—when one goes up, the other goes down. Inevitably."

Tretona started to tell a story about Linus Pauling and his teaching reputation, but Doctor Halfner did not wait to hear the moral (which was a complicated one). "I must go now. My students are waiting." He lifted his left index finger and wagged it from side to side. "Beware of modernism," he said. "Avoid trends," and with a little bow he was gone.

A tall middle-aged man in a sports coat joined her. "Beware of Halfner," he said. "He's a terrible gossip. Anything you say to him is immediately distorted or exaggerated to produce the worst possible effect and then spread all over campus. Permit me—I'm Jack Hunt, Biology."

"Oh yes, Dr. Kripke mentioned you," Tretona said.

"He did? I'm surprised. Sometimes I think he'd like to forget I exist. Did he tell you I was an infidel?"

"No," said Tretona, amused. "Do you stand up on the chapel steps and ask God to strike you dead in order to prove that he exists?"

"No, I dissect frogs and show them that there is no soul to be found. No, seriously—all I do is point out inconsistencies. These kids here are so placid that if you'd let them they'd just keep their fundamentalist religion in one pocket and their biology in another, completely separate. Well, I won't let them do that. When I teach the theory of evolution, I just say it, flat out: 'This theory is inconsistent with the story in *Genesis*. You cannot believe both at once.' I don't tell them which to believe, I just say they've got to make a choice and Kripke hates that. He was going to make a formal complaint about my discussing religion in a biology course, but Halfner talked him out of it. He saw the repercussions immediately. You see they want to mix religion into the history courses and political science and all that kind of stuff because their people are doing those subjects."

"Gee, I wonder why Kripke didn't veto me," Tretona said, and told about her specific disclaimer of religion at the interview.

"Well, you never can tell about Kripke," said Hunt, "Maybe he thought you were just a young woman he could intimidate. Hey, it's okay. You don't seem that way to me, but that might be the way he'd think. You know the girls here are really passive and apathetic. All of our students are, of course, but the girls are the worst—as a group—there are a few exceptions. Not that it's their fault—it probably starts with the family background—and by now it's too late, they're just cut out to be pious little mothers."

Tretona felt her face getting red and she was on the verge of sputtering something inane about the whole point of education being to widen perspectives, to encourage people to develop their potential. Jack Hunt droned on, steamrolling any attempt at a reply. "And that's what I mainly try to prepare them for—being good wives and mothers. Of course, some can be nurses."

"Jack Hunt, are you at it again?" The voice was deep and smooth and firm. "As Halfner would say: 'Beware of defeatism!'

Now, if you'll excuse us," and the tall woman in a smart tweed suit, beige sweater, and pearls escorted Tretona out of the faculty lounge.

"You must be—President Steiner mentioned you."

"Diane Sorensen. Call me Di." The woman smiled and offered her hand. Tretona was so pleased to be rescued that without thinking she gave it a good old Methodist handshake. (Brother Jode used to say that you could tell the quality of a person's religion by the way he or she shook hands. As a result, everyone in Cheaney developed a very vigorous handshake.)

"Gee, I'm glad to meet you," said Tretona. "Everyone in there was trying to be nice but almost right away Halfner started a sermon about teaching and the perils of research. I thought Jack Hunt was going to be okay, but then he started this whole business about female stereotypes, which was even worse."

Di laughed. "Well, it sure didn't take you long to get their numbers." She sighed, "Frankly, I've given up for the most part. For each of my esteemed colleagues I have a little checklist of topics to avoid. With Halfner, the list of No-Nos got so long it's become easier to remember what the safe subjects are: food (he fancies himself a bit of a gourmet), music in prewar Austria, and gardening. With Wahlpuhl it's travel and photography, period. If you stay off gender differences, Jack Hunt isn't so bad."

"Yeah, he was doing okay on religion versus evolution and that sort of thing," said Tretona.

"Well, within limits," said Di. "You know he's Catholic—went to Notre Dame—the whole bit."

"But that needn't mean he's religious now," said Tretona.

"Well, all I can say is that he's secretary of the Faculty Council. (They wanted Miss Sorensen to take that job, of course—I told them that *Dr.* Sorensen was too busy to oblige.) Anyway, he's the secretary and every meeting before he takes minutes he puts 'J.M.J.' at the top of the page."

"Really?" said Tretona. "Jesus!"

"And Mary and Joseph," said Di. "But forget about them. Let's go have lunch." In the next two hours Tretona learned that Di had been to Europe several times, that she drove a Saab sedan, which was free-wheeling and had front-wheel drive, that she liked martinis even before lunch, that there was a group of Young Turks on the faculty who were conspiring to turn Lake View College into a true liberal arts college. "There're really only four of us," said Di. "But we started attending faculty meetings regularly and we'd pick up allies, according to what the issue was, and we really started getting some good motions passed until the Old Guard caught on and started staying awake."

"What sort of motions?" Tretona asked.

"Oh, everything from abolishing mandatory attendance at chapel to not letting geography count as fulfilling the Lab Science requirement," said Di. So that was what she would be thinking about here at Lake View, thought Tretona, geography requirements and chapel attendance. Big deal. For a moment she wished she were back on the Near North Side. The guy they all called Belladonna would just be getting up, putting on make-up, starting to wander around the coffeeshops looking for handouts so he could buy drugs. If you gave him a quarter he was your friend for life. Jackie would be sweeping out the Volleyball—actually, someone else would—that's right, Jackie would be playing elevator boy. Maria would be finishing serving lunch—maybe she would have set up a trick for later. Those were real people—and the problems they faced were real ones. Why wasn't she there with them, helping? But she hadn't helped—not really. All she had done was to get dragged down herself. Here at least she was making money—good money, too, well, good compared to before. The important thing was to keep on her toes, to keep learning and figuring things out.

She looked at Di. "I want to change the subject. You're in social psych, right? Well, can you explain to me why some minority groups or subcultures make it big and others get defeated or assimilated? Take the Jews—they aren't very well liked but they do okay—get into *Who's Who* and all that stuff while the Poles stay down in Cicero and work in the steel mills—and the blacks—they're even worse off. What makes the difference? Is it a case of native intelligence or cultural heritage or what?"

It was obviously a good conversational set-up for Di. She tore off eagerly into a little lecture on aspiration levels, community support systems, congruence of values of the minority group with those of the dominant society, attitudes toward assimilation. . . . It was all interesting and aptly put, but as the chain of explanations unrolled, Tretona's thought turned to the gnawing question that lay underneath her inquiry: Why were homosexuals such losers? Wait, correction—the ones she'd met were. Who knew how many of those *Who's Who* people were queers? No one ever told you that statistic—all you ever heard about was Oscar Wilde and Sappho, along with a bunch of rumors about David and Jonathan, Tony Curtis, and maybe your gym teacher. And it wasn't even true that all homosexuals she knew were losers—Red wasn't. Hell, she wasn't—though it had been close for awhile. And Lu? Well, Lu had a good job and was doing okay, but still the crowd she hung around with wasn't very inspiring. Maybe that was the thing—as long as a homosexual was fully assimilated into straight society, as Red was, as she was now, they were as healthy as the next person. It was only when they got together that things fell apart—maybe it was homosexual society that was spiritually and psychologically debilitating, not individuals. But why was that?

Di was making a new point. "Mind you, the Jews don't always rise to the top. If the anti-Semitic sentiment is strong enough and if it's institutionalized, the Jews get ground down just like everyone else." And she told about Hebrew schools in Central Europe where they had never heard of Copernicus and used Sacrobosco's medieval treatise in astronomy classes clear up into the nineteenth century and about the big lags in their medical knowledge. "It seems a general rule," said Di. "Anytime a group is *forced* to live apart instead of choosing to be separate, their culture deteriorates. Sometimes it's from a lack of information and economic trading possibilities. Sometimes it's from a lack of internal criticism (an attitude that since everyone else hates us we should give each other unqualified support). Sometimes it's just a sheer lack of resources. If all your time and energy has to go into defending yourself, into surviving oppression, there's not going to be much left over for building libraries."

Yeah, something like that went on at the Volleyball, Tretona decided. People came there desperate because they'd spent the whole day pretending to be straight. They had to come because there was no place else to let down their hair and be with people of their own kind. And when they got there, it wasn't really all that great—competition for lovers, paranoia about their presence at a gay bar getting back to their families or teachers or bosses or commanding officers. And since it was a bar, nothing really got started until ten o'clock and they'd stay too late and drink too much and oversleep, and then they'd lose their jobs. And there'd be one more hard-luck story to contribute to the overall depression and paranoia. It was one big vicious spiral downward. Tretona sighed from remembering it all.

"Hey, you're looking like Atlas," said Di. "Like you're bearing the weight of the world on your shoulders."

"Nah, I'm just thinking about all I've got to do to get ready for that lab class tomorrow," said Tretona. "Say, I appreciated your talking to me about minorities. Maybe sometime we could talk about why people hate minorities and anyone who's different."

"Love to," Di said. "It's rather a nice change for me—getting away from Lake View politics."

And they did continue to have good talks, but soon Tretona's whole existence became dominated by the affairs and ambience of a small church-affiliated liberal arts college located a convenient but safe distance from the wicked city. There were lots of activities on campus, like the "Firesides" in which faculty members would discuss books with the students (Tretona chose *The Myth of Sisyphus* and went into a funk for days wondering if her eternal rock was going to be teaching at Lake View College), and frequent informal gatherings of the Young Turks to bitch and complain and plot battle strategy. Tretona called it the Ph.D.–L.L.D. war (pronounced "fud-lud") because the rebels had Ph.Ds and at least paid lip service to doing research. She was the exception, of course, on both counts and maybe that was the reason she remained on fairly good terms with the old-timers, who had L.L.Ds and really were Luddites when it came to educational innovation. However, her effectiveness as a spy was pretty well ruined when she started teaching in slacks.

When the weather got bad and she'd saved up a little money, Tretona bought a car, a beautiful second-hand TR-2, bright red, with a black top and side curtains. It was drafty as hell—even with the heater on full blast her breath frosted the windshield—and it broke loose on icy roads something terrible. She once did a 360 degree turn at the four-way stop out by the Oakbrook shopping center!

It was great in good weather, though. Tretona took the top down at the slightest hint of sunshine—even though it took two people and a horse to get it back up—and drove around in the forest preserves. Muffler flying, leather gloves, the car so low you could reach out at stop signs and strike a match on the pavement.

A community service—that's what she was providing by adding such a splendid flash of color and elegance to the suburbs.

She drove the car in one Sunday afternoon to see Lu. It had been only three months but the distance between their two worlds soon became obvious. Tretona asked about all her old friends. No one had seen Natasha—maybe she had gone back to Tacoma (Tretona could picture her with long hair and apple cheeks scootering around Mount Rainier) or maybe she had finally driven off the pier into the lake as she occasionally threatened to do (Tretona censored that picture). Bobbie was in a mental hospital, rumors of shock treatments (Tretona took down the address but knew damn well she would be too afraid and squeamish to visit). And Maria? Not too bad, but she had a black eye from a trick who wanted to date her—"on the level," he said. Finally, to get rid of him Maria had told him she could only love women, so he'd said, "Goddamn lesbian" and decked her. "So you see, everything's as fucked up and exciting as ever," said Lu. "But tell me about Lake View."

And then Tretona realized how incommensurable the two worlds were. What was she supposed to say, "I finally got up enough nerve to wear slacks to class? One night during final exams some kids moved the president's yellow VW up on the porch of the chapel? Jack Hunt saw Dr. Halfner wink at a senior girl who wants to be a missionary?"

Late in April, a faculty apartment on campus became vacant and Di was next on the waiting list. They moved her harp in the back of the TR. What a splendid sight that was! The red rumble seat looked tailor-made for the elegant golden instrument. If they went faster than ten miles an hour the strings all vibrated hysterically. So it was at a stately pace and with a faint Aeolian whir that they drove through Lake View. That night while leaning against unpacked boxes and eating herring roll-mops on Triscuits Di asked Tretona to be her apartment mate. Tretona said yes, of course, and proceeded to get slightly tipsy on the cold German wine. Well, this completes the domestication of Tretona Getroek, she thought. Here I am snug as can be in a respectable college, sharing housing with the other single woman on the faculty, getting my kicks by shocking middle-aged ex-pastors. And the hell of it was, it was all quite pleasant—satisfying even. Is this what happened to you when you got old and settled? She thought of Lara and Lu and Lorrie and Belinda and Tiia. . . . "Sure, I'll move in, Di. I think we'll get along just great. I ought to warn you though, I don't think you really know me very well."

"What do you mean?"

"Well, some of my friends are kind of different," said Tretona, the masked woman.

*   *   *

There is something paradoxical about the romantico-sex instinct. Once aroused, it drives us on almost inexorably—meals are skipped, work neglected, songs composed, fantasies created and then played and replayed incessantly. Once the love condenser is charged up, everything trembles and blushes until discharge comes, be it through ecstasy or despair. Yet that great unruly sexual-romantic engine can lie dormant for months—not dead, not repressed, but somehow just not called for.

So it was during Tretona's next two years at Lake View. She and Di went off on a canoeing trip, swam together, slept nude in their sleeping bags—and never once did Tretona come close to feeling out of control. She would speak to Lu on the phone occasionally and say, yes, she really had to come into town for some action—but she never did. She noted how the science librarian was always smiling at her and thought about asking her out to coffee. She even winked at Di's senior thesis student. But nothing was moving inside.

What induces these periods of hibernation? (Or might we better ask, why do we sometimes become so vulnerable to romance?) True, she was busy as could be, setting up a college facility for the use of radio isotopes. And she was swamped with affection from Di and students, who were constantly in and out of their apartment.

It was quite peaceful, but it made her wonder a little. If you were in love, most of the time you felt anxious and insecure as hell. Yet it was irresistibly exciting. No one ever turned it down. At least she never did. It wasn't even something you had a choice about. She was obviously a lot happier as she was now, just being busy and enjoying life in the faculty apartments, but yet she kept thinking her life was missing something—not just excitement, not just sex, but something more special. She also wondered whether the pressures against celibacy in our society might not just be as irrational as all the other sexual taboos. Well, at least as long as it was temporary celibacy. . . .

It was Di who finally roused Tretona from her quiescent state. "Let's go to Turkey," she said one Sunday afternoon, halfway through the *New York Times*.

"Would you settle for a movie instead?" Tretona was grading papers.

"No, seriously. The Near East College Association is advertising a bunch of openings in Istanbul."

Once the possibility was raised, Tretona found she had an almost painful desire to travel. She'd see Canadian Club ads and get huge waves of nostalgia for places she'd never been to. She remembered how when her mother had told them stories about Jean Valjean in the sewers of Paris she would always ask, "Can one still see the sewers, Mama?" And her mother would always say, "Yes and maybe you can go there someday—I never will."

"Why not, Mama?"

"Well, because I married a farmer and became a mother, but someday you can go and tell me all about it."

Tretona remembered how much she had loved reading about the Nile and the Pyramids in third grade geography. So what was she doing here in boring Lake View College? And what had she studied all those languages for—not just to pass the Ph.D. reading requirements, that was for sure.

It was preposterous to believe that the two of them would get jobs at the same place, but they both took it for granted. (After all, didn't the water wings come on time? If it was something you really wanted. . . .) So even before their interviews in New York at Christmas, Di and Tretona were reading up on Sultan Ahmet and Atatürk.

Shortly after, Tretona's contract arrived. She would be supervising two Turkish lab assistants, both former graduates of the lycée, and a storeroom man who spoke no English but was evidently very good at getting clean ice, clearing chemicals through customs, and coping with the local fire inspectors who considered chemistry laboratories to be very dangerous indeed.

But there was no word for Di. Suddenly, Tretona realized how important it was that they go together. Faculty friends brought over a jug of Chianti to celebrate Tretona's letter and everyone kept saying that of course Di's letter would come. The secretary couldn't type everything at once, could she? Probably they were still reading all the reprints in Di's fat dossier. No problem. Not to worry.

But Tretona couldn't help worrying. After the others went home the two of them sat on the couch listening to their latest find, a crackly album of Turkish folk dances, recorded from old 78's. Their hands touched, and shoulders. Suddenly, Tretona burst into tears and hugged Di fiercely. "I won't go without you, Di. If you can't come too, I'm staying here at Lake View with you." Tretona felt dumb, but determined. Di patted her on the shoulder and they went off to their separate bedrooms. Soap opera suspense rarely lasts more than one day—a weekend at most. Sure enough, magic struck for the second time and Di was hired, too. Now the only problem was somehow to last out the lame duck period.

Most of the Lake View old-timers were glad to be getting rid of two troublemakers at once. ("Send the Young Turks off to Turkey. What could be more appropriate?" was the way Dr. Steiner put it.) A couple of the other research types would be away on sabbatical so those good-byes were pretty painless. However, Di had a group of senior girls who were all doing special projects in psych and she was definitely going to miss them. She invited them over one evening for wine and cheese and on impulse Tretona had Lu and Maria drive out from Chicago. It was a mad idea. She did it partly out of rebellion, a final fling in which Lake View students (Christian psychologists that they were) would be confronted with a little taste of real life. Also she dreaded saying good-bye to Lu, because they were supposed to be good friends, yet they hadn't spent any time together all year long. It would be phony to say, "I'll miss you—let's keep in touch" and all that jazz when they couldn't even seem to make a toll-free phone call.

The gathering started out okay. Christians are friendly—at least they are at a religious school where some premium is placed on being cheery, trusting the Lord, and loving your neighbor. And psychologists are open and sensitive—well, the young ones are. The old ones become arrogant and aggressive as hell and then claim everyone else is being defensive. Lu was right in her element—lots of new women to impress and Maria started flirting with Di. "Why didn't you tell me you were living with such a divine butchy lady?" she whispered to Tretona. Di was in good form. She had matched the jacket to her tweed suit with a pair of brown flannels. For once she didn't have hose on underneath but a nice pair of argyle socks. And she was wearing penny loafers instead of those little round-toed Belgian pumps with bows. Meanwhile, Lu was playing bartender, so quite a bit of wine was drunk.

Tretona sat in the corner sulking. There was no one for her to make time with. She was annoyed that the two sides of her life, which were supposedly so incompatible, were getting along so well. Had all of her compartmentalization been unnecessary? Now Di was trying to "involve her in the group" or whatever the psychological jargon for being nosey was. "Hey, Tretona, come help me explain the way Turkish forms the negative. I think it may be pretty significant from a psycholinguistic point of view and Maria thinks there is a similar construction in Spanish. . . ."

"Naw, thanks. I'll just sit here. I'm kind of drowsy from the booze."

So what does good old sensitive Di do but propose a late-night plunge in the pool. Strictly forbidden, of course, but she knows where the matron keeps the key. No swim suits? *Pas de problem* (or as we say in Turkish, *Problemlar yok,*). Everyone could go nude. "After all, we're all girls."

Yes, indeed. We're all girls, but two of us are lesbians (in her confusion, Tretona forgot to count herself) and lord knows what they'll do. Visions of Lu eye-raping the lot—or worse, Lu and Maria mating like dolphins under the diving board.

Panicked, Tretona pointed out the danger of night watchmen, how miserable it would be afterwards going home with wet hair, Di should be careful of that cough, why not make popcorn instead, etc., but she was outnumbered. She tried to get Lu alone on the way over, but Lu just said, "Don't worry, I'll leave some for you," and ran ahead.

Women in locker rooms go through strange little modesty rituals—undressing in front of everybody but then carefully wearing a towel into the open showers. Or standing around naked to dry their hair but covering up with a towel when they're on the scales. That night, though, there was no semaphoring with towels. Maria probably set the tone when she made a comment about the body being the temple of the holy spirit. Besides, none of the psychology types wanted to appear repressed. Lu was staring openly. Tretona knew what she was doing. Lu was big on butts and was doing a comparison of roundness-to-firmness ratios. Then Di had to start talking about cross-cultural breast typologies. Tretona broke that up by saying the last one in the pool was a big fat tomato.

She started swimming laps furiously, hoping others would follow, but they were standing around in the water giggling about how good it felt. When she stopped to catch her breath what should she see but Maria lolling on the edge of the pool, her legs spread and stretched straight out so that only her heels touched the water. Suddenly Lu surfaced, her sleek head bobbing between Maria's knees. Then Maria put her feet on Lu's shoulders and tried to dunk her and Lu caught hold of Maria's thighs and tried to pull her in. Maria squealed and spread her legs to get loose and you could see everything—and believe me, everyone was watching.

Lu, determined to keep the audience, swam to the side and pulled herself out. Meanwhile, Maria had collapsed flat onto the floor, her hands stretched over her head—which made her breasts look nice, as she very well knew. Lu strode over to her, straddled Maria's outstretched arms and then walked down until the water dripping from her pussy was falling straight into Maria's mouth. Maria blew her a kiss and slowly lifted her hands to grab Lu's buttocks. Then she raised her legs, slowly, powerfully, tantalizingly. Her toes touched Lu's shoulders. Lu just stood there, hands on her hips, her eyes watching the approaching little furry. Maria continued to roll up on her shoulders. Now her ankles were across Lu's shoulders. Tretona watched, horrified, fascinated. Now Lu lifted Maria's knees even higher with her hands, and began to drop her head. Would she dare? Was she really going to. . . ? But Lu thrust the legs down and away and made a perfect racing dive over Maria's body.

There were cheers and cries of "More! More! Do some more tricks!" Tretona couldn't take it and went down to the shallow end to work out with a kickboard. Pretty soon Di came down and said, "Hey, what's eating you?" Tretona mumbled something about her friends shocking all of Di's Christians and Di said, "Hey, they don't read Freud in my class for nothing and besides, don't you see they love it. Don't take the responsibility for other people's scenes. Come on, I don't like to see you mope."

The party ended without problems but that night after she went to bed Tretona was still stewing. It wasn't fair, she decided.

Everyone had had a great time at the party except for her. The straight people had fun because they didn't even know what was going on, so they didn't feel threatened. Lu and Maria couldn't care less what people thought of them, so they weren't scared. Only Tretona was nervous. I'm neither fish nor fowl, she thought. It was like trying to stand with one foot in a rowboat and the other on the pier—if you weren't damn careful every second, you'd fall in the brink. She sighed and got up to go to the john.

"Tretona, is that you?" Of course, it's me, who in the hell else would it be. "Yeah, what do you want, Di?"

"Will you come in and talk for a minute?" The warm flesh smell of another person's bedroom met her as she wondered where to stand. Or should she sit? On the bed? Why not? Di taking her hand, touching her arm, "I was concerned about you tonight—you seemed so worried." Tretona, blasé now, saying, well, her friends Lu and Maria were a little different, might shock Lake Viewers. Di professing to understand.

"I know what's bothering you, Tretona. Really I do. I know about Lu and Maria—and I know about you, too."

"Do you really?" Tretona was incredulous.

"Of course, you big dope. I'm no dummy, you know." And Tretona buried her face on Di's shoulder and was crying big hot tears of frustration and fatigue and relief that she wouldn't have to work so hard keeping her guard up. And then anger came, anger at this smooth competent psychology woman who was so fucking tolerant and so fucking sure that she "understood." I'll expose her shallowness. Fuck you, little liberal, and she grabbed Di and kissed her hard and fondled her breasts roughly and then Di was breathing hard and moaning, oh my dear, oh my dear one, be gentle, oh it feels so good. So what was Tretona to do, her bluff had been called, and being too proud to admit that her advances had been from hostility and thinking, I *do* like Di and I know I used to be attracted to her. Into the familiar routines, like bicycle riding, a skill never forgotten, playing the woman instrument before her, listening to the tuning, strumming now light, now intensely, getting into it a little, until feeling the paunchy belly—Di's only concession to middle age—and then snapping off in her head. I do not desire this woman. But can't be a cunt tease. Remembering Casanova's guilt over any and all women lying alone in their beds at night. Now feeling guilty over being so mechanical, so uninvolved. Remembering the great wheel in dirty songs, the great big fucking machine. Her hand hurt. And now Di pulling her close, feeling the sweat on Di's forehead and tiny, happy tears. Now I know what's worse than being an animal carried away by passion, thought Tretona. What's worse is being a robot, driven by pride and duty and triggered by hostility.

The nice soft robot stayed in Di's room and made nice postcoital conversation until a decent interval had passed and she could go back to bed.

17 Turkish Delight

Kirpiklerini ok eyle ("Make arrows from your eyelashes")
                                    —*Anatolian Folk Song*

The splendor of the wrinkled lapis lazuli sea . . .
                                    —*E. Coxon*

AMERICA IS SO vast and homogeneous that the sharply defined cultural areas in Europe seem like adjacent movie sets. Cross a river and suddenly the language, architecture, and ambience are all different. The ferry from Sweden to East Germany, the tunnel from Switzerland to Italy—sauna bath shocks to the jaded traveler.

Asia had been making her presence felt for some miles now—a sort of spiritual equivalent to the foothills of the Rockies which dominate the Kansas plains hours before you reach Denver. The smell of Turkish tobacco began at Trieste. One drank *çai* in Yugoslavia and ate *baklava* in Greece. There were other reminders, too—the tower of skulls constructed by Turkish invaders at Niz and drawings in the Acropolis Museum of the Parthenon as mosque and munitions dump.

Last night in Thessalonica, they had eaten roast chicken in a restaurant run by a Greek from Chicago and then joined in the evening promenade by the sea. On the unofficial advice of the British consul they had laid in an illegal supply of cheap Turkish lira. Now they were driving north and east. CONSTANTINOPLE: 300 KM, said the road sign. "You can't go back to Constantinople," sang Di.

Suddenly a wire barrier—a dilapidated little shed, drab dusty soldiers outside, inside a fat bureaucrat sitting under an oversized Turkish flag too wrinkled for its fierce, passionate logo to be effective. There was a faded picture of Atatürk on the side wall. Silent, unsmiling examination of the car's papers, much stamping and punching, and they were waved through.

The road led through barren, slightly rolling plains—occasional wagons of hay on the road coming from nowhere and with no visible destination. Now the road signs read ISTANBUL. Di continued her imitation of Eartha Kitt: "Why did Constantinople get the works? It's nobody's business but the Turks!"

"How's the gas?" Tretona asked anxiously. They had expected a BP station at the border. There was hardly any traffic other than the oxcarts. She tried to remember whether the bandits were only on the Syrian border or if they came over on the European side, too.

Try the radio. Human contact and civilization, courtesy of Blaupunkt. Crackles and then a thread of music—winding, wavering Oriental music, shimmering in the heat, buzzing, monotonous, circular melodies, like flies cruising a manure pile.

Suddenly, Tretona sat upright and turned up the volume. "It's Turkish," she said. "I caught a word. Listen." Sure enough, clear as could be. "Şe-ke-rim," moaned the woman vocalist. The syllables drawn and pulled like tough taffy. "Darling," she was saying— literally, "my sugar." Tretona tried to learn the melody (the rest of the words were too difficult), but there was something odd about the time and she kept falling off the beat.

Now an erect pointer on the horizon, pencil thin, faint rosy stone almost blending into the thick hazy heat. It was the great mosque of Edirne, worth a visit according to *Le Guide Bleu*. Minarets were more phallic than church steeples, especially with the soft round mosque domes underneath. An archetypal fairy-tale landscape until one drew near enough to see the rusty cable running up the minaret to a loudspeaker. No longer need the imam scramble up five times daily to call the faithful to prayer. A microphone at the base—hooray for technological progress! And the crippled beggar at the entrance was on a sort of skateboard and knew some German. No backward country, this.

Now that they were well away from the border, traffic picked up. Mostly there were trucks of varied sizes, all belching black exhaust and covered with blue beads; then lurching buses, bundles piled high on the roof tops, shock absorbers long gone and the springs in serious doubt; next the occasional Mercedes Benz private sedan still bearing German export plates (duty on

190

cars was over 100 percent—Tretona and Di's car had to be bonded when they came in as a guarantee that they wouldn't sell it). In the fields there were storks and camels and blindfolded mules walking in circles threshing grain. It was bad country for farming—not enough summer rain, parching winds, red dirt, erosion from flash floods.

Finally they reached Istanbul—the crumbling fifteenth-century walls; Black Sea boats in kindergarten colors, eyes painted on each side of the prow; the Blue Mosque, hovering in the haze like a story-book castle; *hamals* around the train station—they were human beasts of burden, carrying everything from refrigerators to ten-foot-high stacks of bird cages; donkeys, taxicabs (old American Fords), *Çai* boys with swinging trays of tea, *simitcis* carrying hot circular pretzels stacked high on a long stick; ferries tooting up the Golden Horn and crisscrossing the Bosphorus. Now up past Dolmababçe and Atatürk's palace; roars from the soccer stadium; then the hauntingly beautiful carved wooden houses along the Bosphorus.

Not that Tretona and Di could take it all in—just glimpses for now as they desperately read the road map and flinched at the audacity of *dolmuş* drivers and gawked at men walking along the sidewalk holding hands and giggled as they transliterated the billboard which advertised limousines for rent with *şöför* included. Speeding by all the tantalizing landmarks in search of the school.

That had to be it—huge iron gates, decorative but functional, too (the Dean feared anti-American riots), a discreet sign in Turkish, AMERIKAN KIZ KOLEJI), a Turkish flag displayed prominently. The guard touched his cap respectfully and swung open the gates. A winding road through trees so green they were a refreshing shock in this arid country, a steep hill, better put the VW in first gear. Finally, tennis courts and a parking lot. Wide stairs leading up to the main building. As they locked the car and started in, Di remarked that except for the Turkish flag they could just as well be in the middle of America, at Lake View College, even. "Don't be so sure," said Tretona and began to quote Kipling: "East is East and West is West. . . ." She was interrupted by a blast of music from what appeared to be a dormitory window: "I Wanna Hold Your Hand!" "They may not have Coca-Cola, but the Beatles are here," said Di. "Let's go in."

Two weeks later Tretona felt perfectly at home in the

classroom, but after four weeks she had decided that Turkish students were completely inscrutable. And after six weeks she finally understood what people meant by "culture shock." A bunch of new teachers and a few old Turkish hands were sitting around the lounge, discussing as usual the culture characteristics of the native population.

"Before I came out here," said Tretona, "I expected the culture to be totally foreign, but the *people* to be basically the same as us. You know—there wouldn't be any Cokes or Kleenex or detergents, but the basic values of friendship and honesty and kindness would all be the same, although their ways of expressing them might be different."

"Well, isn't that right?" asked Margaret. "That's what I've found." She was a preacher's daughter and instinctively took a Pollyanna position on every conceivable question. Betsy groaned and held her stomach. She was the most acculturated of all the old-timers—her Turkish was passable and she depilated her legs and armpits as the Turks did, by sticking on a sort of taffy goop and pulling the hair out by the roots. (People wondered if she also followed the Turkish custom of removing her pubic hair, but no one dared ask.) At the same time she was the most cynical about the Turkish mentality. "Do you know what I mean, Betsy?" asked Tretona.

"You're preaching the sermon tonight, carry on, honey." And Betsy lifted her glass of *rakı*.

"I'll give a 'for instance,'" said Tretona. "Well, two 'for instances,' actually. The first day I walk into class to face the dusky daughters of the Seljuk nomads, right? I don't want to introduce any confusing Western content, so I've been careful to prepare a list of Turkish examples. I begin by describing the differences between compounds, solutions, and mixtures and then start on the illustrations. 'I have an example of a solution, miss,' volunteers the littlest girl there. 'Yes, Gülgün?' I say. 'A martini is a solution! It's three parts gin to one part vermouth.' 'No, it's not,' screams Ayşe. 'The ratio is four to one!' 'No, you're both wrong,' says one of the Armenian girls. 'A martini is a mixture, not a solution.' I take up the last remark eagerly, hoping to get back to the main point. 'Now remember the definition of *solution,* Nadine. Are you quite sure a martini isn't a solution?' 'Oh, yes, miss. Because it has an olive in it.' And then they all started babbling about gimlets and having your drink 'up' versus 'on-the-rocks.' I swear they knew more about cocktails than most American fifteen-year-olds would."

"Oh, they're sophisticated, there's no doubt about that," said Margaret. "They all go to Paris shopping—or if they don't, they read *Elle* and *Vogue*."

"Yeah, that's what's so misleading," said Tretona. "Their English is excellent; they love Western music and movies; they wear cashmere sweaters—well, not the scholarship kids, but a lot of them do. But they don't *think* at all Western. Like that shocking business with Safiye. I still can't understand it."

The incident in question had started when Tretona decided to make up two sets of exam questions to cut down on cheating. Someone had asked Safiye to pass her answers over two rows and she had refused. Afterwards, a big gang had dragged her out to the plateau on the far side of campus and literally stoned her. Luckily, Betsy had found out about it before the girl was seriously hurt.

"What you have to realize," Betsy said, "is that these people are very serious about questions of loyalty." "I know that," said Tretona. "But there are other values, too. Like not cheating or sheer self-interest. I would have flunked her if I caught her."

"But you know what the strangest thing of all was," said Di. "I was there when Dean Tanner called everyone in—you know, to act as the resident shrink in case anyone had hysterics. The strange thing was that it was *Safiye* who kept acting guilty, not the kids who chucked stones at her. She kept saying in a sad voice, 'I was just afraid—I was just afraid.' Finally, I said, of course, she was afraid. Who wouldn't be when people were throwing stones at you. And she said, 'Oh, no, Dr. Sorensen. I was *afraid* to cheat!' I couldn't understand that at all!"

"But that's just it," said Tretona. "She felt bad because she was too big a coward to help her friends cheat on an exam! That's what I mean by there being a basic difference in values. Safiye is no sociopathic juvenile delinquent. She's just an ordinary all-American Turkish girl—if you know what I mean."

"Well, there is one thing worth noticing," said Betsy. "Safiye is Greek—her real name is Sophia—but she's trying to pass. She was adopted by a Turkish army officer—*very* unusual—and she wants desperately to be accepted by the Turkish Turks. But of course that makes her an especially good indicator of Turkish values—converts are always the most doctrinaire, you know."

"On the contrary," said Di. "That just means that she's a little socially immature. She's experiencing the sort of conflict of loyalties ten-year-olds undergo when they start moving out of the family and establishing strong peer relationships."

Tretona barely kept from snorting—she was getting fed up with all of Di's developmental explanations. First it had been Piaget, now it was Freud. Di was trying to wangle research money to test the effect of Muslim circumcision rites on traumas of the Oedipal stage. Di figured that getting your foreskin whacked off at about age six, just when castration anxiety was high, ought to show up in Rorschach tests or dreams or something.

But as Tretona thought about it, while munching *fıstık* nuts and half-listening to the conversation, what really pissed her off was Di's analysis of the blatant homosexual goings-on around the school. It was wild. Everyone held hands constantly and "best friends" would walk each other to class and kiss good-bye right at the door. There were all sorts of rumors about bed-sharing in the dorms, which Tretona hadn't taken too seriously until one noon hour she had discovered two of the middle-school students lying intertwined on one of the lab tables. When she walked in they just giggled and ran away.

Di explained all this in terms of slow development caused by sexual segregation in Turkish society as a whole and aggravated by the fact that this was a girls' school. Tretona agreed that those factors were relevant, but why not speak of an *alternative* development instead of *slow* development? Was it really a sign of immaturity when all those big swarthy workmen held hands in the park on their lunch break? But Di described *that* stuff as a cultural difference in ways of expressing friendship or camaraderie. "American men slap each other on the back," she said, "and Turks hold hands. It doesn't mean anything." "But the Turkish men slap each other on the back, too," protested Tretona. It did mean *something*—men holding hands, girl students kissing, all those tales about what went on in the harem when the sultan got old or was overworked, vague allusions her students had made about women's steam baths and special belly dance performances where the audience was all women. It meant something, all right, but she didn't yet know exactly what.

Tretona would have liked to pump the students a little more on such topics. She had lots of opportunities—there was a pretty raucous gang of sophomores that always tried to sit at her table in the dining hall (faculty ate with students in order to enforce the

"English only" rule) and some of the seniors hung around after lab was over. But she really didn't trust them yet. These kids could be plenty two-faced. Of course, the situation fostered it. Because of the culture and language barriers, it was hard for the American teachers to compare notes with their parents or even their other teachers. And some of the Americans were so credulous and brainwashed by the cultural difference talk that they'd believe anything. (It was rumored that Margaret almost got talked into believing that Turkish vaginas ran sideways.) But Betsy claimed that "sly as a Turk" was a saying throughout the lands which were once part of the Ottoman Empire. Tretona sure couldn't figure them out half the time. A big part of it was the unfamiliar body language. They would keep their faces wooden no matter what. Tretona reckoned it might have something to do with centuries of wearing veils. They might as well be wearing veils as far as communicating anything with their faces was concerned. They'd laugh, of course—but missing were the Western expressions of surprise, concern, encouragement, puzzlement—all the little cues that give you feedback on where you are and keep the conversation going. Some of the kids, especially the younger ones, would imitate Western facial expressions, but they wouldn't get them quite right and they'd come across as phony or duplicitous. As Tretona said to Di, "Speaking with a foreign accent isn't so bad, but if you *smile* with a foreign accent, then everyone really gets confused."

A whole other side of the Turkish persona emerged in November. Di and Tretona came back to the faculty rooming house late that Friday night—they'd gone downtown to eat disappointing chop suey at a Turkish-Chinese restaurant because they were homesick. Betsy's door was open when they got back and she appeared in her nightgown carrying a glass of milk—or was it *rakı?* Her glasses were off and her hair was straggling out of the normally tight, neat bun. Tretona started to make a joke about being drunk and disorderly, but Di grabbed her arm and asked "What on earth's wrong, Betsy?"

"Kennedy's dead—shot by a sniper. It just came in on the Air Force station."

"Shot? Who on earth—was it some nut? Did they catch him?"

"It *had* to be some nut." Margaret appeared, red-eyed and tense.

The four of them huddled around the shortwave receiver.

The announcements were brief, short on detail and devoid of speculation. "They're being super cautious because it's a government station broadcasting overseas," said Betsy. "People must be going nuts at home," said Tretona. "Kennedy was the big hope. He was going to turn things around—" "I'm going to call home," said Margaret. But she didn't. She sat there like the rest of them, glued to the radio, listening to slow brass band marches, and waiting to hear the terse repetition: "Today . . . Dallas . . . Johnson flying back . . . stand-by for further. . . ."

All weekend the American teachers were barraged by condolences from the staff. Dimitros, the headwaiter, brought a special Greek coffeecake for the Sunday morning faculty breakfast. Miss Fetva, the Armenian head housekeeper, put a flower in each of their rooms. She dabbed at her eyes and patted people on the shoulder as they passed. Even Mustafa, the sullen *kapıcı* at the foot of the hill, came over to Di and Tretona's VW and made a little bilingual speech: "Türk, Amerikan—friend, arkadaş" and pressed two fingers tightly together to show how close the relationship was.

Sunday night they were all invited to Betsy's room for popcorn and real American beer (Betsy had a connection at the PX).

"Why are the staff being so nice?" asked Tretona.

Margaret didn't like her tone. "Because it's tragic, that's why! And they at least are sensitive enough to realize it."

Betsy responded to Tretona. "I think there are several things going on. Sure, it's a tragedy and all the Near Eastern peoples really dig drama. As far as the minority staff are concerned, they have a genuine affection and admiration for Americans and especially for the school. I'll never forget Dimitros' face that night back in '57 when the Turks were throwing bricks at all the shops owned by "foreigners"—by which they meant the Greeks and Armenians who had lived here for generations. Some fires broke out and there were lots of rumors about pogroms and massacres. Anyway, Dean Farley opened up the gym for any of the staff who wished to bring their families here. It was a bit of a dicey thing to do, politically, but Farley had balls. You can bet ole Tanner wouldn't have done it. Dimitros has twins, you know—a boy and a girl—they couldn't have been over two at the time. Well, he showed up here about midnight, a baby in each arm, his wife trotting along behind carrying any number of baskets. They probably walked all the way from Beşiktaş—took back streets or something. Fetva was translating and assigning sleeping spaces while Farley was serving up pita and peanut butter sandwiches. Dimitros walked straight over to Farley without even putting the kids down. He said that Farley was a good woman and that Americans were good people and that he would always tell his boy and girl the story of how Dean Farley had saved their lives, and they would teach their children and grandchildren, and her good name would live forever."

"Wow," said Tretona. "What happened?"

"Well, Farley made a little bow and say, 'You are very kind. . . .'"

"No, I mean what happened about the pogroms?" said Tretona.

"Oh, nothing," said Betsy. "It blew over—that time. If you want some real horror stories, get Fetva talking sometime about the Armenian massacres of 1915. The Nazis didn't invent genocide, you know."

Margaret sighed and then said brightly, "It just goes to show America isn't such a bad place, after all."

Tretona didn't like Margaret's smug tone, but she had to agree with her statement. Lynching by red-neck vigilantes wasn't the same as organized army massacres. And although informal racism was plenty bad, it still wasn't the same as explicit race laws. As soon as the thought crossed her mind, she felt a bit uneasy. Travel was supposed to be broadening, teach you alternative ways of looking at things and here she was feeling more pro-American than she would have dreamed possible back home.

Dean Tanner had decided that classes would meet as usual on Monday, but when the students congregated they all started crying and it soon became clear that there would have to be some sort of special ceremony. So at eleven o'clock the whole school met in the assembly hall. Tanner started with a sort of eighth-grade civic lecture about how elections worked, the two-party system, the bicameral legislature, and ended with an analysis of the order of Presidential succession, which sounded rather macabre given the occasion. ("And if the Vice-President should die, then. . . .")

Then Neriman Saydam, the "student president," took over. She was dark, serious, not very lively, and not too pretty. She was a scholarship student from the provinces. None of the Americans could understand why she had been elected school president and had almost decided it was another sign that the students didn't give two hoots about student government—probably none of the popular kids would serve.

However that may have been, Neriman certainly rose to this occasion. On very short notice she had put together a fine little program—Tengün played a couple of somber Chopin preludes on the piano, the little Orta students who could barely speak English yet gave a choral reading of "Sail on Oh Ship of State" and Algın sang and played "Sometimes I Feel Like a Motherless Child" on the guitar. By that time the sniffles were audible. Tretona felt detached from the proceedings, partly out of embarrassment (teachers shouldn't cry in front of students), partly because she couldn't understand why the Turks were taking it all so hard.

Then, speaking with great dignity, Neriman announced the last number: "We always close the assembly by singing the 'Istiklal Marsı' and we will sing it also today. But afterwards, I will ask you all to sing 'The Star Spangled Banner.' A great buzz went through the crowd. Dean Tanner was adamant that the American national anthem never be sung at official school functions. "We are not here to proselytze. We are here to teach English." Neither were Americans allowed to join in the Turkish national anthem—"It isn't yours to sing." Neriman was breaking two rules at once.

As usual, Tretona got goose bumps during the "Istiklal." The music was martial, yet haunting and the girls sang it with such intensity. No matter how they giggled or whispered during assembly they always became fiercely attentive when their flag was presented. The pianist struck the chord for the American national anthem. We'll never make it, thought Tretona, and sure enough by the time they got to "what so proudly we hailed" all the Americans were choked with tears. Even Alice MacCruthers, the music director who was playing the piano, started sobbing. But the Turkish accents carried on, each syllable carefully pronounced, their voices soaring effortlessly up to "the rocket's red glare." Tretona dug in her nails and managed to help sing the final line.

Some senior science students saved a table for Tretona at lunch. She didn't really want to eat with anybody, but they waved insistently. They all sat quietly, eyes dark and sad, nibbling bread off the table Turkish fashion. Somehow their faces seemed more expressive than usual. Always before, Tretona had continued to eat off a plate Western-style, but today she too laid her bread on the table cloth and pulled little pieces off of it delicately with her fingers.

"That was a beautiful program," she said. "It was very thoughtful of Neriman and all of you. . . ." Their silence stopped her. Finally, her best senior chemistry student spoke. "Excuse me. May I please ask a personal question?"

"Of course, Filiz. What is it?"

"Are you—is your family Democrat or Republican?" Filiz spoke quietly.

"Democrat," said Tretona. "Mostly Democrat."

Filiz sighed. "And Dr. Sorensen's family?"

"I expect they're Democrats, too. Yeah, I'm sure they would be—they're immigrants and her dad's in a union."

Filiz sighed again. "Kennedy was the Democratic leader, wasn't he?"

"Well, yes. But Filiz, that doesn't matter. Everyone will be mourning him—Democrats *and* Republicans. Political parties don't matter that much."

"But aren't you afraid for your family?" said Filiz. "If there's a coup or civil war. . . ."

Tretona's mouth dropped open and she laughed for a split second before the solemnity of the room and Filiz's seriousness stopped her. "There won't be a *coup,* Filiz. For God's sakes, this is America—I mean, we don't do things like that in my. . . ." There was no way to finish. What *was* she trying to say? That Americans were too civilized to have political coups, but not too civilized to let deranged people run around with guns?

Tretona glanced up at Filiz, trying to frame an apology, but Filiz was looking quite relaxed. "I'm so relieved to hear you say that, miss. Some of my friends—those from the university—say there will be a right-wing coup. I am glad to hear different—differently?"

Suddenly everyone at the table had an American story to tell. Sirani told how all their history books described Atatürk as the Jorj Vasinkton of Turkey because he led their fight for independence. Tengün, who was a translator at the tourist office during the summer, reported that everyone said that Americans were the nicest tourists. "The Arabs are the worst," she said. "So arrogant. The French people never understand anything and Germans are very stubborn."

"All the Turkish people love American people very much," said Nesli.

"Except for the Marxist students," corrected Filiz. "They say all the Amerikan Kız Koleji teachers are CIA agents," she added. Then Filiz said that the Turks admired Americans very much because their country was so advanced. "We are still a developing country," she said.

"Yes," agreed Tengün. "We have only one advantage over America—in Turkey we have no race problem."

Tretona's brain whirred. She looked at Sirani—Sirani Nabalkiyan. Wasn't that an Armenian name? "No race problems?" she finally asked in as neutral a voice as she could manage.

"That is right," said Sirani. Her black eyes were earnest. "It is because we never had slaves."

Tretona let it pass. Whatever the status of the Armenians, it certainly wasn't that of ex-slaves. During the Ottoman Empire most of the civil service jobs were filled by Greeks, Armenians, and Jews. Then there were the Janissaries—the Sultan's special crack army corps comprised of kidnapped Christian children who were raised in the palace. They retained their religion yet were fiercely loyal—more trustworthy in fact than aristocratic Moslems who might have aspired to the throne. No melting pot ideology here; no push for assimilation.

Tretona remembered how proud her granddad had been that he *couldn't* remember much German: "My father said we are Americans now and he never let us speak it at home although sometimes he and your great-grandmother would speak *Deutsch* when they were alone." Tretona imagined her grandfather squatting by their bedroom naughtily listening to the forbidden tongue. How strange the different ways people chose to define themselves. Turkish-Armenians who saw no racial prejudice, German-Americans proud of their German descent and equally proud that they couldn't speak the language. It was all confusing. And Tretona—what was she?

"One thing is for sure—the Turks are the best cooks in the world," said Tretona. It was true. Dimitros proudly bore in the dessert—*kestane püresi,* a wonderful pudding of chestnuts and cream.

The girls were delighted. "What is your favorite Turkish dish?" asked Tengün.

"*Ali paşa pilaf*—sorry, *pilavı.*" Tretona carefully added the correct noun ending.

After lunch Tretona gave everyone the slip and snuck off to the far side of the campus where there was a sit-and-think place overlooking the Bosphorus. It was a beautiful view—the Rumeli Hısarı fortress just visible to the far left and with binoculars you could see people on the decks of the ferry boats drinking tea from little glasses. From this height the traffic noise was a barely audible hum. There were occasional shouts from the *gecekondu* shacks (literally "night built"). Once squatters had a roof over their head it was difficult to evict them, so villagers who had come to the city would invade unused tracts of ground and throw together little houses. Occasionally, there was a loud intermittent sound, which Tretona now knew was a donkey's bray. When she had first come she'd swore it was someone using a rusty pump.

Tretona tried to sort out the mixture of intense feelings jostling inside her. It had something to do with being American— what that meant, both to her and to the Turks, what Kennedy had meant to the country, what his death would mean. What if the Turks were right? What if his assassination opened a new era of political violence? It was funny. She had been gone only since June—five months—yet already much of the time she was feeling quite detached from her own country. America—and American superhighways and supermarkets and super-bowl games—all seemed strange and faraway. With just a touch of amnesia she could easily be convinced that the whole damn country was simply a cardboard set in some super-Hollywood located on Mars—or Andromeda.

And yet—here was the irony—though America was fading, she herself had never had such a strong feeling of *being* American, not even when she was writing all those patriotic essays for the Elks. Some of it came from realizing how different the Turks were. But mostly it was seeing herself reflected in their eyes. Any place she went, she was immediately identified—not as a redhead, not as a beatnik, not as a sportscar driver, but as an American—which meant affluent, powerful, and different. You were automatically an outsider and there was not a thing you could do about it. Samantha Özgen, who was married to a Turk, had lived here twenty years and was still called *Ingiliz*—"the English lady"—by the very shopkeepers who swore her Turkish was perfect! Being an American was a highly visible, immutable characteristic, an indelible label. Tretona was surprised to find that she didn't care. Actually, it gave one a tremendous feeling of freedom. It didn't really matter whether your grammar was good, or what your folks did, or how well you dressed. All that was fine structure, completely swamped by the blatant fact that *you were American*. And there was no premium on being tactful or quiet—you got stared at mercilessly whatever you did. Just existing was enormously indiscreet. In comparison, any other idiosyncrasy was irrelevant.

Any other? Could Turks tell when Americans were queer? Probably not. And if they could, would they care? What *did* all that kissing in the halls really mean? Damn. She had to know. She had to have an informant. Maybe Filiz? At least if it didn't work, they could talk about chemistry.

Serendipity favors the prepared mind and manipulation is the mother of invention. By that weekend Tretona had maneuvered Filiz into volunteering to show her the best place in town to buy *baklava*. (Tretona was laying in supplies for Di's thirty-fifth birthday.) So began a series of pleasant outings and rendezvous. The *Konakı* (which had twenty-seven varieties of *baklava*—Tretona told Filiz about Baskin and Robbins) was followed by a Viennese pastry shop, the Russian tea room, a ride on Istanbul's one-stop subway, fittingly called *Tünel*. One afternoon Tretona played guide for a change and took Filiz to the Hilton Hotel. Filiz swore that Turks weren't allowed to enter by the front door but Tretona said that was ridiculous and dragged her in to try a chocolate milk shake—"A real milk shake, not those horrid *melk şek* concoctions they sell down by the Galata bridge."

They were sitting close together in a semicircular booth. (Filiz had never seen one before and scooted clear around to Tretona's side.) The conversation turned, as it often did, to national differences. In general, Filiz had been very informative. The only subject on which Tretona had drawn a complete blank was the size of the apartment where she and her half-dozen brothers and sisters (some married), mother, and aunt lived. Emboldened by the power and affluence which the Hilton reflected on her (12 Turkish lira for a drink was outrageous), Tretona started fishing.

"Guess what? People here could tell we weren't both American even if all they could see were our silhouettes!"

Filiz was flustered. "Why? My hair? My glasses frames? What's wrong?"

Tretona quickly reassured her. "No, no. Everything's fine. It's just that—well—two American women would probably not be sitting this close to each other." She took Filiz's arm to stop her from slipping away immediately. "No, please don't move. I like sitting like this. You know, everyone says the British are so cold, but they'll sit side by side in a booth and think nothing of it. I guess Americans are still infected with that good old frontier spirit—when you see smoke on the horizon, it's time to move on West."

By the time Tretona had explained that last remark, Filiz seemed at ease again. As casually as possible, Tretona brought up the subject of kissing in the corridors at school.

"Oh, but they are both girls," said Filiz. "Girls always kiss, when they are friends and especially when they are young."

"So it is quite socially acceptable for girl friends to kiss? But then why do they act embarrassed and run away when one of the teachers comes up?"

"I guess they are shy," said Filiz. "Maybe they do not want to admit that they like somebody very much."

"But would that happen if the school were coed? If there were boys around?" Tretona pressed on.

"Oh, no, never."

"Why not?"

"Because if a boy saw girls kissing he would think—that they would kiss him—I mean, that they were—I don't know how to say it—that they were warm for love." Filiz was struggling to find the right idiom.

"Ah, so it does have some sexual significance," said Tretona.

"No," said Filiz firmly. "When girls kiss, it only means they are friends."

Tretona let it drop and told Filiz how milk shakes were made. Later that afternoon when she drove Filiz to the corner near where she lived (Filiz was always vague about precisely which building their apartment was in), Tretona gave her a kiss on the cheek ("because we are becoming friends"). Filiz took it calmly enough.

But the following week when Tretona started to arrange an

appointment, Filiz asked *if* she could bring along a friend. Well, I've scared her off, thought Tretona. It was just as well, really—Filiz wasn't that exciting. But now she would be stuck buying milk shakes for two little Turkish students. She hoped they wouldn't giggle—or worse, smoke cigarettes in a terribly adult fashion.

They were to meet at the Divan Oteli at four P.M. on Friday. It was a posh place—much more cosmopolitan and sophisticated than the Hilton. The pastries in the coffee shop looked good. Tretona sat down in the lounge to wait. Of course they were late. Betsy swore the official motto of the Turkish bureaucracy was: *Yarın, Yavaş, Yok*—"tomorrow, slowly, never." Annoyed with herself for failing to adjust and for always being on time, Tretona went over and bought a *Time* magazine. There was Filiz now, getting out of a cab. With her was a tall well-dressed woman in enormous sunglasses. Well, well, thought Tretona, and pretended to read her magazine. She waited until they were standing in front of her and then slowly scanned up the newcomer's body. Just as she reached her face, the thought struck her, be careful, maybe this is Filiz's mother, but as soon as she saw Filiz's excited expression, Tretona decided it was okay.

"This is my friend, Nükhet. Perhaps you have seen her at AKK. She is assisting in psychology with Dr. Sorensen."

No foolin, thought Tretona. Di never told me about you, my beauty. The greetings were barely over before Filiz excused herself and scurried out the door.

"I didn't know Filiz had something else on this afternoon," said Tretona. "I wonder where she's going?"

"I told her to leave," said Nükhet in a matter-of-fact voice. She took off her sunglasses, tossed them into an enormous black leather handbag-cum-bookbag. "Shall we go in?" she said, gesturing toward the bar.

Her eyes were enormous—almond-shaped, Oriental, slightly hooded.

"Oh well, yes—I had assumed we were going to the coffee shop."

Nükhet stopped in the middle of the lobby. "Muslims don't drink. And Turkish women especially do not drink. Isn't that what they told you at AKK? Well, I must inform you that there are lots of things Dean Tanner does not know—especially about Turkish women."

Nükhet murmured something to the waiter and they were

seated at a table in the shadows, overlooking the terrace. "A good place for people-watching—without being watched yourself," observed Tretona.

"Are you a natural spy, or did the CIA teach you?" asked Nükhet.

Tretona floundered, trying to diagnose the level of seriousness, but then the drinks arrived.

"What is this stuff?" asked Tretona as the waiter deftly dumped a jigger of green liquid over ice and put it gracefully in front of her.

"Absinthe," said Nükhet. "Americans have trouble liking *rakı* at the beginning. So it is good to begin with absinthe. They both are anise-flavored." (Her English was excellent but she did say a-*nize*.)

"But isn't absinthe dangerous? I think it's made out of wormwood or something."

"I am not going to poison you, my dear," said Nükhet. "We Turks are not so violent as you Americans. Or at least not openly so. It would not be subtle to invite a CIA agent—agentette?—to the Divan Oteli in the middle of Istanbul and poison her—especially before the *fıstık* arrived."

At which point the pistachio nuts did arrive—and with them a dish containing a packet marked *çips*.

As Nükhet opened them, her voice seemed a little tired: "You see we even have crisps—or do you say potato chips? (You must forgive my confused English; I studied in a British high school.) Are we not advanced for an underdeveloped country?"

Tretona ignored the remark. The *çips* were good (she said so), although quite different tasting because they were cooked in olive oil (she did not say so). Nükhet was playing with her—she was sure of it, though she didn't know why. The best strategy, Tretona decided, was to be completely innocent and open.

"Do you work with Di full-time or just part-time?" Tretona asked politely.

"Di? Di? Oh, you must mean Dr. Sorensen. You Americans are so informal. No, that is, of course, only a little part of the day. I teach painting at the psychiatric hospital in Ortaköy. In addition, there is my theater work—make-up, stage design, and—yes—a little acting. And then there are my studies. Now I am doing research on T. S. Eliot."

Tretona was impressed, and said so. Nükhet's smile seemed

incongruous. Tretona wondered if it were a Turkish imitation of an American smile. Then Nükhet batted her eyelids once, lowered her glance, and said quietly, "Perhaps you are surprised that a young girl from a poor underdeveloped country could do so many things? We do not work as hard and efficiently as Americans, of course, but we do the little bits which we can."

"Oh, cut out that 'underdeveloped country' stuff," said Tretona. "Look, I'm not in the Peace Corps and I'm not an Ugly American—or at least I try hard not to be one—and I haven't been patronizing with you, have I? So just stop the dumb native act, okay?"

"Did you have an Irish grandmother?" asked Nükhet. Again, there was that strange smile, friendly but somehow dissonant with the rest of her face, which remained Oriental and blank.

Tretona struggled to follow the conversation—non sequiturs made her nervous. "Well, a Scotch-Irish-English mixture on my mother's side. Why?"

Nükhet kept the interrogator's initiative. "Why did you kiss Filiz?"

"Hey, wait a minute," protested Tretona. "I didn't really—it was just a peck. Anyway, that's absolutely none of your business."

"Filiz is a young Turkish girl and I am a Turk," said Nükhet quietly. "Furthermore, she is my friend. So it is natural that I be interested whan an older American, a teacher at AKK no less, and a very *intimate* friend of Dr. Sorensen, I might add, begins to make inquiries about the sexual-affectional patterns of Turkish adolescents and then proceeds to initiate certain. . . ." She finished the sentence with a vague wave of the hand.

That last gesture was French, not Turkish, thought Tretona. This woman was an amazing synthesis of disparate elements and totally unfathomable. How to deal with her? Tretona spoke calmly and carefully:

"Look, I really don't think there is any cause for concern. I was merely . . ."

"I am not *concerned,*" said Nükhet. "You did not listen. I said I was *interested.*"

"Interested?" Tretona was puzzled and searched Nükhet's eyes for a clue as to where the conversation was going.

For the first time, Nükhet retreated. "Interested just to know, of course. . . ." she beckoned the waiter.

Tretona decided to gamble. She leaned forward, gently, earnestly and she hoped, invitingly. "You see, I guess I *am* very curious about diverse—what did you call them?—sexual-affectional patterns, not just in Turkey, but everywhere. And so naturally I sought a—well, what the anthropologists would call an 'informant.' But what I'd really like much more is a Turkish friend—I mean a *real* friend, not just an acquaintance." Tretona beamed as much intensity across the cocktail table as she dared.

Nükhet's eyes traced Tretona's face. I wonder if we are as inscrutable to them, thought Tretona. The obvious symmetry of the communication gap had never struck her before.

"To Turks, friendship is a very serious matter," said Nükhet, "so that is perhaps too much to hope. In the meantime, for a while, I will be your guide. Filiz is too young, too naive—you must abandon her."

Tretona started to propose a qualification to that order, but decided not to challenge the "guide's" authority. "Wonderful," she said. "May I invite you to dinner? On condition that you will pick the place?"

"How impetuous you Americans are!" Now the smile seemed genuine. "I have other obligations tonight—on such short notice, it is impossible. But perhaps the day after tomorrow I might find a little time. . . ."

"Sunday? Well, Di and I had planned something—but maybe all three of us could go. . . ?"

"No, no, I think you *and* Dr. Sorensen would be too much, entirely too much. You must remember that we people from underdeveloped countries—our English is not good—and the contrast of American intensity with our Turkish ambience. . . ." There came the magical French hands again.

Di was not pleased that Tretona cancelled their Sunday plans. Neither could she understand Tretona's fascination with Nükhet. "You mean Nükhet Altın? Tall? Wears big sunglasses? She's not my assistant; she's a student—a senior here at AKK. Well, once she 'assisted' me in demonstrating an experiment for the sophomores, but that was all."

Tretona wondered why Nükhet would exaggerate, especially when it was inevitable that the truth would come out. Maybe it was a language problem: people who help are helpers; why shouldn't people who assist be called "assistants"?

From then on, Tretona saw Nükhet nearly every other day. They drove out on the Çanakkale road to look for storks and eat *döner kebab* at a roadside place which Nükhet insisted on calling a "drive-in restaurant." They visited the Osmanli forest and watched the Black Sea surf at Kilios. Nükhet showed her the holy mosque where Eyüp, a disciple of Mohammed, was buried. One warm afternoon they took a ferry boat up the Golden Horn to look at turbaned tombstones and drink coffee at Pierre Loti's café. Nükhet knew the best *meze-evis* and there they would stuff themselves on little dishes of fish and olives and all sorts of appetizers. They observed women feeding eggs to the eels in a sacred pool on the Bosphorus close to the submarine nets. Tretona wanted to buy some eggs, too, but Nükhet insisted she would become pregnant if she did so. "Not bloody likely, given my life-style," laughed Tretona. Nükhet recorded the message but responded with a remark about the power of Turkish rituals.

Nükhet seemed eager to share all aspects of her country with Tretona, but she refused to go to the covered bazaar. "I suppose you want me to help you bargain for goat hair rugs and swinging tea trays. I find it all disgusting, Americans haggling down to the last lira, begrudging an extra coin for the poor peasants who spin the yarn for those blankets. Then they walk away, so smug, not realizing, that despite their greed, they have paid three times the going rate."

"Well, so much the better for the peasants then," said Tretona.

"No, it is the shopkeeper who profits."

"So why blame the Americans?" But it was no use arguing with Nükhet. She would plead poor English or insuperable cultural differences or boredom. What worried Tretona was the realization that she really didn't give a damn about Nükhet's exaggerations or phoniness or defensiveness about Turkey or her refusal to debate rationally. Instead, she found all the weaknesses and inadequacies charming and endearing. Here we go again, thought Tretona. I'm smitten. I'm down for the count. Maybe it was lucky that Christmas break was coming.

The night before the last day of school Tretona talked Di out of the car, even though it wasn't her turn. ("I suppose I *will* see you when we go to Lebanon," Di said grumpily.) For once

Nükhet had accepted an evening invitation. She always professed to have "pressing obligations" at night, but Tretona conjectured the real story was that her parents wouldn't let her go out. Anyway, tonight they were going to use a couple of Betsy's passes to see *Zorba the Greek* at the army base. Nükhet acted blasé, but Tretona knew she was excited. *Zorba* was censored, like anything else too sexy or even the slightest bit anti-Turkish, and Nükhet had never been on the base before.

Strictly speaking, Turkish guests weren't allowed for security reasons, but Betsy said no one would question a couple of women going to a movie. Tretona teased Nükhet about needing all of her theatrical skill to pose as an American. "The eyes will give you away, for sure," she said. "No American girl has eyes like yours." As it turned out, it was Tretona who needed acting lessons, for as soon as the lights went out Nükhet's presence beside her nearly drove her insane. First, it was her aura, the smell of a new perfume or sachet—had the hairs on their arms touched or had she just imagined it?—there, could that brush of the knee really have been accidental? Tretona, emboldened, moved her shoulder gently but positively against Nükhet's. But then, oh so subtly, the shoulder receded—was it a rejection or a natural settling of the body? No, there it was again, but maybe only as a result of Nükhet's sigh when the peasant women in the film started to keen.

And so it went, Tretona making socially acceptable positive advances, Nükhet fading away, but then reapproaching if Tretona did nothing. During the intermission for a reel change Tretona tried to decipher some message from Nükhet's eyes, but couldn't stand to look into them too long. Her cunt was as tense as an overwound alarm clock. On the way to fetch another box of "popcorns," as Nükhet insisted on calling it (she had trouble getting her mass nouns straight—the fact that her British teachers said "the Government *are* . . ." didn't help any), Tretona resolved to cool down and be completely unresponsive. But is it possible to share popcorn in the dark without touching? Popcorn perhaps, but with "popcorns" it is definitely *olamaz* (as the Turks say) or "impossible" (as the Americans say). And each brush, jostle, and bump sent reverberations through Tretona's body. A final close-up of Anthony Quinn and the sweet tense agony was over. Steer Nükhet swiftly though the transplanted southern accents and tennis shoes to the car. With one hand on the wheel and the other already shifting down and back into reverse, Tretona turned to ask Nükhet if she liked the movie, but instead somehow their lips met and clung and with her last ounce of rationality Tretona turned off the motor and got the parking brake on. Meanwhile, Nükhet was holding Tretona's neck and ears with her hands and kissing her face all over with little glides and very imperatively but yet languorously or was it languidly?— Tretona's mind inexplicably set off stubbornly on a search for the right word—lips like yogurt, she thought. And then to keep from feeling silly and overcome and incredulous because Turks really *did* kiss differently—ot at least Nükhet did—Tretona finally got her arms around Nükhet and drew her carefully but strongly over toward the driver's side. But it was like embracing a marshmallow—a toasted one where the fragile golden shell slips off the molten interior—because Nükhet's arms and breasts shifted without resistance but the rest of her body remained positioned squarely in the passenger's seat.

Oops, thought Tretona, necking in a VW is obviously an acquired art. How strange Nükhet's body felt. She was rounded but not really chubby; yet her body felt like silly putty—it seemed to be devoid of muscle tone. In fact, it reminded Tretona of those fake Persian miniatures in the bazaar with engravings of effete sultans "voluptuing" on divans.

"Do all Americans make love like John Wayne?" Nükhet was obviously experiencing some culture shock, too. Tretona was a teeny bit insulted but decided to try to save the situation. "Only when there's a horse waiting outside. But you must remember that America is a very underdeveloped country when it comes to the art of love."

Nükhet picked up the ball and ran with it. "Then I must teach you the secrets of the harem," she said. "Oils, scents, mysterious herbs and potions and other skills so secret that you must wear a blindfold. . . ." She placed her long cool fingers over Tretona's eyes and stopped up Tretona's ears with her thumbs. Thus deprived of extraneous sensory input, Tretona was free to concentrate completely on Nükhet's mouth, which had enveloped hers, and now on her tongue, which was gliding with agonizing slowness and incredible delicacy. When Tretona curled her own tongue in response, Nükhet pressed a little on her eyes. When it got to the point that Tretona could feel Nükhet's ring on her eyelids, she finally stopped moving and let her own tongue go limp which seemed to be what Nükhet had wanted all along, for now her mouth assumed complete control, stroking, kneading, teasing, until Tretona's lips and tongue were bruised and even her teeth seemed to be throbbing with desire.

Desperately, Tretona clutched at Nükhet, trying to draw her closer but then from what seemed to be a great distance came Nükhet's voice, "Touch yourself. Don't touch me; touch *yourself!* Now!"

And somehow knowing what Nükhet meant—but not caring if she was mistaken—Tretona immediately slid her left hand down into her crotch and relief was on the way even before her right hand had finished unbuttoning the levis. And now Nükhet was cradling her, very gently, and warming her and caressing her. With shock waves and reverberations Tretona penetrated the sound barrier into that otherworldly stillness where you're going faster than any message can travel. . . . The winter quarter was spent reading T. S. Eliot, whose poetry eventually came to provide a special language for them. "I have saved this afternoon for you. . . ." the quote would appear in Tretona's mailbox.

"Why can't you tell me ahead of time when I can see you?" Tretona would complain.

"Oh my impatient, impetuous American," Nükhet would reply. "In the East things are not so simple. . . ."

Nükhet would now sometimes even invite her home. They would sit on a glassed-in porch overlooking Beyoğlu, and Nükhet's grandmother would bring in plate after plate of little snacks. Tretona called her "Anna" and always asked her in Turkish how she was. "*Iyi, hocam. Iyi,*" the grandmother would reply but there were cataracts on her eyes and she had arthritis in her hands.

Nükhet would become a little defensive. "You must not learn Turkish from my grandmother. She is a simple woman and very old-fashioned. *Hoca* means religious teacher. She does not quite understand what goes on at AKK."

Tea with Nükhet was a delicious agony of teasing glances and love play. Tretona would try to kiss the fingers which fed her olives and dolmas. "Do I dare to eat a peach?" Nükhet would quote while holding the lush fruit from Izmir as gently as a breast.

Sometimes, but certainly not always, Tretona would be invited into Nükhet's room and then they would sit together on the bed and look at art books or Nükhet's grotesque sketches of crucifixions and dismembered limbs. Sometimes, but not always—and Tretona could *never* predict when her luck would strike—Nükhet would allow herself to be kissed and embraced (not too hard, though), but soon she would take charge and stroke Tretona so sensually (but never touching the primary erogenous zones) that the juices would flow from her mouth and vagina and Tretona would whimper and beg for satisfaction.

"But would it be worth it, after all?" Nükhet would say completely seriously. "After all the cakes and ices, should I push the moment to its crisis?" And sometimes Tretona would get in a huff and leave and sometimes she would cry bitterly into Nükhet's pillow.

"You Americans—you do not know the meaning of *sacrifice,*" Nükhet would say. "How can there be love without sacrifice?" And twice Tretona got Nükhet down and raped her thigh, humping and rubbing against that foam cylinder, hot breath rasping harshly in her throat. An ugly sound accompanying an ugly movement, but how else to vent her frustration and anger? Such excesses always led to Nükhet's being unreachable for several days. So Tretona would ask, Are you mad? and apologize profusely for her crudeness and promise never, never—but Nükhet would become impatient and insist that she was simply *too busy* to spend any time with Tretona.

Feeling more and more helpless, Tretona finally talked to Di about it, putting her problem in obscure terms—having to do with teasing and what to do when you liked someone more than they liked you. Di gently extracted the structure of the situation from her, though not the sweaty details.

"So Nükhet has access to you practically any time she wants, while you can see her only on her terms," Di summarized.

"Well, yes—I guess that's about it," said Tretona glumly.

Then Di launched into a little lecture on the relationship of access to power, how housemothers can walk into student dormitory rooms anytime they please, but not vice versa, and so on. She talked about the importance of being able to say no, of the power that comes from saying no.

"But I *want* to give Nükhet access to my life," protested Tretona. "I always want to see her. I don't *want* to say no, so why should I?"

Di exploded and said nonsense, surely there were occasions on which the time and place Nükhet selected for a rendezvous were not the most convenient ones for Tretona.

"But I don't mind adapting. I don't mind making a little sacrifice for Nükhet's sake. Isn't that what love is about, making sacrifices?"

Tretona had never seen Di so exasperated. "Don't confuse sacrifice with sabotage," she snapped. "What good are all these little sacrifices doing you? Does playing Miss Mamby-Pamby-Always-Available make Nükhet like you any more?"

"Well, she probably couldn't see me as often if we didn't meet on her terms," said Tretona. "Besides, I'm not as busy as she is and honestly, Di, I don't mind sacrificing. . . ."

Di groaned. "Don't devalue yourself, Tretona. Your time and convenience are every bit as important as dear little Nükhet's. Okay, I realize you don't feel that way, but look at it practically. Use a little bit of that scientific training. Do your sacrifices get you what you want? Is your strategy effective? Is there any direct correlation between how obsequious you are to Nükhet and how nice she is to you?"

Tretona, thinking of those totally unpredictable bedroom scenes, had to admit that there wasn't. "Except that if I become too frustrated and get pushy, then she withdraws." Tretona was close to tears. "But what I can't understand, Di, is why I keep liking her so much. I mean she holds out on me so much and won't explain why—sometimes, of course, she is very nice but I never know when it's going to be—I just can't figure it out."

"It's sort of like playing an emotional roulette wheel," said Di. "You never know exactly what number's going to turn up."

"Yeah—it's frustrating as hell. But of course in a funny way, that's part of the excitement." Tretona was getting more and more puzzled.

So Di put on a Skinnerian hat and gave a lecture about how those situations in which the rewards are random and intermittent are more reinforcing than cases where you know what is going to happen. "Obviously, the unpredictable can add a lot of spice to life," said Di. "That's why we're moved so much by unexpected kindness—we tend to value them more highly than the constant flow of nice things members of our families or good friends do for us. At least our gut level response is more intense. Sometimes, people can get really addicted by partial-reinforcement schedules. Take compulsive gamblers—on an overall basis they lose money steadily, but those rare, unexpected jackpots are *so* rewarding that they get hooked."

It was time to eat dinner at the dining hall. Thank God,

Nükhet doesn't live in the dorm, thought Tretona. I'd never survive. Or maybe it'd be better. She couldn't play so much cat-and-mouse stuff then. On the way over to eat, Tretona took hold of Di's arm. "You're a wonderful friend to me, Di," she said. "Thanks for being so accessible—I mean, thanks for being so willing to help when I need you. I'm afraid I haven't been very . . . to you . . . I mean." Tretona flushed, realizing the unfairness of it all, but Di just gave her a little hug. Nükhet is a one-armed bandit, Tretona thought, a Turkish torture device—but I love her—sort of.

The link between having a rational insight and coming to feel differently about things is every bit as mysterious and obscure as Descartes' pineal gland. Sometimes, emotional liberation rolls in like thunder right after the lighning flashes in the mind. More often, time and patience are required—and sometimes a bit of luck. Would Tretona on her own ever have learned to say no to Nükhet? The answer lies in the unfolding of some other possible world for on the fourth of April, 1963, in Istanbul, Turkey, the administration of the American College for Girls unwittingly intervened on Tretona's behalf.

The identical typewritten notes Tretona and Di received at dinner were terse to the point of rudeness: "Come to the Deanery at 7:30 tonight. Do not discuss this engagement with anyone." Tretona had a date right after dinner with Nükhet and thought about ignoring the summons—after all, she rarely got to see Nükhet after dark. But Di talked her out of it. "Obviously, some emergency has come up. I think you'd better come." So when the faculty adjourned to the lounge for coffee, Tretona phoned Nükhet. Her voice went dead when she heard Tretona wasn't coming, but all she said was, "It doesn't matter—I've got work to do." For once, Tretona didn't fall all over herself apologizing and it seemed to work, a little bit at least, because Nükhet closed by saying *she'd* phone Tretona to see what had happened at the Deanery. It was nice to think that Nükhet was genuinely interested and might take the initiative and put some effort into their relationship. Of course, it could have been a command for Tretona *not* to get in touch with her until summoned. There was no outguessing a Turk, especially Nükhet.

Tretona and Di walked down the marble stairs of Old Main and cut across the lawn to Dean Tanner's cottage. Di was nervous, "I can't imagine why they called us so mysteriously."

For some reason, maybe it was the big Asian moon hanging over Usküdar, Tretona wasn't worried, but her mood changed as soon as they got there.

Tanner opened the door without a word of greeting, merely a tense, "You've come," and ushered them into the living room. All the senior staff were there, Turkish as well as American, but only Betsy smiled and nodded. The rest sat like wax figures looking at the floor.

Tanner motioned them to sit in a couple of easy chairs. She herself perched on the circular library ladder. "There's no need to prolong this," she said. "The Advisory Council has concluded that you two set a bad example for the students and that you" (here she seemed to be looking mainly at Tretona) "are a disrupting influence."

Oh boy, here it comes, thought Tretona. She composed her body for the attack—toes turned in a little, upper body erect (damn this overstuffed chair), and face turned to a solemn blank expression. I wonder who complained, Nükhet? Nükhet's mother? Or maybe Filiz acting out of jealousy?

Tanner started reading out her list of charges against Tretona: wearing knee socks to the dress-up Thanksgiving dinner, repeated failure to enforce the English rule at lunch ("But I only inquire about the Turkish names for . . ."—Di reached over and squelched Tretona's interruption.) The more serious accusations were evidently to come: "teaching religious and socialist politics at the folk song club" (Tanner forestalled another outburst by giving examples: "Christian spirituals and those so-called labor-union songs"), "blasphemy, and inciting the sophomore class to rebel against the properly constituted school authorities."

Tretona's look of complete bewilderment must have moved Dr. Rabahat, the Turkish sociology teacher, because she gestured for Tanner to explain.

The story unfolded rather slowly, what with Tretona's denials and Tanner's refusal to listen. Roughly what had happened was that the sophomores, in a fit of spring fever, had challenged a bunch of the dormitory regulations and Tanner had responded by asking the student council to enforce the rules more strictly. There had been an *ad hoc* strike meeting, which Tretona had attended in her capacity as sophomore class advisor. In trying to calm them down, Tretona had presented both sides of the issue as she saw it and at one point had said (Tanner had the quote in her

215

report): "I'd be damned if I'd help enforce rules which I hadn't made and about which I had absolutely no say."

Tretona admitted saying the quoted sentence, but claimed that she had followed it up immediately by saying something like: "However, you *do* have some input into the content of the rules and you could probably increase your input if . . ."

Tanner seemed not to hear. Di's list of sins was similar: "unfortunate remarks made while discussing the authoritarian personality in her Intro Pysch class (which all the sophomores took) describing civil disobedience as a legitimate form of protest instead of as law-breaking," etc.

Tretona's exasperation was modulated by her intense relief that nothing more explosive had come up—like "seducing . . ." or "public self-pollution. . . ." Phew!

The charges having been read and the defendants having duly pleaded Not Guilty, Tanner moved on immediately to the sentence. It seemed no evidence or discussion was deemed relevant.

"Duties to be terminated immediately . . . passage home already arranged. Fetva is on hand to help you pack. . . ." And so exactly one hour and thirty-five minutes after their arrival at the Deanery, Di and Tretona were out once again under the beautiful Bosphorus moon.

During the next couple of hours Tretona sat numb as a prisoner on Death Row waiting for execution—she was unable to move and unable to think about anything except how she would say good-bye to Nükhet. Di, on the other hand, was starting a counterattack. She telephoned the British high school and got the names of some influential liberals at Robert College. She ordered a taxi and got Dimitros to go down to the Hilton with an emergency telegram to send off to the Board of Trustees in New York. Fetva was coaxed into phoning the airport, finding out if the plane reservations had been made (they had), and cancelling them. "That fucker," said Di. "Did she really think she could bully us into leaving our car here?"

Finally, they heard Betsy come back. Tretona was for staying away, but Di said, nonsense, we've got to find out what's going on, and so down they went. Betsy was calm, seemingly not the least bit sheepish over her membership in the Star Council.

"There's really not much to explain," she said. "Tanner is insecure as hell—she's really scared shitless that the sophomores are getting out of hand. You know the older teachers—they're all frustrated nun-types and frankly, they think you both are too frisky and iconoclastic. One of you they could probably take, but two—well, I guess it was just too much."

Di was just as calm. "Well, we're going to challenge the decision. After all, we have a three-year contract. I've just found out that there's a branch of the AAUP over at Robert College—they're willing to investigate. And whatever happens, we are not leaving here until this business has been dealt with properly—legally, if need be."

Tretona was becoming more and more apprehensive. "Wait, Di," she said. And then to Betsy: "Are you sure that we've heard all their accusations? Is there maybe something else at the bottom of all this?"

Betsy looked puzzled. "If Tanner had any other beefs, I'm sure she would have aired them. She hates both your guts."

Di was impatient. "What does it matter, Tretona? We have nothing to hide. All we need is a fair hearing."

If you only knew, thought Tretona. Eventually, they did get a hearing with quite favorable results—the dismissal was postponed until the end of the term and the board agreed to honor their contract for the next two years if they couldn't find equivalent jobs. The news leaked out, of course, and the sophomore class quit rebelling and diverted all their rambunctious energy into planning a series of farewell events for Di and Tretona. Dimitros and Fetva beamed about how wonderful American justice was. Di's lawyer back home said that if they couldn't find another job in Turkey they could just take two years off and collect full salary.

So everything turned out all right, although Tretona was too paranoid to have any more dates with Nükhet—except once they drove out on the Bursa road and checked into a hotel room at three P.M. and made love—in both directions—and Nükhet was a wonderful lover, but so much crap had already gone under the bridge and there was the tension of having been apart and thinking about saying good-bye. As T. S. Eliot said, "Would it have been worth it after all?"

18 Tea and Communitas

I'll take you by the hand
And lead you through the streets of London
I'll show you something
To make you change your mind.
                    —*As sung by Cleo Laine*

Culture . . . is an atmosphere and a heritage.
                    —*H. L. Mencken*

LOO. LORRY. LIFT. Dustbin. Ice lollies. Strangers who said, "Thanks, love." Pencils with and without rubbers. Fellow students who came down the hall to "knock you up for lunch." Muted voices and omnipresent queues. Beans on toast. Half pints of bitter. England was every bit as foreign as Turkey.

Even here in Western Europe it was practically impossible to pass as anything other than American. "I can always pick your lot out," said Benjamin Cartwright as they sat outside a café watching tourists parade up and down the King's Road.

"Sure, it's easy when they're fresh off a charter plane, saddled with cameras and backpacks," said Tretona. "But what about someone like me, someone who's lived here a while? This pullover came from Marks and Sparks. I got the jeans here in the King's Road and I'm wearing sandals from India. So there's no way you could pick me out as American. I mean if I didn't *say* anything, you couldn't."

"In your case it'd be rather easy, actually. You're sitting like an American."

Tretona flushed. What did he mean? For once, she didn't

have her feet propped up or her legs sprawled apart. She surreptitiously brought her knees closer together and straightened her back. "My mother would consider this to be a very ladylike pose—for me, at least. So what are you picking up on?"

"It's hard to explain," said Benjamin. "It has something to do with the amount of space you occupy. No, not *occupy*—that's too passive a word. You really *fill* space—something about your air of confidence, your enthusiasm. No, don't protest—it's true— and I think it's rather marvelous, really."

Benjamin Cartwright sat primly on the bench, tall and thin, his long legs somehow folded up and stowed away under the table, wrists protruding from his jacket sleeves like those of a growing schoolboy.

"Yankee know-how, Yankee confidence, eh? Glad to hear you finally admit it, Ben." He hated being called anything but Benjamin, so it was a good way to tease him. "At least you're on to something more basic about Americans than their deodorant."

"I know you think we Brits are a grotty lot," he replied, "but don't forget we've got a much lower child mortality rate than you do—even though we use midwives."

"What do you mean, *even* with midwives?" protested Tretona. "I'd trust them over an M.D. any day." But the first part was true—she *did* think the Brits were "grotty." Look at Benjamin: his cravat was of good quality—it might even have come from Liberty's—but it hung around his neck like a limp greasy dishrag. Not that it was easy to keep clean over here. The landlady at that bed-sitter place in South Ken where she and Di had stayed when they first arrived last summer had not only charged extra for baths but had also rationed them.

"Tuesday'll be your bath night, love." And when Di complained, she launched into a tirade about how wasteful foreigners were. According to her, Australians were the worst. "They'll draw a hot tub every bloody night if you don't keep a sharp lookout."

Whatever the explanation—maybe the British had just missed out on the cleanliness-is-next-to-Godliness brand of Puritanism—the people here were pretty sloppy—not that she'd ever thought of herself as particularly fastidious.

That was the nice thing about living abroad. You found out who you really were, which of your characteristics were unusual ones and—this was more interesting—which things about yourself you either couldn't or wouldn't change. Like this business about "filling space," as Benjamin had described it. True, she didn't sprawl all over park benches and scatter her books around on the library tables anymore—that behavior she had modified. After all, this really was a tight little island, there simply wasn't as much room to go around. But there was no way she was going to start melting into the wallpaper and trying to be invisible in class like the British students. Hell, if she was interested in what the lecturer was saying, she was going to show it. And if he was coming out with a right load of old poppycock she was going to register that, too. "Lecturer"—"he." Funny she should say that because her favorite lecturer was very much a "she"—disturbingly so. Tretona wondered if her face transmitted those reactions as well.

"Shulamith Elkana." She liked saying the name.

"Your favorite philosophical midwife?" Benjamin was trying to keep the conversation going.

"She sure is. Isn't she just marvelous as a discussion leader?" Tretona couldn't help gushing. "I mean the way she keeps making you be precise about what problem we're working on and exactly what our criticisms are and stuff."

"In my opinion, our dear Dr. Elkana does philosophy like a Zionist terrorist. She's a methodological dogmatist, she bullies people, she uses dirty arguments, *and* she's intellectually irresponsible."

Tretona realized she was being baited; nevertheless, she couldn't keep from swelling up like a little irate red hen. Words of praise and defense and love poured out like a well-rehearsed litany.

"Shulamith is *not* dogmatic. She just has strong ideas about how to conduct an intellectual discussion, that's all. She announced them at the beginning of class: 'Always state the problem you're trying to solve. Never ask What-is questions. Never ask people to justify their conjectures. Always be grateful for criticism.' You know the list. She was absolutely clear about what the rules are *and* she explicitly said that nothing was immune to criticism—not even the rules. You can hardly call *that* being dogmatic. And talk about playing dirty—what do you call your little slur about her being an Israeli?"

Benjamin, as usual, kept his dignity and reserve. Arguing

with him was like playing Ping Pong with a foam rubber mattress. No matter how hard she slammed home a point, some reply would come dribbling back. Here it came now, sane-sounding talk about the importance of constructive suggestions as a complement to negative criticism, the necessity of confirmation and evidential support, blah, blah. She knew it all already.

What she couldn't quite say to Benjamin—not yet at least—was how emotionally important for her Shulamith's philosophy class had become. Practically ever day Shulamith would come out with some slogan, ostensibly about the growth of science, but which seemed to speak directly to Tretona personally. "We learn from our mistakes," Shulamith would say, the ordinary English words gaining significance because of her careful foreigner's intonation. "Successful predictions teach us nothing. We only know we are touching reality when our expectations are violated."

It was true, oh so true, and in so many ways. You could never be sure that someone loved you. It was exactly as in science—just because a theory was working well right now didn't mean that it always would. And when the refutations came, when the theory failed, you didn't need to feel guilty, not if you'd been scrupulous on a methodological level. For example, you had to record negative results carefully and honestly, and not try to relabel them or explain them away with what Shulamith called "conventionalist stratagems."

Sometimes, Tretona could hardly breathe when she thought about how much mislabeling she had done in the past, all in the name of false optimism or trying to think well of someone.

But, "We *learn* from our mistakes." That was the healing part of Shulamith's philosophy. Everybody makes mistakes. Scientists and lovers alike make all kinds of mistakes—both substantive and methodological errors. It was inevitable because we're all fallible. The thing is to *learn* from our mistakes, not begrudge them or feel guilty over them.

Another thing Shulamith stressed was how long it sometimes takes scientists to understand matters that in retrospect seem so elementary. "Aristotle was no dummy," (as Benjamin sarcastically summarized one of her lectures), "but he thought water could be turned into wine and believed metals grew in the bowels of the earth." And it took centuries for people to get straight on really basic stuff like the circulation of the blood and atmospheric pressure. So she shouldn't feel too bad about taking so long to figure out who she was and what she wanted to be.

Sometimes Tretona would sit there in class and almost swoon from the insights she was getting—and the relief. She wondered if Shulamith realized how powerful and how widely applicable her philosophical theory was. Maybe someday they could have coffee together and. . . . There she went again, getting a teenage crush on her teacher.

Benjamin was twiddling with his tea cup, watching the never-ending parade along the King's Road—trendy teenagers bopping along from one jeans shop to the next, upper-class Chelsea mums in tweeds and sturdy oxfords, foreign students from Kensington College, school boys from St. Luke's wearing maroon and tan uniforms, tradespeople, Americans, even the occasional bowler hat.

Finally, with a shade of irritation, he turned back to Tretona. "You seem rather far away today. If it were spring, I'd say you were in love."

"I *am* in love," Tretona found herself saying. "With Britain, with Chelsea, with the Philosophy and Science program, with our lecturers. I'm even getting used to that flat warm stuff you guys pretend is beer!"

Benjamin looked uncomfortable. "Too much enthusiasm again?" Tretona asked.

He smiled. "Well—no. I'm *glad* you like it, I suppose. It's just that I get so impatient. I don't know why I came here. I had a good job teaching physics in that comprehensive school you know, trying to motivate all the chaps, convince them they could make it into trade school, university even, make a better living than their parents could—giving them the standard old upward mobility line. Sometimes I really believed what I was saying—other times it was damn depressing. Once I was telling them about the debate between Galileo and the Aristotelians over where a cannon ball would land if dropped from the mast of a moving ship. I was dramatizing it a bit, making Galileo sound like a working-class Bristol boy and doing posh accents for the Aristotelian Establishment types, but at the same time trying to get the physics right Gradually   became aware that I'd lost Foster—his face had that dead look he always gets when he's not following. Well, Foster was one of my better students—wretched background—I gather his old man used to beat the children, but by some mercy he finally ran off or got put in jail or something. Anyway, Foster gets discouraged easily but is really bright. So I stopped and said, 'I feel like I'm not explaining this very well.' (That was the way I always phrased it so as not to put them off.) 'Help me out, Foster. Ask me a question so I get back on the track.' I watched his face. I could see he was trying to decide whether to get involved or just lay back and play dead. 'I'm sorry, sir,' he said. 'But what is a *mast?*' "

"Jesus, what did you do?" asked Tretona.

"I'm afraid I became very flustered," said Benjamin. "At first, I thought he was asking a question about *mass* and so I reviewed Aristotle's reasons for thinking that heavy bodies fall faster, but when his face went blank again it finally dawned on me. So then I told him what a *mast* was and some of the boys looked like they were going to snicker, so I got tough and said they all needed to know basic things about ships and navigation and I threw every damned technical term I could think of at them—lanyard, halyard, port, starboard, stays, spars—and mast, too."

"Probably Foster's ancestors knew what a mast was," said Tretona. "Well, unless they spent the whole voyage down in the hold."

Benjamin snapped his head up quickly. "Foster's not West Indian, you know. He's English—Cockney—lives in the East End—probably not more than two miles from the docks. So much for the British Empire—its native sons don't know a mast from a Maypole. And there I was telling chaps like Foster they could catch up, compete with those rich twits who've been sailing on Daddy's yacht at Cowes ever since they crawled out of their fur-lined prams. What a lot of old malarky that was."

"Well, it's not *all* false—some people *do* make it that way. You did."

As Benjamin's hands tightened, his arms receded until his jacket almost fit. "Oh, I made it, all right, by going to a Catholic school where the good Christian brothers cracked your palm with a ruler once for every misspelled word. And then the strap at home if you got a bad report. God, how I hated it—evaluations every six weeks. Our mum always tried to have something special for tea on report day, sausages maybe or even a meat pie, but none of us could eat. After he d finished stuffing himself, Dad would throw some coal on the fire and light up a Woodbine. Cigarettes were his only luxury. 'I've worked at their factory twenty-five years now,' he'd say, 'smelling that good Woodbine tobacco smell all the day long. A man can only take so much.' Most of the men stole their fags from the factory but he was too proud to do that. He'd walk down to the tobacconist's every payday and buy a pack of ten to last him out the week.

"He'd get the fire poked up and his cigarette going and then he'd look at our marks. God, I can still see him. Cigarette drooping from his lips, eyes squinting from the smoke, as he fumbled at his belt buckle."

Benjamin's pain came out in splinters—it was too old and petrified ever to be dissolved by tears. Tretona moved her hands forward, but did not quite manage to touch his sleeve.

"Benjamin, you *did* make it, though. You passed your eleven-pluses and you got a first-class in physics at Bristol. Okay, so it's not Oxford or Cambridge, but it's a damn good university—and now you're writing an M.Phil. here. You're doing real well."

Benjamin's face was calm now—maybe even dead like Foster's. "I'll always be an outsider. I'll always have the wrong accent. And I'll always feel angry and embarrassed around Oxbridge types. I'd be miserable in any Senior Common Room. Not that they'd ever hire me in the first place. Not bloody likely."

"Maybe you should join the Brain Drain," said Tretona. "Americans would be impressed to hell with your Bristol accent."

"Save my own skin? What about Foster and all the rest?"

"Well, what about them? You aren't doing anything for Foster sitting in a café feeling miserable." Tretona was immediately sorry that she'd said that. Sure enough, Benjamin went off on a tirade about how useless the Philosophy and Science program at Kensington was, how he shouldn't be there wasting both his time and the taxpayer's money, etc. etc.

"Benjie, stop." Tretona had never used the diminutive of his name before, but she suddenly felt motherly or big-sisterly or something. "I don't know why I yelled at you."

"It's perfectly all right, Tretona. I deserved it. I'm always moaning. To put Marx in the vernacular, 'The thing to do is get off one's ass and change the world, not sit around complaining about it.'"

"Listen," said Tretona. "Let me tell you about this debate I keep having with Di about social responsibility and individual happiness. Maybe you can help me sort it all out, 'cause I think there's something important here—something that would apply to you—although maybe I'm just trying to shove my own rationalizations off onto other people.

"Here's the background. As you know, we came here under unusually carefree circumstances. After the blow-up in Turkey, they guaranteed us our salaries if we didn't find jobs. We didn't have to save up money to come here—it was just a big magic present from out of nowhere with no strings attached."

"Some people have all the luck," said Benjamin.

"Isn't it the truth?" said Tretona, "and you're worried about taking a free ride on the taxpayers! Well, anyway, it's terribly nice being an expatriate. We don't have to take any responsibility for Britain's problems—not much anyway, because we aren't citizens. And as for America—the bus strike in Montgomery, Vietnam, nuclear testing—we aren't there, so there's little we can do about them either.

"So here I am, simply ecstatic over the Philosophy and Science program. I'm learning answers to all the big questions I never quite knew how to formulate before. God, I can't think of a more important subject. And Di's having a ball hanging around Anna Freud's operation up in Hampstead and sitting in on seminars at the Tavistock Clinic.

"So what should creep into our little subsidized expatriate paradise, but guilt. It hit Di first. Maybe it comes from subscribing to the *Bulletin of Atomic Scientists.* Anyway, she started nagging at me—and herself, 'If you aren't part of the solution, you're part of the problem,' and, 'There are no personal solutions, only political ones.' Then she got all in a snit about our easy life here, bopping by Big Ben on the way to the theater, doing the pubs and having a grand time in Merrie Old England while the rest of the world is going to hell in a hand basket.

"I didn't know what to reply. I still don't. All I have to defend myself with is my good old masturbation principle."

"What's that?" asked Benjamin. He seemed to be cheering up, so Tretona rushed on feeling a little giddy.

"Why, it's very simple," said Tretona, "and I'll pass it on to you for free: 'Anything that feels *that* good can't be all bad.' You'll find it in any hedonistic calculus book."

"Well, that doesn't help me out," said Benjamin. "I don't

feel a bit good sitting around in class learning about conditional probabilities and natural deduction while Foster is back in the East End wondering what a *mast* is."

"But your pain is on the meta-level, isn't it?" said Tretona. "I mean you *like* probability theory and logic. You *enjoy* it. No, you do—admit it. You love it as much as I do. Even that British reserve can't hide it. What causes your pain is the guilt you feel *about* liking it as much as you do."

"I'm afraid you're right," said Benjamin. "I seem to be afflicted with decadent intellectual bourgeois tastes."

"Oh cut out the cant," said Tretona. "Look. Your studying logic doesn't hurt anyone and it brings you happiness. There's no reason to deprive yourself of something nice just because other people in our society are unhappy."

"But I should be—I *want* to be—doing something for the Fosters in this world," said Benjamin.

"Wonderful," said Tretona. "That's what you should do."

Benjamin's forehead was wrinkled so tight that his scalp looked stretched. "But I don't know *what* to do. I tried teaching, but I got so miserable that I gave it up and came here."

Tretona no longer knew whether she was talking to Benjamin or to herself. "So rest, relax, learn, prepare yourself, heal yourself. If you do sacrifice yourself, make it have a point, make it purposeful. It's no use suffering just to feel solidarity with the downtrodden."

Benjamin's brow smoothed a little, but he made one last remonstration. "But it's so easy to become complacent, to get seduced into a comfortable, selfish existence."

Tretona had the answer to that, too. All in all, it was amazing how wise and confident she felt when talking to Benjamin. Was it because she was older than he? He was probably twenty-three or twenty-four. Five years made a big difference sometimes. Or maybe Americans *were* more confident.

"With *your* social sensitivity, I don't think you need to worry about getting complacent, Benjamin. The main thing to do is to keep alert—whenever the occasion arises, strike a blow for what you believe, no matter how small. It'll keep you sharp, keep you in practice until the time comes for a big play."

Wise advise, but damned if she could follow it. What was it Professor Spinner had said the other day? Something about

"Kepler pursuing the correct orbital description of Mars with the zeal usually reserved for wooing members of the opposite sex?"

She'd wanted to intervene, but couldn't think of anything, and then a little later got caught whispering to Benjamin. "Was there a question?" snapped Professor Spinner.

"No, I was just remarking that Mars, in as much as he was the god of war, was surely a member of the *same* sex," said Tretona. Of course, Professor Spinner didn't get the political point—no one did. They probably just marked it up as another example of her being an American smart aleck.

Tretona hadn't quite figured out yet what the British attitude toward homosexuality was. They talked about it a lot—every other joke on a comedy show seemed to be about faggots. Most of them were derogatory, but sometimes they would get off some really good puns.

Although in general one had to be pretty careful with slang. Once in a pub garden she had described an energetic two-year-old who was crawling all over the place as a "feisty little booger" and Benjamin had nearly collapsed. Later he told her that "booger" was the North Country pronunciation of "bugger" and that it was *not* a term to apply to other people's children. Then he told her about Winston Churchill's *bon mot*. When a famous homosexual in Parliament finally got married to a rather ugly woman, Winston had puffed on his cigar and harrumphed, "Well, buggers can't be choosers, you know."

All in all, there was quite a bit of verbal queer-bashing. Tretona was surprised at Di's reaction to it one night when they went to a Rag Day Review at the college. One of the skits had some funny business in it about English judges and their wigs. When the last member of the Queen's Council took off his barrister's robe and turned out to be in full drag, Di got disgusted and almost walked out.

"Hey, it was just a joke," said Tretona over drinks at the pub afterward. "Don't get so uptight."

"Jokes are one of the ways in which a society puts down minorities," said Di. "That skit helps perpetuate the myth that all homosexual men are effeminate or transvestites. It was full of hostility and contempt."

"Oh, for God's sake—they were just a bunch of irreverent college kids goofing off. They were taking the mickey out of everything sacred in those routines. You saw them—the Queen, upper-class snobs, officers at Sandhurst, TV announcers—everybody was getting their comeuppance."

"Exactly. And the way they made fun of judges was by implying they were queer, which is obviously a laughable thing to be. I'm surprised that you, of all people, aren't more sensitive."

Tretona took up the gauntlet and started inventing counter arguments, not pausing to decide whether she believed them 100 percent or not. "Well, as far as I'm concerned, I think it's a lot healthier for people to at least be able to joke about it. I get the impression that in Britain anti-queer jokes are about on a par with jokes about mothers-in-law and Irishmen. Sure, there's some hostility involved, but at least the subject is not totally beyond the pale. In America you'd never hear any explicit jokes about queers on television and radio because the whole subject is so taboo. It's like child molesting or incest—too frightening even to joke about."

"On the contrary, I think the British are even more frightened of homosexuality than Americans are. Because of what goes on in boarding schools they realize it could happen to anyone. Jokes are one very effective form of social control: 'Don't be queer or everyone will laugh at you.' That's the real message that comes through loud and clear."

"Yeah, that message is there all right, but there're a lot of other points being made, too. Like tonight we learned that *judges* might be queer—it's not just hairdressers and make-up men at the BBC. That's even more clear in the Winston Churchill anecdote Benjamin told me. The story doesn't get off the ground unless the listener believes that there are MP's who are not only gay but also *known* to be gay. That sure wouldn't be a plausible assumption about the American government. There's no way you could translate that joke by giving, say, Harry Truman the punch line."

"Look, I'm not trying to make any comparisons," said Di. "All I said was that I find anti-queer jokes in bad taste and I detest them, just like—. Well, do you remember that rash of sick jokes about using Thalidomide babies for first base? Absolutely intolerable."

Tretona felt herself getting angry, though she didn't know why until after she'd spoken, "Well, I'll tell you one thing, Di Sorensen, I'd a hell of a lot rather people *laugh* at me because they think queers are odd and eccentric than *pity* me because they think queers are sick—with a psyche as misshapen as a Thalidomide baby's body."

"Hey, Tretona. Sounds like we better talk about that."

"What's there to say?" said Tretona. "Want another round?" And without waiting for an answer, "I'll get it."

She worked her way carefully through the crowd to the bar. An English pub was no place to have a heated argument, especially if you were sporting a big brassy American accent. It was amazing how many British you could pack into a small space, all drinking and talking animatedly, and yet how quiet it would be.

The two ends of the social scale were the noisiest, according to Benjamin—jolly working-class women and pompous upper-class twits. This was a fairly chic Chelsea pub, but not for swingers. The clientele were well-heeled middle-aged types with respectably old Jaguars parked outside and well-behaved Corgis lying at their feet. Tretona and Di liked it because the annex was a sort of orangerie with plants and wooden tables. Definitely not a suitable place for a tiff.

Tretona ordered two halves of special bitter. Then so as to be conciliatory to Di, she changed it: "Make that two full pints, would you?"

As usual, the bartender looked slightly disapproving. In England women did not drink beer from pint mugs. According to Benjamin, it just wasn't done. Sometimes bartenders would get adamant about it and if you ordered a pint, they'd give it to you in two half-pint glasses!

Tretona had long since conformed to the local custom, partly so as not to embarrass Benjamin and the others. But Di resented it like hell and *always* ordered a pint, even when she couldn't drink it all. Di was always taking on the British, trying to ride in first-class railway carriages on a second-class ticket, sneaking up into better seats at the cinema, walking on the grass in the middle of Trinity College quadrangle at Cambridge, trying to take a photograph of Newton's rooms. And she always got caught by some uniformed official and then would deliver a lecture to the conductor, usher, or university don on the stupidity of the rule or custom involved.

On such occasions Di would be triumphant afterward, but Tretona always felt mortified. Still, she had to admit you should be able to buy a large beer if you wanted one.

Tretona turned on a smile as she returned to their table.

"Here's enough mud for both your eyes! Cheers."

"Ooh, you got pints. Cheers, my dear. Cheers—to queers!"

Oops. The subject of conversation hadn't changed. If anything, Di seemed to have prepared a speech.

"Tretona, I've felt for a long time that you feel—now correct me if I'm wrong—that you feel that I feel homosexuals are psychologically inferior."

"Jesus, you've been reading too much R. D. Laing—you're even starting to talk like him."

"Quit weaseling out. Tell me, am I right? Don't you feel hostile toward psychologists in general and maybe me in particular? Tretona, I want us to face this issue. I know you're pissed at the Freudians and their retarded theories of homosexuality. But why take it out on me? I don't believe that stuff."

"Well, frankly, Di, I have no idea what you believe. When I first met you it was all Piaget; then you started flirting with Skinner. And in Turkey you were even some sort of Freudian. Jesus, remember when you burned your arm with the iron that time and went around for days wondering why you were punishing yourself with fire? Now you're hanging around the Tavistock Clinic drooling over the Laingians and Melanie Klein. Your ideas about psychology change faster than the fashions in skirt lengths. I guess I find both pretty disgusting."

"Now hold up a little. Let's get this straight. Look, I admit I'm eclectic. I like to sample lots of different approaches and sort out what seems convincing from the rest. But I don't think I'm intellectually fickle. Sure, sometimes I change my mind—who doesn't? But mainly what I'm doing is expanding my earlier ideas, qualifying old thoughts and theories. In a way it's just Piaget's processes of assimilation and accommodation carried out on an abstract level."

Tretona felt herself getting grumpier and grumpier. Hell, maybe a pub *was* a good place to have a showdown after all. Things couldn't get too out of control with all these civilized people around. It reminded her of how she would try to bring Bernice home for dinner after Sunday school whenever her folks were quarreling. It generally worked.

"Well, that's another thing that pisses me off. You're always trying to make up theories about people—about me, especially. Always getting me to tell stories so you can collect more data—

'Oh, so your mother wouldn't let you wear white bucks because they made your feet look bigger? Tell me, what was your body image like at that time? How did you feel? Were you experiencing peer alienation?' Honestly, Di, sometimes I feel like a dissected frog. How's that for a nice body image?"

Di was silent. Then she took a deep breath and spoke very calmly. "My impression was that you rather liked telling anecdotes and were interested in my little attempts to. . . ." Her voice broke. "You big lummox. Don't you understand that I love you—very much—and I just want to help you all I can."

Tretona's heart poised on a knife edge, wanting to trust this person, this woman who had been her friend, and a *good* friend, too, for three or four years now. But some instinct (survival? fear? a faint whiff of phoniness about Di?), some instinct made her veer away.

"Well, maybe it's time you found a new case to study."

Tretona knew that look of hurt pride that crossed Di's face. She tried to soften her remark:

"Look, we're just basically too different, Di. It'd never work."

Di shrugged coldly. Tretona was now falling all over herself to explain. "Our basic response patterns are just really different. Like that business in Turkey. When we got called up on the carpet, you immediately launched a counterattack, calling in the AAUP and getting a lawyer. I remember your saying at the time, 'The best defense is a good offense.' Remember that? You're always fighting for what you think is right—even when you're bound to lose—like that time with the customs' official in Switzerland.

"I really admire that, though sometimes I think you get too pushy and it's counterproductive. I admire your spunk, but I'm just not that way. Oh, sure, I rebel sometimes—and I generally get clobbered when I do—but mainly I'm more—well, conciliatory, prone to compromise. I don't know what it is, maybe I'm just a coward underneath."

Di still looked hurt and angry, but she wasn't going to let any data escape. "I must admit that I found your whole attitude to the Turkey troubles very puzzling. There we were being falsely accused, harassed over the pettiest imaginable crimes—knee socks at Thanksgiving dinner, for God's sake—remember? And all through it, you just sat there looking like a sheep who wished they'd slaughter her quick and get it over with. Boy, talk about compliant victims—I was starting to think that they'd put opium in your tea. I just couldn't believe how docile you were being."

"Well, since the case they made against us was so ridiculously flimsy, I just naturally assumed that they had some other charges in mind, charges they didn't want to make public unless we forced them to."

"What sort of charges? You mean witnesses who wanted to remain anonymous?"

"Di, don't play so damn dumb. You know what Nükhet and I were doing. We were pretty careful, but any number of people might have complained—her mom, Filiz, even the hotel desk clerk. . . ." She stopped. Di's mouth was signaling complete astonishment. "Why are you looking like that? Surely you knew—or at least suspected."

"Yeah, I knew—well, I guessed that you and Nükhet were having an affair, but I never connected *that* up with the dean's little Inquisition. It never occurred to me! Of course! How stupid I am. No wonder you were frightened and passive. Why didn't I think of that before?"

"Because you aren't queer—not really," said Tretona. "Being queer is like being on a lifetime assignment as a secret agent in some foreign country. No matter how careful you are, no matter how practiced you are at emulating the natives, you know that at any minute you may be uncovered. So you walk around gingerly, trying not to look furtive. And once in a while, if you're brave enough, or lonesome enough, you slyly scrutinize the passersby, searching for some signal, some secret sign that they're a secret agent, too. But that's always risky."

Di's face softened and she spontaneously reached out to touch Tretona's hand. Midway her face grew sterner and her fingers ended up on the table instead. "But not everyone hides— Lu was very forthright about the nature of her sexuality."

"Yes, she was." Tretona had to admit that, but then a wave of self-defensiveness swept over her. "But she was rich. For some miraculous reason her folks didn't disinherit her. She didn't care about a career and she had pull at the apartment house where she stayed. But even Lu was scared of the police. Even with her Mafia connections, she had a good healthy respect for the fuzz."

"Tretona," Di's voice was almost pleading. "Tretona, you're in England now." Tretona shrugged, puzzled. "Don't you see?

It's not against the law in England. Queen Victoria couldn't believe that women were capable of such a thing, so there's never been a law against lesbianism."

"Fat lot of good that did Radclyffe Hall when she faced an obscenity trial for writing a lesbian love story. Illegal or obscene, what does it matter?"

"It ought to matter a hell of a lot to you. You aren't writing a novel. You're a foreign student at a big commuter college in one of the most cosmopolitan cities of the world. You're three thousand miles from Cheaney or Chicago or Dean Tanner. Nobody knows you here and nobody could care less about your life-style."

"Well, except *you*. You seem pretty fucking interested—in what I am, how I got that way, whom I'm attracted to. You want to know every goddamn thing about me. I wish you'd just stop snooping. . . ."

Tretona had never seen Di cry before. Maybe she'd thought Di was too rational or psychologically well-adjusted or some damn thing or other to cry. But now the tears were spurting out, quiet, gentle tears, silent, unpretentious, and therefore all the more moving. But when Di spoke, her voice was steady and strong. "I love you, Tretona. I want you to be happy. No, more than that, because I think you're basically happy now. What I wish for you is all the happiness and joy which you're capable of."

Tretona couldn't speak, so she just sat and grinned at Di until the wrinkles around her eyes made *her* start to cry, too. And then the publican rang the bell for last drinks and it was time to go.

Outside it was a beautiful London autumn evening, not too cold, mist and fog making mysterious halos around the street lamps—a good evening for Mr. Hyde to set forth from Dr. Jekyll's rooms, or for Sherlock Holmes to lie in wait for his suspect. Yet there is something basically healthy and safe about the London atmosphere. Jack the Ripper *feels* less real than the Boston Strangler.

And so without hesitation Di and Tretona threaded their way home through the back streets of Chelsea. Bravely past the tombstones in the gardens by St. Luke's, merrily past the art nouveau ceramic tiles on the Michelin building, solemnly past the eroded lions protecting an antique shop on Walton Street.

Just as they reached the stairs to their basement flat in Ovington Square, Tretona turned to Di:

"I just wanted to tell you that you're a wonderful friend," and for once Tretona did not feel embarrassed or inadequate because she could not speak of love.

*   *   *

"My old man said, 'Follow the van—but don't dilly dally on the way.'" Tretona whistled the old music hall tune at full volume all the way down Sloane Street. It was a Monday morning. The sun was beating down with a very un-British directness and on such a day even Londoners looked at each other and smiled.

There was a policeman standing at the intersection where Sloane ran into the King's Road. "Hey, Bobby," Tretona felt like saying. "Hey bobolink, bobolink, spink, spank, spink, I'm not a criminal in your country. What do you think!" But instead she just looked straight at him and smiled so big that he touched the brim of his helmet in a little semi-salute.

Hello, Mary Quant shop. Hello, greengrocer and flower vendor. Hello, strange man with a purple stripe in your hair and one gold earring. Somewhere in this menagerie there are women like me and *I'm* going to find them.

But how? Maybe she should just bounce up to a butch-looking traffic warden and say, "Lovely Rita, where do the meter maids go at night?" Or maybe sidle up to that older woman wearing tweeds and inquire as to the whereabouts of stable girls and keen horsewomen. "Mind you," she would add, "they must be well-spoken and reliable."

More realistically, she could ask Benjamin about that club in *The Killing of Sister George*. She was almost sure he'd once said something about its being in the environs of Kensington College. She wondered what London lesbians would be like. Real posh and standoffish? Or cockney and jolly? Well, just as long as it wasn't depressing like Chicago. . . .

Better drop by Professor Spinner's office and see if that essay was graded yet. So far, studying in England was a snap. No exams hardly, just lots of reading—yummy books, though—and a little paper due every two weeks. She always tried to do her business in the office early, before Professor Spinner arrived. Besides, Dr. Elkana generally came in early, too. Sometimes Tretona would hang around for a while talking to Spinner's secretary, waiting for Shulamith to come by and pick up her mail. The encounters were always minimal. Shulamith would burst in the door, say a warm good morning to Hélène-Claire (Spinner's secretary was from France), look questioningly at Tretona ("Were you waiting to see me?" her glance said. "Oh, yes—I mean no." Tretona's eyes would answer), stretch out her tanned hand for the bundle of letters and then leave.

Tretona had always said "Helen," when talking to Spinner's secretary as all the English did, but this fine clear, queer, liberated morning in London she decided to imitate Dr. Elkana's Israeli accent.

"Goot mornink, Hélène-Claire," she said throatily as she sauntered through the office door. Tretona's great imitation was all in vain for Hélène-Claire's head was buried in her arms on the typewriter. She straightened up immediately and dried her eyes.

"Helen, what's wrong?"

"Nothing. Some trouble at home."

"Not too serious, I hope."

Hélène-Claire had been in England twelve years—long enough to pick up English reserve, but not long enough to just sit passively when someone pried. Intead, she gave a Gallic shrug.

Tretona was sort of curious about Hélène-Claire's living situation. There were kids in the house—not hers—and two poodles—Tretona found that out when Hélène-Claire came to work one day with dog hairs on her navy blue French fisherman's sweater. But Hélène-Claire didn't seem to want to talk about the rest of the family. Tretona wondered if maybe she was a part-time governess or an au pair girl and too proud to admit it.

"Hey, let's go get some coffee. Old Spinner's not going to show up for quite a while yet."

Hélène-Claire started to refuse—her wonderful French hands had already begun to say no—but she stopped and looked intently at Tretona, as if it were the first time she had ever really noticed her. "Of course. Why not? I'll take you to the jug and bottle where the staff get morning coffee."

Tretona was surprised at how tall Hélène-Claire was; she had a long stride, too. After they had each picked up a coffee and a cheese roll, Hélène-Claire led the way to a little ledge under the stairs.

"This is where I *hide* if Professor Spinner gives me a *hard* time." Her *h*'s were carefully aspirated.

"Or when you *have* trouble at *home*?" Tretona unintentionally imitated the French intonation.

Hélène-Claire shot her a quick glance.

"I'm sorry. I do sound nosey. But you seemed so sad."

"It was nothing, really. Gillian and I had planned a party. But now she's decided to pack up the kids and go to the country for the whole weekend. It's a bloody bore, really—I've already asked lots of people over."

"That leaves you with all the work to do, doesn't it?"

Hélène-Claire was looking sad again, so after a pause Tretona changed the subject.

"Do you think Dr. Elkana wears a wig?"

That at least made Hélène-Claire look up. "Why would you think so?"

"Well, her hair is so perfectly groomed, the same way every day, pulled back into a completely symmetric bun, and it's almost too black to be true. And have you noticed how clean the line is where her hair—or the wig—or whatever it is—meets her forehead?"

"I guess I really haven't looked that closely," said Hélène-Claire with a smile.

"Oh, *I* have," said Tretona, pleased that Helen was cheering up. "I look at her all through lecture. I guess I have a crush on her."

"Ooh, la, la!" Now Hélène-Claire was laughing. "Aren't you too old for that?"

"Oh, no," said Tretona. "I always get crushes on my teachers—especially if they're female." Oops, Tretona thought—and then kept on going. "Plato recommended it, you know—helps the learning process."

"I'd better get back. Spinner's liable to pop in any minute."

Well, I've shocked her good and proper, thought Tretona. Never mind, crushes aren't illegal in any country, let alone in England!

But on the way back upstairs Hélène-Claire suddenly said, "Would you like to come to our—to my party? I can explain how to get there—it's not at all difficult."

Tretona almost asked if she could bring Di, but then found herself saying, "I'd love to come! And maybe I can help you get ready or clean up or something, seeing that Gillian won't be around to help." They sort of bumped as they got to the office. Tretona would have sworn that Hélène's hair had brushed her cheek, but maybe that was just a tactile hallucination.

Do I love England! Tretona thought, as she caught her breath for a moment while sitting in the loo at Hélène-Claire's place. She didn't know whether to call it old-fashioned Edwardian etiquette or just commonsense consideration—whatever it was, the British had it and it really made a difference to the quality of life.

It had first struck her forcibly that evening at Professor Spinner's house. The graciousness with which he had taken her coat, given her a drink, and introduced her had been unusual but not startling. But then at dinner she gradually became aware of an interesting pattern—for a while, she found herself talking to the person on her right, then later to the person on her left—and there were never any embarrassing moments when neither of her neighbors was talking to her or both were. She eventually figured out how it worked—everyone at the table was switching conversation partners at once! She couldn't tell what the signal was, but the whole thing was orchestrated—that she was sure of. Later Benjamin said that at high table at Oxford and Cambridge it went by courses—lady on your left during soup, lady on your right when the fish came and so on.

Similar things happened in the living room afterward—quite a bit of seemingly spontaneous changes in seating between dessert and coffee and more shifting around later when the brandy was served. Professor Spinner and his crowd were sort of old fuddy-duddies so it wasn't surprising to find lots of formal rituals there, but similar little smooth things were happening here at this lively gathering. Tretona didn't know any of Hélène-Claire's friends—there was no one here from the department—yet she never ended up standing alone, feeling stranded. Either someone would wander up to talk or Hélène-Claire would come by with yet another tray of goodies.

Better hurry back down so as not to miss any of those hors d'oeuvres. The people were really interesting, too—like Susan, the social worker who worked at a shelter for battered women. She said her biggest problem was to keep them from going back right away for more—all in the name of love. Then there was Alison, who had on a sailor suit, and was a very flashy dancer. She picked out films for the BBC's matinees. Tretona talked to her about censorship—and eventually found out that the real reason the British had rejected *Sesame Street* was not the expense but because the grammar the characters used was so poor! "Even the adults on the show split infinitives and repeatedly make errors involving relative pronouns," said Alison disdainfully. After the mauling her essays had received from Professor Spinner, Tretona was almost prepared to believe that she and other Americans *were* illiterate—at least by British standards—but she was always game for a fight.

"Well, I think there is altogether too much emphasis placed on the stylistic or cosmetic aspects of language. What you want little kids to do is to *communicate,* to express what they feel—the grammerians' little orthodoxies just aren't that important."

Tretona was expecting a reply along the lines of "sloppy language encourages sloppy thinking," but Alison's objection was quite different: "It's mainly a matter of knowing what's proper. One wouldn't offer a guest a drink from a chipped glass, would one? Speaking the language properly is simply a matter of courtesy."

How very British of you, Tretona thought—and for the life of her, couldn't think of a retort.

Her favorite character so far was Jacqueline (or Jacký, as she seemed to be called). She had a strong chiseled face—rather reminiscent of Gertrude Stein's. Her forearms were tan and muscular, her hands wonderfully large. Even the most superficial glance would tell you *she* wasn't British. She was an old friend of Hélène-Claire's and was French from the flair of her neck scarf down to the bow on her neat little pumps. What a delightful mixture of style and toughness she was—expensive accessories teamed with a denim shirt and blue jeans. Her language seemed to consist of equal parts of elegant abstractions and gutter jargon, all coated in the thickest of French accents. "Eh, Hélène-Claire! Why do you buy this piss of woodpecker?" (She was holding up a bottle of Bulmer's cider, which had a woodpecker on the label.) "Apples are only for pigs, for pigs and woodpeckers. Not very elégante, my dear. What would your maman. . . ?"

Hélène-Claire responded with a very Gallic gesture of the middle finger. Jacký laughed and carried on her conversation with Tretona and some woman from Northern Ireland about the esthetic advantages of using fabrics for wall coverings instead of paint or wallpaper. She was evidently an interior decorator who worked for rich people in Chelsea.

As usual, Tretona asked questions about methodology. "When you go into a new place—suppose someone calls you in to redo one of those trendy little mews houses behind the Brompton Oratory—how do you get your ideas? Do you just walk in and sort of get an intuitive feel for. . . ."

Jacký wagged a finger to interrupt. "No, no, non!" she said, her accent thickening as she proceeded. "I am artiste, not animale. Animals must live spontaneously by feeling, because they have no mind, non? Only a brain. But I am a human be-ing. I can calculate. So when I walk in, I analyze. I say, 'What is the esthetic problème of this room?' I say, 'What personnes live in this room?' I say, 'Where is this room situa-ted?' I ask many things and then I make one answer for all the questions."

Vive Descartes, thought Tretona. How wonderful—Descartes had died over three hundred years ago and yet his philosophy still survived, incarnated in a French woman living in London talking to an American. I really *am* an American, she thought. I am Benjamin Franklin and Huck Finn and Horatio Alger and Louisa May Alcott—that part of me will never change, not even if I were to live abroad for a thousand years.

Tretona glanced at her watch—it was time to tell Hélène-Claire good-bye. She sank down on the couch beside her exhausted hostess: "Hey, this has been a great party, but I've got to catch the last train from Hammersmith." Hélène-Claire shoved over the footstool for Tretona to share. "No need to go—you could overnight here."

Tretona stared at their four feet propped up on the hassock—one pair of black Swedish clogs and one pair of blue American tennies. Her head felt like a Bozo clown punching bag—tippy but heavy at the bottom.

"Besides, you can't leave before the baked potatoes are served."

It was true. Once she and Di had invited people over and put out the ordinary American chips and dips stuff. People had stayed and stayed and stayed—they seemed restless, but they still stayed. Finally, just to be doing something, Tretona made popcorn and after eating everyone left! Benjamin said it was traditional to have a hot savory dish at the end of a party.

"Okay. But can I use your phone?" Tretona dreaded calling Di, but felt she'd better. It hadn't been too bad telling her about the party. For some reason, she felt freer around Di these days—

maybe it was because she no longer felt she should love Di in some way other than what she did.

Di's voice was low and anxious. "Oh, Tretona, it's just you. I'm so relieved."

"Why? What'd you expect?"

"Well—well, you never know, so late at night."

"Well, it's me. I'm fine. Hey, I'm having a wonderful time, meeting lots of real neat people—thought I might stay over. I'll be back early, though."

Di's voice was flat. "Early? You mean tomorrow morning?" Then she became animated. "Yes, actually that's a very good idea. I'll be ready for you then."

Be *ready* for me? Wonder what that means? thought Tretona.

She had her potato back on the couch with Hélène-Claire. "This sour cream stuff is unbelievable, what's in it?"

"A little garlic—some yogurt, basil, fresh rosemary—a little this and that."

"Oh, ho—la cuisine française," said Tretona with admiration. Hélène-Claire smiled, made a little bow, and then settled deep into the couch, her head lolling against the back, leaning a little toward Tretona, watching her face. Tretona deliberately kept talking.

"I really like your friends—Jacký, the BBC woman, those two Irish women—where did you ever meet so many interesting people? They're fascinating."

"Jacqueline is an old friend. I knew her in Lyon before I even came to England. The others? I guess I met them all at the Lesbos."

"The Lesbos?" Tretona fought to keep her voice and appearance casual.

"The Lesbos Club. Meets once a week in the back room of a pub. We have discussions and little programs. Mainly, though, it's just a social club. Maybe you'd like to come along some time—we meet on Thursday nights."

Tretona's throat was tight with excitement. "Yes, very much," was all she could say.

Now Hélène-Claire was sitting up straight again. "Looks as if Alison is leaving. I better go say cheerio." Once again Tretona thought she felt a brush against her cheek.

"I'll get up, too. Need some more of that woodpecker juice."

Her mind whirred, busily assimilating this new bit of information and drawing out all its implications: So Hélène-Claire is obviously not the governess here—she and Gillian must be lovers. No, not necessarily—after all, look at me and Di. So all these neat women I've been talking to are lesbians! Wow, and I never even guessed. That makes a shambles out of the "takes-one-to-know-one" theory.

Then Tretona felt a little giddy—the cider was probably stronger than she realized—so she went back to the couch, leaned her head back, and happily hummed, "This Is My Island in the Sun," thinking partly of the British Isles and partly of the Lesbos Club with all its Sapphic islanders.

The smell of Hélène-Claire's hair roused her. "Everyone's gone home. Do you want to go to bed now?" Tretona struggled to clear her brain. For some reason a bit of GI French drummed through her mind: "Voulez-vous coucher avec moi?" Was Hélène-Claire propositioning her? And was she up for it?

"I'm not sure. I guess so," said Tretona, stalling for time.

"Don't worry, ma petite. I'll take care of everything," said Hélène, ruffling her hair.

She was gone for ages. Tretona got up, took off her shoes, put on a Cleo Laine album, straightened her hair, then spit on a Kleenex and bathed her eyes with it. Breath should be pretty much okay after all that alcohol—and the French of all people shouldn't mind garlic.

Hélène-Claire returned wearing a flannel nightgown. She was carrying a sleeping bag in one hand and precariously balancing a tray in the other.

Wide awake now and feeling gallant (would the French be *gallante?*), Tretona jumped up to help, "I've fixed us some Bosco," said Hélène-Claire.

"Bosco?" (Could it be *Basqueaux?*) "What on earth is that?"

"Ask the English. You make it with hot milk—absolutely super for hang-ovaires" (As Hélène got tired, her almost perfect English accent faltered a little.) "I hope you'll be comfortable here on the couch. I'd put you in the children's room, but they've left the hamsters untended and it's not very nice in there."

And what of the double bed I saw on the way to the loo? thought Tretona. Hélène studied her face a second and then added, "You understand?" Their fingers touched during the transfer of the Bosco. For just a sec, Tretona felt acutely disappointed about the sleeping arrangements, but then she quickly reconsidered. This wasn't the Volleyball crowd in Chicago, after all. This was the start of a friendship, the discovery of a community. She should build her new network of relationships carefully and considerately.

And so they chatted easily about the party and the Resistance in France during World War II and the bargains in Goldhawk Road market and exchanged stories about how snotty the clerks were in Harrod's—until neither one could stay awake and then Hélène-Claire went off to bed.

* * *

Di was hemming up a navy blue dress when Tretona got home. Her eyes were red.

"How was the party?" she asked. So Tretona told her about everything—the people, the food, the Bulmer's Woodpecker cider and especially about the Lesbos Club.

Finally, she paused for breath. "I never saw that dress before—are you going some place special?"

"To my father's funeral," said Di, calmly enough. But as she told the story, her hands trembled, though she kept sewing determinedly. The undertaker had phoned—the death was totally unexpected. He had been out digging in the garden on an unseasonably warm day—her mother heard him fall and rushed out, but he had died instantly.

Tretona was numb, not knowing how to cope or what to say, mechanically asking for irrelevant details just to keep talking. When had it happened? Odd to be gardening so late in the fall, a wonder it hadn't snowed, how old was he. . . ?

"Seventy-eight," said Di and then she finally started to cry.

"Well, he was a pretty old man then," said Tretona. "And it's nice that he went while he was still healthy instead of being bedfast. . . ."

Di burst into sobs. "That's just it—he was *so* healthy. He could have lived for *years* to come."

Tretona felt completely helpless. "Why didn't you let me know when I telephoned last night?" she asked accusingly, "I would have taken a taxi."

Di looked calmer. "I thought about it but I needed some time to think—to compose myself. And now I'm really glad I didn't. It'll be easier to leave knowing that you've found some new friends."

Tretona smiled reassuringly. "Hey, they'll be your friends, too. When you get back maybe we'll have a party. . . ."

Di shook her head. "I'm not coming back."

"Of course, you'll be back—I mean, after the funeral. . . ?"

Di kept shaking her head while Tretona clutched for arguments. "But you can get a cheap ABC round-trip ticket. What about Anna Freud and the Tavistock? What about our plans to go to Spain at Christmas?" When Di spoke, her voice seemed far away, like a trans-Atlantic phone call, trying to touch, trying to communicate, trying in vain to overcome the vast separating distances.

"I'm needed at home. My mother is an old woman . . . bad health . . . pinched a nerve in her leg when she rushed out to help Dad . . . crutches now . . . maybe traction later. And America needs me, too—I guess I just want to be there now."

Tretona, trying to understand, trying to let go, but feeling kicked in the stomach, feeling her face go dead like Foster's, wanting to shriek, "But what about *me? I* need you too," clamping down on her tears, pulling the tough turtle shell up over her ears until it shaded her eyes. But suddenly an amazing calmness fell over her—she would be going home, too . . . eventually. But right now her place was in England. Her work was here—becoming a professional philosopher, learning to feel secure about her sexual identity, preparing to go home strong, and whole, and ready to shoulder that Sisyphean rock.

Finally she spoke:

"I'll miss you like everything, Di. But we'll write. I'll tell you everything that happens."

Di squeezed both her upper arms in gratitude and for a minute they stood there, hands gripping each other's shoulders, strong, close, yet firmly separate, not daring to meld their bodies even for a moment.

Then the welcome distractions of suitcases, tickets, calls to British Rail and a shipping company, stacks of Di's library books to be returned to the Tavistock, bank account to be closed, money for the phone bill, arrangements for what to give away, what to throw away.

Tretona driving her to the airport, "Try to get some sleep on the plane."

Di, anxiously, "I did give you Mom's address and phone number, didn't I?"

"Now I probably won't ever phone, Di. You know how I hate talking long distance, anyway—and at eight dollars a minute, I'd be hopeless."

"But we will write, won't we? Promise?"

"Promise."

* * *

They *did* write, regularly, which could not have been predicted. Our best friends or favorite conversationalists do not always make the best correspondents. But these two wrote, Di reporting funny things that went on in a women's discussion group she'd joined and Tretona describing her conversations with Shulamith about concepts of personal identity. Di sent clippings about Betty Friedan and Tretona described the BBC coverage of Martin Luther King's funeral.

And after enough time had passed and jealousy was no longer a problem, Di started writing about a fascinating guy she'd met who was in comparative literature and swore he was a real feminist. And about the same time, Tretona's letters contained more and more stuff about Hélène-Claire and lots of theorizing about the nature of relationships.

And eventually Tretona found a great job back in America and even achieved a détente with the folks in Cheaney.

But that's quite another story.